In
Times Of Peril
A Tale Of India

by

G. A. Henty

Double 9
BOOKS

In
Times Of Peril
A Tale Of India
by G. A. Henty

ISBN: 978-93-59393-09-4

Published by

DOUBLE 9 BOOKS

2/13-B, Ansari Road
Daryaganj, New Delhi – 110002
info@double9books.com
www.double9books.com
Tel. 011-40042856

ABOUT THE AUTHOR

English author and war correspondent George Alfred Henty lived from 8 December 1832 to 16 November 1902. He is most well-known for his historical fiction and adventure books, including The Dragon & The Raven (1886), For The Temple (1888), Under Drake's Flag (1883), and In Freedom's Cause (1883). (1885). He was a British journalist who served as G. A. Henty's war correspondent. He was raised in Cambridge and finished his education there at Gonville and Caius College. He continued to cover important wars that followed, such as the Italian and Austro-Italian Wars. He wrote 122 books, most of which were geared toward young readers. He also wrote non-fiction, adult fiction, and short tales. In Henty's stories, the main character is a boy or young man who is going through a challenging situation. His characters are consistently low-key, astute, courageous, truthful, and resourceful with a lot of "pluck." The date was put at the bottom of the title page of each of Henty's 122 historical fiction works in their first printings.

CONTENTS

CHAPTER I.
LIFE IN CANTONMENTS.

Very bright and pretty, in the early springtime of the year 1857, were the British cantonments of Sandynugghur. As in all other British garrisons in India, they stood quite apart from the town, forming a suburb of their own. They consisted of the barracks, and of a maidan, or, as in England it would be called, "a common," on which the troops drilled and exercised, and round which stood the bungalows of the military and civil officers of the station, of the chaplain, and of the one or two merchants who completed the white population of the place.

Very pretty were these bungalows, built entirely upon the ground floor, in rustic fashion, wood entering largely into their composition. Some were thatched; others covered with slabs of wood or stone. All had wide verandas running around them, with tatties, or blinds, made of reeds or strips of wood, to let down, and give shade and coolness to the rooms therein. In some of them the visitor walked from the compound, or garden, directly into the dining-room; large, airy, with neither curtains, nor carpeting, nor matting, but with polished boards as flooring. The furniture here was generally plain and almost scanty, for, except at meal-times, the rooms were but little used.

Outside, in the veranda, is the real sitting-room of the bungalow. Here are placed a number of easy-chairs of all shapes, constructed of cane or bamboo—light, cool, and comfortable; these are moved, as the sun advances, to the shady side of the veranda, and in them the ladies read and work, the gentlemen smoke. In all bungalows built for the use of English families, there is, as was the case at Sandynugghur, a drawing-room as well as a dining-room, and this, being the ladies' especial domain, is generally furnished in European style, with a piano, light chintz chair-covers, and muslin curtains.

The bedroom opens out of the sitting-room; and almost every bedroom has its bathroom—that all-important adjunct in the East—attached to it. The windows all open down to the ground, and the servants generally come in and out through the veranda. Each window has its Venetian blind, which answers all purposes of a door, and yet permits the air to pass freely.

The veranda, in addition to serving as the general sitting-room to the family, acts as a servants' hall. Here at the side not used by the employers, the servants, when not otherwise engaged, sit on their mats, mend their clothes, talk and sleep; and it is wonderful how much sleep a Hindoo can get through in the twenty-four hours. The veranda is his bedroom as well as sitting-room; here, spreading a mat upon the ground, and rolling themselves up in a thin rug or blanket from the very top of their head to their feet, the servants sleep, looking like a number of mummies ranged against the wall. Out by the stables they have their quarters, where they cook and eat, and could, if they chose, sleep; but they prefer the coolness and freshness of the veranda, where, too, they are ready at hand whenever called. The gardens were all pretty, and well kept, with broad, shady trees, and great shrubs covered by bright masses of flower; for Sandynugghur had been a station for many years, and with plenty of water and a hot sun, vegetation is very rapid.

In two of the large reclining chairs two lads, of fifteen and sixteen respectively, were lolling idly; they had been reading, for books lay open in their laps, and they were now engaged in eating bananas, and in talking to two young ladies, some three years their senior, who were sitting working beside them.

"You boys will really make yourselves ill if you eat so many bananas."

"It is not that I care for them," said the eldest lad; "they are tasteless things, and a good apple is worth a hundred of them; but one must do something, and I am too lazy to go on with this Hindoo grammar; besides, a fellow can't work when you girls come out here and talk to him."

"That's very good, Ned; it is you that do all the talking; besides, you know that you ought to shut yourselves up in the study, and not sit here where you are sure to be interrupted."

"I have done three hours' steady work this morning with that wretched Moonshi, Kate; and three hours in this climate is as much as my brain will stand."

Kate Warrener and her brothers, Ned and Dick, were the children of the major of the One Hundred and Fifty-first Bengal Native Infantry, the regiment stationed at Sandynugghur. Rose Hertford, the other young lady, was their cousin. The three former were born in India, but had each gone to England at the age of nine for their education, and to save them from the effects of the climate which English children are seldom able to endure after that age. Their mother had sailed for England with Dick, the youngest, but had died soon after she reached home. Dick had a passion for the sea, and his father's relations having good interest, had obtained for him a berth as a midshipman in the royal navy, in which rank he had been serving for upward of a year. His ship being now in Indian waters, a month's leave had been granted him that he might go up the country to see his father. The other lad had arrived from England three months before, with his sister and cousin. Major Warrener had sent for his daughter, whose education was finished, to take the head of his house, and, as a companion, had invited Rose Hertford, who was the orphan child of his sister, to accompany her. Ned, who had been at Westminster till he left England, was intended for the Indian army. His father thought that it would be well for him to come out to India with his sister, as he himself would work with him, and complete his education, to enable him to pass the necessary examination—then not a very severe one—while he could be at the same time learning the native languages, which would be of immense benefit to him after he had entered the army. Coming out as they had done in the cold season, none of the four exhibited any of that pallor and lassitude which, at any rate during the summer heats, are the rule throughout the Anglo-Indian community.

As Ned finished his sentence the sound of the tread of two horses was heard along the road.

"Captains Dunlop and Manners," Dick exclaimed; "a shilling to a penny! Will either of you bet, girls?"

Neither his sister nor cousin replied to this offer; and the boys gave a sly nod of intelligence to each other, as two horsemen rode up to the veranda and dismounted; throwing their reins to the *syces*, who, whatever the pace at which their masters ride, run just behind, in readiness to take the horses, should they dismount.

"Good-morning, Miss Warrener; good-morning, Miss Hertford: we have brought you some interesting news."

"Indeed!" said the girls, as they shook hands with the newcomers, who were two as good specimens of tall, well-made, sunburnt Anglo-Saxons as one would wish to see. "What is it?"

"We have just got the news that a family of wild boars have come down, and are doing a lot of damage near Meanwerrie, four miles off. I suppose they have been disturbed somewhere further away, as we have not heard of any pig here for months; so to-morrow morning there is going to be grand pig-sticking; of course you will come out and see the fun?"

"We shall be delighted," said Kate; but Rose put in: "Yes; but oh! how unfortunate! it's Mrs. Briarley's garden party."

"That has been put off till next day. It is not often we get a chance at pig, and we have always got gardens. The two need not have interfered with each other, as we shall start at daylight for Meanwerrie; but we may be out some hours, and so it was thought better to put off the party to a day when there will be nothing else to do."

"Hurrah!" shouted Dick; "I am in luck! I wanted, above all things, to see a wild boar hunt; do you think my father will let me have a spear?"

"Hardly, Dick, considering that last time you went out you tumbled off three times at some jumps two feet wide, and that, were you to fall in front of a pig, he would rip you up before you had time to think about it; besides which, you would almost certainly stick somebody with your spear."

Dick laughed.

"That was the first time I had ever been on a horse," he said; "will you ride, Ned?"

"No," said Ned; "I can ride fairly enough along a straight road, but it wants a first-rate rider to go across country at a gallop, looking at the boar instead of where you are going, and carrying a spear in one hand."

"Do you think papa will ride?" Kate asked.

"I don't know, Miss Warrener; the major is a famous spear; but here he is to speak for himself."

Major Warrener was in uniform, having just come up from the orderly-room. He was a tall, soldierly figure, inclining to stoutness. His general expression was that of cheeriness and good temper; but he was looking, as he drove up, grave and serious. His brow cleared, however, as his eye fell upon the group in the veranda.

"Ah! Dunlop, brought the news about the boar, eh?"

"You will take us with you?" the girls asked in a breath.

"Oh, yes, you shall go; I will drive you myself. I am getting too heavy for pig-sticking, especially with such responsibilities as you about. There, I will get out of this uniform; it's hot for the time of year. What are you drinking? nothing? Boy, bring some soda and brandy!"

Then, producing his cigar-case, he took a cheroot.

"Ag-low!" he shouted, and a native servant ran up with a piece of red-hot charcoal held in a little pair of tongs.

"There, sit down and make yourselves comfortable till I come back."

The lads, finding that their society was not particularly required, strolled off to the stables, where Ned entered into a conversation with the *syces* as to the distance to Meanwerrie and the direction in which that village lay. Like all Anglo-Indian children brought up in India, the boys had, when they left India, spoken the language fluently. They had almost entirely forgotten it during their stay in England, but it speedily came back again, and Ned, at the end of three months' work, found that he could get on very fairly. Dick had lost it altogether.

When they went back to the veranda they found that the girls had gone indoors, and that their father was sitting and smoking with his brother officers. When the lads came up the conversation ceased, and then the major said:

"It is as well the boys should know what is going on."

"What is it, father?" Ned asked, struck with the grave tone in which the major spoke, and at the serious expression in all their faces.

"Well, boys, for some months past there have been all sorts of curious rumors running through the country. Chupatties have been sent round, and that is always considered to portend something serious."

"Do you mean the chupatties we eat—flat cakes, father?"

"Yes, Ned. Nobody knows who sends them round, or the exact meaning of the signal, but it seems to be an equivalent for to 'prepare,' 'make ready.' Chupatties are quickly prepared; they are the bread eaten on a journey, and hence probably their signification. At any rate, these things have been circulated among the native troops all over the country. Strangers are known to have come and gone, and there is a general uneasy and unsettled feeling prevalent among the troops. A ridiculous rumor has circulated among them that the new cartridges have been greased with pig's fat, in order that the caste of all who put it to their lips might be destroyed. To-day I have received news from Calcutta that the Nineteenth native regiment at Berhampore has behaved in a grossly mutinous manner, and that it is feared the regiments at Barrackpore and Dumdum will follow their example. The affair has been suppressed, but there is an uneasy feeling abroad, and all the troops in Bengal proper appear tainted with paltry disaffection. We have no reason for believing that the spirit has spread to the northwest, and are convinced that as far as our own regiment is concerned they can be relied on; but the affair, taken in connection with the previous rumors, is very strange, and I fear that there are lots of trouble ahead. I wish now that I had not had the girls out for another year; but I could not foresee this, and, indeed, until this morning, although there has been a good deal of talk, we all hoped it would have passed off without anything coming of it. One hopes still that it will spread no further; but should it do so, it is impossible to say what may happen. All we have to do is to be watchful, and to avoid with care anything that can offend the men's prejudices. We must explain to the native officers the folly of the greased cartridge story, and tell them to reassure the men. You don't see anything else to do, Dunlop?"

"No, major; I trust that the regiment is to be depended upon; it has always been well treated and the men have seemed attached to us all. We will do our best to reassure them; but if there is any insubordination, I hope that the colonel will give the men a lesson which will put an end to the nonsense in the bud."

"Of course you will stay to tiffin?" the major said, as the *kitmagar*, or head servant, announced that tiffin was ready.

"Many thanks, major, but we promised to tiff with Bullen, and he would be mad if we did not turn up. How are you thinking of going to-morrow? I intend to drive over, and send my horse on; so I can give one of your boys a lift in my buggy."

"Thank you," the major said, "that would suit us exactly. I shall drive in my dog-cart, which will carry four of us; and if you will take Dick, that will make it all right."

"What time do we start?"

"We are to be there by seven; we set it so late to give the ladies time to breakfast comfortably before starting. I will call here at half-past six for Dick; it will be all in my way. Good-morning."

Two minutes later the girls, Ned, and Dick came into the dining-room, and the party sat down to luncheon—a meal always called tiffin in India. It is a great mistake to suppose that people in India cannot eat because of the heat; in the extreme heat of summer their appetites do, no doubt, fall off; but at other times, they not only eat, but eat more largely than is good for them; and a good deal of the liver complaint which is the pest of India is in no small degree due to the fact that, the appetite being unnaturally stimulated by hot and piquant food, people eat more than in such a climate as this can be properly digested. The meal consisted of curries, with which were handed round chutney and Bombay ducks—a little fish about the size of a smelt, cut open, dried, and smoked with assafoetida, giving it an intolerably nasty taste to strangers, but one which Anglo-Indians become accustomed to and like—no one knows why they are called Bombay ducks—cutlets, plantains sliced and fried, pomegranates, and watermelons. They were waited upon by two servants, both dressed entirely in white, but wearing red turbans, very broad and shallow. These turbans denoted the particular tribe and sect to which their wearers belonged. The castes in India are almost innumerable, and each has a turban of a peculiar color or shape, and by these they can be at once distinguished by a resident. On their foreheads were lines and spots of a yellowish white paint, indicating also their caste, and the peculiar divinity to whose worship they were specially devoted. On their feet they wore slippers, and were as noiseless as cats in all their movements. There are no better or more pleasant waiters in the world than the natives of Hindostan.

Early as the hour named for the start would appear in England, it was by no means early for India, where every one is up and about soon after daylight—the morning hours up to eight o'clock being the most pleasant of the whole day.

Kate and Rose were up, and all had had "chota hazaree" (little breakfast) by half-past six, and were ready when Captain Dunlop drew up in his buggy—a conveyance which will only hold two. The dog-cart was already at the door, and the whole party were soon in motion. On the road they passed several of their friends, for every one was going out to the hunt, and merry greetings were exchanged.

The scenery round Sandynugghur resembles that which is common to all the great plains of India watered by the Ganges and Jumna. The country is for the most part perfectly flat, and cut up into little fields, divided by shallow ditches. Here and there nullahs, or deep watercourses, with tortuous channels and perpendicular sides, wind through the fields to the nearest stream. These nullahs constitute the great danger of hunting in the country. In the fields men may be noticed, in the scantiest of attire, working with hoes among their springing crops; women, wrapped up in the dark blue calico cloth which forms their ordinary costume, are working as hard as the men. Villages are scattered about, generally close to groves of trees. The huts are built of mud; most of them are flat-topped, but some are thatched with rushes. Rising above the villages is the mosque, where the population are Mohammedan, built of mud like the houses, but whitewashed and bright. The Hindoo villages generally, but not always, have their temples. The vegetation of the great plains of India is not tropical, according to the ideas of tropical vegetation gathered from British hothouses. There are a few palms and many bananas with their wide leaves, but the groves are composed of sturdy trees, whose appearance at a distance differs in no way from that of ordinary English forest trees. Viewed closer, the banian with its many stems is indeed a vegetable wonder; but, were it not for the villages and natives, a traveler might journey for very many miles across the plains of India without seeing anything which would specially remind him that he was out of England.

There were a considerable number of traps assembled when Major Warrener drew up, and some eight or ten gentlemen on horseback, each carrying a boar-spear—a weapon not unlike the lance of an English cavalryman, but shorter in the handle. The riders were mostly dressed in coats of the Norfolk jacket type, and knee-breeches with thick gaiters. The material of their clothes was a coarse but very strong cloth of native make, gray or brown in color. Some wore round hats and forage caps with puggarees twisted round them.

A chorus of greeting saluted the party as they drove up.

"Well, young ladies," the colonel said, "so you have come out to see the death of the boar,

"'The boar, the boar, the mighty boar,'

as the song says? So you are not going to take a spear to-day, major? Think it's time to leave it to the youngsters, eh?"

"Where are the wild boars, Mrs. Renwick?" Kate asked of the colonel's wife.

"Pig, my dear; we always call them pig when we speak of them together, though we talk of the father of the family as the boar. Do you see that clump of long grass and jungle right across the plain? That's where they are. They have been watched all night. They went out to feed before daybreak and have just gone back again. Do you think we are in the best place for seeing the sport, Major Warrener?"

"I think, Mrs. Renwick, that if you leave your trap and go up to the top of that knoll, two hundred yards to the right, you will get a really good view of the plain."

Mrs. Renwick alighted from the dog-cart in which the colonel had driven her, and the whole party, following her example, walked in a laughing group to the spot which Major Warrener had indicated, and which was pronounced as just the place. The *syces* stood at the heads of the horses, and those who were going to take part in the sport cantered off toward the spot where the pigs were lurking, making, however, a wide *détour* so as to approach it from the other side, as it was desired to drive them across the plain. At some distance behind the clump were stationed a number of natives, with a variety of mongrel village curs. When they saw the horsemen approach they came up and prepared to enter the jungle to drive out the pigs.

The horsemen took up their position on either side of the patch in readiness to start as soon as the animals were fairly off. A number of villagers, in whose fields of young rice the family had done much damage during the few days that they had taken up their abode in their present quarters, were assembled on such little rises of ground as were likely to give a good view of the proceedings. There were about a dozen horsemen with spears; of these, three or four were novices, and these intended to try their skill for the first time upon the "squeakers," as the young pigs are called, while the others prepared for a race after the old ones.

Great nerve, considerable skill, and first-rate horsemanship are required for the sport of pigsticking. The horse, too, must be fast, steady, well-trained and quick, for without all these advantages the sport is a dangerous one. The wild boar is, at the start, as fast as a horse. He is very quick at turning, and when pressed always attacks his pursuers, and as he rushes past will lay open the leg or flank of a horse with a sweeping cut with his sharp tusk. If he can knock a horse down the position of his rider would be serious indeed, were not help to arrive in time to draw off the attention of the enraged animal from his foe. Heavy falls, too, take place over watercourses and nullahs, and in some parts of India the difficulties are greatly increased by bowlders of all kinds being scattered over the ground, and by the frequent occurrence of bushes and shrubs armed with most formidable spines and thorns. Conspicuous among these is the bush known as the "wait-a-bit thorn," which is furnished with two kinds of thorn—the one long, stiff, and penetrating, the other short and curved, with a forked point almost like a fishhook. When this once takes hold it is almost necessary to cut the cloth to obtain a release.

Scarcely had the beaters, with much shouting and clamor, entered the patch of bush in which the pigs were lying, than the porcine family, consisting of a splendid boar and sow, and eight nearly full-grown squeakers, darted out on the open, and in a moment the horsemen were off in pursuit. The ground was deep and heavy, and the pigs at the first burst gained fast upon their pursuers. There was no attempt on the part of the pigs to keep together, and directly after starting they began to diverge. The old boar and sow both kept across the plain—one bearing toward the left, the other to the right. The squeakers ran in all directions—some at right angles to the line that the old ones were taking. The object of one and all was to gain cover of some kind.

With their hats pressed well down upon their heads, and their spears advanced with the head some two or three feet from the ground, the hunters started after them—some making after the boar, some after the sow, according to the position which they occupied at the commencement of the chase, while some of the young hands dashed off in pursuit of the squeakers.

There were five, however, after the boar; Captain Dunlop, a young ensign named Skinner, the Scotch doctor of the regiment, and two civilians. For a short time they kept together, and then Captain Dunlop and Skinner began to draw ahead of the others.

The boar was a stanch one, and a mile had been passed before his speed began sensibly to diminish. The young ensign, who was mounted on a very fast Arab, began to draw up to him three or four lengths ahead of Captain Dunlop, bearing his horse so as to get upon the left side of the boar, in order to permit him to use his spear to advantage.

He was nearly up to him when Captain Dunlop, who saw the boar glancing back savagely, cried:

"Look out, Skinner! he will be round in a moment; keep your horse well in hand!"

A moment later the boar was round. The horse, young and unbroken at the work, started violently, swerved, and, before his rider could get him round, the boar was upon him. In an instant the horse was upon the ground, with a long gash upon his flank, and Skinner, flying through the air, fell almost directly in the boar's way.

Fortunately for the young ensign, Captain Dunlop, as he shouted his warning, had turned his horse to the left, so as to cut off the boar when he turned, and he was now so close that the boar, in passing, had only time to give a vicious blow at the fallen man, which laid his arm open from his shoulder to his elbow.

At that instant Captain Dunlop arrived, and his spear pierced the animal's flank. His aim was, however, disconcerted by his horse, at the moment he struck, leaping over the fallen ensign; the wound, therefore, was but a glancing one, and in a moment the boar was round upon his new assailant. Fortunately the horse was a well-trained one, and needed not the sharp touch of his master's rein to wheel sharp round on his hind legs, and dart off at full speed. The boar swerved off again, and continued his original line of flight, his object being to gain a thick patch of jungle, now little over a quarter of a mile distant; the detention, however, was fatal to him, for the doctor, who was close on Captain Dunlop's heels, now brought up his horse with a rush and, with a well-aimed thrust, ran the animal through, completely pinning him to the earth. The honor of his death was therefore divided between the doctor and Captain Dunlop, for the latter had drawn first blood, or, as it is termed, had taken first spear, while the former had scored the kill.

The sow had been more fortunate than her lord. She had taken a line across a part of the plain which was intersected by several nullahs. She, too, had been wounded, but one of the nullahs had thrown out several of her pursuers: one rider had been sent over his horse's head and stunned; and the sow, turning sharp down a deep and precipitous gully, had made her escape. Three of the squeakers fell to the spears of the Griffs—young hands—and the rest had escaped. The boar had been killed only a short distance from the rise upon which the spectators from Sandynugghur were assembled, and the beaters soon tied its four legs together, and, putting a pole through them, six of them carried the beast up to the colonel's wife for inspection.

"What a savage-looking brute it is!" said Kate; "not a bit like a pig, with all those long bristles, and that sharp high back, and those tremendous tusks."

"Will you accept the skin, Miss Warrener?" Captain Dunlop said to her afterward; "I have arranged with the doctor. He is to have the hams, and I am to have the hide. If you will, I will have it dressed and mounted."

"Thank you, Captain Dunlop, I should like it very much;" but, as it turned out, Kate Warrener never got the skin.

The boar killed, the doctor's first care was to attend to the wounded, and Skinner's arm was soon bound up, and he was sent home in a buggy; the man who was stunned came to in a short time. The unsuccessful ones were much laughed at by the colonel and major, for allowing half the game started to get away.

"You ought not to grumble, colonel," Captain Manners said. "If we had killed them all, we might not have had another run for months; as it is, we will have some more sport next week."

There was some consultation as to the chance of getting the sow even now, but it was generally agreed that she would follow the nullah down, cross the stream, and get into a large canebrake beyond, from which it would take hours to dislodge her; so a general move was made to the carriages, and in a short time the whole party were on their way back to Sandynugghur.

CHAPTER II.
THE OUTBREAK.

A week after the boar-hunt came the news that a Sepoy named Mangul Pandy, belonging to the Thirty-fourth Native Infantry, stationed at Barrackpore, a place only a few miles out of Calcutta, had, on the 29th of March, rushed out upon the parade ground and called upon the men to mutiny. He then shot the European sergeant-major of the regiment, and cut down an officer. Pandy continued to exhort the men to rise to arms, and although his comrades would not join him, they refused to make any movement to arrest him. General Hearsey now arrived on the parade ground with his son and a Major Ross, and at once rode at the man, who, finding that his comrades would not assist him, discharged the contents of the musket into his own body.

Two days later the mutinous Nineteenth were disbanded at Barrackpore. On the 3rd of April Mangul Pandy, who had only wounded himself, was hung, and the same doom was allotted to a native officer of his regiment, for refusing to order the men to assist the officer attacked by that mutineer, and for himself inciting the men to rise against the government.

"What do you think of the news, papa?" Dick asked his father.

"I hope that the example which has been set by the execution of these ringleaders, and by the disbandment of the Nineteenth, may have a wholesome effect, Dick; but we shall see before long."

It needed no great lapse of time to show that this lesson had been ineffectual. From nearly every station throughout Bengal and the northwest provinces came rumors of disaffection; at Agra, at Umballah, and at other places incendiary fires broke out with alarming frequency, letters were from time to time intercepted, calling upon the Sepoys to revolt, while at Lucknow serious disturbances occurred, and the Seventh Regiment were disarmed by Sir Henry Lawrence, the Commissioner of Oude. So the month of April passed, and as it went on the feeling of disquiet and danger grew deeper and more general. It was like the anxious time preceding a thunderstorm, the cloud was gathering, but how or when it would burst none could say. Many still maintained stoutly that there was no danger whatever, and that the whole thing would blow over; but men with wives and families were generally inclined to take a more somber view of the case. Nor is this to be wondered at. The British form an almost inappreciable portion of the population of India; they are isolated in a throng of natives, outnumbered by a thousand to one. A man might therefore well feel his helplessness to render any assistance to those dear to him in the event of a general uprising of the people. Soldiers without family ties take things lightly, they are ready for danger and for death if needs be, but they can always hope to get through somehow; but the man with a wife and children in India, at the time when a general outbreak was anticipated, would have the deepest cause for anxiety. Not, however, that at this time any one at Sandynugghur looked for anything so terrible. There was a spirit of insubordination abroad in the native troops, no doubt, but no one doubted but that it would, with more or less trouble, be put down. And so things went on as usual, and the garden parties and the drives, and the friendly evening visiting continued just as before. It was at one of these pleasant evening gatherings that the first blow fell. Most of the officers of the station, their wives, and the two or three civilians were collected at Major Warrener's. The windows were all open. The girls were playing a duet on the piano; five or six other ladies were in the drawing-room and about the same number of gentlemen were standing or sitting by them, some four or five were lounging in the veranda enjoying their cheroots; native servants in their white dresses moved noiselessly about with iced lemonade and wine, when a Sepoy came up the walk.

"What is it?" asked Major Warrener, who was one of the group in the veranda.

"Dispatch for the colonel, Sahib."

The colonel, who was sitting next to the major, held out his hand for the message, and was rising, when Major Warrener said:

"Don't move, colonel; boy, bring a candle."

The servant brought it: the colonel opened the envelope and glanced at the dispatch. He uttered an exclamation which was half a groan, half a cry.

"Good Heaven! what is the matter, colonel?"

"The native troops at Meerut have mutinied, have murdered their officers and all the European men, women, and children they could find, and are marching upon Delhi. Look after your regiment."

A low cry broke from the major. This was indeed awful news, and for a moment the two men sat half-stunned at the calamity, while the sound of music and merry talk came in through the open window like a mockery on their ears.

In Times Of Peril A Tale Of India | 19

"Let us take a turn in the compound," said the major, "where no one can hear us."

For half an hour they walked up and down the garden. There could be no doubt about the truth of the news, for it was an official telegram from the adjutant at Meerut; and as to the extent of the misfortune, it was terrible.

"There is not a single white regiment at Delhi," exclaimed the colonel; "these fiends will have it all their own way, and at Delhi there are scores of European families. Delhi once in their hands will be a center, and the mutiny will spread like wildfire over India. What was the general at Meerut about? what were the white troops up to? It is as inexplicable as it is terrible. Is there anything to be done, major, do you think?" But Major Warrener could think of nothing. The men at present knew nothing of the news, but the tidings would reach them in two or three days; for news in India spreads from village to village, and town to town, with almost incredible speed, and Meerut was but a hundred and fifty miles distant.

"Had we better tell them inside?" the major asked.

"No," answered the colonel; "let them be happy for to-night; they will know the news to-morrow. As they are breaking up, ask all the officers to come round to the messroom; I will meet them there, and we can talk the matter over; but let the ladies have one more quiet night; they will want all their strength and fortitude for what is to come."

And so, clearing their brows, they went into the house and listened to the music, and joined in the talk until ten o'clock struck and every one got up to go, and so ended the last happy evening at Sandynugghur.

The next morning brought the news of the rising at Delhi, but it was not till two days later that letters giving any details of these terrible events arrived, and the full extent of the awful calamity was known.

The flame broke out at Meerut at seven o'clock in the evening of Sunday, the 10th of May. On the previous day a punishment parade had been held to witness the military degradation of a number of men of the Third Native Cavalry, who had been guilty of mutinous conduct in respect to the cartridges. The native regiments at the station consisted of the Third Cavalry, the Eleventh and Twentieth Infantry; there were also in garrison the Sixtieth Rifles, the Sixth Dragoon Guards, and two batteries of artillery; a force amply sufficient, if properly handled, to have crushed the native troops, and to have nipped the mutiny in the bud. Unhappily, they were not well handled. The cantonments of Meerut were of great extent, being nearly five miles in length by two in breadth, the barracks of the British troops were situated at some distance from those of the native regiments, and the action of the troops was paralyzed by the incompetency of the general, an old man who had lost all energy, and who remained in a state of indecision while the men of the native regiments shot their officers, murdered all the women and children, and the white inhabitants whose bungalows were situated at their end of their cantonment, opened the jail doors, and after setting fire to the whole of this quarter of Meerut, marched off toward Delhi, unmolested by the British troops. Even then an orderly sent off with dispatches to the officer commanding at Delhi, informing him of what had happened, and bidding him beware, might have saved the lives of hundreds of Englishmen and women, even if it were too late to save Delhi; but nothing whatever was done; the English troops made a few meaningless and uncertain movements, and marched back to their barracks. No one came forward to take the lead. So the white troops of Meerut remained stationary under arms all night, and the English population of Delhi were left to their fate.

From Meerut to Delhi is thirty-two miles, and the mutineers of Meerut, marching all night, arrived near the town at eight in the morning. Singularly enough, the ancient capital of India, the place around which the aspiration of Hindoos and Mohammedans alike centered, and where the ex-emperor and his family still resided, was left entirely to the guard of native troops; not a single British regiment was there, not a battery of white troops. As the center of the province, a large white population were gathered there- the families of the officers of the native infantry and artillery, of the civil officers of the province, merchants, bankers, missionaries, and others. As at all other Indian towns, the great bulk of the white inhabitants lived in the cantonments outside the town; had it not been for this, not one would have escaped the slaughter that commenced as soon as the Third Cavalry from Meerut rode into the town. The Fifty-fourth Native Infantry, who had hastily been marched out to meet them, fraternized with them at once, and, standing quietly by, looked on while their officers were murdered by the cavalrymen. Then commenced a scene of murder and atrocity which is happily without parallel in history. Suffice to say, that with the exception of some half-dozen who in one way or other managed to escape, the whole of the white population inside the walls of Delhi were murdered under circumstances of the most horrible and revolting cruelty. Had the news of the outbreak of Meerut been sent by a swift mounted messenger, the whole of these hapless people would have had time to leave the town before the arrival of the mutineers. Those in the cantonments outside the city fared somewhat better. Some were killed, but the greater part made their escape; and although many were murdered on the way, either by villagers or by bodies of mutineers, the majority reached Meerut or Aliwal. The sufferers of Delhi did not die wholly unavenged. Inside the city walls was an immense magazine containing vast stores of powder, cartridges, and arms. It was all-important that this should not fall into the hands of the mutineers. This was in charge of Lieutenant Willoughby of the royal artillery, who had with him Lieutenants Forrest and Rayner, and six English warrant and non-commissioned officers, Buckley, Shaw, Scully, Crow, Edwards, and Stewart. The following account was given by Lieutenant Forrest:

"The gates of the magazine were closed and barricaded, and every possible arrangement that could be made was at once commenced. Inside the gate leading to the park were placed two six-pounders doubly charged with grape. These were under acting sub-conductor Crow and Sergeant Stewart, with lighted matches in their hands. Their orders were that if any attempt was made to force the gate the guns were to be fired at once, and they were to fall back to that part of the magazine where Lieutenant Willoughby and I were posted. The principal gate of the magazine was similarly defended by two guns and by the *chevaux-de-frise* laid down in the inside. For the further defense of this gate and the magazine in its vicinity, there were two six-pounders so placed as to command it and a small bastion close by. Within sixty yards of the gate, and commanding two cross roads, were three six-pounders, and one twenty-four pound howitzer, which could be so managed as to act upon any part of the magazine in that neighborhood. After all these guns and howitzers had been placed in the several positions above named, they were loaded with a double charge of grape. After these arrangements had been completed a train was laid ready to be fired at a preconcerted signal. On the enemy approaching the walls of the magazine, which was provided with scaling ladders, the native establishment at once deserted us by climbing up the sloped sheds on the inside of the magazine and descending the ladders on the outside."

When the attack began the mutineers climbed the walls in great numbers, and opened fire upon the little garrison; these replied by an incessant fire of grape-shot, which told severely upon the enemy. There were but two men to each gun, but they stood nobly to their pieces until all were more or less wounded by the enemy's fire. Finding that no more could be done, Lieutenant Willoughby gave the order, Conductor Scully fired the several trains, and in another instant a tremendous explosion took place which shook all Delhi, and covered the city with a cloud of black smoke. It was calculated that from fifteen hundred to two thousand of the mutineers and rabble of the town were killed by the falling walls, or crushed under the masses of masonry. Lieutenants Willoughby, Forrest, Rayner, and Conductor Buckley survived the explosion, and effected their retreat in the confusion through a small sallyport on the river face. The mutineers were so enraged by their misfortune that they rushed to the palace and demanded of the king a number of European officers and ladies who had sought refuge under his protection. They were handed over to the mutineers, and at once slaughtered.

The Warreners listened with pale faces as their father, on his return from the orderly-room, where the news had been discussed, told them the sad story.

"There is nothing to be done, I suppose, papa?" Ned said gently.

"No, my boy; we are in the hands of God. We must wait now for what may come. At present the regiment professes its fidelity, and has now volunteered to march against the mutineers. The colonel believes them, so do some of the others; I do not; it may be that the men mean what they say at present, but we know that emissaries come and go, and every fresh rising will be an incentive to them. It is no use blinking the truth, dear; we are like men standing on a loaded mine which may at any moment explode. I have been thinking, indeed for the last week I have done nothing but think, what is best to be done. If the mutiny breaks out at night or at any time when we are not on parade, we have agreed that all the whites shall make at once for Mr. Thompson's house. It is the strongest of any of the residences—for there would of course be no getting to the messhouse—and then we will sell our lives as dearly as we may. If it happens when we are on parade, defense by the rest of the residents would be useless. There are but six civilians, with you two boys—for we have counted you—eight. Probably but few of you could gain Thompson's house in time; and if all did, your number would be too small to defend it. There remains then nothing but flight. The rising will most likely take place on parade. The residents have agreed that each day they will, on some excuses or other, have their traps at their door at that hour, so that at the sound of the first shot fired they may jump in and drive off."

"But, you, papa?" Kate asked.

"My dear," said her father, "I shall be on duty; so long as a vestige of the regiment remains as a regiment, I shall be with it; if the whole regiment breaks up and attacks us, those who do not fall at the first volley will be justified in trying to save their lives. The colonel, the adjutant, and myself are mounted officers, and two or three of the others will have their dogcarts each day brought up to the messhouse, as they often do. If there is a mutiny on parade, the unmounted officers will make for them, and we who are mounted will as far as possible cover their retreat. So it is arranged."

"But will the road be open to Meerut, uncle?" Rose asked after a pause, for the danger seemed so strange and terrible that they felt stunned by it.

"No, my dear; it certainly will not. There are three garrison towns between us, and they also will probably be up. The only thing is to keep to the road for the first ten or twelve miles, and then take to the woods, and make your way on foot. I have spoken to Saba this morning. We can trust her; she nursed you all, and has lived with me ever since as a sort of pensioner till you came out. I have asked her to get two dresses of Mussulman country women; in those only the eyes are visible, while the Hindoo dress gives no concealment. I have also ordered her to get me two dresses: one, such as a young Mussulman *zemindar* wears; the other, as his retainer. They are for you boys. Keep the bundles, when you get them, in that closet in the dining-room, so as to be close at hand; and in case of alarm, be sure and take them with you. Remember my instructions are absolute. If by day, escape in the trap at the first alarm; if the trap is not available, escape at once on foot. If you hear the enemy are close, hide till nightfall in that thick clump of bushes in the corner of the compound, then make for that copse of trees, and try and find your way to Meerut. I trust I may be with you, or that I may join you on the road. But in any case, it will relieve my anxiety greatly to know that your course is laid down. If I had to return here to look for you, I should bring my pursuers after me, and your chance of escape would be gone—for I rely upon you all to follow my instructions to the letter."

"Yes, indeed, papa," was the unanimous answer of the young Warreners, who were deeply affected at the solemn manner in which their father spoke of the situation.

"I have a brace of revolvers upstairs," he said, "and will give one to each of you boys. Carry them always, but put them on under your coats, so that they may not be noticed; it would be as well for you to practice yourselves in their use; but when you do so, always go some distance from the station, so that the sound will not be heard."

"Can you give Rose and me a pistol each, too, papa?" Kate said quietly.

Major Warrener kissed his daughter and niece tenderly.

"I have a pair of small double-barreled pistols; you shall each have one," he answered with a deep sigh.

That afternoon the young Warreners and their cousin went out for a walk, and, fixing a piece of paper against a tree, practiced pistol shooting for an hour. Any passer-by ignorant of the circumstances would have wondered at the countenances of these young people, engaged, apparently, in the amusement of pistol practice. There was no smile on them, no merry laugh when the ball went wide of the mark, no triumphant shout at a successful shot. Their faces were set, pale, and earnest, Scarcely a word was spoken. Each loaded in silence, took up a place at the firing point, and aimed steadily and seriously; the boys with an angry eye and frowning brow, as if each time they were firing at a deadly foe; the girls as earnestly, and without any of the nervousness or timidity which would be natural in girls handling firearms for the first time. Each day the exercise was repeated, and after a week's practice all could hit, with a fair amount of certainty, a piece of paper six inches square, at a distance of ten yards.

During this time Captains Dunlop and Manners spent their whole time, when not engaged upon their military duties, at Major Warrener's. They were now the recognized lovers of Kate and Rose; and although, in those days of tremendous anxiety and peril, no formal engagements were entered upon, the young people understood each other, and Major Warrener gave his tacit approval. Very earnestly all the party hoped that when the dread moment came it might come when they were all together, so that they might share the same fate, whatever it might be. The young officers' buggies now stood all day in Major Warrener's compound, with the patient *syces* squatting near, or talking with the servants, while the major›s horses stood ready saddled in the stables.

However much the party might hope to be together when the crisis came, they felt that it was improbable that they would be so, for at the first symptoms of mutiny it would be the duty of the officers to hasten to the barracks to endeavor to quell it, even if certain death should meet them there.

In the face of the tidings from Meerut and Delhi, all the pretense of confidence, which had hitherto been kept up at the station, came to an end; and even had there been implicit confidence in the regiment, the news of such terrible events would have caused an entire cessation of the little amusements and gatherings in which Sandynugghur had previously indulged.

As is usual in cases of extreme danger, the various temperaments of people come strongly into relief at these awful times. The pretty young wife of the doctor was nearly wild with alarm. Not daring to remain at home alone, she passed the day in going from house to house of her female friends. Advice and example she obtained from these, but poor comfort. The colonel's wife was as brave as any man in the station; she hardly shared her husband's opinion that the regiment would remain faithful in the midst of an almost general defection; but she was calm, self-possessed, and ready for the worst.

"It is no use crying, my dear," she said to the doctor's wife. "Our husbands have enough to worry them without being shaken by our tears. Death, after all, can only come once, and it is better to die with those we love than to be separated."

But there were not many tears shed in Sandynugghur. The women were pale and quiet. They shook hands with a pressure which meant much, lips quivered, and tears might drop when they spoke of children at home; but this was not often, and day after day they bore the terrible strain with that heroic fortitude which characterized English women in India during the awful period of the mutiny. Ten days after the news came in of the rising at Delhi Major Warrener told his family, on his return from parade, that the regiment had again declared its fidelity, and had offered to march against the mutineers.

"I am glad of it," he said, "because it looks as if at present, at least, they have not made up their minds to mutiny, and I shall be able to go to mess with a lighter heart; as I told you yesterday, it is the colonel's birthday, so we all dine at mess."

In the meantime Saba had faithfully carried out her commission as to the dresses, and had added to the bundles a bottle containing a brown juice which she had extracted from some berries; this was to be used for staining the skin, and so completing the disguise. The Warreners knew that if their old nurse had any information as to any intended outbreak she would let them know; but she heard nothing. She was known to be so strongly attached to the major's family that, had the other servants known anything of it, they would have kept it from her.

The hour for the mess-dinner was eight, and the young Warreners had finished their evening meal before their father started.

"God bless you, my children, and watch over and protect us all till we meet again!" such was the solemn leave-taking with which the major and his children had parted—if only for half an hour—since the evil days began.

For an hour and a half the young Warreners and their cousin sat and read, and occasionally talked.

"It's time for tea," Kate said, looking at her watch; and she struck a bell upon the table.

Usually the response was almost instantaneous; but Kate waited two minutes, and then rang sharply twice. There was still no reply.

"He must be asleep," she said, "or out of hearing; but it is curious that none of the others answer!"

Dick went out into the veranda, but came in again in a minute or two:

"There is no one there, Kate; and I don't hear any of them about anywhere."

The four young people looked at each other. What did this mean? Had the servants left in a body? Did they know that something was going to happen? Such were the mute questions which their looks asked each other.

"Girls!" said Ned, "put your dark shawls round you. It may be nothing, but it is better to be prepared. Get the bundles out. Dick, put a bottle of wine in your pocket; and let us all fill our pockets with biscuits."

Silently and quietly the others did as he told them.

"There is that great biscuit-tin full," Ned said when they had filled their pockets; "let us empty it into that cloth, and tie it up. Now, if you will put your shawls on I will look in at the stables."

In a couple of minutes he returned.

"The horses are all unharnessed," he said, "and not a soul is to be seen. Ah, is that Saba?"

The old nurse had been found asleep in her favorite place outside the door of her young mistresses' room.

"Do you know what is the matter, Saba? All the servants are gone!"

The old nurse shook her head. "Bad news; no tell Saba."

"Now, Saba, get ready to start," for the nurse had declared that she would accompany them, to go into the villages to buy food; "Dick, come with me; we will put one of the horses into the dogcart."

They were leaving the room when they heard the sound of a rifle. As if it were the signal, in a moment the air rang with rifle shots, shouts, and yells. The boys leaped back into the room and caught up the bundles.

"Quick, for your lives, girls! some of them are not fifty yards off! To the bushes! Come, Saba!"

"Saba do more good here," the old nurse said, and seated herself quietly in the veranda.

It was but twenty yards to the bushes they had marked as the place of concealment; and as they entered and crouched down there came the sound of hurrying feet, and a band of Sepoys, led by one of the jemadars, or native officers, rushed up to the veranda from the back.

"Now," the jemadar shouted, "search the house; kill the boys, but keep the white women; they are too pretty to hurt."

Two minutes' search—in which furniture was upset, curtains pulled down, and chests ransacked—and a shout of rage proclaimed that the house was empty.

The jemadar shouted to his men: "Search the compound; they can't be far off; some of you run out to the plain; they can't have got a hundred yards away; besides, our guards out there will catch them."

The old nurse rose to her feet just as the Sepoys were rushing out on the search.

"It is of no use searching," she said; "they have been gone an hour."

"Gone an hour!" shouted the enraged jemadar; "who told them of the attack?"

"I told them," Saba said steadily; "Saba was true to her salt."

There was a yell of rage on the part of the mutineers, and half a dozen bayonets darted into the faithful old servant's body, and without a word she fell dead on the veranda, a victim to her noble fidelity to the children she had nursed.

"Now," the jemadar said, "strip the place; carry everything off; it is all to be divided to-morrow, and then we will have a blaze."

Five minutes sufficed to carry off all the portable articles from the bungalow; the furniture, as useless to the Sepoys, was left, but everything else was soon cleared away, and then the house was lit in half a dozen places. The fire ran quickly up the muslin curtains, caught the dry reeds of the tatties, ran up the bamboos which formed the top of the veranda, and in five minutes the house was a sheet of flame.

CHAPTER III.
THE FLIGHT.

The young Warreners and their cousin, hurrying on, soon gained the thick bush toward which they were directing their steps. As they cowered down in its shelter the girls pulled their shawls over their heads, and with their hands to their ears to keep out the noise of the awful din around them, they awaited, in shuddering horror, their fate. The boys sat, revolver in hand, determined to sell their lives dearly. Ned translated the jemadar's speech, and at his order to search the compound both felt that all was over, and, with a grasp of each other's hand, prepared to sally forth and die. Then came Saba's act of noble self-sacrifice, and the boys had difficulty in restraining themselves from rushing out to avenge her.

In the meantime the night was hideous with noises; musket shots, the sharp cracks of revolvers, shouts, cries, and at times the long shrill screams of women. It was too much to be borne, and feeling that for the present Saba's act had saved them, the boys, laying down their weapons, pressed their hands to their ears to keep out the din. There they sat for half an hour, stunned by the awful calamity, too horror-stricken at what had passed, and at the probable fate of their father, to find relief in tears.

At the end of that time the fire had burned itself out, and a few upright posts still flickering with tongues of fire, and a heap of glowing embers marked where the pretty bungalow, replete with every luxury and comfort, had stood an hour before.

Dick was the first to move; he touched Ned's arm.

"All is quiet here now, but they may take it into their heads to come back and search. We had better make for the trees; by keeping close to that cactus hedge we shall be in shadow all the way."

The girls were roused from their stupor of grief.

"Now, dears, we must be brave," said Ned, "and carry out our orders. God has protected us thus far; let us pray that He will continue to do so."

In another five minutes the little party, stealing cautiously out from their shelter, kept along close to the wall to a side door, through which they issued forth into the open. Ten steps took them to the cactus hedge, and stooping low under its shelter, they moved on till they safely reached the clump of trees.

For some time the little party crouched among the thick bushes, the silence broken only by the sobs of the girls. Ned and Richard said nothing, but the tears fell fast down their cheeks. The crackling of the flames of many of the burning bungalows could be distinctly heard; and outside the shadow of the trees it was nearly as light as day. Yells of triumph rose on the night air, but there was no firing or sounds of conflict, and resistance was plainly over. For a quarter of an hour they sat there, crushed with the immensity of the calamity. Then Ned roused himself and took the lead.

"Now, dears, the fires have burned down, and we must be moving, for we should be far away from here before morning. No doubt others have hidden in the woods round this place, and those black fiends will be searching everywhere to-morrow. Remember what our orders are;" and he paused for a moment to choke down the sob which would come when he thought of who had given the order, and how it was given. "We were to make for Meerut. Be strong and brave, girls, as father would have had you. I have gone over the course on the district map, and I think I can keep pretty straight for it. We need not change our clothes now; we can do that when we halt before daylight. We must walk all night, to be as far as possible away before the search begins. We know this country pretty well for some miles round, which will make it easier. Come, girls, take heart; it is possible yet that some of the officers have cut their way out, and our father may be among them. Who can say?"

"I knew that he had talked over with Dunlop and Manners the very best course to take whenever they might be attacked," Dick said in a more cheerful tone, "so they were sure to keep together, and if any one has got away, they would." Neither of the boys had at heart the least hope, but they spoke as cheerfully as they could, to give strength and courage to the girls. Their words had their effect. Kate rose, and taking her cousin's arm said:

"Come, Rose, the boys are right. There is still some hope; let us cling to it as long as we can. Now let us be moving: but before we go, let us all thank God for having saved us from harm so far, and let us pray for His protection and help upon the road."

Silently the little group knelt in prayer, and when they rose followed Ned—who had naturally assumed the position of leader—out into the open country beyond the grove, without a word being spoken. The moon was as yet quite young, a favorable state for the fugitives, as it afforded light enough to see where they were going without giving so bright a light as to betray them to any one at a distance.

"The moon will be down in a couple of hours," Ned said; "but by that time we shall be beyond where any sentries are likely to have been placed on the road, so we can then trust ourselves on that till it begins to get daylight. We must keep in the fields till we are past Nussara, which is five miles by the road; then we can walk straight on. There is a nullah a few yards on; we had better keep in that for a quarter of a mile; it does not go quite the way we want, but it will be safer to follow it till we are well out of sight of any one who may be watching the plain."

They scrambled down into the bed of the nullah. Then Kate said, "Walk on as fast as you can, Ned; we can keep up with you, and if we hurry on we shan't be able to think."

"All right," Ned answered; "I will go fast for a bit, but you must not knock yourselves up; we have a long journey before us."

Walking fast, however, was impossible at the bottom of the nullah, for it was pitch dark between its steep banks, and there were bowlders and stones lying here and there. After half an hour's walking Ned scrambled up and looked back.

"It is quite safe now," he said; "let us make as straight as we can for Nussara."

Kate Warrener and Rose Hertford have never been able to recall any incidents of that night's walk. Mechanically, as in a dreadful dream, they followed Ned's guidance, stumbling across little watercourses, tramping through marshy rice-fields, climbing into and out of deep nullahs, now pausing to listen to the barking of a village dog, now making their way through a thick clump of trees, and at last tramping for hours—that seemed ages—along the dead flat of the highroad. This at the first faint dawn of morning they left, and took refuge in a thick grove a quarter of a mile from the highway. Before throwing themselves down to rest, the girls, at Ned's earnest request, tried to eat a piece of biscuit, but tried in vain, they, however, each sipped a little wine from the bottles, and then, utterly worn out and exhausted, soon forgot their misery in a deep and heavy sleep.

The sun was upon the point of setting when their companions aroused them, and they woke up to their sorrows and dangers. The day had passed quietly; the boys, after both sleeping for some four or five hours, had watched by turns. No one had approached the wood; but a party of four Sepoys, mounted on horses, had passed from Sandynugghur; and a larger party had, later in the afternoon, come along in the other direction. From this the boys guessed that a successful revolt had also taken place at Nalgwa, the next station to Sandynugghur.

"Now, girls, the first thing to do is to eat. Here are biscuits for some days, and the two bottles of wine, which we must be sparing of. Dick and I have eaten lots of biscuits, and have had some water from a well at a little distance behind the wood. There was a large gourd lying by it which we have taken the liberty of borrowing. You can drink some water if you like, but you must each take a glass of wine. You must keep up your strength. There is no one in sight, so if you like you can go to the well and have a wash. Don't be longer than you can help; it would be ruin to be seen before we have changed our clothes. While you are away washing, Dick and I will put on our dresses, and when you come back you can do the same. We can stain our faces and hands afterward."

The girls chose to have their wash first and their meal afterward, and felt refreshed and brighter after they had done so. Then they dressed in the clothes Saba had provided for them, and could, at any other time, have laughed at the comicality of their aspect, muffled up in white, with only their eyes visible. The awkward shoes were the only part of the costume to which they objected; but the sight of European boots below the native dress would have betrayed them instantly; however, they determined to adopt them for walking in at nights, or when crossing the fields, and to put the native shoes in a bundle, to be worn in public.

The boys presently joined them, Ned in the dress of a young Mussulman zemindar, Dick as his follower.

"I should not have known you in the least," Rose said; "as far as appearances go, I think we are all safe now."

When it was quite dark they again started, regained the road, and kept steadily along it. After two hours' walking they approached a village. After some consultation it was decided that Dick, whose dress was the darkest and least noticeable, should steal forward and reconnoiter. If every one was indoors they would push boldly through; if not, they would make a circuit round it. In ten minutes he returned.

"Ned, there are two troopers' horses standing before the largest house of the place. I suppose they belong to some of the men of the cavalry regiment at Nalgwa. If we could but steal them!"

"Splendid, Dick; why should we not? I can get on one, you on the other; one of the girls can sit behind each of us, with her arms round our waists. What do you say, girls? With our dress it would be natural for us to be on horseback, and no one would ask any questions. We are pretty safe, because if they come out there are but two of them, and we are more than a match for them with our pistols."

"It seems a terrible risk to run, Ned; but I do think it would be our best plan. What do you say, Rose?"

"I think we had better try, Kate."

"Now let us settle everything before we start," said Ned. "We must mount first, I think, that we may be able to help you more easily; and you would have less risk of falling off if you get up in front of us. We can change when we have gone half a mile. Will you stand close to Dick, Kate, when he mounts; Rose, you keep close to me. The moment we are fairly in the saddle, and have got the reins in our hands, you put your foot on mine, and take hold of my hand, and climb up in the saddle in front of me. Put your arms round our necks and hold us, because we shall want one hand for the reins, the other for a pistol."

"Let us cut a stick, Ned, to give them a lick and make them start at a gallop."

Very gently, and with bated breath, they stole up the village. The horses were still standing with their reins thrown over a hook in the wall. Very quietly the boys unhooked the reins, but the horses moved uneasily, and objected to their mounting them, for horses accustomed to natives dislike to be touched by Europeans. However, the boys had just managed to climb into their seats when a shutter of the house opened, and a voice said in Hindostanee, "What is fidgeting the horses?" Then a head looked out.

"Some one is stealing the horses," he shouted.

"Quick, girls, up with you," Ned said; and the girls, as light as feathers, sprang up. "Go along," the boys cried, bringing down their sticks on the animals' sides. Dick's at once leaped forward, but Ned's horse only backed. Ned gave his stick to Rose and seized his pistol, which was cocked and ready for use. As he did so a native trooper rushed from the house. As he came out Ned fired, and the man fell forward on his face.

Startled by the shot, the horse darted off after his companion. For a few minutes they went forward at a gallop, the boys holding on as well as they could, but expecting every moment to be thrown off. For awhile shouts and cries were heard from the village, and then all was quiet again. The two boys reined in their horses.

"That was awful," Dick said; "I would rather sit on the yardarm in a storm than ride on that beast any further at the pace we have been going."

In Times Of Peril A Tale Of India | 33

The girls had not spoken a word since they started, and they now slipped to the ground. It was not an easy thing for them to get up behind, and several slips were made before their attempts were successful. Once seated, they were more comfortable, and they again went on, this time at an easy canter. After half an hour's ride they came to a crossroad, and turned up there, going now at a walk. After awhile they took a well-marked path running in a parallel direction to the road; this they followed for some time, passing fearlessly through one or two small villages.

Then, feeling by the flagging walk of their horses that they were becoming fatigued, they plunged deep into a thick wood, dismounted, and prepared for the night. Attached to the saddle of each horse was a nose-bag with some forage. These were put on, the horses fastened up, and the little party were soon asleep again.

Before starting next morning the first care of the boys was to take off the embroidery of the horse-cloths, and as much of the metal work on the bridles as could be possibly dispensed with, in order to conceal the fact that the horses had belonged to a British cavalry regiment; then they mounted, with the girls behind them, and rode quietly forward, taking care not to travel by the main road, as the news of the carrying off the horses would have been generally known there.

They passed through several villages, attracting but little attention as they did so, for there was now nothing unusual in the appearance of a Mohammedan zemindar and follower riding with two closely-veiled women *en croupe*. Late in the afternoon they stopped at a village store, and Ned purchased, without exciting any apparent suspicion, some grain for the horses. That night they slept as usual in a wood, and congratulated themselves on having made fully twenty-five miles of their journey toward Meerut.

The next morning, after two miles' riding, they entered a large village. As they were passing through it a number of peasants suddenly rushed out into the road, and shouted to them to stop. They were armed with sticks and hoes, and a few had guns. Looking behind, Ned saw a similar body fill up the road behind them, cutting off their escape.

"Look, Ned, at that old fellow with the gun; that's the man who sold us the grain last night," Dick said.

"We must charge them, Dick; there's nothing else to do. Hold tight, girls. Now for your revolver, Dick! Now!"

And, digging their heels into their horses' side, the boys rode at the crowd of peasants. There was a discharge of guns, and Dick felt as if a hot iron had been drawn suddenly across his cheek; then they were in the midst of the crowd, emptying their revolvers with deadly effect among them; some fell, and the horses dashed forward, followed by the yells of their assailants. A minute later three or four more guns were discharged, the rear party having now joined the other, and being therefore able for the first time to fire.

Dick heard a little startled cry from Kate.

"Are you hurt, darling?" he cried in alarm.

"Nothing to speak of, Dick. Ride on."

In a quarter of a mile they drew rein, and found that a ball had passed through the upper part of Kate's arm, as it went round Dick's body. Fortunately it had gone through the flesh only, without touching the bone. Dick was bleeding copiously from a wound across the cheek.

"Another two inches to the right," he said, "and it would have taken me fairly in the mouth. It's well it's no worse."

Kate's arm was soon bandaged up, and a handkerchief tied round Dick's face. Ned proposed that for Kate's sake they should make a halt at the first wood they came to, but Kate would not hear of it.

"On the contrary, Ned, we ought to press forward as hard as we can, for it is very possible that at that village where we were recognized—I suppose because they had heard about the horses—they may have dispatched people to the main road, as well as further on to stop us here; and we may be pursued at any moment, if there happens to be any native cavalry upon the road. Evidently they are very much in earnest about catching us, and have sent word to look after four people on two horses all over the country, or they could not have known about it at the village yesterday evening."

"I am afraid you are right, Kate; if we could turn off this road I should not fear, but the river cannot be far to our right, and the main road is to our left. There is nothing for it but to press straight on. Fortunately, the country is not thickly populated, and there is a good deal of jungle. If the worst comes to the worst, we must leave our horses and go on foot again. I fear that is more fatiguing for you, but we can hide ourselves a good deal better."

It was late in the afternoon when Rose cried. "They are coming, Ned; there is a party of cavalry behind!"

Ned looked round; and far back, along the straight road, he saw a body of horsemen.

"They are a long distance behind," he said; "now for a race!"

The boys plied their sticks, and the horses sprang on at full gallop.

"How much are they gaining, Rose?" he asked, after twenty minutes' hard riding.

"They are nearer, Ned—a good deal nearer; but they have not gained half their distance yet."

"The sun set fully ten minutes ago," Ned said; "in another half-hour it will be dark. Their horses must be done up, or they would gain faster on us, as ours have to carry double, and are getting terribly blown; but there is a wood, which looks a large one, a couple of miles ahead. If we can get there five minutes before them, we are safe."

By dint of flogging their horses they entered the wood while their pursuers were half a mile behind.

"Another hundred yards," Ned said, "and then halt. Now, off we get."

In an instant they leaped off, and gave a couple of sharp blows with their sticks to the horses, who dashed off at a gallop down the road.

It was already perfectly dark in the wood, and the fugitives hurried into the thickest part. In five minutes they heard the cavalry come thundering past.

"We must push on," Ned said; "fortunately, we have done no walking, for we must be far away by to-morrow morning. They will come up with the horses before very long, and will know we are in the wood, and they will search it through and through in the morning."

A quarter of a mile, and the wood grew thicker, being filled with an undergrowth of jungle.

"If you will stop here, Ned, I will push on through this jungle, and see how far it goes. The girls can never get through this. I think we are near the edge of the wood; it looks lighter ahead."

In ten minutes he came back.

"Ned, we are on the river; it is not fifty yards from here."

This was serious news.

"What a pity we did not take to the left instead of the right when we left the horses. However, they won't know which way we have gone, and must watch the whole wood. We must push forward, and, by keeping as close as we can to the river, shall most likely pass them; besides, they will be some time before they decide upon forming a chain round the wood, and as there are only about twenty of them they will be a long way apart. There! Do you hear them? They are coming back! Now let us go on again!"

In ten minutes they reached the edge of the wood. They could see nothing of the horsemen. Keeping in the fields, but close to the line of jungle that bordered the river, they walked onward for upward of an hour. Then they came upon the road. The river had made a bend, and the road now followed its bank.

"Shall we cross it, and keep in the open country, or follow it, girls?"

"Follow it as long as we can keep on walking," Kate said. "It is in the right direction, and we can go on so much faster than in the fields. If we hear them coming along we can get into the jungle on the bank."

"Listen, Kate," Rose said a few minutes afterward; "they are following!"

"I expect," Ned said, "they find that the wood is too big to be watched, and some of them are going on to get some help from the next garrison, or, perhaps, to rouse up a village and press them in the work. Trot on, girls; the jungle is so thick here you could hardly squeeze yourself in. We have plenty of time; they won't be here for five minutes yet."

CHAPTER IV.
BROKEN DOWN.

They ran at the top of their speed, but the sound of the horses' feet grew louder.

"There is a path leading to the river," Ned said; "let us turn down there; we can hide under the jungle on the bank."

Breathlessly they ran down to the river.

"Hurrah! here is a boat, jump in;" and in another minute they had pushed off from the bank, just as they heard a body of cavalry—for that they were troops they knew by the jingling of their accouterments—pass at a gallop. The stream was strong; and the boys found that with the rude oars they could make no way whatever.

"We had better land again, and get further from the river," Ned said. "We will push the boat off, and it will be supposed that we have gone off in it."

This was soon done, and having regained the road, they crossed it and struck over the fields.

The moon, which had been hitherto hidden under a passing cloud, was soon out fully, and for some time they kept across the country, carefully avoiding all villages. These were here more thinly scattered; patches of jungle and wood occurred more frequently; and it was evident that they were getting into a less highly cultivated district. It was long before daybreak that Rose declared that she was too fatigued to go further, and they entered a large wood. Here they lay down, and were soon fast asleep. It was broad daylight when the Warreners woke. Rose still slept on.

Presently Kate came to her brothers. "I am afraid Rose is going to be ill. She keeps talking and moaning in her sleep; her face is flushed, and her hands as hot as fire."

As they were looking sadly at her she opened her eyes.

"Is it time to get up?" she asked. "Oh, my head! it is aching terribly. Is the trap at the door?"

Then she closed her eyes again, and went on talking incoherently to herself.

"She has fever," Kate said, "and we must get her under shelter, at whatever risk."

"I heard a dog bark not far off, just as I went to sleep," Ned said. "I will go and reconnoiter. Dick, you had better stay here."

Dick nodded, and Ned advanced cautiously to the edge of the wood. There he saw a farmhouse of a better class than usual. Three peons were just starting for work, and an elderly man with a long beard was standing at the door. Then he went in, and after a few minutes reappeared with a long staff in his hands, and went out into the fields. He did not, however, follow the direction which the peons had taken, but took a line parallel with the edge of the wood. "He looks a decent old fellow," Ned said to himself; "I can but try; at any rate, at the worst I am more than a match for him."

So saying, he stepped out into the field. The farmer started with surprise at seeing a young Mussulman appear before him.

"I am English," Ned said at once. "I think you are kind by your face, and I tell you the truth. There are two English girls in the wood, and one is ill. We can go no further. Will you give them shelter?"

The old man stood for some time in thought.

"I have no complaint against the Feringhees," he said; "in my fathers time the country was red with blood, but all my life I have eaten my bread in peace, and no man has injured me. Where are the English ladies?"

Ned led the way to the spot where Rose was still lying. The old man looked at her flushed face, and then at Kate, and said:

"The English ladies have suffered much, and can have done harm to no one. I will shelter them. My wife and daughter will nurse the sick one. They will be in the women's chamber, and my servants will not know that there is a stranger there. I believe that they would be faithful, but one who knows nothing can tell no tales. On the other side of the wood there is a shed. It is empty now, and none go near it. The English sahibs can live there, and each day I will bring them food. When their sister is well they can go on again."

Ned translated the old man's words, and Kate, who was kneeling by Rose, caught his hand and kissed it in her gratitude. He patted her head and said, "Poor child!"

"How are we to carry Rose? I don't think she can walk," Kate asked.

The farmer solved the difficulty by motioning them to stay where they were. He then went off, and in ten minutes returned, bearing a dried bullock's skin. On this Rose was laid. The Hindoo took the two ends at her feet, the boys each one of those by her head, and then, slung as in a hammock, Rose was carried to the house, where the wife and daughter of their host, prepared by him for what was coming, received them with many expressions of pity, and she was at once carried into the inner room. The farmer then placed before the boys two bowls of milk and some freshly made chupatties, and then gave them some food for the day. With an expression of fervent gratitude to him, and a kiss from Kate, who came out to tell them that Rose would be well nursed and cared for, the boys started for the hut in the direction the Hindoo pointed out to them. It was a small building, and had apparently been at some time used as a cattle shed. The floor was two feet deep in fodder of the stalks of Indian corn. Above was a sort of rough loft, in which grain had been stored.

The boys at once agreed that, to prevent suspicion, it was safer to occupy this, and they soon transferred enough of the fodder from below to make a comfortable bed. Then, feeling secure from discovery, even if by chance some passer-by should happen to glance into the shed, they were soon deep in a sounder sleep than they had enjoyed since they left Sandynugghur.

The next day, when the old man came to see them, he was accompanied by Kate. She looked pale and wan.

"How is Rose?" was their first question.

"She is as bad as she can be, dears. She has been delirious all night, and is so this morning. I did not like to leave her for a moment. But this kind old man wanted me to go with him, as I think he has something to say to you."

"Have you any news?" Ned asked him.

"My servants tell me that the Sepoys are searching the whole country, some of the officers have escaped from Sandynugghur, and also from Nalgwa, where the troops rose on the same night; some of the residents have escaped also. There is a reward offered for them alive or dead, and any one hiding them is to be punished with death. The white lady is very ill. She is in the hand of God; she may get better, she may die. If she gets better it will be weeks before she can go through the hardships of the journey to Meerut. I think it better that you should go on alone; the white ladies will be as my daughters. I have told my servants that my daughter is ill, so that if they hear cries and voices at night they will think that it is she who is in pain. You can do no good here. If the woods are searched you may be found; if you are found they will search everywhere closely, and may find them. I will hide them here safely. The orders are, I hear, that the captives taken are to be carried to Delhi; but if they should be found I will myself journey to Meerut to bring you the news. You will give me your names, and I will find you; then you may get help and rescue them on the way."

Ned translated the old man's opinion and kind offer to his brother and sister, and said that he was very unwilling to leave the girls—a sentiment in which Dick heartily joined.

Kate, however, at once expressed her warm approval of the plan.

"It will be weeks, dears, before Rose can walk again, and I shall have an anxious time with her. It would add greatly to my anxiety if I knew that you were near, and might at any time be captured and killed. If dear papa has escaped he will be in a terrible state of anxiety about us, and you could relieve him if you can join him at Meerut, and tell him how kindly we are treated here. Altogether, boys, it would be so much better for you to go; for if the Sepoys do come, you could not defend us against more than two or three, and they are sure to come in a stronger party than that."

In spite of their disinclination to leave the girls without such protection as they could give them, the boys saw that the course advised was the best to be pursued, and told their Hindoo friend that they agreed to follow his counsel, thanking him in the warmest terms for his kindness.

He advised them to leave their Mohammedan dresses behind, and to dress in the simple costume of Hindoo peons, with which he could supply them. They would then attract far less attention, and could even by day pass across the fields without any comment whatever from the natives at work there, who would naturally suppose that they belonged to some village near at hand. "Englishmen could not do this," he said; "too much leg, too much arm, too much width of shoulders; but boys are thinner, and no one will notice the difference. In half an hour I will come back with the things." Ned gave him the rest of the berries, which they had preserved, and asked him to boil them up in a little water, as they would now have to color their bodies and arms and legs, in addition to their faces.

It was a sad parting between Kate and her brothers, for all felt that they might never meet again. Still the course decided upon was, under the circumstances, evidently the best that could be adopted.

In an hour the Hindoo returned. The boys took off their clothes, and stained themselves a deep brown from head to foot. The farmer then produced a razor and a bowl of water and some soap, and said that they must shave their hair off their heads, up to a level with the top of the ears, so as to leave only that which could be concealed by their turban. This, with some laughter—the first time they had smiled since they left Sandynugghur—

they proceeded to do to each other, and the skin thus exposed they dyed the same color as the rest of the body. They then each put on a scanty loincloth, and wrapping a large piece of dark blue cotton stuff first round their waists and then over one shoulder, their costume was complete, with the exception of a pair of sandals and a white turban. The old Hindoo surveyed them gravely when their attire was completed, and expressed his belief that they would pass without exciting the slightest suspicion. Their pistols were a trouble. They were determined that, come what might, they would not go without these, and they were finally slung behind them from a strap passing round the waist under the loin-cloth; the spare ammunition and a supply of biscuit were stowed in stout cotton bags, with which their friend provided them, and which hung by a band passing over one shoulder. Their money and a box of matches they secured in a corner of their clothes. A couple of stout staves completed their outfit.

Bidding a grateful farewell to their friendly Hindoo, the boys started on their journey. The sandals they found so difficult to keep on that they took them off and carried them, except when they were passing over stony ground. They kept to bypaths and avoided all villages. Occasionally they met a native, but either they passed him without speech, or Ned muttered a salutation in answer to that of the passer. All day they walked, and far into the night. They had no fear of missing their way, as the road on one hand and the river on the other both ran to Meerut; and although these were sometimes ten miles apart, they served as a fair index as to the line they should take. The biscuits, eked out with such grain as they could pluck as they crossed the fields, lasted for two days; but at the end of that time it became necessary to seek another supply of food.

"I don't know what to ask for, Dick; and those niggers always chatter so much that I should have to answer, and then I should be found out directly. I think we must try some quiet huts at a distance from the road."

The wood in which they that night slept was near three or four scattered huts. In the morning they waited and watched for a long time until one of the cottages was, as far as they could judge, deserted, all its inmates being gone out to work in the fields. They then entered it boldly. It was empty. On hunting about they found some chupatties which had apparently been newly baked, a store of rice and of several other grains. They took the chupatties, five or six pounds of rice, and a little copper cooking-pot. They placed in a conspicuous position two rupees, which were more than equivalent to the value of the things they had taken, and went on their way rejoicing.

At midday they sat down, lit a fire with some dried sticks, and put their rice in the pot to boil. As Ned was stooping to pick up a stick he was startled by a simultaneous cry of "Look out!" from Dick, and a sharp hiss; and looking up, saw, three or four feet ahead of him, a cobra, with its hood inflated, and its head raised in the very act of springing. Just as it was darting itself forward Dick's stick came down with a sharp tap on its head and killed it.

"That was a close shave, Ned," the boy said, laughing; "if you had stooped he would have bit you on the face. What would have been the best thing to do if he had bitten you?"

"The best thing is to suck the wound instantly, to take out a knife and cut deeply in, and then, as we have no vesuvians, I should break up half a dozen pistol cartridges, put the powder into and on the wound, and set it alight. I believe that that is what they do in some parts of Eastern Europe in the case of the bites of mad dogs; and this, if no time is lost after the bite is given, is almost always effectual in keeping off hydrophobia."

"Well, Ned, I am very thankful that we had not to put the virtue of the receipt to a practical test."

"Would you like to eat the snake, Dick? I believe that snake is not at all bad eating."

"Thank you," Dick said, "I will take it on trust. We have got rice; and although I am not partial to rice it will do very well. If we could have got nothing else we might have tried the snake; but as it is, I had rather not. Two more days, Ned, and we shall be at Meerut. The old Hindoo said it was a hundred miles, and we go twenty-five a day, even with all our bends and turns to get out of the way of villages."

"Yes, I should think we do quite that, Dick. We walk from daylight to sunset, and often two or three hours by moonlight; and though we don't go very fast, we ought to get over a lot of ground. Listen! There is music!" Both held their breath. "Yes, there are the regular beats of a big drum. It is on the highroad, I should say, nearly abreast of us. If we go to that knoll we shall have a view of them; and there cannot be the least danger, as they must be fully a mile away."

Upon gaining the rise in question they saw a regiment in scarlet, winding along the road.

"Are they mutineers, Dick, or British?"

It was more than any one could say. Mounted officers rode at the head of the regiment; perfect order was to be observed in its marching; there was nothing that in any way differed from its ordinary aspect.

"Let us go back and get our rice and lota, Dick. We can't afford to lose that; and if we go at a trot for a couple of miles we can get round into some trees near the road, where we can see their faces. If the mounted officers are white it is all right; if not, they are mutineers."

Half an hour's trot brought them to such a point of vantage as they desired. Crouched in some bushes at the edge of a clump of trees, not fifty yards from the road, they awaited the passage of the regiment. They had not been in their hiding-place five minutes when the head of the column appeared.

"They march in very good order, Ned; do you think that they would keep up such discipline as that after they had mutinied?"

"I don't know. Dirk; but they'll want all their discipline when they come to meet our men. For anything we know we may be the two last white men left in India; but when the news gets to England there will be such a cry throughout the land that, if it needed a million men to win back the country, I believe they would be found and sent out. There! There are two mounted officers; I can't see their color, but I don't think they are white."

"No, Ned; I am sure they are not white; then they must be mutineers. Look! Look! Don't you see they have got three prisoners? There they are, marching in the middle of that column; they are officers; and oh! Ned! I do think that the middle one's father." And the excited boy, with tears of joy running down his cheeks, would have risen and dashed out had not Ned forcibly detained him.

"Hush! Dick! and keep quiet. Yes! It is father! and Dunlop and Manners. Thank God!" he said, in deep gratitude.

"Well, let's go to them, Ned; we may as well be all together."

"Keep quiet, Dick," the elder said, holding him down again; "you will destroy their chance as well as ours. We must rescue them if we can."

"How, Ned, how?"

"I don't know yet, Dick; but we must wait and see; anyhow, we will try. There goes the bugle for a halt. I expect they have done their day's march. Come on, Dick; we must get out of this. When they have once pitched their tents they will scatter about, and, as likely as not, some will come into this wood. Let us get further back, so as to be able to see them pitch their tents, and watch, if we can, where they put the prisoners."

The regiment piled arms, and waited until the bullock-carts came up with the tents. These were taken out and pitched on the other side of the road, and facing the wood. The ground being marked out, the men were told off to their quarters, and the poles of the tents aligned with as much regularity and exactness as could have been used when the regiment possessed its white officers.

Near the quarter-guard tent—that is, the tent of the men engaged upon actual duty—a small square tent was erected; and into this the three officers, who were handcuffed, were thrust; and two sentries, one in front, the other at the back of the tent, were placed.

"Now, Dick, we know all about it; let us get further away, and talk over how it is to be managed."

The task was one of extreme difficulty, and the boys were a long time arranging the details. Had there been but one sentry, the matter would have been easy enough: but with two sentries, and with the quarter guard close at hand, it seemed at first as if no possible scheme could be hit upon. The sentry at the back of the tent must be the one to be disposed of, and this must be done so noiselessly as not to alarm the man in front. Each marched backward and forward some eight paces to the right, and as much to the left, of the tent, halting occasionally. When both marched right and left at the same time, they were in sight of each other except during the time of passing before and behind the tent; when they walked alternately, the tent hid them altogether from each other.

"I suppose there is no chance of our being able to gag that fellow, Ned? It's horrid to think of killing a man in cold blood."

"There is no help for it, Dick. If he were alone, we might gag him; as it is, he must be killed. These scoundrels are all mutineers and murderers. This regiment has, no doubt, like the others, killed its officers, and all the men, women, and children at the station. I would not kill the man unless it could be helped, but our father's life depends upon it; and to save him I would, if there were no other way, cut the throats of the whole regiment while they were asleep! This is no ordinary war, Dick; it is a struggle for existence; and though I'm sure I hate the thought of it, I shall not hesitate for an instant."

"I shan't hesitate," the midshipman said; "but I wish the fellow could make a fight of it. However, as he would kill me if he had a chance, he mustn't grumble if I do the same for him. Now, Ned, you tell me exactly what I am to do, and you may rely on my doing it."

Every minute detail of the scheme was discussed and arranged; and then, as the sun set, the boys lit a fire in a nullah and boiled some rice, and ate their food with lighter hearts than they had done since they left Sandynugghur, for the knowledge that their father had escaped death had lifted a heavy burden from their hearts. As to the danger of the expedition that they were about to undertake, with the happy recklessness of boys they thought but little of it.

Across the plain they could see the campfires, but as the evening went on these gradually died away, and the sounds which had come faintly across the still night air ceased altogether. As patiently as might be, they waited until they guessed that it must be about ten o'clock. The night was, for the country, cold—a favorable circumstance, as the natives, who are very chilly, would be less likely to leave their tents if they felt restless. The moon was now half full and shining brightly, giving a light with which the boys could well have dispensed.

"Now, Dick, old boy, let's be moving. May God help us in our night's work!"

They made a considerable detour to approach the camp in the rear, where they rightly judged that the Sepoys, having no fear whatever of any hostile body being near, would have placed no sentries.

"Listen!" Dick said, as they were pausing to reconnoiter; "that sounded like a cannon in the far distance."

There was no doubt of it; faintly, but quite distinct, across the air came the sound of heavy cannon fired at regular intervals.

"Those cannon must be fired as a salute to some great chief newly arrived at Delhi—we should not fire so late, but I suppose they are not particular," Ned said; "we calculated it was not more than twenty-five miles off, and we should hear them at that distance easily. We had better wait a few minutes to see if any one comes out to listen to it."

But there was no movement among the white tents. Then they stole quietly into the camp.

The tents of the Indian native regiments are large, oblong tents, with two poles, holding thirty men each. They are manufactured at the government prison at Jubbalpore, and are made of thick cotton canvas, lined with red or blue cotton. In the daytime they open right along one side, the wall of the tent being propped outward, with two slight poles, so as to form a sort of veranda, and shade the inside of the tent while admitting the air. At night-time, in the cool season, this flap is let down and the tent closed. In front of the tents the muskets of the men inside are piled.

Into one of these tents Dick crawled, Ned watching outside. When Dick first entered it was so dark that he could see nothing; but the moonlight penetrated dimly through the double cotton, and he was soon able to discover objects around. The ground was all occupied by sleeping figures, each wrapped up from head to foot in his blanket, looking like so many mummies. Their uniforms were folded, and placed between their heads and the wall of the tent. Six of these, with the same number of caps, and six ammunition pouches and belts, and a uniform cloak, taken carefully off one of the sleepers, Dick collected and passed out through the door of the tent to Ned. Not a sleeper stirred while he did so, and he crept quietly out, with the first part of his task accomplished. Gathering the things together, the boys made all speed back to a clump of trees half a mile in the rear of the camp. Here Ned put on one of the uniforms and the cloak, and they then started back again for the camp.

The sentries upon the prisoners' tent were changed at twelve o'clock, and a few minutes later the sentry at the rear of the tent saw one of his comrades come out of one of the large tents close to the end of his beat. He was wrapped in his blanket, and his face was tied up with a cloth. Coughing violently, he squatted himself in front of his tent, and rocked himself to and fro, with his hands to his face, uttering occasional groans. This was all so natural—for the natives of India suffer much from neuralgia in the cold weather—that the sentry thought nothing of the matter. He continued to pace his beat, turning back each time when within a yard or two of the sufferer. The third time he did so the figure dropped off his blanket, and, with a sudden bound, threw himself on the sentry's back; at the same moment a Sepoy in uniform darted out from the tent. One hand of the assailant—in which was a damp cloth—was pressed tightly over the mouth and nostrils of the sentry; the other grasped the lock of his musket, so that it could not be discharged. Thrown backward off his balance, taken utterly by surprise, the sentry was unable even to struggle, and in an instant the second antagonist plunged a bayonet twice into his body, and he fell a lifeless mass on the ground. It was the work of an instant to drag the body a yard or two into the shadow of the tent, and before the other sentry appeared from the opposite side of the prisoner's tent the native was rocking himself as before; the sentry, wrapped in his cloak, was marching calmly on his beat. The whole affair had lasted but twenty seconds, and had passed as noiselessly as a dream.

The next time the sentry in front was hidden from view the native started from his sitting position and stole up behind the tent. Cautiously and quietly he cut a slit in the canvas and entered. Then he knelt down by the side of one of the sleepers, and kissed him. He moved in his sleep, and his disturber, putting his hand on his mouth to prevent sudden speech, shook him gently. The major opened his eyes.

"Father, it is I—Richard; hush! do not speak."

In Times Of Peril A Tale Of India | 47

Then, as the bewildered man gradually understood what was said, his son fell on his neck, kissing him with passionate delight.

After the first rapturous joy of the recognition was over, "Ned and the girls?" Major Warrener asked.

"The girls are at present safe," Dick said; "Ned is outside behind. He is the sentry. Now, father, wake the others, and then let us steal off. Take off your boots; the men's tents are only ten yards behind; once there, you are safe. I will let Ned know when you are ready, and he will occupy the sentry. We can't silence him, because he is within sight of the sentry of the quarter-guard."

Major Warrener aroused his sleeping companions, and in a few whispered words told them what had happened. In silence they wrung Dick's hand, and then taking off their boots, stole one by one out of the tent. As Ned passed he exchanged a silent embrace with his father. The next time the sentry in front was passing before the tent, a heavy stone, hurled by Ned, crashed into a bush upon the other side of the road. The sentry halted instantly, and, with gun advanced, listened, but he could hear nothing, for his comrade was at that instant seized with a fit of coughing.

After standing in a listening attitude for three or four minutes the Sepoy supposed that the noise must have been caused by some large bird suddenly disturbed in the foliage.

"Did you hear anything?" he asked Ned, as their path crossed.

"Nothing," Ned answered, continuing his march.

For another quarter of an hour he passed backward and forward, his only fear being that the sentry might take it into his head to open the tent and look in to see if the prisoners were safe. In a quarter of an hour he knew that the fugitives would have gained the trees, and would have time to put on the Sepoy uniforms before he reached them; and also, by the aid of a couple of large stones, have got rid of their handcuffs, lie might therefore be off to join them.

Waiting till the sentry was at the other end of his beat, he slipped round the tent, stripped off his cloak, lay down his musket and belt—for Dick had arranged that they should carry off five muskets in their retreat—threw off the Sepoy jacket, and in light running order, darted through the tents. He calculated that he should have at least a couple of minutes start before his absence was discovered, another minute or two before the sentry was sufficiently sure of it to hail the quarter-guard and report the circumstance. Then would follow the discovery of the escape of the prisoners; but by that time he would be far out on the plain, and even if seen, which was unlikely, he was confident that he could outrun any native.

His anticipations turned out correct; he was already some distance off when he heard the call of the sentry to the quarter-guard, followed almost immediately by a still louder shout, that told that he had discovered the flight of the prisoners; then came the sound of a musket shot, a drum beat the alarm, and a babel of sounds rang on the still air. But by this time Ned was halfway to the clump of trees, and three minutes later he was in his father's arms. There was no time to talk then. Another coat was hurried on to him, an ammunition belt and pouch thrown over his shoulder, and Captain Manners carrying his musket until he should have quite recovered breath, the five went off at a steady trot, which after a quarter of an hour broke into a walk—for there was no fear of pursuit—in the direction in which they knew Delhi to lie.

CHAPTER V.
BACK UNDER THE FLAG.

"How far is it to Delhi? We heard the guns there just now."

"Not thirty miles."

"Have you heard how things are going on there?" Dick asked.

"According to the Sepoy reports, fresh regiments are pouring in from all quarters; and they boast that they are going to drive us out of the country. Our troops are still at Meerut, and a force is gathering at Umballah; but they are after all a mere handful."

"Do you think there is any chance of help coming to us?"

"None for the present. The Sepoys say that every station has gone down except Agra, Allahabad, and Benares, and that these are soon to go too. Cawnpore and Lucknow have risen."

"Are all the whites killed everywhere?"

"I am afraid they are all killed where there are no white troops; but there, we must hope that they are making a stand. We shall be a long time before we know anything. It is but a week yet since our station went; seven days longer since Delhi rose."

"It seems ages ago," Ned said. "You don't mean to try and get to Meerut to-night, I hope; we could walk as far if it were absolutely necessary, but we have done a long day's walk already."

"No, no, Ned. I only want to get well away from our late camp. To-morrow we will get near the river, hide all next day, and cross after nightfall. There is a clump of trees; we will pass the night there; I think we are safe enough now. The mutineers are too anxious to be at Delhi to spend much time in looking for us. Now, first of all, let us get a fire."

"We have never had a fire at night," Dick said, "since we started; we have been too much afraid of being seen."

"There is not much chance of its being observed in a wood; especially if the bushes are thick. We are four miles at least from the camp, and we are all wet through with dew. Now for sticks."

The whole party soon collected a pile of sticks; and the major was about to scatter some powder among the dead leaves, when Ned said, "We have matches, father."

"Oh, that's all right, Ned. There we are, fairly alight. Yes, we have chosen the place well; there are bushes all around. Now," he said, when the fire had burned up brightly, "let us hear the full story of what has passed; you gave us a short account when we first got free. Now let us hear all about it."

Ned and Dick told the story—sometimes one taking it up, sometimes the other. There were many questions from their auditors, and expressions of warm approval of their conduct; and Captain Dunlop threatened under his breath that if he ever had a chance he would not leave one cake of mud upon another in the village where Kate was wounded. He and Captain Manners proposed that they should go back, and afford what protection they could to the girls. But Major Warrener at once negatived this idea.

"If they could come straight back with us, I should say yes," he said, "for with us five we might hope to get them through safely; but even that would be very risky, for the larger the party is, the more easily it attracts attention, and the whole country is alive with rebels marching to Delhi. But as Rose cannot be fit to travel for weeks, we have no choice in the matter. They must remain where they are, and we can only hope and pray for their safety. Our duty lies clearly at Meerut, where every man who can sight a rifle will be wanted most urgently. Now let us be off to sleep; the fire has burned low, and in another hour or two it will be daybreak; however, there will be no reveille, and we can sleep on with lighter hearts than we have had for some time."

"What figures you are in those uniforms!" Dick said, laughing, next morning; "you can scarcely move in them, and they won't meet by eight or nine inches. It does not seem to me that they are any disguise at all. Any one could see in a moment that they were not made for you."

"They are wretchedly uncomfortable, Dick." his father said; "and, as you say, any one could see they were not made for us. But they are useful. As we go along, any one who saw us at a distance would take us for a straggling party of mutineers making our way to Delhi; while the bright scarlet of our own uniform would have told its tale miles off."

"I shall be glad enough to get rid of mine, Dick; I feel as if I had got into a boy's jacket by mistake. Jack Sepoy has no shoulders to speak of; as far as height goes he is well enough; but thirty Sepoys on parade take up no more room than twenty English. I had to take my jacket off last night and lay it over my shoulders; I might as well have tried to go to sleep in a vise. There! major; do you hear the music? These rascals are on the march again."

The strains of music came very faintly to the ear, for the bivouac was nearly a mile from the road.

"That is all right," the major said. "Now they have gone by, we can be moving. We must give them an hour's start."

"Now, father, we have not heard your adventures yet; please tell us all about them."

"Well, we have not had so much variety as you, but we have gone through a good deal. You know we had talked over the best possible course to take in case of an attack, come when it might. We had arranged what each should do in case of a night attack, or of a rising upon parade; and we had even considered the probability of being set upon when gathered in the messroom. We had all agreed that if taken by surprise, resistance would mean certain death; they would shoot us down through the doors and windows, and we should be like rats in a cage. We agreed, therefore, that in case of an attack, a simultaneous attempt to break out must be made, and we had even settled upon the window by which we should go. The married men were, of course, to make for their bungalows, except where, as in my case, I had made other arrangements; and the rest to various bungalows agreed upon, where traps were to be in readiness. Dunlop, Manners, and myself had agreed to make for Dunlop's, as it was the nearest, and his trap was to be ready that evening.

"There were not many who believed in a mutiny that night. The villains, only in the morning, having sworn to be faithful, deceived most of us, for it was very hard to believe they could be capable of such diabolical treachery. Swords and pistols were, of course, taken off, but instead of being left in the anteroom, were brought into the messroom. Some fellows put theirs in a corner, others against the wall behind them. I was sitting between Dunlop and Manners, and we were, as it happened, at the corner nearest the window fixed upon for the bolt. Things went on all right till dinner was over, There was an insolent look about some of the servants' faces I did not like, but nothing to take hold of. I pointed it out to Dunlop, and we agreed that the plan arranged was the best possible; and that, as resistance would be of no use, if at each of the eight large windows and the two doors a stream of musketry fire were being poured in, we would make a rush straight for the window. Presently the colonel rose and gave 'The Queen.' We all rose, and as if—as I have no doubt it was—the toast was the signal, there was a sudden trampling in the veranda outside, and at every window appeared a crowd of Sepoys, with their arms in their hands. I shouted,

'To the window for your lives!' and without stopping to get my sword, I dashed at the Sepoys who were there. Dunlop and Manners were with me, and before the scoundrels had time to get their guns to their shoulders, we were upon them. We are all big men; and our weight and impetus, and the surprise, were too much for them; we burst through them, standing as they did four or five deep, as if they had been reeds. They gave a yell of rage and astonishment as they went down like ninepins; but we scarcely saw it, for as we went through them the musketry fire broke out round the messroom.

"Whether any of the others tried to follow us, we don't know. I think most of them forgot their arrangement, and rushed to their arms: certainly some of them did so, for we heard the crack of revolvers between the rifle shots. We made straight across the parade for Dunlop's bungalow, with musket balls flying in all directions, as soon as the fellows we had gone through recovered from their first astonishment; but they are not good shots at the best, and a man running at his top speed is not an easy mark by moonlight. We heard yells and musket shots all round, and knew that while a part of the regiment was attacking us, parties were told off to each bungalow. By the time we had got over the few hundred yards to Dunlop's, the whistling of the bullets round us had pretty well ceased, for the fellows had all emptied their muskets; besides, we were nearly out of range. None of them were near us, for they had stopped in their run to fire; they were too much interested in the massacre going on inside, and we seemed pretty safe; when, just as I entered the gate of the compound, a stray bullet hit me on the head, and down I went like a log.

"Happily, the syce had proved faithful; he had been with Dunlop ever since he joined the regiment, and Dunlop once risked his life to save him from a tiger. There was the syce with the trap. He had not dared bring it out till the first shot was fired, lest his fellow-servants, who were all traitors, should stop it; but the instant it began, he came round. They ran the horse up to where I was lying, lifted me in, and jumped in, and drove out of the gate as a score of fellows from the mess-house came making toward the bungalow. We had fifty yards' start, but they fired away at us, a ball passing through the syce's leg as he scrambled up behind. The horse went along at a gallop; but we were not safe, for parties were carrying on their hellish work in every bungalow, Dunlop and Manners were maddened by the screams they heard; and if it had not been for having me under their charge, and by the thoughts of the girls, I believe they would have jumped out and died fighting. A few of the black devils, hearing wheels, ran out and fired; but we kept on at a full gallop till we were well out of the place. A mile further Dunlop found the horse begin to slacken his speed, and to go very leisurely. He jumped out to see what was the matter, and found, as he expected, that the horse had been hit. He had one bullet in the neck, another in the side. It was evident that it could not go much further. They lifted me out and carried me to a patch of bushes thirty yards from the road. The syce was told to drive on quietly till the horse dropped. Dunlop gave him money and told him to meet us at Meerut."

"Why did you not keep him with you? he would have been very useful?" Dick asked.

"You see I wanted to get the trap as far away as possible before the horse fell," Captain Dunlop said. "We did not know how severely wounded the major was; indeed, we both feared he was killed; but the mutineers, when they found the dead horse in the morning, were certain to make a search in its neighbourhood, and would have found your father had he been close by laid up with a wound."

"Happily I now began to come to," the major went on, continuing his story. "The ball was nearly spent, and had given me a nasty scalp wound, and had stunned me, but I now began to come round. The instant I was able to understand where I was or what had happened, Dunlop and Manners, who were half-wild with excitement and grief, made me promise to lie quiet, while they went back to see what had become of you all. Of course I consented. They were away about three hours, for they had to make a circle of the cantonments, as our bungalow was quite at the other end. They brought cheering news. They had first been to the house, and found it utterly destroyed as they expected. That told them nothing; for if you had been killed, your bodies would probably have been burned with the house. Then they went out to the tope of trees where it was agreed that you should, if possible, first fly. Here they found a pocket-handkerchief of Rose's; and going round to the other side, found by the marks upon the soil that four of you had started together. With hearts immensely lightened by the discovery that you had, at any rate, all escaped from the first massacre, they hurried back to gladden me with the news. I was past understanding it when they arrived, for the intense pain in my head and my terrible anxiety about you had made me delirious. It would have been certain death to stay so near the road, so they dipped their handkerchiefs in water, and tied them round my head; and then supporting me, one on each side, they half-dragged, half-carried, me to a deserted and half-ruinous cottage, about a mile away.

"Next day I was still feverish, but fortunately no one came near us. Dunlop and Manners went out at night, and got a few bananas. Next morning our regiment marched away; and Dunlop then appealed to an old cottager for shelter and food for us all. He at once promised to aid us, and I was removed to his cottage, where everything in his power was done for me. I was now convalescent, and a day later we were talking of making a move forward. That night, however, the cottage was surrounded—whether the peasant himself or some one else betrayed us, we shall never know—but the men that we saw there belonged to a regiment of mutineers that had marched in that afternoon from Dollah. We saw at once that resistance was useless, and we were, moreover, without arms. Had we had them, I have no doubt we should have fought and been killed. As it was, we were bound and marched into the camp at Sandynugghur. It was resolved to take us in triumph into Delhi; and we were marched along with the regiment till you saw us. We had talked over every conceivable plan of escape, and had determined that we would try to-night, which will be the last halt before they get to Delhi. It is very unlikely that we should have succeeded, but it was better to be shot down than to be taken to Delhi and given over to the mob to torture before they killed us. I am convinced we had no chance of really getting off, and that you have saved our lives, just as Dunlop and Manners saved mine, at the risk of their own, on that first night of our flight. And now let us be on the march."

They had not gone far before the three officers found that it was impossible to walk in their Sepoy jackets. They accordingly took them off, and slung them from their muskets. Ned and Dick were fairly fitted. They halted for the night near the river, about ten miles above Delhi. In the morning they were off early. By nine o'clock they stood on the bank of the river, five miles higher up.

The river is wide, or rather the bed of the river is wide, half a mile at least; this in the rainy season is full to the brim, but at other times the stream is not more than half that width. After crossing the river they would have fifteen miles still to traverse to arrive at Meerut; and it was probable that the whole intervening country was in the hands of the Sepoys.

"Had we not better keep this side of the river for a bit, father?" Ned asked.

"No, my boy; we will cross here after dark, and make straight for Meerut. If we can't find a boat, we will each cut a large bundle of rushes, to act as a lifebuoy and carry your guns and ammunition, and so swim across after it is dark."

"Well, major, as the sun is getting awfully hot, I vote we get into the shade of those stunted trees, and have a nap till the afternoon. It won't do to begin even to make the raft till the sun is down."

Captain Dunlop's proposition was carried into effect; but it is questionable whether any of the party slept much, for they were excited by the thought that in a few hours they would be with friends, once more soldiers instead of fugitives, with power to fight in defense of their sovereign's dominions, and of the helpless women and children exposed to the fury of the atrocious mutineers. With these thoughts mingled the anxiety which was wearing them all, although each refrained from talking about it, as to the safety of the girls, whose lives wore dependent upon the fidelity of a native and his servants.

Over and over again, since they met the boys, had they regretted that they had not gone back to watch over them; but the fact that Rose might be weeks before she was able to stand, and that, as their protector had said, the presence of Europeans near them might be detected, and would be a source of constant danger, convinced them that they had taken the proper course. They knew, too, that in acting as they had done they were performing their duty; and that at a moment when the fate of British India trembled in the balance, the place of every soldier was by the side of the British troops who still maintained the old flag flying in the face of increasing numbers of the enemy. Still, although they knew that they were doing their duty, and were, moreover, taking the wisest course, the thoughts of the girls alone in the midst of danger, with one of them down with fever, tried them terribly, and they longed with a fierce desire for the excitement of work and of danger to keep them from thinking of it.

"Here, boys, is a ear of Indian corn apiece; eat that and then get to work."

The frugal meal was soon over, and they then set to work, cutting down, breaking off, and tearing up large reeds with which to make floats. The boys had knives, but the others had been stripped of everything they had at the time of their capture. In about an hour, however, five bundles were made, each some six feet long and nearly three feet thick. The muskets and ammunition pouches were fastened on these, and soon after it was quite dark they entered the water.

"There are no crocodiles, I hope," Dick whispered to Ned.

"Nothing to fear in these large rivers; the chances of meeting one are very small."

"All right," Dick said. "Of course we've got to risk it. But they're as bad as sharks; and sharks, as the Yankee said, is pison. Well, here goes."

When the bundles were placed in the water they were lashed side by side with long trailing creepers which grew abundantly among the rushes; and they were thus secured from the risk of turning over from the weights on the top. Upon the raft thus formed their clothes were placed, and then, side by side, pushing it before them, the party shoved off from shore. In twenty minutes they touched ground on the other side. They dressed, examined their muskets to see if they were in good order, and then started in the direction in which they knew Meerut to be. Several times they paused and listened, for they could occasionally hear the noise of galloping men, and it was evident that there were troops of some kind or other moving about.

They walked for some hours until they thought that they could not be far from their destination, and had begun to congratulate themselves upon being near their friends, when the sound of a strong body of men was heard sweeping along the level plain across which they were now passing.

"There is a small building ahead," the major said; "run for that; they are coming across here."

They were seen, for a shout of "Who goes there?" in Hindostanee was heard.

"Give me your musket, Dick," Captain Dunlop exclaimed. For the lad, with the weight of his musket and ammunition, could hardly keep up with the others.

Just in time they reached the building in front of them, rushed in, and closed the door as the cavalry swept up. It was a small temple; a building of massive construction, with one little window about six inches square, and on the same side a strong door.

"Pile everything against the door," the major cried. "Dunlop, fire at once at them. Our only chance is to hold out with the hope that we may be heard, and that some of our fellows may come to the rescue."

Captain Dunlop fired just as the troopers dashed up to the door.

"Now, Manners, steady, pick off your man," the major said, as, aided by the boys, he jammed a beam of wood between the door and the wall, at such an angle that, except by breaking it to pieces, the door could not be forced.

"Now," he said, "it's my turn;" and he fired into the enraged enemy. "Now, Ned, steady. Are you loaded again, Dunlop?"

"Yes, major; just ready."

"Dick, you follow; take good aim."

The cavalry answered their fire, every shot of which was taking effect, by a confused discharge of their pistols at the door and window.

"Draw off!" their leader shouted; "rear-rank men hold the horses, front-rank men dismount and break in the door."

The order was obeyed; and the troopers rushed forward on foot, and were met by a steady fire, to which the straggling return of their pistols was but an inefficient answer. Vainly the mutineers hacked at the door with their sabers and struck it with their pommels.

"Throw yourselves against it, all at once," cried their leader; and a dozen men sent themselves against the door; it creaked and strained, but the beam kept it in its place.

"You keep up the fire through the window," said the major; "the boys and I will fire through the door."

Yells and shrieks followed each shot through the door, and after three or four minutes the troopers drew off.

"Any one hurt?" the major asked.

"I have got a bullet in my shoulder," said Captain Dunlop.

But that was the only reply. There was a shout outside, and Manners exclaimed: "Confound the fellows, they have got a big log of wood that will soon splinter the door."

"We must stop them as long as we can," said the major, as he fired among the men who were advancing with the log.

Several Sepoys fell before they got up to the house, but they pressed on, and, at the first blow given by the battering-ram driven by the men, the door split from top to bottom.

"Fix bayonets," the major said. "Now, Manners, you and I will hold them back. Not more than two can come at once, and their swords are of no use against bayonets in a narrow space. Dunlop, will you stand in reserve? you have still got your right hand; use your bayonet as a dagger if a rush comes. Boys, you go on loading and firing; put in four balls each time. If they get in, of course use your bayonets; there goes the door!"

A shout burst from the natives as the last portion of the door dropped from its hinges, and the doorway was open. There was, however, no inclination betrayed to make a rush.

"Forward! Death to the infidel dogs!" shouted their officer.

"Suppose you lead us," said one of the troopers; "the officers always show the way."

"Come, then," cried an old officer, on whose breast hung several medals; "follow me!"

Drawing his sword, he rushed forward, followed by twenty of his men. But as he passed over the threshold he and the trooper next to him fell beneath the bayonet thrusts of Major Warrener and his companion. The next two, pushed forward by their comrades, shared the same fate; while, as they fell, the muskets of Ned and Dick sent their contents into the mass. The rest recoiled from the fatal doorway, while the defenders set up a cheer of triumph. It was drowned in a crash of musketry, mingled with a cry of surprise and despair from the natives, as a body of British soldiers leaped from the wood, and followed their volley by an impetuous charge. The cavalry on the plain turned and fled at a gallop; and in five minutes, but for a few dark figures prostrate on the plain, not an enemy was in sight.

"Well, gentlemen, you have made a stout defense," the officer in command said, as he returned to the shrine, outside which the little party had gathered. "It seems as if you could have done without my help. Who are you, may I ask? And where have you sprung from?"

"Why, Sibbold, is it you? You haven't forgotten Warrener? And here are Dunlop and Manners."

"Hurrah!" shouted the officer. "Thank God, old fellows, you are saved; we fancied that you had all gone down. I am glad;" and he shook hands enthusiastically with his friends; while two of the officers, coming up, joined in the hearty greeting.

"Do those two men belong to your regiment?" Captain Sibbold asked. "If so, they are wonders; for I don't know a case as yet where any of the men proved true when the rest mutinied."

"They are my sons," Major Warrener answered.

"What?" exclaimed the other, laughing—believing that the major was joking.

"It's a fact, as you will see when they have got rid of the stains on their faces," he replied; while Captain Dunlop added, "and two as fine young fellows as ever stepped. Do you know that we three were prisoners, and that these lads rescued us from the middle of a pandy regiment. If they hadn't we should have been dead men before now. And now have you got anything to eat at Meerut, for we are famishing? In the next place, I have got a bullet in my shoulder, and shall enjoy my food all the more after it has been taken out. Our stories are long and will keep. How go things here?"

"Not very brightly, Dunlop; however, that will keep, too; now let us be off. Have we any casualties, sergeant?" he asked a non-commissioned officer who came up for orders.

"None, sir."

"What is the enemy's loss?"

"There are fifteen which can be fairly counted to us, sir, and nineteen here."

"That's a respectable total. Fall in, lads," he said to the men who had gathered round, "and let us get back. You will be glad to hear that these officers have escaped from the massacre at Sandynugghur."

There was a hearty cheer of satisfaction from the men, for Englishmen were knit very closely together in those terrible days. Then, falling in, the two companies of the Sixtieth Rifles marched back again to their cantonments at Meerut.

CHAPTER VI.
A DASHING EXPEDITION.

On arriving at the cantonments, the party were soon surrounded by the troops, who had been called under arms at the sound of distant firing, but had been dismissed again on the arrival of a message to the effect that the enemy had fled. The news had spread rapidly that some fugitives had escaped from Sandynugghur, where it was supposed that the massacre had been general; and officers pressed forward to shake their hands, and the men uttered words of kindly congratulation and welcome. The greeting swelled into a cheer as the detachment fell out, and, scattering among their comrades, told of the desperate defense, and of the slaughter inflicted upon the enemy by this handful of men. The fugitives were, of course, taken first to the messroom, Captain Dunlop being, however, carried off by the surgeon to his quarters, to have his wound examined and attended to.

It seemed almost like a dream to the worn and weary party, as they sat down again to a table laid with all the brightness and comfort of civilization, and felt that they were indeed safe among friends. Many were the questions asked them by officers who had friends and acquaintances among the military and civilians at Sandynugghur; and the fugitives learned that they were, so far as was known, the only survivors from the massacre. The story of their escape, and the safety of the girls, was told briefly, and listened to with eager interest; and very deep and hearty were the congratulations which the boys received for their share in the history. In return, Major Warrener learned what had taken place in the last ten days.

The story was not reassuring; tidings of evil were coming from all parts. As yet the number of stations where risings had taken place was comparatively small; but the position was everywhere critical. In Agra, Allahabad, and Benares, the attitude of the native troops and population was more than doubtful. At Lucknow and Cawnpore every precaution was being taken, but a rising was regarded as inevitable. In fact everywhere, save in the Punjab, trouble had either come or was coming. General Anson was collecting in all haste a force at Umballah, which was intended to advance upon Delhi—where the ex-king had been proclaimed Emperor of India—but his force would necessarily be an extremely small one; and no help could possibly arrive up country for many weeks. There was therefore only the Punjab to look to for aid. Happily, the troops of the Madras and Bombay presidencies had so far remained faithful.

"I suppose you have a good many men from Delhi, civilians and military, as well as from other places?"

"Oh, yes, we are crowded; every bungalow has been given up to the ladies, and we all sleep under canvas."

"I intend to ask leave to get up a troop of volunteers," Major Warrener said; "in the first place to go out and bring in my daughter and niece, and afterward to do any scouting or other duty that may be required."

"There has already been a talk of forming the unattached officers and civilians into a sort of irregular cavalry, so I should think that you will get leave; but it will be a hazardous business to make your way eighty miles through the country, especially as the mutineers are marching in all directions toward Delhi."

The next morning Major Warrener obtained permission, without difficulty, to carry out his scheme; and the news no sooner was known through the cantonments that a body of irregular horse was to be formed for scouting and general purposes, and that unattached officers might, until they received further orders, join it, than the tent which had been assigned to Major Warrener was besieged by men anxious to join a corps which seemed likely to afford them a chance of striking an early blow at the mutineers.

Hitherto, the officers who had escaped from Delhi and other stations, those who had come in from police duties in isolated districts, and civilians, both merchants and government officials, had been fretting that they could not be doing something to aid the great work of holding India, and punishing those who had murdered their friends and relations. Major Warrener's Light Horse, as it was to be called, afforded the opportunity desired, and by the next morning eighty-five volunteers had enrolled themselves. Some thirty-five of these were officers, the rest civilians. Many of them had ridden in, others had driven, so that most of them were already provided with horses. An appeal was made to the officers of the Meerut garrison, and to the civilians resident there, to give up any horses they might be able to spare for the public service, while others were bought from friendly zemindars. In a week the troop were all mounted, and during this time they had worked hard to acquire a sufficient amount of cavalry drill to enable them to perform such simple evolutions as might be necessary. Major Warrener divided the squadron into two troops, each with a captain and subaltern; all these officers being cavalrymen, as were the officers who did duty as sergeants. Thus Major Warrener had the general command, each troop being maneuvered by its own officers. In the ranks as simple privates were two majors and a dozen captains—among these latter, Captain Manners. Captain Dunlop was for the present in the surgeon's hands; but he was resolved that when the time came for a start for the rescue of the girls he would take his place in the ranks. The boys of course formed part of the troop. The uniform was simple, consisting simply of a sort of Norfolk jacket made of karkee, a kind of coarse brown holland of native make. Each man carried a revolver, and sword belt of brown leather. Their headgear was a cap of any kind, wrapped round and round with the thick folds of a brown puggaree. Beyond the Norfolk jacket and puggaree there was no actual uniform. Most of the men had hunting breeches, many had high boots, others had gaiters; but these were minor points, as were the horses' equipments.

Nothing had been said as to the intended expedition to bring in the fugitives, as native spies might have carried the news to the rebels, and so caused a renewed search to be made for their hiding-place. There was, therefore, a deep feeling of satisfaction, as well as of surprise, when, on the tenth day after the formation of the corps, the men were told, on being dismissed from morning parade, that the squadron would parade for duty at evening gunfire; that each man was to be provided with a blanket and a haversack, with cooked food sufficient for four days, and a bag with twenty pounds of forage for his horse, each horse to be well fed before coming on parade.

Had the route been free from enemies, the distance might have been done in two long night marches; but it would be necessary to make a detour on starting, so as to avoid striking the main road, as on the way out it was all-important to avoid detection, as the enemy might muster in such strength that their return would be difficult and dangerous in the extreme. The girls once in their hands, the return journey would be easy, as they could avoid any infantry, and had no fear of being able to cut their way through any body of cavalry whom they might accidentally come across, especially as they would have all the advantage of a surprise. Half an hour after sunset the squadron rode out from the lines at Meerut, amid a hearty cheer from the many troops at the station, who, hearing that Warrener's Light Horse were off on an expedition against the mutineers, had assembled to see the start. Major Warrener rode at the head of the squadron, with Captain Kent, who commanded the first troop, by his side, and behind them came two native guides well acquainted with the country. These had been dressed in the uniform of a native cavalry regiment, in order that if they passed any village and were challenged, they could ride forward and represent the troop as a body of native cavalry sent out from Delhi on a mission to a friendly rajah. The precaution was unnecessary. During two long night marches, with occasional halts to rest the horses, they rode without interruption. They passed through several villages; but although the tramp of the horses and the rattle of sabers must have been heard by the inhabitants, none stirred, for the mutineers took what they wanted without paying, and were already behaving as masters of the country; and even thus early the country people were beginning to doubt whether the fall of the English Raj, and the substitution of the old native rule, with its war, its bloodshed, and its exactions, was by any means a benefit, so far as the tillers of the soil were concerned. Just before morning, on the third day, the troop halted in a thick grove, having watered their horses at a tank a half-hour before. They had ridden some seventy miles, and were, they calculated, about fifteen miles from the place where they had left the girls. It might have been possible to push on at once, but the day was breaking, and it would have been inexpedient to tire out the horses when they might want all their speed and strength on the return journey. Very slowly passed the day. Most of the men, after seeing to their horses and eating some food, threw themselves down and slept soundly. But Major Warrener, his sons, and Captains Dunlop and Manners were far too anxious to follow their example, for some time. It was more than a fortnight since the boys had left the ladies, and so many things, of which they hardly dare think, might have happened since.

"Don't let us talk about it any more," Major Warrener said at last; "we only add to each other's anxiety. Now, Dunlop, you must positively lie down; you know Johnson said it was mad in you to get on horseback till your bone had set firmly, and that it was ten to one in favor of inflammation coming on again. You have much to go through yet."

Gradually sleepiness overcame excitement, and with the exception of ten men told off as sentries and to look after the horses, the whole party slept quietly for some hours. It had been determined to start in time to arrive at the farmhouse before it was dark, as the boys required daylight to enable them to recognize the locality; besides which it was advisable to get as far back upon the return journey as possible before daybreak. The boys were now riding in front with their father.

"That is the wood," Ned said presently. "I know by those three palm trees growing together in a clump, at a short distance in advance. I noticed them particularly."

"Where is the house?" Major Warrener asked.

"We ought to see the house," Dick said, and he looked at his brother apprehensively.

"Yes," Ned said; "we certainly ought to see it."

"You are sure you are not mistaken in the locality?" their father asked.

"Quite sure," the boys answered together; "but the house— —"

"Let us gallop on," Major Warrener said, catching the fear which was expressed in each of his sons' faces.

Five minutes' riding, and they drew up their horses with a cry of dismay. A large patch of wood ashes marked the spot where the house had stood. No words were needed; the truth was apparent; the fugitives had been discovered, and the abode of their protectors destroyed. Their two friends joined the little group, and the rest of the troop dismounted at a short distance, respecting the deep pain which the discovery had caused to their leader.

"What is to be done?" Major Warrener asked, breaking the deep silence.

For a moment no one answered; and then Dick said:

"Perhaps we may find some of the farmer's people in the hut where we slept, and we may get news from them."

"A capital thought, Dick," said Major Warrener. "We must not give up hope; there are no bodies lying about, so the farm people are probably alive. As to the girls, if they are carried off we must rescue them. Where is the hut?"

A few minutes' walking brought them to it. Even before they reached it it was evident that it was inhabited, for two or three peons were squatted near the door. These rose on seeing the group of Englishmen, but made no attempt at flight. They entered the hut without ceremony, and Ned and Dick hurried to the side of an old man lying on a heap of straw, while some females standing near hastily veiled themselves at the entrance of the strangers.

"Where are the girls? what has happened? are you hurt?" were the three questions poured out rapidly by Ned, as the boy seized the old man's hands.

"Is it you, sahibs? I am glad, indeed. I did not break my promise to come and tell you; but as you see," and he pointed to the bandage which enveloped his head, "I was wounded, and am still ill."

"But the girls?" asked Ned.

"They have been carried off by the troops of the Rajah of Nahdoor."

"How long since?"

"Thursday, sahib."

"How far off is Nahdoor?"

"Ten miles, sahib."

Major Warrener now took up the interrogation.

"How is the one who was ill?"

"She was better, and was getting stronger again when they carried her off."

"Do you think they are still at Nahdoor? or that they have been sent into Delhi?"

"They are still there," the Hindoo said. "I have sent a man each day to watch, so that directly I got better I might be able to tell you the truth of the matter. My servant has just returned; they had not left at three o'clock, and they would be sure not to start after that hour. The rajah will go with his troops in a few days to pay his respects to the emperor; he will probably take the *mem* sahibs with him.»

"Thank God for that," Major Warrener said. "If they have not yet been taken to that horrible den of murder we will save them. I am the father of one, and the other is my niece," he said to the zemindar; "and I owe their lives so far to you. The debt of gratitude I can never pay to you—or to your wife and daughter," he added, turning to the women, who, their first impulse of alarm over, had now, in the presence of friends, uncovered their faces, for it is only the higher class of Hindoo women who closely veil—"for your care in nursing my niece, and for giving them shelter, when to do so was to risk your lives. This debt I can never pay; but the losses you have sustained in the destruction of your house, and the loss of animals, I can happily more than replace. And now tell me how it happened."

"It was late in the afternoon," the Hindoo said, "when a body of horse galloped across the field to my door. Their captain rode up to me. 'Are there any Feringhees hid here, old man?' he asked. 'I have seen no man of the white race since the troubles began,' I said; and you know I spoke not falsely. 'I must search the house,' he said; 'there are a party of fugitives hiding somewhere in this district, and the orders from Delhi are strict that every Feringhee is to be hunted down and sent there.' 'You will find no one here,' I said, 'but my women, one of whom is sick.' 'I must see them,' he said; and he knocked loudly at the door of the women's room, and ordered them to come out. My wife and daughter came to the door. 'Where is the one who is said to be sick?' he said; 'I must see her too.' Then, seeing that he was determined to enter, the young *mem* sahib came to the door. The captain gave a shout of pleasure; calling in his men, he entered the room, and, in spite of the entreaties of her sister, brought the one who was sick out also. She was able to walk, but, as we had agreed between us should be done if discovery was made, she pretended that she was almost at the point of death. Some poles were got; a hammock was made; and borne by four bearers, she was carried away, her sister being placed on a horse closely guarded. As he turned to ride off the captain's eye fell upon me. 'Ah! old traitor!' he said; 'I had forgotten you!' and he drew a pistol and fired at me. I know no more; his men put fire to the barn and granaries, and drove off our cattle and horses. When he had ridden off my servants—who thought I was dead—by order of my sorrowing wife carried me here. Happily, however, by the will of Brahma, the bullet, instead of going through my skull, glanced off, and I was only stunned. I had lost much blood, but I determined to set out as soon as I could walk to bring you the news, and in the meantime have had a watch kept upon Nahdoor."

Major Warrener and his sons thanked the old peasant and his family in the warmest terms for what they had done, and the former pressed upon the farmer a sum of money which would cover all the losses he had sustained.

"Your conduct," he said, "will be reported to the government, and you will find when these troubles are over that England knows how to reward those who proved faithful when so many were faithless. Now we will say adieu. When the war is over the ladies you have so kindly treated will themselves return to thank you."

In a few minutes the troop was in the saddle again, and directed its march toward Nahdoor.

On the way Major Warrener questioned his guide as to the strength and position of the fortress, which lay away from the main road, and had not been visited by any of the troop—as the major had ascertained before starting. The account was not reassuring. The guide reported that it stood on a rock, which rose perpendicularly some eighty or a hundred feet from the plain; the only access being by a zigzag road cut in the face of the cliff, with a gateway defended by a gun, and loopholed walls at each turn, and with a very strong wall all round the edge of the rock. The garrison, they had learned from the persons at the farm, was some three hundred strong, the ordinary number of retainers being at present increased by many fighting men, who had within the last few days joined the rajah, on hearing that he was going to march to Delhi to fight under the emperor against the Feringhees.

The troop halted in a wood three miles from Nahdoor; as the guide said that there was no place nearer where they could be concealed without a certainty of discovery.

Before morning Major Warrener and his second in command put on native clothes, which the former bad brought with him, in case it should be necessary to open communication with the girls, and left the wood with one of the native guides. The disguises were not meant to deceive close investigation, and no attempt was made to change the color of the skin, but they were sufficient to enable the wearers to pass without exciting suspicion by any one who only saw them at a distance.

When morning broke they stood within half a mile of the fortress, which answered exactly to the description they had received of it. Gradually—keeping always at a distance, and availing themselves as far as possible of cover—they made a circuit of the place, and then returned to the troop, who were anxiously awaiting their report.

"It is a very hard nut to crack," Major Warrener said to his sons. "There is no possibility of climbing the rock anywhere, or of attacking in any way except by the regular ascent. There are eight gateways to be forced before arriving at the main entrance through the walls. We should require petards to blow in gates, and ought to have field guns to drive them out of the gate-houses. I do not say it would be absolutely impossible, because before now British troops have done what seemed impossible in India; but the difficulties would be so enormous, the risk of failure so great, and the loss certainly so crushing, that I should not be justified in undertaking such a desperate adventure on my own responsibility, and for my own private ends. We have no right, boys, to cause the loss of some thirty or forty of these fine young fellows, even to rescue the girls. An attack by surprise is the only possibility. At present we don't see the way, but something may turn up to help us. Failing that, our only plan is to wait till the rajah starts with his following and the girls for Delhi, and then to attack them on their way. The drawback to this is that he may not leave for days, and that at any moment we may be discovered. Besides, there is the difficulty of feeding the horses and ourselves. Now, boys, you know as much as I do. Think it over while I have a talk with Dunlop and Manners."

"Manners is at the other end of the wood, father, half a mile away. We found, after you had gone, that the main Delhi road ran through the further skirts of the wood, so Manners suggested to Lieutenant Simmons that he should go with ten men and hide there, so that they could see who went along the road and perhaps intercept some messenger between Delhi and Nahdoor."

"A capital idea," Major Warrener said.

Two hours later Captain Manners returned with his party, bringing in two prisoners.

"Who have you there, Manners?" Major Warrener asked.

"Two of the rascally Third Cavalry, who mutinied at Meerut. This fellow, as you see, is a native officer; there were two of them and two sowars, but they showed fight when we surrounded them, and tried to ride through us, so we had to shoot two of them. They are bearers of a letter from the Delhi prince to the rajah. Here it is."

Major Warrener looked sternly at the prisoners, who were still wearing their British uniform, and then ordered them to be taken away and hung at once.

"What did you do with the others, Manners?"

"We hid their bodies under some bushes at a distance from the road."

"You must go back," the major said, "with another; take Larkin with you. You must strip off the uniforms and bring them here."

Half an hour later Major Warrener summoned the captains of his two troops, and took them into council.

"Nothing could be more fortunate than this capture," he said; "it seems to clear the way for us altogether. What I propose to do is this: that two of the best linguists of the troop, with the two native guides, should dress in the uniforms of these scoundrels. They can then go boldly in with the letter from the prince. They will of course be well received, and will stay for the night. The two who go as officers will be entertained by the rajah, and will learn the plan of the state apartments; the other two will be made welcome by the retainers. When all is quiet at night they must steal out and wait on the wall. That projecting watch-tower that overhangs the cliff on the other side would be the best. We will be below. Then a rope must be lowered. We have two long picketing ropes, either of which would be long enough, but they would be too bulky to carry in without suspicion. Our native guides, however, will soon tear up some cloth, and twist a rope not much thicker than string, but strong enough to hold the rope. Then the string can be twisted round the body without fear of detection, and when the time comes lowered, with a stone at the end. We shall be below with a strong rope ladder, made with the picket-ropes and bamboo staves; and once fixed, we shall be up in no time. I leave it to you to decide who are the best linguists. They must of course be asked if they are willing to undertake it. I will speak to the guides. What do you think of the general plan?"

"Excellent," the officers said. "It might be as well," one suggested, "that each of the party should have a light rope wound round him, so that if one, two, or even three could not slip away, the fourth could still carry out the plan."

Some other details were arranged, and then the officers went to pick out the two men who could best pass as natives. There was no difficulty upon this score, for two of the troop, who had for years commanded large police districts, spoke the language as perfectly as natives, and these, upon being asked, readily accepted the duty. The work of making the rope ladders, and the light ropes for hauling them up, was entered upon, and by sunset all were ready for the expedition.

It was fortunate that they had no longer to stay in the wood, for during the day five or six natives who came in to gather wood had to be seized and bound, and it was certain that a search would be set on foot there next morning. Fortunately a large field of Indian corn bordered one side of the wood, and from this both man and horse had satisfied their hunger.

Every detail of the plan was carefully considered and discussed, so that no mistake could occur; and each of the principal actors in the piece had his part assigned to him. The two native guides, who had themselves served as soldiers in native regiments, consented willingly to perform their parts, and just at sunset the two officers and men rode off to Nahdoor, bearing the letter from the prince of Delhi to the rajah.

There was high feasting in Nahdoor that night. The rajah had received with all honor the officers from Delhi. The letter from the prince had promised him a high command in the army which was to exterminate the last infidel from the land. It had thanked him for the capture of the white women, and had begged him to bring them on with him to Delhi, and to come at once with his own force. From the officers the rajah had heard how the mutiny was everywhere a success, and that at Lucknow and Cawnpore the troops would rise in a day or two and massacre all the whites. The evening ended early, for the officers from Delhi were fatigued with their long ride, and being shown into a little square marble-lined room off the great hall where they had supped, were soon apparently asleep on the cushions and shawls spread for them. The rajah retired to his apartments, and his officers to their quarters; and although for another hour talking and laughing went on round the little fires in the courtyard, presently these too were hushed, and a profound stillness fell upon Nahdoor. Then, barefooted, the officers from Delhi stole out of their apartment and made for the outer wall. As they had anticipated, they found no one about; beyond a sentry at the lower gate there would be no watch kept, and they reached the watch-tower on the wall without the slightest interruption. Here two other figures had already arrived, and after throwing down some small stones as a signal, which was answered by a faint whistle, the ropes were lowered without delay. One of them was soon seized from below, and the others being also found and fastened to the rope ladder, the weight of which was considerable, those above began to draw up. Everything succeeded admirably. One by one fifty men appeared at the top of the wall. Quietly they made their way down to the courtyard, and broke up into parties, taking their places at the entrance to the various buildings; then, all further need for concealment being at an end, a bugle call sounded loud in the air. It was answered by another down upon the plain near the gate. The rajah himself was one of the first to rash out. He was seized and disarmed before he was aware of what had happened.

"Tell your men to throw down their arms and surrender," Major Warrener said to him, "or we will put you and every soul here to the sword. The place is surrounded, and there is no escape. Do you not hear our bugles on the plain?"

It needed not the rajah's order; the garrison, taken utterly by surprise, and finding the castle captured by an enemy of unknown strength, threw down their arms as they came out of their quarters. Orders were sent by the rajah to the men at the various gates on the hill to come up and lay down their arms, and the sentry at the lowest of all was to open it to the troops there. A bugler and ten men were left below, and the rest joined the party in the castle.

Long ere they had arrived, the joyful meeting of the captives and their friends had taken place. Rose and Kate had awoke at the sound of the bugle, but had heeded it little, believing that it was only a Sepoy call. Even the stir and commotion outside had not disturbed them, and they had lain quiet until they heard a loud knocking at the door of the women's apartments, followed by screams from the women, and then—they could scarcely believe their ears—their names shouted in Major Warrener's voice. With a cry of delight both sprang up, and seizing shawls, rushed to the door, and in another moment Kate was in the arms of her father.

"We are all here, dear," he said, after the first wild greeting—"the boys, and Dunlop, and Manners. Hurry on your clothes, darlings; they are longing to see you."

The garrison of the castle were all collected in one of the smaller courts, where twenty troopers, revolver in hand, kept guard over them. The whole of the arms found in the castle were broken to pieces and thrown over the walls, and the cannon planted there were first spiked and then pitched over. The guns on the gates were similarly rendered useless, and the stores of gunpowder all wetted. The rajah and his two sons, boys of six and eight, were then told to prepare to accompany the troops, and warning was given that they would be shot in case an attack was made upon the force as it returned to Meerut.

"Tell your followers this," Major Warrener said, "and order them to give no alarm, or to spread the news; for if we are caught your life and that of your sons will pay forfeit. As it is, you may hope for clemency. You have as yet taken no part in the insurrection; and although there is no doubt of your intention, your good conduct in the future may, perhaps, wipe out the memory of your faults."

It needs not to say anything of the rapturous greeting of the girls and their brothers and lovers, or the happy half-hour which was spent together in the great hall while the preparations for the departure were being made outside. Captain Kent saw to all that there was to be done, leaving the major free to join the happy party within.

"Are you strong enough to ride, Rose?"

"Oh, I think so, uncle; I have been shamming ill, and they thought I could not walk; but I am pretty strong, and if I can't ride by myself I must be tied on to some one else."

"I dare say my horse will carry double," Captain Manners said, laughing.

"Have the women here been kind?" Major Warrener asked.

The girls shook their heads:

"Not very, papa; they have been talking of Delhi;" and Kate shuddered.

The major frowned; he could guess what they must have suffered. He went to the door.

"Kent, order the women out of the *zenana* into one of the other rooms. Tell them that they will all be searched as they come out, and that if one brings out an ornament or a jewel with her she will be put to death. Of course you will not search them; but the threat will do. Let no insult be offered them. Then let Rivers take four men, and go in, and take all the loot you can find. The jewels we will divide among the men when at Meerut. Tell off another party to loot the rest of the rooms, but only take what is really valuable and portable. We cannot cumber ourselves with baggage. It would serve the rajah right if I were to burn his castle down; he may think himself lucky to get off with his life."

The girls pleaded for the women. "We bear them no ill-feeling," they said. "They are very ignorant; they only acted as they were taught."

"Well, well," said the major, "we will take the jewels alone; they are a fair loot."

Another hour and the troops were already well on their way on the Delhi road. The good luck which had attended them so far followed them to the end. Anxious to avoid an encounter with the enemy, they took an even more circuitous route than that by which they had come, and on the fourth afternoon after leaving rode into Meerut, where their arrival after the long and successful expedition created quite an excitement. A comfortable house was found for the girls, with some old friends of the major, who resided permanently at Meerut; as for the major and his troops, they prepared to accompany the column which was on the point of marching against Delhi.

CHAPTER VII.
DELHI.

Never did a government or a people meet a terrible disaster with a more undaunted front than that displayed by the government and British population of India when the full extent of the peril caused by the rising of the Sepoys was first clearly understood. By the rising of Delhi, and of the whole country down to Allahabad, the northern part of India was entirely cut off from Calcutta, and was left wholly to its own resources. Any help that could be spared from the capital was needed for the menaced garrisons of Allahabad, Benares, and Agra, while it was certain that the important stations of Cawnpore and Lucknow, in the newly-annexed province of Oude, would at best be scarcely able to defend themselves, and would in all probability urgently require assistance. Thus the rebel city of Delhi, the center and focus of the insurrection, was safe from any possibility of a British advance from the south. Nor did it look as if the position of the English was much better in the north. At Sealkote, Lahore, and many other stations, the Sepoys mutinied, and the Sikh regiments were disturbed, and semi-mutinous. It was at this all-important moment that the fidelity of two or three of the great Sikh chieftains saved British India. Foremost of them was the Rajah of Puttiala, who, when the whole Sikh nation was wavering as to the course it should take, rode into the nearest British station with only one retainer, and offered his whole force and his whole treasury to the British government. A half-dozen other prominent princes instantly followed the example; and from that moment Northern India was not only safe, but was able to furnish troops for the siege of Delhi. The Sikh regiments at once returned to their habitual state of cheerful obedience, and served with unflinching loyalty and bravery through the campaign.

Not a moment was lost, as it was all-important to make an appearance before Delhi, and so, by striking at the heart of the insurrection, to show the waverers all over India that we had no idea of giving up the game. The main force was collected at Umballah, under General Anson. Transport was hastily got together, and in the last week of May this force moved forward, while a brigade from Meerut advanced to effect a junction with it. With this latter force were Warrener's irregular horse, which had returned only the evening before the advance from its successful expedition to Nahdoor. On the 30th of May the Meerut force under Brigadier-General Wilson came in contact with the enemy at Ghazee-ud-deen-Nugghur, a village fifteen miles from Delhi, where there was a suspension bridge across the Hindur. This fight, although unimportant in itself, is memorable as being the first occasion upon which the mutineers and the British troops met. Hitherto the Sepoys had had it entirely their own way. Mutiny, havoc, murder, had gone on unchecked; but now the tide was to turn, never to ebb again until the Sepoy mutiny was drowned in a sea of blood. Upon this, their first meeting with the white troops, the Sepoys were confident of success. They were greatly superior in force; they had been carefully drilled in the English system; they were led by their native regimental officers; and they had been for so many years pampered and indulged by government, that they regarded themselves, as being, man for man, fully equal to the British. Thus, then, they began to fight with a confidence of victory which, however great their superiority in numbers, was never again felt by the mutineers throughout the war. Upon many subsequent occasions they fought with extreme bravery, but it was the bravery of despair; whereas the British soldiers were animated with a burning desire for vengeance, and an absolute confidence of victory. Thus the fight at Ghazee-ud-deen-Nugghur is a memorable one in the annals of British India.

The mutineers, seeing the smallness of the British force, at first advanced to the attack; but they were met with such fury by four companies of the Sixtieth Rifles, supported by eight guns of the artillery, by the Carbineers and Warrener's Horse, that, astounded and dismayed, they broke before the impetuous onslaught, abandoned their intrenchments, threw a way their arms, and fled, leaving five guns in the hands of the victors, and in many cases not stopping in their flight until they reached the gates of Delhi. The next day considerable bodies of fresh troops came out to renew the attack; but the reports of the fugitives of the day before, of the fury and desperation with which the British troops were possessed, had already effected such an impression that they did not venture upon close fighting, but after engaging in an artillery duel at long distances, fell back again to Delhi.

On the 7th of June the Meerut force joined that from Umballah, at Alipore, a short march from Delhi; and the next morning the little army, now under the command of Sir H. Barnard—for General Anson, overwhelmed by work and responsibility, had died a few days before advanced upon the capital of India, After four miles march they came at Badulee-Ka-Serai upon the enemy's first line of defense, a strong intrenched position, held by three thousand Sepoys with twelve guns. These pieces of artillery were much heavier than the British field guns, and as they opened a heavy fire, they inflicted considerable damage upon our advancing troops. The British, however, were in no humor for distant fighting; they panted to get at the murderers of women and children—these men who had shot down in cold blood the officers, whose only fault had been their too great kindness to, and confidence in them. Orders were given to the Seventy-fifth to advance at once and take the position; and that regiment, giving a tremendous cheer, rushed forward with such impetuosity through the heavy fire that, as at Ghazee-ud-deen-Nugghur, the Sepoys were seized with a panic, and fled in wild haste from their intrenchments, leaving their cannon behind them.

At the foot of the steep hill on which the signal tower stands, another and stronger line of defense had been prepared; but the mutineers stationed here were infected by the wild panic of the fugitives from the first position, and so, deserting their position, joined in the flight into the city.

The British troops had marched from their encampment at Alipore at one in the morning, and by nine A.M. the last Sepoy disappeared within the walls of the town, and the British flag flew out on the signal tower on the Ridge, almost looking down upon the rebel city, and the troops took up their quarters in the lines formerly occupied by the Thirty-eighth, Fifty-fourth, and Seventy-fourth native regiments. As the English flag blew out to the wind from the signal tower, a thrill of anxiety must have been felt by every one in Delhi, from the emperor down to the lowest street ruffian. So long as it waved there it was a proof that the British Raj was not yet overthrown—that British supremacy, although sorely shaken, still asserted itself—and that the day of reckoning and retribution would, slowly perhaps, but none the less surely, come for the blood-stained city. Not only in Delhi itself, but over the whole of India, the eyes of the population were turned toward that British flag on the Ridge. Native and British alike recognized the fact that English supremacy in India depended upon its maintenance. That England would send out large reinforcements all knew, but they also knew that many an anxious week must elapse before the first soldier from England could arrive within striking distance. If the native leaders at Delhi, with the enormously superior forces at their command, could not drive off their besiegers and pluck down the flag from the Ridge, the time must come when, with the arrival of the reinforcements, the tide would begin to flow against them. So India argued, and waited for the result. The Delhi leaders, as well as the English, felt the importance of the issue, and the one never relaxed their desperate efforts to drive back the besiegers—the other with astonishing tenacity held on against all odds; while scores of native chiefs hesitated on the verge, waiting, until they saw the end of the struggle at Delhi. It was called the siege of Delhi, but it should rather have been called the siege of the Ridge, for it was our force rather than that of the enemy which was besieged. Never before in the history of the world did three thousand men sit down before a great city inhabited by a quarter of a million bitterly hostile inhabitants, and defended moreover by strong walls, a very powerful artillery, and a well-drilled and disciplined force, at first amounting to some ten thousand men, but swelled later on, as the mutineers poured in from all quarters, to three times that force. Never during the long months which the struggle lasted did we attempt to do more than to hold our own. The city was open to the enemy at all sides, save where we held our footing; large forces marched in and out of the town; provisions and stores poured into it; and we can scarcely be said to have fired a shot at it until our batteries opened to effect a breach a few days before the final assault.

The troops with which Sir H. Barnard arrived before Delhi consisted of the Seventy-fifth Regiment, six companies of the Sixtieth Rifles, the First Bengal Fusiliers, six companies of the Second Fusiliers—both composed of white troops—the Sirmoor battalion of Goorkhas, the Sixth Dragoon Guards (the Carbineers), two squadrons of the Ninth Lancers, and a troop or two of newly-raised irregular horse. The artillery consisted of some thirty pieces, mostly light field-guns.

Upon the day following the occupation of the Ridge a welcome accession of strength was received by the arrival of the Guides, a picked corps consisting of three troops of cavalry and six companies of infantry. This little force had marched five hundred and eighty miles in twenty-two days, a rate of twenty-six miles a day, without a break—a feat probably altogether without example, especially when it is considered that it took place in India, and in the hottest time of the year.

The Ridge, which occupies so important a place in the history of the siege of Delhi, is a sharp backed hill, some half a mile long, rising abruptly from the plain. From the top a splendid view of Delhi, and of the country, scattered with mosques and tombs—the remains of older Delhi—can be obtained. The cantonments lay at the back of this hill, a few posts only, such as Hindoo Rao's house, being held in advance. Until the work of building batteries and regularly commencing the siege should begin, it would have been useless putting the troops unnecessarily under the fire of the heavy guns of the city bastions.

When the troops had fairly taken possession of the old native lines on the 8th of June many of them, as soon as dismissed from duty, made their way up to the flagstaff tower, on the highest point of the Ridge, to look down upon Delhi. Among those who did so were Major Warrener and his two sons. Both uttered an exclamation of pleasure as the city came into view:

"What a superb city!"

Delhi is indeed a glorious city as viewed from the Ridge. It is surrounded by a lofty crenelated wall, strengthened with detached martello towers, and with eleven bastions, each mounting nine guns, the work of our own engineers, but in admirable architectural keeping with the towers. Conspicuous, on a high table rock rising almost perpendicularly in the heart of the city, is the Jumma Musjid, the great mosque, a superb pile of building, with its domes and minarets. To the left, as viewed from the Ridge, is the great mass of the king's palace—a fortress in itself—with its lofty walls and towers, and with its own mosques and minarets. These rise thickly, too, in other parts, while near the palace the closely-packed houses cease, and lofty trees rise alone there. The Ridge lies on the north of the city, and opposite to it is the Cashmere gate, through which our storming parties would rush later on; and away, a little to the right, is the Lahore gate, through which the enemy's sorties were principally made. On the left of the Ridge the ground is flat to the river, which sweeps along by the wall of the town and palace. There are two bridges across it, and over them the exulting mutineers were for weeks to pass into the city—not altogether unpunished, for our guns carried that far, and were sometimes able to inflict a heavy loss upon them as they passed, with music playing and flags flying, into the town.

"A glorious city!" Ned Warrener said, as they looked down upon it. "What a ridiculous handful of men we seem by the side of it! It is like Tom Thumb sitting down to besiege the giant's castle. Why, we should be lost if we got inside!"

"Yes, indeed, Ned," said his father; "there will be no possibility of our storming that city until our numbers are greatly increased; for if we scaled the walls by assault, which we could no doubt do, we should have to fight our way through the narrow streets, with barriers and barricades everywhere; and such a force as ours would simply melt away before the fire from the housetops and windows. There is nothing so terrible as street fighting; and drill and discipline are there of comparatively little use. The enemy will naturally fight with the desperation of rats in a hole: and it would be rash in the extreme for us to make the attempt until we are sure of success. A disastrous repulse here would entail the loss of all India. The news is worse and worse every day from all the stations of the northwest; and as the mutineers are sure to make for Delhi, the enemy will receive reinforcements vastly more rapidly than we shall, and it will be all we shall be able to do to hold our own here. We may be months before we take Delhi."

"I hope they won't keep us here all that time," Dick said, "for cavalry can't do much in a siege; besides, the ground is all cut up into gardens and inclosures, and we could not act, even if we had orders to do so."

"We may be very useful in going out to bring convoys in," Major Warrener replied, "and to cut off convoys of the enemy, to scout generally, and to bring in news; still, I agree with you, Dick, that I hope we may be sent off for duty elsewhere. Hullo! what's that?"

As he spoke a sudden fire broke out from the walls and bastions; shot and shell whizzed over their heads, many of them plunging down behind the Ridge, among the troops who were engaged in getting up their tents; while a crackling fire of musketry broke out in the gardens around Hindoo Rao's house, our advanced post on the right front.

"A sortie!" exclaimed the major. "Come along, boys." And those who had gathered around the flagstaff dashed down the hill to join their respective corps. The Sixtieth Rifles, however, of whom two companies held Hindoo Rao's, repulsed the sortie, and all calmed down again; but the enemy's artillery continued to play, and it was evident that the foe had it in his power to cause great annoyance to all our pickets on the Ridge.

Fortunately our position could only be assailed on one side. Our cavalry patrolled the plain as far as the river, and our rear was covered by a canal, possessing but few bridges, and those easily guarded. It was thus from our right and right front alone that serious attacks could be looked for.

The next afternoon a heavy firing broke out near Hindoo Rao's house, and the troops got under arms. The enemy were evidently in force.

An aid-de-camp rode up:

"Major Warrener, you will move up your troop, and fall in with the Guide cavalry."

At a trot Warrener's Horse moved off toward the right. The guns on the walls were now all at work, and our artillery at Hindoo Rao's were answering them, and the shots from a light battery placed by the flagstaff went singing away toward the right.

Warrener's Horse were now at the station assigned to them. The musketry fire in the gardens and broken ground near Hindoo Rao's was very heavy, and a large body of the enemy's cavalry was seen extending into the plain, with the intention of pushing forward on the right of the Ridge.

"You will charge the enemy at once," an aid-de-camp said; and with a cheer the Guides and Warrener's Horse dashed forward.

It was the moment they had longed for; and the fury with which they charged was too much for the enemy, who, although enormously superior in numbers, halted before they reached them, and fled toward the city, with the British mixed with them, in a confused mass of fighting, struggling men. The pursuit lasted almost to the walls of the city. Then the guns on the wall opened a heavy fire, and the cavalry fell back as the balls plunged in among them.

There were but two or three hurt, but among them was Lieutenant Quentin Battye, a most gallant young officer, a mere lad, but a general favorite alike with other officers and the men. Struck by a round shot in the body, his case was hopeless from the first; he kept up his spirits to the last, and said with a smile to an old school-friend who came in to bid him farewell:

"Well, old fellow, *Dulce et decorum est pro patriá mori*, and you see it's my case."

Such was the spirit which animated every officer and man of the little army before Delhi; and it is no wonder that, day after day, and week after week, they were able to repulse the furious attacks of the ever-increasing enemy.

On the 9th, 10th, and 11th fresh sorties were made. Before daybreak on the 13th a large force of the mutineers came out quietly, and worked their way round to the left, and just as it began to be light, made a furious assault on the company of the Seventy-fifth who were holding the flagstaff battery. Warrener's Horse were encamped on the old parade-ground, immediately behind and below the flagstaff, and the men leaped from their beds on hearing this outburst of firing close to them.

There was a confused shouting, and then the major's voice was heard above the din:

"Breeches and boots, revolvers and swords, nothing else. Quick, lads; fall in on foot. We must save the battery at all hazards."

In a few seconds the men came rushing out, hastily buckling on their belts, with their pouches of revolver ammunition, and fell into rank; and in less than two minutes from the sound of the first shot the whole were dashing up the steep ascent to the battery, where the tremendous musketry fire told them how hardly the Seventy-fifth were pressed.

"Keep line, lads; steady!" shouted the major as they neared the crest. "Now get ready for a charge; go right at them. Don't fire a shot till you are within five paces, then give them three barrels of your revolvers; then at them with the sword; and keep your other shots in case you are pressed. Hurrah!"

With a thundering cheer the gallant little band fell on the mutineers, many of whom had already made their way into the battery, where the handful of white troops were defending themselves with desperation. Struck with terror and surprise at this sudden attack, and by the shower of pistol bullets which swept among them, the enemy wavered and broke at the fierce onslaught, sword in hand, of these new foes; while the Seventy-fifth, raising a shout of joy at the arrival of their friends, took the offensive, swept before them the mutineers who had made their way into the battery, and, joining the irregulars, drove the mutineers, astounded and panic-stricken at the fierceness of the assault, pell-mell before them down the hill.

The reinforcements had arrived but just in time, for Captain Knox, who commanded at this post, and nearly half his force, had fallen before Major Warrener's band had come up to their aid. The next day, and the next, and the next, the sorties from the city were repeated, with ever-increasing force and fury, each fresh body of mutineers who came into the city being required to testify their loyalty to the emperor by heading the attack on his foes. Desperately the little British force had to fight to maintain their position, and their losses were so serious, the number of their enemies so large, so rapidly increasing, that it was clear to all that the most prodigious efforts would be necessary to enable them to hold on until reinforcements arrived, and that all idea of an early capture of the city must be abandoned.

Warrener's Horse, however, had no share in these struggles, for on the day after the fight at the flagstaff a report spread among them that they were again to start upon an expedition. A note had been brought in by a native to the effect that several English ladies and gentlemen were prisoners at the fortress of Bithri, in Oude, some hundred and fifty miles from Delhi. The instructions given to Major Warrener were that he was to obtain their release by fair means, if possible; if not, to carry the place and release them, if it appeared practicable to do so with his small force; that he was then to press on to Cawnpore. Communications had ceased with Sir H. Wheeler, the officer in command there; but it was not known whether he was actually besieged, or whether it was merely a severance of the telegraph wire. If he could join Sir H. Wheeler he was to do so; if not, he was to make his way on, to form part of the force which General Havelock was collecting at Allahabad for an advance to Cawnpore and Lucknow. It would be a long and perilous march, but the troops were admirably mounted; and as they would have the choice of routes open to them, and would travel fast, it was thought that they might hope to get through in safety, and their aid would be valuable either to Sir H. Wheeler or to General Havelock.

It was a lovely moonlight evening when they started. During their stay at Delhi they had, profiting by their previous expedition, got rid of every article of accouterment that could make a noise. Wooden scabbards had taken the place of steel, and these were covered in flannel, to prevent rattle should they strike against a stirrup. The water bottles were similarly cased in flannel, and the rings and chains of the bits in leather. Nothing, save the sound of the horses' hoofs, was to be heard as they marched, and even these were muffled by the deep dust that lay on the road. Each man, moreover, carried four leathern shoes for his horse, with lacings for fastening them. Under the guidance of two natives, the troop made their first six stages without the slightest adventure. The country was flat, and the villages sparsely scattered. The barking of the dogs brought a few villagers to their doors, but in those troubled times the advantages of non-interference were obvious and the peasant population in general asked nothing better than to be let alone.

The troop always marched by night, and rested by day at villages at a short distance from the main road. Upon a long march like that before them, it would have been impossible to maintain secrecy by resting in woods. Food for men and horses was requisite, and this could only be obtained in villages. So far no difficulty had been met with. The head men of the villages willingly provided provender for the horses, while flour, milk, eggs, and fowls were forthcoming in sufficient quantities for the men, everything being strictly paid for.

The last night march was as successful as the preceding, and crossing the river by a bridge at Banat, they halted some five miles from the fortified house, or castle, which was the immediate object of their expedition. They were now in Oude, and had, since crossing the river, avoided the villages as much as possible, for in this province these are little fortresses. Each is strongly walled and guarded, and petty wars and feuds are common occurrences. The people are warlike, and used to arms, and without artillery even a small village could not be carried without considerable loss. The troops therefore had made circuits round the villages, and bivouacked at the end of their march in a wood, having brought with them a supply of food and grain from the village where they had halted on the previous day. They had not slept many hours when one of the vedettes came in to say that there was a sound of beating of drums in a large village not far away, and that bodies of peasantry had arrived from other villages, and that he believed an attack was about to take place.

Major Warrener at once took his measures for defense. The first troop were to defend the front of their position with their carbines against an attack. The second troop were to move round to the extreme end of the tope, were to mount there, and when the enemy began to waver before the musketry fire, were to sweep round and take them in flank. Major Warrener himself took command of the dismounted troop, and posted the men along behind a bank with a hedge, a short distance in front of the trees. Then, each man knowing his place, they fell back out of the scorching sunshine to the shade of the tree's, and waited. In half an hour a loud drumming was heard, and a motley body, two or three thousand strong, of peasants in a confused mass, with a tattered banner or two, made their appearance.

The "Avengers," as Warrener's Horse called themselves, took their places behind the bank, and quietly awaited the attack. The enemy opened a heavy fire, yet at a long distance. "Answer with a shot or two, occasionally," Major Warrener had ordered, "as they will then aim at the bank instead of tiring into the wood. We don't want the horses hurt."

Slowly and steadily the rifled carbines spoke out in answer to the heavy fire opened on the bank, and as almost every man of Warrener's Horse was a sportsman and a good shot, very few shots were thrown away. The enemy beat their drums more and more loudly, and shouted vociferously as they advanced. When they were within three hundred yards Major Warrener gave the word:

"Fire fast, but don't throw away a shot."

Astonished at the accuracy and deadliness of the fire which was poured into them by their still invisible foe, the enemy wavered. Their leaders, shouting loudly, and exposing themselves bravely in front, called them on, as slowly, and with heavy loss, the main body arrived within a hundred yards of the hedge. Those in front were, however, falling so fast that no efforts of their leaders could get them to advance further, and already a retrograde movement had begun, when there was a yell of fear, as the mounted troop, hitherto unnoticed, charged furiously down upon their flank.

"Empty your rifles, and then to horse," shouted Major Warrener; and the men dashed back through the tope to the spot in the rear, where four of their number were mounting guard over the horses.

In three minutes they were back again on the plain, but the fight was over. The enemy in scattered bodies were in full flight, and the cavalry, dashing through them, were cutting them down, or emptying their revolvers among them.

"Make for the village," Major Warrener said. "Gallop!"

At full speed the troop dashed across the plain to the village, whose gate they reached just as a large body of the fugitives were arriving. These gave a yell as this fresh body of horsemen fell upon them; a few tried to enter the gates of the village, but the main body scattered again in flight. The cavalry dashed in through the gates, and sabered some men who were trying to close them. A few shots were fired inside, but resistance was soon over, and the male inhabitants who remained dropped over the wall and sought refuge in flight. A bugle call now summoned the other troop from pursuit, and the women and children being at once, without harm or indignity, turned out of the village, the conquerors took possession.

"This will be our headquarters for a day or two," the major said, as the troop gathered round him; "there is an abundance of food for horse and man, and we could stand a siege if necessary."

Warrener's Horse was the happiest of military bodies. On duty the discipline was severe, and obedience prompt and ready. Off duty, there was, as among the members of a regimental mess, no longer any marked distinction of rank; all were officers and gentlemen, good fellows and good comrades. The best house in the village was set aside for Major Warrener, and the rest of the squadron dispersed in the village, quartering themselves in parties of threes and fours among the cleanest-looking of the huts. Eight men were at once put on sentry on the walls, two on each side. Their horses were first looked to, fed and watered, and soon the village assumed as quiet an aspect as if the sounds of war had never been heard in the land. At dark all was life and animation. A dozen great fires blazed in the little square in the center of the village, and here the men fried their chickens, or, scraping out a quantity of red-hot embers, baked their chupatties, with much laughter and noise.

Then there was comparative quiet, the sentries on the walls were trebled, and outposts placed at a couple of hundred yards beyond the gates. Men lighted their pipes and chatted round the fires, while Major Warrener and a dozen of the oldest and most experienced of his comrades sat together and discussed the best course to be pursued.

CHAPTER VIII.
A DESPERATE DEFENSE.

"Well, major, what do you think of the situation?" one of the senior captains asked, after the pipes had begun to draw.

"It looks rather bad, Crawshay. There's no disguising the fact. We shall have the country up in force; they will swarm out like wasps from every village, and by to-morrow night we shall have, at the very least, ten thousand of them round us. Against a moderate force we could defend the village; but it is a good-sized place, and we have only twenty-five men for each wall, and a couple of hundred would be none too little."

"But surely, major, we might prevent their scaling the walls. It is not likely that they would attack on all sides at once, and without artillery they could do little."

"They will have artillery," said Captain Wilkins, an officer, who had served for some time in Oude. "These talookdars have all got artillery. They were ordered to give it up, and a good many old guns were sent in; but there is not one of these fellows who cannot bring a battery at the very least into the field. By to-morrow night, or at the latest next day, we may have some thirty or forty pieces of artillery round this place."

"It will not do to be caught like rats in a trap here," Major Warrener said. "For to-night it is a shelter, after that it would be a trap. But about Bithri; I don't like to give up the idea of rescuing our country-people there. Still, although the matter has been left to my discretion, I cannot risk losing the whole squadron."

"What is the castle like, Warrener? have you heard?" Captain Crawshay asked.

"A square building, with high walls, and a deep moat. Beyond the moat is another wall with a strong outwork and gate. There are believed to be a couple of guns on the outwork, and eight on the inner wall."

"Do you think they will attack us to-morrow, Wilkins? You know these Oude fellows."

"They will muster strong, no doubt, and be prepared to attack us if we sally out; but I should think if we remain quiet they would wait till next day, so as to gather as many men and guns as possible."

"Then you think we ought to be out of this early?" Major Warrener asked.

"I don't say we ought to be, major; I only say we ought to be if we intend to get off without having to fight our way through them. I suppose the Bithri man is sure to come out to attack us?"

"Oh, no doubt," Major Warrener answered; "he has openly declared against us."

"The thing would be to pop into his place, just as he is thinking of popping in here," Captain Dunlop said, laughing.

"That's a good idea, Dunlop—a capital idea, if it could be carried out. The question is, is it possible?"

Then gradually the plan was elaborated, until it finally was definitely arranged as afterward carried into execution.

The night passed quietly, but fires could be seen blazing in many directions over the plain, and occasionally a distant sound of drums, or a wild shout, came faintly on the still air. Next morning Major Warrener started early, with half a troop, to reconnoiter the country toward Bithri. The party got to a spot within two miles of the castle, and had a look at it and its surroundings, and were able to discern that a great deal of bustle was going on around it, and that considerable numbers of horse and footmen were gathered near the gate. Then they rode rapidly back again, having to run the gantlet of several bodies of natives, who fired at them. One party indeed had already placed themselves on the road, about a mile from the village; but Captain Kent, seeing with his glass what was going on, rode out with his troop to meet the little reconnoitering party, and the enemy, fearing cavalry on the open, fell back after a scattering fire, but not quickly enough to prevent the horse from cutting up their rear somewhat severely.

At eight o'clock large bodies of men could, be seen approaching the village. These, when they arrived within gunshot, discharged their long matchlocks at the walls, with much shouting and gesticulation. Major Warrener's order was that not a shot should be returned, as it was advisable to keep them in ignorance as to the long range of the Enfield carbine.

"Let all get their breakfasts," he said, "and let the horses be well groomed and attended to; we shall want all their speed to-morrow."

At eleven some elephants, surrounded by a large body of horse, could be seen across the plain.

"Here come some of the talookdars," Captain Wilkins said. "I suspect those elephants are dragging guns behind them."

"Yes, the fun will soon begin now," Captain Dunlop answered. "Now, Dick," he went on to young Warrener, "you are going to see a little native artillery practice. These fellows are not like the Delhi pandies, who are artillerymen trained by ourselves; here you will see the real genuine native product; and as the manufacture of shell is in its infancy, and as the shot seldom fits the gun within half an inch, or even an inch, you will see something erratic. They may knock holes in the wall, but it will take them a long time to cut enough holes near each other to make a breach. There, do you see? there are another lot of elephants and troops coming from the left. We shall have the whole countryside here before long. Ah! that's just as we expected; they are going to take up their position on that rising ground, which you measured this morning, and found to be just five hundred yards off. Our carbines make very decent practice at that distance, and you will see we shall astonish them presently."

The two forces with elephants reached the rising ground at the same time, and there was great waving of flags, letting off of muskets, and beating of drums, while the multitude of footmen cheered and danced.

By this time the greater portion of the little garrison were gathered behind the wall. This was some two feet thick, of rough sun-dried bricks and mud. It was about fourteen feet high. Against it behind was thrown up a bank of earth five feet high, and in the wall were loopholes, four feet above the bank. At the corners of the walls, and at intervals along them, were little towers, each capable of holding about four men, who could fire over the top of the walls. In these towers, and at the loopholes, Major Warrener placed twenty of his best shots. There was a great deal of moving about on the rising ground; then the footmen cleared away in front, and most of the elephants withdrew, and then were seen ten guns ranged side by side. Close behind them were two elephants, with gaudy trappings, while others, less brilliantly arrayed, stood further back.

Major Warrener was in one of the little towers, with his second in command, and his two sons to act as his orderlies.

"Run, boys, and tell the men in the other towers to fire at the howdahs of the chief elephants; let the rest of them fire at the artillery. Tell them to take good aim, and fire a volley; I will give the word. Make haste, I want first shot; that will hurry them, and they will fire wild."

The boys started at a run, one each way, and in a minute the instructions were given. The major glanced down, saw that every carbine was leveled, and gave the word:

"Fire!"

The sound of the volley was answered in a few seconds by a yell of dismay from the enemy. One of the state elephants threw up its trunk, and started at a wild gallop across the plain, and a man was seen to fall from the howdah as it started. There was also confusion visible in the howdahs of the other elephants. Several men dropped at the guns; some, surprised and startled, fired wildly, most of the balls going high over the village; while others, whose loading was not yet complete, ran back from the guns. Only one ball hit the wall, and made a ragged hole of a foot in diameter.

"That's sickened them for the present," Captain Dunlop said, "I expect they'll do nothing now till it gets a bit cooler, for even a nigger could hardly stand this. Ah, we are going to give them another volley, this time a stronger one."

Fifty carbines spoke out this time, and the wildest confusion was caused among the elephants and footmen, who were now trying to drag the guns back. Again, a third volley, and then the garrison were dismissed from their posts, and told to lie down and keep cool till wanted again.

Half an hour later another large train of elephants, ten of them with guns, came from the direction of Bithri, and proceeded to a tope at about a mile from the village. There the elephants of the first comers had gathered after the stampede, and presently a great tent was raised in front of the tope.

"Bithri is going to do it in style," Dick laughed to his brother. "I shouldn't mind some iced sherbet at present, if he has got any to spare."

"Look, Dick, there is a movement; they are getting the guns in position on that knoll a little to the right, and a hundred yards or so in front of their tent."

Dick took the field-glass which his brother handed him.

"Yes, we shall have a salute presently; but they won't breach the wall this afternoon at that distance."

Twenty guns opened fire upon the village, and the shot flew overhead, or buried themselves in the ground in front, or came with heavy thuds against the wall, or, in some instances, crashed into the upper parts of the houses. After an hour's firing it slackened a little, and finally died out, for the heat was tremendous.

At three o'clock there was a move again; ten of the guns were brought forward to a point about a thousand yards from the wall, while ten others were taken round and placed on the road, at about the same distance, so as to command the gate. Again the fire opened, and this time more effectually. Again the men were called to the loopholes. The greater portion of them were armed, not with the government carbines, but with sporting rifles, shortened so as to be carried as carbines; and although none of the weapons were sighted for more than six hundred yards, all with sufficient elevation could send balls far beyond that distance. Ten of the best-armed men were told off against each battery of artillery, and a slow, steady fire was opened. It was effective, for, with the field-glasses, men could be seen to fall frequently at the guns, and the fire became more hurried, but much wilder and even less accurate, than it had hitherto been. The rest of the men, with the exception of ten told off for special duty, were dispersed round the walls, to check the advance of the footmen, who crept daringly to within a short distance, and kept up a rolling fire around the village.

At five o'clock half of the men were taken off the walls, and several were set to build a wall four feet high, in a semicircle just inside the gate, which had been struck by several shots, and showed signs of yielding. Two or three of the nearest huts were demolished rapidly, there being plenty of native tools in the village, and a rough wall was constructed of the materials; a trench five feet deep and eight feet wide was simultaneously dug across the entrance. At six o'clock, just as the wall was finished, an unlucky shot struck one of the doorposts, and the gate fell, dragging the other post with it. A distant yell of triumph came through the air.

The gates fell partly across the trench. "Now, lads, push them back a bit if you can; if not, knock the part over the ditch to pieces; it's half-smashed already."

It was easier to knock the gate, already splintered with shot, to pieces, than to remove it.

"Now, Dunlop, fetch one of those powder-bags we brought for blowing up the gates; put it in the trench, with a long train. You attend to the train, and when I give the word, fire it. Bring up those two big pots of boiling water to the gate-towers. Captain Kent, thirty men of your troop will hold the other three walls; but if you hear my dog-whistle, every man is to leave his post and come on here at a run. Thirty men more will man this front wall and towers. They are to direct their fire to check the crowd pushing forward behind those immediately assaulting. The remaining forty will fire through the loopholes as long as possible, and will then form round the breastwork and hold it to the last. One man in each gate-tower, when the enemy reach the gate, will lay down his carbine, and attend to the boiling water. Let them each have a small pot as a ladle. But let them throw the water on those pressing toward the gate, not on those who have reached it. Those are our affair."

In five minutes every man was at his post, and a sharp fire from the seventy men along the front wall opened upon the masses of the enemy, who came swarming toward the gate. The effect on the crowd, many thousand strong, was very severe, for each shot told; but the Mussulmen of Oude are courageous, and the rush toward the gate continued. Fast as those in front fell, the gaps were imperceptible in the swarming crowd. Major Warreners band of forty men were called away from the loopholes, and were drawn up behind the ditch; and as the head of the assaulting crowd neared the gate volley after volley rang out, and swept away the leaders, foremost among whom were a number of Sepoys, who, when their regiments mutinied, had returned to their homes, and now headed the peasantry in their attack upon the British force. When the dense mass arrived within thirty yards of the gate Major Warrener gave the word, and a retreat was made behind the breastwork. On, with wild shouts, came the assailants; the first few saw the trench, and leaped it; those who followed fell in, until the trench was full; then the crowd swept in unchecked. The defenders had laid by their carbines now, and had drawn their revolvers. They were divided into two lines, who were alternately to take places in front and fire, while those behind loaded their revolvers. The din, as the circle inclosed by the low wall filled with the assailants, was prodigious; the sharp incessant crack of the revolver; the roll of musketry from the walls; the yells of the enemy; the shrieks, which occasionally rose outside the gate as the men in the towers scattered the boiling water broadcast over them, formed a chaos. With the fury and despair of cornered wild beasts, the enemy fought, striving to get over the wall which so unexpectedly barred their way; but their very numbers and the pressure from behind hampered their efforts.

If a man in the front line of defenders had emptied his revolver before the one behind him had reloaded, he held his place with the sword.

"The wall's giving from the pressure!" Dick exclaimed to his father; and the latter put his whistle to his lips, and the sound rang out shrill and high above the uproar.

A minute later the front of the wall tottered and fell. Then Major Warrener held up his hand, and Captain Dunlop, who had stood all the time quietly watching him, fired the train. A thundering explosion, a flight of bodies and fragments of bodies through the air, a yell of terror from the enemy, and then, as those already rushing triumphantly through the breach stood paralyzed, the British fell upon them sword in hand; the men from the other walls came rushing up, eager to take their part in the fray, and the enemy inside the gate were either cut down or driven headlong through it!

The crowd beyond, already shaken by the murderous fire that the party on the walls kept up unceasingly upon them, while they stood unable to move from the jam in front, had recoiled through their whole mass at the explosion, and the sight of the handful of their comrades flying through the gate completed the effect. With yells of rage and discomfiture, each man turned and fled, while the defenders of the gateway passed out, and joined their fire to that of their comrades above on the flying foe.

"Thank God, it is all over!" Major Warrener said; "but it has been hot while it lasted. Have we had many casualties?"

The roll was soon called, and it was found that the besieged had escaped marvelously. One young fellow, a civil servant, had been shot through the head, by a stray ball entering the loophole through which he was firing. Thirteen of the defenders of the gateway were wounded with pistol shots, or with sword cuts; but none of the injuries were of a serious character.

It was now rapidly becoming dark, and Major Warrener mounted one of the towers to have a last look.

The enemy had rallied at a distance from the walls, and two fresh bodies of troops, with elephants, were to be seen approaching from the distance.

"That is all right," he said. "They will wait, and renew the attack to-morrow."

An hour afterward it was night. The moon had not risen yet, and Major Warrener had a huge bonfire lighted outside the gate, with posts and solid beams from the fallen gates and from the houses.

"That will burn for hours," he said, "quite long enough for our purpose."

Lights could be seen scattered all over the side of the plain on which the tents were erected, some of them coming up comparatively close to the walls. On the road in front, but far enough to be well beyond the light of the fire, voices could be heard, and occasionally a shout that they would finish with the infidel dogs to-morrow rose on the air. Evidently by the low buzz of talk there were a large number here, and probably the guns had been brought closer, to check any attempt on the part of the little garrison to dash through their enemies. The blazing fire, however, throwing as it did a bright light upon the empty gateway through which they must pass, showed that at present, at least, the besieged had no idea of making their escape.

At nine o'clock the whole of the garrison stood to their horses. Not only had their feet been muffled with the leather shoes, but cloths, of which there were plenty in the village, had been wound round them, until their footfalls would, even on the hardest road, have been noiseless. Then Major Warrener led the way to the spot where ten men had been at work during the afternoon.

At this point, which was on the side furthest from that upon which was the main camp of the enemy, a clump of trees and bushes grew close to the wall outside; behind them a hole in the wall, wide enough and high enough for a horse to pass through easily, had been made, and the ditch behind had been filled up with rubbish. There was no word spoken; every one had received his orders, and knew what to do; and as silently as phantoms the troop passed through, each man leading his horse. Once outside the bushes, they formed fours and went forward, still leading their horses-as these were less likely to snort with their masters at their heads.

Ten minutes' walking convinced them that they had little to fear, and that no guards had been set on that side. It was regarded by the enemy as so certain that the English would not abandon their horses and fly on foot, only to be overtaken and destroyed the next day, that they had only thought it necessary to watch the gateway through which, as they supposed, the British must, if at all, escape on horseback.

The troop now mounted, and trotted quietly away, making a wide detour, and then going straight toward Bithri. The moon had risen; and when, about a mile and a half in front, they could see the castle, Major Warrener, who with Captain Kent and the native guides was riding ahead, held up his hand. The troop came to a halt.

"There are some bullock-carts just ahead. Take the mufflings off your horse's feet and ride on by yourself," he said to one of the native guides, "and see what is in the wagons, and where they are going."

The man did as ordered, but he needed no questions. The wagons were full of wounded men going to Bithri. He passed on with a word of greeting, turned his horse when he reached a wood a little in front, and allowed them to pass, and then rode back to the troop.

"Four bullock-carts full of wounded, sahib."

"The very thing," Major Warrener exclaimed; "nothing could be more lucky."

Orders were passed down the line that they were to ride along until the leaders were abreast of the first cart, then to halt and dismount suddenly. The drivers were to be seized, gagged, and bound. The wounded were not to be injured.

"These men are not mutinous Sepoys, with their hands red with the blood of women," Major Warrener said; "they are peasants who have fought bravely for their country, and have done their duty, according to their light."

CHAPTER IX.
SAVE BY A TIGER.

The drivers of the bullock-carts were startled at the noiseless appearance by their side of a body of horsemen; still more startled, when suddenly that phantom-like troop halted and dismounted. The rest was like a dream; in an instant they were seized, bound, and gagged, and laid down in the field at some distance from the road; one of them, however, being ungagged, and asked a few questions before being finally left. The wounded, all past offering the slightest resistance, were still more astonished when their captors, whom the moonlight now showed to be white, instead of cutting their throats as they expected, lifted them tenderly and carefully from the wagons, and laid them down on a bank a short distance off.

"Swear by the Prophet not to call for aid, or to speak, should any one pass the road, for one hour!" was the oath administered to each, and all who were still conscious swore to observe it. Then with the empty wagons the troops proceeded on their way. At the last clump of trees, a quarter of a mile from the castle, there was another halt. The troop dismounted, led their horses some little distance from the road, and tied them to the trees. Twenty men remained as a guard. Four of the others wrapped themselves up so as to appear at a short distance like natives, and took their places at the bullocks' heads, and the rest crowded into the wagons, covering themselves with their cloaks to hide their light uniforms. Then the bullocks were again set in motion across the plain. So careless were the garrison that they were not even challenged as they approached the gate of the outworks, and without a question the gate swung back.

"More wounded!" the officer on guard said. "This is the third lot. Those children of Sheitan must have been aided by their father. Ah, treachery!" he cried, as, the first cart moving into the moonlight beyond the shadow of the gateway, he saw the white faces of the supposed wounded.

There was a leap from the nearest driver upon him, and he was felled to the ground. But the man at the open gate had heard the cry, and drew a pistol and fired it before he could be reached. Then the British leaped from the carts, and twenty of them scattered through the works, cutting down those who offered resistance and disarming the rest. These were huddled into the guardroom, and five men with cocked revolvers placed at the door, with orders to shoot them down at the first sign of movement.

The garrison in the castle itself had been alarmed by the shots; and shouts were heard, and loud orders, and the sentries over the gate discharged their muskets. There was little time given them to rally, however; for Captain Kent, with four of his men, had, on leaping from the cart, made straight across the drawbridge over the moat, for the gateway, to which they attached the petards which they had brought with them. Then they ran back to the main body, who stood awaiting the explosion. In a few seconds it came, and then with a cheer the troops dashed across the drawbridge, and in through the splintered gate. There was scarcely any resistance. Taken utterly by surprise, and being numerically inferior to their assailants—for nearly all the fighting men had gone out with their lord—the frightened retainers tried to hide themselves rather than to resist, and were speedily disarmed and gathered in the courtyard.

Major Warrener, informed by the bullock drivers of the quarter in which the Europeans were confined, followed by a dozen men, made his way straight to it, and had the delight of being greeted by the voices of his countrymen and women. These were, as reported, three officers and five ladies, all of whom were absolutely bewildered by the surprise and suddenness of their rescue.

There was no time for explanation. The stables were ransacked and eight of the rajah's best horses taken. Then, when all was ready for starting, Major Warrener proceeded to the door of the women's apartments. Here, in obedience to the order he had sent her, the wife of the talookdar, veiled from head to foot, and surrounded by her attendants, stood to await the orders of her captor.

"Madam," said Captain Wilkins, who spoke the dialect in use in Oude, "Major Warrener, the British officer in command, bids me tell you that this castle, with you and all that it contains, are in his power, and that he might give it to the flames and carry you off as hostage. But he will not do this. The Rajah of Bithri is a brave man, but he is wrong to fight against fate. The English Raj will prevail again, and all who have rebelled will be punished. We treat him as a brave but mistaken enemy; and as we have spared his castle and his family, so we hope that he in turn will behave kindly to any Englishman or woman who may fall into his hands or may ask his aid. Lastly, let no one leave this castle till daybreak, for whoever does so we will slay without mercy."

Then, turning round again, Warrener and his companions returned to the courtyard. The moment the castle was entered and opposition quelled, half the troops had run back for the horses, and in twenty minutes from the arrival of the bullock-carts at the gateway of Bithri the last of its captors filed out from its walls and trotted off into the darkness. Day broke before any of the inhabitants of Bithri dared issue from its walls. Then a horseman took the news on to the camp. The artillery, increased now to thirty-six guns, had already opened upon the village ere he reached the great tent on the plain. The rajah could not credit the intelligence that the enemy had escaped, that his castle had been attacked and carried, and the white prisoners released; but his surprise and fury were overpowered by the delight he felt at the news that his women and children were safe and his ancestral dwelling uninjured. "The English are a great people," he said, stroking his beard; then, issuing from his tent, he told the news. Like wildfire it ran through the camp, and as none of the thousands gathered there had his feelings of gratitude and relief to soften their anger and disappointment, the fury of the multitude was unbounded.

With a wild rush they made for the gate-almost blocked with their dead-scoured the little village, and soon discovered the hole through which the besieged had escaped. Then with wild yells three thousand horsemen set off in pursuit; but it was six o'clock now, and the fugitives had got seven hours' start. The Rajah of Bithri's contingent took no part in the pursuit. On issuing from his tent he had, after telling the news, briefly given orders for his tents to be struck and for all his troops to return at once to the castle, toward which he himself, accompanied by his bodyguard, set out on his elephant of state.

Major Warrener and his troops had no fear of pursuit. New foes might be met; but with horses fresh and in good condition, and six hours' start—for they were confident that no pursuit could commence before daybreak at the earliest—they felt safe, from the enemy who had just attacked them, especially as these could not know the direction which they were pursuing, and would believe that their aim would be to return with their rescued friends to Delhi, instead of proceeding through the heart of Oude. The party whom they had found at Bithri consisted of Mr. Hartford, a deputy commissioner, with his wife and two daughters; of a Mrs. Pearson and her sister, the former the wife of a district magistrate, who had been absent on duty when the rising at the little station at which they lived took place; and of Captain Harper and Lieutenant Jones, who were the officers of the detachment there. The men, native cavalry, had ridden off without injuring their officers, but the fanatical people of the place had killed many of the residents and fired their bungalows. Some had escaped on horseback or in carriages; and the present party, keeping together, had, when near Bithri, been seized and brought in to the chief, who intended to take them with him to Lucknow, when—an event of which he daily expected news—the little body of English there were destroyed by the forces gathering round them. The captives had heard what was doing, both at Lucknow and Cawnpore. At the latter place not only had the native troops mutinied, but the Rajah of Bithoor, Nana Sahib, whom the English had regarded as a firm friend, had joined them. Sir Hugh Wheeler, with the officers of the revolted regiments the civilians of the station, and forty or fifty white troops, having some eight hundred women and children in their charge, were defending a weak position against thousands of the enemy, provided with artillery.

When after riding thirty miles, the party stopped at daybreak at a ruined temple standing in its grove at a distance from the main road, Major Warrener called his officers into council, to determine what was the best course to adopt under the circumstances. Should they dash through the lines of the besiegers of Cawnpore, or should they make for Agra, or endeavor to join the force which was being collected at Allahabad to march to their relief?

Finally, and very reluctantly, the latter course was decided upon. It was agreed—and the truth of their conclusion was proved by the fact that throughout the mutiny there was no single instance of the rebels, however numerous, carrying a position held by any body of Englishmen—that Sir Hugh Wheeler and his force could probably hold the intrenchments against any assault that the enemy could make, and that if forced to surrender it would probably be from want of supplies. In that case the arrival of a hundred men would be a source of weakness rather than of strength. The reinforcement would not be of sufficient strength to enable the garrison, incumbered as it was with women and children, to cut its way out, while there would be a hundred more mouths to fill. It was therefore resolved to change their course, to avoid Cawnpore, and to make direct for Allahabad, with the news of the urgent strait in which Sir Hugh Wheeler was placed, and of the necessity for an instant advance to his relief.

Cawnpore was now but forty miles away, and Lucknow was about the same distance, but in a different direction; and as they stretched themselves on the ground and prepared for sleep, they could distinctly hear the dull, faint sounds that told of a heavy artillery fire. At which of the stations, or if at both, the firing was going on, they could not tell; but in fact it was at Cawnpore, as this was the 25th of June, and the siege of the Lucknow Residency did not begin in earnest until the 30th of that month.

The course had now to be decided upon, and maps were consulted, and it was determined to cross the river at Sirapore. It was agreed, too, that they should, at the first village they passed through that evening, question the inhabitants as to the bodies of rebels moving about, and find out whether any large number were stationed at any of the bridges.

At nine o'clock in the evening they were again in the saddle, and an hour later halted at a village. There several of the men were examined separately, and their stories agreed that there were no large bodies of Sepoys on the line by which they proposed to travel, but that most of the talookdars were preparing to march to Lucknow and Cawnpore, when the British were destroyed. Having thus learned that the bridge by which they intended to cross was open to them, the troop again proceeded on their way, leaving the village lost in astonishment as to where this body of British horse could have come from.

Upon this night's ride Ned and Dick Warrener were on rearguard—that is to say, they rode together some two hundred yards behind the rest of the squadron.

An hour after leaving the village, as they were passing through a thick grove of trees some figures rose as from the ground. Ned was knocked off his horse by a blow with the butt-end of a gun; and Dick, before he had time to shout or make a movement in his defense, was dragged from his horse, his head wrapped in a thick cloth, and his arms bound. Then he could feel himself lifted up and rapidly carried off. After a time he was put on his legs and the covering of his head removed. He found Ned beside him; and a word of congratulation that both were alive was exchanged. Then a rope was placed round each of their necks, and surrounded by their captors, two of whom rode their horses, they were started at a run, with admonitions from those around them that any attempt to escape or to shout would be punished with instant death.

For full two hours they were hurried along, and then the party halted at the edge of a thick jungle, lighted a fire, and began to cook. The prisoners were allowed to sit down with their captors. These were matchlock-men, on their way to join the forces besieging the Residency at Cawnpore, toward which town they had been making their way, as the boom of the guns sounded sharper and clearer every mile that they traveled. Ned gathered from the talk that their capture was the effect of pure accident. The party had sat down in the wood to eat, when they heard a troop of horsemen passing. A word or two spoken in English as the leaders came along sufficed to show the nationality of the troop, and the band lay quiet in the bushes until, as they supposed, all had passed. They had risen to leave when the two last horsemen came in view, and these they determined to capture and carry off, if possible, hoping to get a considerable reward from Nan a Sahib on their arrival at Cawnpore.

Nana Sahib's name had not as yet that terrible history attached to it which rendered it execrated wherever the English tongue is spoken; but the boys had heard that after pretending to be the friend of the whites, he was now leading the assault against them, and that he was therefore a traitor, and fighting as it were with a rope round his neck. At the hands of such a man they had no mercy to expect.

"It is of no use trying to make a bolt, Ned?"

"Not the least in the world. The two fellows next to us are appointed to watch us. Don't you see they are sitting with their guns across their knees? We should be shot down in a moment."

There was a debate among the band whether to push on to Cawnpore at once; but they had already made a long day's journey, and moreover thought that they could create a greater effect by arriving with their prisoners by daylight. The fire was made up, and the men wrapped themselves in their cloths—the native of India almost invariably sleeps with his head covered, and looking more like a corpse than a living being. Anxiously the boys watched in hopes that their guards would follow the example. They showed, however, no signs of doing so, but sat talking over the approaching destruction of the English rule and of the restoration of the Mohammedan power.

Two hours passed; the fire burned low, and the boys, in spite of the danger of their position, were just dropping off to sleep, when there was a mighty roar—a rush of some great body passing over them—a scream of one of the natives—a yell of terror from the rest. A tiger stood with one of the guards in his mouth, growling fiercely, and giving him an occasional shake, as a cat would shake a mouse, while one of his paws held down the prostrate figure of the other.

There was a wild stampede—men tumbled over and over each other in their efforts to escape from the terrible presence, and then, getting to their feet, started off at full speed. For a moment the boys had lain paralyzed with the sudden advent of the terrible man-eater, and then had, like the rest, darted away.

"To the jungle!" Ned exclaimed; and in an instant they had plunged into the undergrowth, and were forcing their way at full speed through it. Man-eating tigers are rarely found in pairs, and there was little fear that another was lurking in the wood; and even had such been the case, they would have preferred death in that form to being murdered in cold blood by the enemy. Presently they struck on a track leading through the wood, and followed it, until in five minutes they emerged at the other side. As they did so they heard the report of firearms in the direction of their last halting-place, and guessed that the peasants were firing at hazard, in hopes of frightening the tiger into dropping his prey. As to their own flight, it was probable that so far they had been unthought of. The first object of the fugitives was to get as far as possible from their late captors, who would at daybreak be sure to organize a regular hunt for them, and accordingly they ran straight ahead until in three-quarters of an hour they came into a wide road. Then, exhausted with their exertions, they threw themselves down, and panted for breath.

Dick was the first to speak. "What on earth are we to do now, Ned? These uniforms will betray us to the first person we meet, and we have no means of disguise."

"We must get as far away as we can before daylight, Dick, and then hide up. Sooner or later we must throw ourselves on the hospitality of some one, and take our chance. This is evidently the main road to Cawnpore, and, judging from the guns, we cannot be more than ten or twelve miles away. It will not do to go back along this road, for the fellows we have got away from may strike it below us and follow it up. Let us go forward along it till we meet a side road, and take that."

Ten minutes' walking brought them to a point where a side road came in, and, taking this, they walked steadily on. They passed two or three villages, which the moonlight enabled them to see before they reached them; these they avoided by a detour, as the dogs would be sure to arouse the inhabitants, and it was only in a solitary abode that they had a chance of being sheltered. Toward morning they saw ahead a building of considerable size, evidently the abode of a person of consequence. It was not fortified; but behind it was a large inclosure, with high walls.

"I vote we climb over that wall, Ned; there are several trees growing close up to it. If they hunt the country round for us they will never look inside there; and I expect that there is a garden, and we are sure to find a hiding-place. Then, if the owner comes out, we can, if he looks a decent chap, throw ourselves on his hands."

"I think that a good idea, Dick; the sooner we carry it out the better, for in another half-hour day will be breaking."

They made a detour round to the back of the building, and after some search found a tree growing close enough to the wall to assist them. This they climbed, got along a branch which extended over the top of the wall, and thence dropped into the garden. Here there were pavilions and fountains, and well-kept walks, with great clumps of bushes and flowering shrubs well calculated for concealment. Into one of these they crept, and were soon fast asleep.

It was late in the afternoon when they awoke, roused by the sound of laughter, and of the chatter of many voices.

"Good gracious!" Ned exclaimed; "we have got into the women's garden."

In another minute a group of women came in sight. The principal figure was a young woman of some twenty-two or twenty-three, and with a red wafer-like patch on her forehead, very richly dressed.

"She is a Hindoo," Ned whispered; "what luck!"

There are indeed very few Hindoos in Oude, and the Mohammedan being the dominant race, a Hindoo would naturally feel far more favorably inclined toward a British fugitive than a Mohammedan would be likely to do, as the triumph of the rebellion could to them simply mean a restoration, of Mohammedan supremacy in place of the far more tolerant British rule.

Next to the ranee walked an old woman, who had probably been her nurse, and was now her confidante and adviser. The rest were young women, clearly dependants.

"And so, Ahrab, we must give up our garden, and go into Cawnpore; and in such weather too!"

"It must be so indeed," the elder woman said. "These Mohammedans doubt us, and so insist on your highness showing your devotion to the cause by taking up your residence in Cawnpore, and sending in all your retainers to join in the attack on the English."

The ranee looked sad.

"They say there are hundreds of women and little children there," she said, "and that the English who are defending them are few."

"It is so," Ahrab said. "But they are brave. The men of the Nana, and the old regiments, are fifty to one against them, and the cannon fire night and day, and yet they do not give way a foot."

"They are men, the English sahibs."

While they were speaking the two chief personages of the party had taken their seats in a pavilion close to the spot where the young Warreners were hidden.

Ned translated the purport of the talk to Dick, and both agreed that the way of safety had opened to them.

Seeing that their mistress was not in the humor for laughter and mirth, and would rather talk quietly with her chief friend and adviser, the attendants gradually left them, and gathered in a distant part of the garden.

Then Ned and Dick crept out of their hiding-place, and appeared suddenly at the entrance to the pavilion, where they fell on one knee, in an attitude of supplication, and Ned said:

"Oh, gracious lady, have pity upon two fugitives!"

The ranee and her counselor rose to their feet with a little scream, and hastily covered their heads.

"Have pity, lady," Ned went on earnestly; "we are alone and friendless; oh, do not give us up to our enemies."

"How did you get here?" asked the elder woman.

"We climbed the wall," Ned said. "We knew not that this garden was the ladies' garden, or we might not have invaded it; now we bless Providence that has brought us to the feet of so kind and lovely a lady."

The ranee laughed lightly behind her veil.

"They are mere boys, Ahrab."

"Yes, your highness, but it would be just as dangerous for you to shelter boys as men. And what will you do, as you have to go to Cawnpore to-morrow?"

"Oh, you can manage somehow, Ahrab—you are so clever," the ranee said coaxingly; "and I could not give them up to be killed: I should never feel happy afterward."

"May Heaven bless you, lady!" Ned said earnestly; "and your kind action may not go unrewarded even here. Soon, very soon, an English army will be at Cawnpore to punish the rebels, and then it will be well with those who have succored British fugitives."

"Do you say an English army will come soon?" Ahrab said doubtfully. "Men say the English Raj is gone forever."

"It is not true," Ned said. "England has not begun to put out her strength yet. She can send tens of thousands of soldiers, and the great chiefs of the Punjab have all declared for her. Already Delhi is besieged, and an army is gathering at Allahabad to march hither. It may be quickly; it may be slowly; but in the end the English rule will be restored, her enemies will be destroyed, and her friends rewarded. But I know," he went on, turning to the ranee, "that it needs not a thought of this to influence you, and that in your kind heart compassion alone will suffice to secure us your protection."

The ranee laughed again.

"You are only a boy," she said, "but you have learned to flatter. Now tell us how you got here."

"Your highness," Ahrab interrupted, "I had better send all the others in, for they might surprise us. Let these young sahibs hide themselves again; then we will go in, and I will call in your attendants. Later, when it is dusk, you will plead heat, and come out here with me again, and then I can bring some robes to disguise the sahibs; that is, if your highness has resolved to aid them."

"I think I have resolved that, Ahrab," the ranee said. "You have heard, young sahibs; retire now, and hide. When the sun has set we will be here again."

With deep assurance of gratitude from Ned, the lads again took refuge in the shrubs, delighted with the result of their interview.

"I do hope that the old one will bring us something to eat, Ned. I am as hungry as a hunter! That ranee's a brick, isn't she?"

Two hours later a step was heard coming down the garden, and a woman came and lit some lamps in the pavilion, and again retired. Then in another ten minutes the ranee and her confidante made their appearance. The former took her seat on the couch in the pavilion, the latter remained outside the circle of light, and clapped her hands softly. In a minute the boys stood before her. She held out a basket of provisions, and a bundle of clothes.

"Put these wraps on over your uniforms," she said; "then if we should be surprised, no one will be any the wiser."

The boys retired, hastily ate some food, then wrapped themselves in the long folds of cotton which form the principal garment of native women of the lower class, and went forward to the pavilion.

The ranee laughed outright.

"How clumsy you are!" she said. "Ahrab, do arrange them a little more like women."

Ahrab adjusted their robes, and brought one end over their heads, so that it could, if necessary, be pulled over the face at a moment's notice.

The ranee then motioned to them to sit down upon two cushions near her; and saying to Ahrab, "It is very hot, and they are only boys," removed the veil from her face. "You make very pretty girls, only you are too white," she said.

"Lady, if we had some dye we could pass as natives, I think," Ned said; "we have done so before this, since the troubles began."

"Tell me all about it," the ranee said. "I want to know who you are, and how you came here as if you had dropped from the skies."

Ned related their adventures since leaving Delhi, and then the ranee insisted upon an account of their previous masquerading as natives.

"How brave you English boys are," she said. "No wonder your men have conquered India. Now, Ahrab, tell these young sahibs what we propose."

"We dare not leave you here," Ahrab said. "You would have to be fed, and we must trust many people. We go to Cawnpore to-morrow, and you must go with us. My son has a garden here; we can trust him, and he will bring a bullock-cart with him to-morrow morning. In this will be placed some boxes, and he will start. You must wait a little way off, and when you see him you will know him, because he will tie a piece of red cloth to the horns of the bullock; you will come up and get in. He will ask no questions, but will drive you to the ranee's. I will open the door to you and take you up to a little room where you will not be disturbed. We shall all start first. You cannot go with us, because the other women will wonder who you are. Here is some stuff to dye your faces and hands. I will let you out by a private door. You will see a wood five minutes along the road. You must stop there to-night, and do not come out till you see the ranee and her party pass. There is a little hut, which is empty, in the wood, where you can sleep without fear of disturbance. The ranee is sorry to turn you out to-night, but we start at daybreak, and I should have no opportunity of slipping away and letting you out."

Everything being now arranged, the ranee rose. Ned reiterating the expression of the gratitude of his brother and himself, the ranee coquettishly held out a little hand whose size and shape an Englishwoman might have envied; and the boys kissed it—Ned respectfully, Dick with a heartiness which made her laugh and draw it away.

"You are a darling," Dick said in English, with the native impudence of a midshipman, "and I wish I knew enough of your lingo to tell you."

"What does he say?" she asked of Ned.

"He is a sailor," Ned said; "and sailors say things we on shore would not venture to say. My brother says you are the flower of his heart."

"Your brother is an impudent boy," the ranee said, laughing, "and I have a good mind to hand him over to the Nana. Now good-by! Ahrab will let you out."

CHAPTER X.
TREACHERY.

Of all the names connected with the Indian mutiny, Cawnpore stands out conspicuous for its dark record of treachery, massacre, and bloodshed; and its name will, so long as the English language continues, be regarded as the darkest in the annals of our nation. Cawnpore is situated on the Ganges, one hundred and twenty-three miles northwest of Allahabad, and was at the time of our story a large straggling town, extending nearly five miles along the river. It stands on a sandy plain, intensely hot and dusty in summer, and possesses no fort or other building such as proved the safety of the Europeans in Agra and Allahabad. The force stationed there at the first outbreak of the mutiny consisted of the First, Fifty-third, and Fifty-sixth Native Regiments, the Second Regiment of Bengal Cavalry, and about fifty European invalid artillerymen. When the news of the revolt at Meerut reached Cawnpore, and it was but too probable that the mutiny would spread to all the native regiments throughout the country, Sir Hugh Wheeler, who was in command, at once set to work to prepare a fortified position, in which to retire with the European residents in case of necessity. To this end he connected with breastworks a large unfinished building intended as a military hospital, with the church and some other buildings, all standing near the center of the grand parade, and surrounded the whole with an intrenchment. Within these lines he collected ammunition, stores and provisions for a month's consumption for a thousand persons, and having thus, as he hoped, prepared for the worst, he awaited the event.

Although there was much uneasiness and disquietude, things went on tolerably well up to the middle of May. Then Sir Hugh Wheeler sent to Lucknow, forty miles distant, to ask for a company of white troops, to enable him to disarm the Sepoys; and he also asked aid of Nana Sahib, Rajah of Bithoor, who was looked upon as a stanch friend of the English. On the 22d of May fifty-five Europeans of the Thirty-second Regiment, and two hundred and forty native troopers of the Oude irregular cavalry, arrived from Lucknow, and two guns and three hundred men were sent in by the Rajah of Bithoor.

Nana Sahib was at this time a man of thirty-two years of age, having been born in the year 1825. He was the son of poor parents, and had at the age of two years and a half been adopted by the Peishwa, who had no children of his own. In India adoption is very common, and an adopted son has all the legal rights of a legitimate offspring. The Peishwa, who was at one time a powerful prince, was dethroned by us for having on several occasions joined other princes in waging war against us, but was honorably treated, and an annuity of eighty thousand pounds a year was assigned to him and his heirs. In 1851 the Peishwa died, leaving Nana Dhoondu Pant, for that was the Nana's full name, his heir and successor. The Company refused to continue the grant to Nana Sahib, and in so doing acted in a manner at once impolitic and unjust. It was unjust, because they had allowed the Peishwa and Nana Sahib, up to the death of the former, to suppose that the Indian law of adoption would be recognized here as in all other cases; it was impolitic, because as the greater portion of the Indian princes had adopted heirs, these were all alarmed at the refusal to recognize the Nana, and felt that a similar blow might be dealt to them.

Thus, at this critical period of our history, the minds of the great Indian princes were all alienated from us, by what was in their eyes at once a breach of a solemn engagement, and a menace to every reigning house. Nana Sahib, however, evinced no hostility to the English rule. He had inherited the private fortune of the Peishwa, and lived in great state at Bithoor. He affected greatly the society of the British residents at Cawnpore, was profuse in his hospitality, and was regarded as a jovial fellow and a stanch friend of the English. When the mutiny broke out, it proved that he was only biding his time. Nana Sahib was described by an officer who knew him four years before the mutiny, as then looking at least forty years old and very fat. "His face is round, his eyes very wild, brilliant and restless. His complexion, as is the case with most native gentlemen, is scarcely darker than that of a dark Spaniard, and his expression is, on the whole, of a jovial, and indeed, somewhat rollicking character." In reality, this rollicking native gentleman was a human tiger.

On the very night that the men of the Thirty-second came in from Oude, there was an alarm of a rising, and the ladies and children of the station took refuge in the fortified post prepared for them; and from that time the sufferings of the residents commenced, although it was not for a fortnight afterward that the mutiny took place; for the overcrowding and the intense heat at once began to affect the health of those huddled together in ill-ventilated rooms, and deprived of all the luxuries which alone make existence endurable to white people in Indian cities on the plains during the heats of summer. Scarce a day passed without news of risings at other stations taking place, and with the receipt of each item of intelligence the insolence displayed by the Sepoys increased.

A few English troops arrived from Allahabad and at midnight upon the 4th of June, when the natives broke into revolt, there were in the intrenchments of Cawnpore eighty-three officers of various regiments, sixty men of the Eighty-fourth Regiment, and seventy of the Thirty-second, fifteen of the First Madras Fusiliers, and a few invalid gunners; the whole defensive force consisting of about two hundred and forty men, and six guns. There were under their charge a large number of ladies and children, the wives and families of the officers and civilians at the station, sixty-four women and seventy-six children belonging to the soldiers, with a few native servants who remained faithful. The total number of women, children, and non-effectives amounted to about eight hundred and seventy persons.

During the night of the 4th of June the whole of the native troops rose, set fire to all the European residences outside the intrenchments, and marched to Nawabgunge, a place four miles away. A message was sent by them to Nana Sahib, to the effect that they were marching to Delhi, and inviting him to assume the command. This he at once assented to, and arrived at Nawabgunge a few hours later, with six hundred troops and four guns; and his first act was to divide the contents of the English treasury there, which had been guarded by his own troops, among the mutineers.

Having destroyed the European buildings, the force marched to Kulleanpore, on its way to Delhi; but on its reaching this place the same evening, Nana Sahib called together the native officers, and advised them to return to Cawnpore and kill all the Europeans there. Then they would be thought much of when they arrived at Delhi. The proposal was accepted with acclamation, and during the night the rebel army marched back to Cawnpore, which they invested the next morning; the last message from Sir Hugh Wheeler came through on that day, fighting having begun at half-past ten in the morning.

The first proceeding of the mutineers was to take possession of the native town of Cawnpore, where the houses of the peaceable and wealthy inhabitants were at once broken open and plundered, and many respectable natives slaughtered.

The bombardment of the British position began on the 6th, and continued with daily increasing fury. Every attempt to carry the place by storm was repelled, but the sufferings of the besieged were frightful. There was but one well, in the middle of the intrenchments, and upon this by night and by day the enemy concentrated their fire, so that it might be said that every bucket of water cost a man's life. After four or five days of incessant bombardment, the enemy took to firing red-hot shot, and on the 13th the barracks were set on fire, and, a strong wind blowing, the fire spread so rapidly that upward of fifty sick and wounded were burned. The other buildings were so riddled with shot and shell that they afforded scarcely any shelter. Many of the besieged made holes in the ground or under the banks of the intrenchments; but the deaths from sunstroke and fever were even more numerous than those caused by the murderous and incessant fire.

In the city a reign of terror prevailed. All the native Christians were massacred, with their wives and families; and every white prisoner brought in—and they were many—man, woman, or child, was taken before the Nana, and murdered by his orders.

Day by day the sufferings of the garrison in the intrenchments became greater, and the mortality among the woman and children was terrible. Every day saw the army of the Nana increasing, by the arrival of mutineers from other quarters, until it reached a total of over twelve thousand men, while the fighting force of the garrison had greatly decreased; yet the handful of Englishmen repulsed every effort of the great host of assailants to carry the fragile line of intrenchments.

When Ned and Dick Warrener, having carried out the instructions given by the ranee, arrived next morning at her house at Cawnpore, Ahrab at once led them to a small apartment.

"I have much news to tell you. The fighting is over here. The Nana sent in a messenger to the English sahibs, to say that if they would give up the place, with the guns and treasure, he would grant a free passage for all; and the Nana and his Hindoo officers have sworn the sacred oath of our religion, and the Mohammedans have sworn on the Koran, that these conditions shall be observed. Boats are to be provided for them all. They leave to-morrow at dawn. Her highness the ranee will shelter you here if you like to stay; but if you wish it you can go at daybreak and join your countrymen."

With many thanks for the ranee's offer, the boys at once decided to join their countrymen; and accordingly next morning after a kind farewell from their protectress, they started before daybreak under charge of their driver of the day before, and, still in their disguises of native women, made their way to a point on the line of route outside the town. There were but few people here, and, just as day broke the head of the sad procession came along. The women and children, the sick and wounded—among the latter Sir H. Wheeler, the gallant commander of the garrison—were in wagons provided by the Nana; the remnant of the fighting men marched afterward. Hastily dropping their women's robes, the boys slipped in among the troops, unnoticed by any of the guards of Nana's troops who were escorting the procession.

A few words explained to their surprised compatriots that they were fugitives who had been in shelter in the town, and many a word of welcome was muttered, and furtive handshakes given. In return the boys were able to give the news of the arrival of the British before Delhi, and the commencement of the siege, all of which was new to the garrison, who had been for twenty-two days without a word from the outer world. At last the column reached the ghat, or landing-place, fixed upon for their embarkation.

Here seventeen or eighteen boats were collected. The way down to the river was steep, for the bank of the Ganges is here rather high, and covered with thick jungle. At the top of the ghat is a small Hindoo temple. The wounded and sick were carried down the bank and placed in the boats, the ladies and children took their places, the officers and men then followed. When all was ready, the Nana's officer suddenly called the native boatmen to come ashore to receive their wages for the passage down to Benares.

Then, as if by magic, from out the thick jungle on both sides of the path to the ghat, hundreds of Sepoys rushed; while at the same moment lines of bushes fell to the ground, and showed a number of cannon, all placed in position. In a moment a tremendous fire was opened upon the unhappy fugitives. Numbers of them were at once killed in the boats; some jumped into the water, and, pushing the boats afloat, made for the opposite shore; while others leaped into the river on the deeper side and tried to escape by swimming. But upon the other shore were enemies as bloodthirsty as those they left behind, for there the Sepoys of the Seventeenth Native Regiment, who had mutinied at Azimghur, were posted, and these cut off the retreat of the fugitives there. Then all the boats, with the exception of two or three which had drifted down stream, followed by bands of Sepoys with cannon on either bank, were brought back to the starting-place, which is known, and will be known through all time, as "the slaughter ghat." There all the men still alive were taken on shore and shot; while the women and children, many of them bleeding from wounds, were taken off to a house formerly belonging to the medical department of the European troops, called the Subada Khotee.

Dick and Ned Warrener were in one of the boats which were still ashore when the treacherous Sepoys burst from their hiding-place. "The scoundrels!" burst from Ned indignantly; while Dick, seeing at a glance the hopelessness of their position, grasped his brother's arm.

"We must swim for it, Ned, Take a long dive, and go under again the moment you have got breath."

Without an instant's delay the brothers leaped into the water, as dozens of others were doing; and although each time their heads came up for an instant the bullets splashed around them, they kept on untouched until they reached the center of the stream. They were still within musket range, but the distance was sufficient to render them pretty safe except against an accidental shot. They looked back and saw the Sepoys had many of them entered the river up to their shoulders, to shoot the swimmers: others on horseback had ridden far out, and were cutting down those who, unable to swim far, made again toward shallow water; while cannon and muskets still poured in their fire against the helpless crowds in the boats.

"Look, Ned, it is of no use making for the other shore," Dick said; "there is another body of the wretches there; we must simply float down the stream in the middle. If we keep on our backs, and sink as low as we can, so as to show only our noses and mouths above water, they may fire for a week without hitting us. There, give me your hand, so that we may float together; I will look up from time to time to see that we are floating pretty fairly in the middle, I will do it quickly, so as not to be seen, for if we lie still on our backs they won't watch us after a time, but will take us for two drifting dead bodies. Now, old boy!" So saying, the lads turned on their backs, and occasionally giving a quiet stroke with their legs, or paddling with their hands, drifted down stream, showing so little of their faces above water that they could scarcely have been seen from the shore.

Both the lads were good swimmers, but Dick was perfectly at home in the water; and Ned, knowing his own inferiority in this respect, left himself entirely in his brother's hands. Soon Dick, in his quick glances to note their position, perceived that three boats alone of all the number had got fairly away down stream—that their occupants had got out oars and were quickly coming up to the swimmers; but he saw, too, that on both banks the Sepoy guns kept abreast of them, and that a fire of artillery and musketry was maintained. For a moment he thought of being taken on board; but their chance of escaping the fire centered upon them seemed hopeless, and he judged it was better to keep on in the water. He accordingly paddled himself out of the center of the stream, so as to give the boats a wide berth, trusting that the attention of the enemy would be so much directed at the boats that the floating bodies would be unnoticed. As to keeping afloat for any time, he had no fear whatever. The water of Indian rivers in the heat of summer is so warm that swimmers can remain in them for many hours without any feeling of chill or discomfort.

An hour later Dick lifted his head and looked forward. The firing was two miles ahead now. But one boat of the three still floated, and Dick congratulated himself that he had decided not to join his fate to that of those on board. Hour after hour passed, and still the boys floated on, until at last the sun went down, dusk came and went, and when all was dark they turned on their faces and swam quietly down the stream. For many hours, alternately swimming and floating, they kept their course down the river, until toward morning they gently paddled ashore, crept into the thick jungle of the bank, and fell asleep almost instantly.

It was dusk again before they awoke. They were desperately hungry, but they agreed to spend one more night in the river before searching for food, so as to put as much distance as possible between themselves and Cawnpore. They had been twenty hours in the water before, and allowing two miles an hour for the current, and something for their swimming, they calculated that Cawnpore must be forty-six or forty-seven miles behind. Eight hours' more steady swimming added twenty to this, and they landed again with a hope that Nana Sahib's ferocious bands must have been left behind, and that they had now only the ordinary danger of travel in such times, through a hostile country, to face.

It yet wanted an hour or so of daybreak, and they struck off at right angles to the river, and walked till it became light, when they entered a small wood near to which was a hut. Watching this closely, they saw only an old man come out, and at once made to it, and asked him for food and shelter. Recovered from his first surprise, he received them kindly, and gave them the best which his hut, in which he lived alone with his wife, afforded. A meal of cakes and parched grain greatly revived them, and, after a long sleep, they started again at nightfall, with enough food for the next two days' supply. That they were not ahead of all their foes was certain, from the fact that the peasant said that he had heard firing on the river bank on the previous day. They knew by this also that the one boat ahead of them had at any rate escaped its perils of the first day.

For two more nights they walked, passing one day in a thick wood, the other in a ruined temple, their hopes rising; for, as they knew, the further they got from Cawnpore the loss likely the country people were to be hostile.

The third morning they again entered a hut to ask for food.

"I will give you food," the peasant said, "but you had better go to the rajah's, his house is over there, half an hour's walk. He has four Englishmen there who came from the river, and he is the friend of the Feringhees."

Delighted at the news, the boys went forward. As they entered the courtyard of the house they were greeted with a hearty salutation in English, and their hands were clasped a moment afterward by Lieutenant Delafosse, an officer who had greatly distinguished himself in the defense of Cawnpore, and was one of the few survivors. He took them in to the rajah, who received them most kindly, and after they had been fed Lieutenant Delafosse told them how he and his three comrades had escaped.

The boat had, although many on board had been hit by rifle balls, escaped the first day. She was crowded, and very low in the water, having on board most of those who had been in the two boats sunk by the enemy. The next day they were again fired at without effect by artillery, infantry accompanying the boat all day, and keeping up an incessant fire. On the third day the boat was no longer serviceable, and grounded on a sand-bank. Then the enemy's infantry fired so heavily that those still able to carry arms, fourteen in number, made for the shore and attacked their foes. These fell back, and the handful of Englishmen followed them. Great numbers of the enemy now came up, and the English took refuge in a little temple; here they defended themselves till the enemy piled bushes at the entrance, and set them on fire. Then the English burst through the flames, and made again for the river. Seven out of the twelve who got through the fire reached the river, but of these two were shot before they had swum far. Three miles lower down, one of the survivors, an artilleryman, swimming on his back, went too near the bank and was killed. Six miles lower down the firing ceased, and soon afterward the four survivors were hailed by natives, who shouted to them to come ashore, as their master, the rajah, was friendly to the English. They did so, and were most kindly received by him.

An abundant meal and another good sleep did wonders for the young Warreners, and the next morning they determined to set out to join their countrymen at Allahabad, where they expected to find their father and his troops. The rajah and their fellow-countrymen endeavored in vain to dissuade them, but the former, finding that they were determined, gave them dresses as native women, furnished them with a guide, and sent them across the river in a boat—for they were on the Oude side—with a message to a zemindar there to help them forward.

CHAPTER XI.
RETRIBUTION BEGINS.

The zemindar to whom the Warreners' guide conducted them, after crossing the Ganges, received them kindly, and told them that the safest way would be for them to go on in a hackery, or native cart, and placed one at once at their disposal, with a trusty man as a driver, and another to accompany them in the hackery. He told them that British troops were, it was said, arriving fast at Allahabad, and that it was even reported that an advance had already taken place. Nana Sahib would, it was said, meet them at Futtehpore, a place forty-eight miles from Cawnpore, and seventy-five from Allahabad. As yet, however, none of his troops had reached Futtehpore, which was fortunate, for the main road ran through that place, which was but twenty miles from the point where they had crossed the Ganges; and although they would keep by a road near the river, and so avoid the town, the Nana's troops would be sure to be scouring the country. This news decided them not to accept the zemindar's invitation to stay the night and start the next morning early. It was still but little past noon, and they might do many miles before darkness.

Before they halted the party had made fifteen miles, and in passing through a village learned the welcome news that a small English force had advanced to Synee, some ten miles only beyond Futtehpore. This force had, it was said, met with little resistance as yet, and the country people were full of stories of the manner in which the Sepoys and others who had been engaged with them, as soon as captured, hung up in numbers. Already, in the minds of the peasantry, the idea that the British would be the final conquerors in the strife was gaining ground; and as the whole country had suffered from the exactions and insolence of the triumphant Sepoys, and life and property were no longer safe for a moment, the secret sympathy of all those who had anything to lose was with the advancing British force.

The next day the party followed the road near the river all day, as they feared to fall either into the hands of Sepoys retiring before the English, or of those coming down from Cawnpore. They halted for the night at a village whence a road ran direct to Synee, which was about eight miles distant. The villagers repeated that the Sepoys had all fallen back, and that there would be a great fight at Futtehpore. The English force was small, but a large body were on their way up from Allahabad.

The boys started at daybreak, and had proceeded about three miles when a body of cavalry were seen rapidly approaching.

The driver of the hackery put his head inside the leather curtain of the vehicle.

"English," he said. The boys looked out, and gave a shout of joy as they saw the well-known uniforms; and, regardless of their women's robes, they leaped out and ran to meet them. The advanced guard of the cavalry stopped in surprise.

"Halloo! what is up? who are you?"

"Why, Dunlop, don't you know us?" the boys shouted.

"The Warreners!" exclaimed Captain Dunlop, leaping from his horse and seizing them by the hand. "My dear boys, this is joy."

The men set up a cheer, which was caught up by the main body as they came up, and in another minute the boys were in their father's arms.

The young Warreners had been mourned as dead, for no one doubted that they had been carried to Cawnpore, and had shared the fate of the garrison of that place; and the joy of their father therefore was intense, while the whole corps, with whom the boys were general favorites, were delighted.

After the first rapturous greeting Major Warrener took off his cap reverently, and said a few words of deep gratitude to God, the men all baring their heads as he did so. Then Captain Kent said:

"Shall I push on to the Ganges, major, with my troop? or perhaps your sons can tell us what we are ordered to find out?"

"What is it?" Ned asked.

"Whether there are any bodies of troops pushing down by the river. It would not do for them to get behind us, and threaten our communications."

The boys were able to affirm that there was no body of mutineers near the Ganges below Futtehpore, as they had just come down that way.

"Then we can ride back at once," Major Warrener said. "Major Renaud was on the point of marching when we started, and he will be glad to have us back again. First, though, what have these natives done for you?"

Ned in a few words explained that they came by the instruction of their master, and had been with them for three days.

The major made them a handsome present, and sent a message to the zemindar, to the effect that his kindness would be reported to government; and Dick scribbled a few words to Lieutenant Delafosse, with the news of the British advance, and a kind message to the rajah.

"Now, Dick, you jump up behind me," his father said. "Dunlop can take you, Ned; and you can give us a short account of what has befallen you as we ride back. We must get you a couple of horses of some kind or another at Synee. Can't you cast off these women's clothes?"

"We have got nothing to speak of underneath," Dick laughed; "we got rid of our uniforms in the Ganges, and want a rig out from top to toe."

"Well, we must see what we can do for you tonight. And now," he asked, as they trotted along at the head of the column, amid the smiles of the men at the appearance of their commanding officer carrying, as it seemed, a native woman *en croupe*, "how did you escape, boys? We did not miss you until we halted for half an hour at midnight. Then six of us rode back ten miles, but could find no trace of you, and we gave you up as lost; so we rode on till we met Major Renaud's force coming up, when we sent our rescued friends on to Allahabad, and turned back with just a shadow of hope that we might yet find you alive somewhere or other."

Dick then told the story of the intervention of the tiger in their behalf, and said that afterward an Indian lady had succored them, hinting that at the end of the war it was probable that Ned would present his father with a daughter-in-law.

"That's all very well," Ned laughed. "If Dick had understood the language, I should have been nowhere. You should have seen him kiss her hand."

"Well, anyhow," Dick said, "she was a brick, father, and no mistake."

By this time Synee was reached. In spite of Major Warrener's liberal offers, no horses or even ponies were forthcoming, so completely had the Sepoys stripped the country, most of the villages having been burned as well as plundered by them. From the valises of the troop various articles of clothing were contributed, which enabled the lads again to take their places in the ranks, but riding as before *en croupe*. In two hours after their arrival at Synee they were moving forward again at a trot, and in four hours came up with Major Renaud's force, encamped for the day.

They were glad to get in, for the rain, since they left Synee, had been falling in sheets. The force was fortunately moving now along the grand trunk road, a splendid piece of road-making, extending from Calcutta to Peshawur, for already the country roads would have been almost impassable.

"Do we halt here for the day?" Ned asked his father, as they drew rein in the camp.

"Yes, Dick, the enemy are in force at Futtehpore, which is only some fourteen miles away. Havelock is coming up by double marches. He halted last night fifteen miles the other side of Synee. To-day he will reach Synee; will bivouac there for a few hours, and will march on here in the night. We are to be under arms by the time he will arrive, and the whole of us will push forward to Khaga, five miles this side of Futtehpore. So Havelock's men will have marched twenty-four miles straight off, to say nothing of the fifteen to-day. The troops could not do it, were it not that every one is burning to get to Cawnpore, to avenge the murder of our comrades and to rescue the women and children, if it be yet time."

The boys were at once taken by their father to Major Renaud, who welcomed them warmly. This officer had under his command a force of four hundred British, and four hundred and twenty native troops, with two pieces of cannon.

After being introduced to Major Renaud the boys went to the tents allotted to their corps, which were already pitched, and Major Warrener asked the officers, and as many of the volunteers as his tent would hold, to listen to the account of the massacre of Cawnpore, which was now for the first time authentically told; for hitherto only native reports had come down from the city. Great was the indignation and fury with which the tale of black treachery and foul murder was heard; and when the story was told it had to be repeated to the officers of the other corps in camp.

The terrible tale soon spread through the camp; and men gnashed their teeth in rage, and swore bitter oaths—which were terribly kept—to avenge the deeds that had been committed. Uppermost of all, however, was the anxiety about the women and children; for the boys had heard, when staying at the friendly rajah's, that near one hundred and twenty of these unfortunates—the survivors of the siege, and of the river attack—had been shut up in a room in the Cawnpore lines.

At three o'clock next morning—the 11th of July—the troops were under arms, the tents struck, and all in readiness for an advance. Presently a dull sound was heard; it grew louder, and the head of General Havelock's column came up.

There was a short halt while Major Renaud reported to the general the state of affairs in front, as far as he knew them. He mentioned, too, that two survivors of the Cawnpore massacre had that day come in, and that four others were in shelter with a native rajah on the Oude side of the Ganges. The general at once requested that the Warreners should be brought up to him; and the lads were accordingly presented to the man whose name, hitherto unknown outside military circles, was—in consequence of the wonderful succession of battles and of victories, of which that date, the 12th of July, was to mark the first—to become a household word in England.

"The column had better move forward, Major Renaud; your division will lead. If you will ride by me, gentlemen, you can tell me of this dreadful business as we go."

Fortunately there were several horses in Major Renaud's camp, which had been taken from men of the enemy's cavalry who had been surprised in the upward march, and two of them had been assigned to the boys, so that they were able to feel once more as soldiers.

On arriving at Khaga, an insignificant village, General Havelock said to the lads:

"Thank you very much for your information. You have behaved with great coolness and courage, and Major Warrener, your father, has every reason to be proud of you. I am short of aids-de-camp, and shall be glad if you will act as my gallopers"—an honor which, it need hardly be said, the boys joyfully accepted.

The following was the total force under General Havelock's command when he commenced the series of battles which were finally to lead him to Lucknow: Seventy-six men of the Royal Artillery, three hundred and seventy-six of the Madras Fusiliers, four hundred and thirty-five of the Sixty-fourth Regiment, two hundred and eighty-four of the Seventy-eighth Highlanders one hundred and ninety men of the Eighty-fourth Regiment, twenty-two men of the Bengal Artillery. Total of British regular troops, thirteen hundred and eighty-three, with eight guns. Besides these he had Warrener's Horse. Of natives he had the Ferozepore Regiment (Sikhs), four hundred and forty-eight strong, ninety-five men of the native irregular cavalry, who were worse than useless, and eighteen mounted native police.

The order for a halt was welcome indeed to the troops. Havelock's column had marched twenty-four miles without resting or eating, and fires were speedily lighted, and preparation made for breakfast. Major Tytler, quartermaster-general to the force, had, on arriving at the halting-place, taken twenty of Warrener's Horse, and had gone forward to reconnoiter. The water was growing hot, and the tired soldiers as they lay on the ground, pipes in mouths, were thinking that breakfast would soon be ready, when there was an exclamation:

"Here come the Horse! Something's up!"

The reconnoitering party were seen galloping back at full speed, and a minute or two later a large body of the enemy's cavalry in rapid pursuit emerged from a tope on the edge of the plain. The bugles sounded to arms, and the men grasped their fire-arms and fell in, but not without many a muttered exclamation of disgust.

"Confound them! they might have given us time for breakfast!"

"They need not be in such a hurry; the day's long enough."

"I thought I hated them fellows as bad as a chap could do; but I owe them another now."

A laugh was raised by a young officer saying cheerily to his men, "Nevermind, lads, we'll return good for evil. They won't let us have enough to eat, and we are going to give them more than they can digest."

In a very short time a considerable force of the enemy's infantry appeared, following the cavalry, and with them were some guns, which at once opened on the British force.

Hitherto General Havelock had made no move. He knew that his men urgently needed rest and food. The sun had come out, and was blazing fiercely; and it was of great importance that the troops should eat before undertaking what could not but be a heavy morning's work; but the enemy, who believed that they had only Major Renaud's weak force before them, pressed forward so boldly that there was no refusing the challenge so offered. The order was given to advance, and the men, with a hearty cheer, moved forward against the enemy, whose force consisted of fifteen hundred Sepoys, fifteen hundred Oude tribesmen, and five hundred rebel cavalry, with twelve guns. Their position was a strong one, for on each side of the road the plain was a swamp, and in many places was two and even more feet under water. In front, on a rising ground, were some villages with gardens and mango-groves, and behind this Futtehpore itself, with gardens with high walls, and many houses of solid masonry.

It may, however, be said that the fight was decided as soon as begun. The British artillery silenced that of the enemy; the British rifles drove their infantry before them. Warrener's Horse and the irregular cavalry moved on the flank, the infantry marched straight the swamps, and while some of the guns kept on the solid road, others had to be dragged and pushed with immense labor through the morass. As the British advanced the enemy fell back, abandoning gun after gun. The general of the Sepoy force was on an elephant, on rising ground in the rear of his troops, and Captain Maude, who commanded the artillery, by a well-aimed shot knocked the elephant over, to the great delight of the gunners. After that the rebels attempted no further resistance, and fled to Futtehpore. There they prepared to make a stand in the houses and gardens; but our men, whose blood was now thoroughly up, and who were disgusted at their failure to get at their foe, went forward with a rush, and the enemy fled without hesitation.

The streets of Futtehpore were absolutely choked with the baggage train of the defeated rebels, and the discovery of many articles of attire of English ladies and children raised the fury of the troops to the highest point. Pursuit of the enemy was, however, impossible. The troops were utterly exhausted, and officers and men threw themselves down where-ever a little shade could be found. At three o'clock the baggage came up, and by the forethought of the commissariat officer in charge some camels laden with rum and biscuit came up with it, so that the men were able to have a biscuit and a little spirits and water, which revived them; for whatever be the demerits of spirits upon ordinary occasions, on an emergency of this kind it is a restorative of a very valuable kind.

Singularly enough, in this battle, in which thirty-five hundred men were defeated and twelve guns captured, not a single British soldier was killed, the enemy never waiting until fairly within shot. Twelve soldiers, however, fell and died from sunstroke during the fight.

On the 13th the troops halted to rest. The guns taken from the enemy were brought in, and the great baggage train captured in the town organized for our own service.

On the 14th the force again advanced along a road literally strewn with arms, cartridges, chests of ammunition, shot, clothing, and tents, abandoned in their flight by the insurgents. The most welcome find to the army were forty barrels of English porter, part of the Sepoys' loot at one of the scenes of mutiny. That night the force encamped at Kulleanpore, twenty-seven miles from Cawnpore.

"So far it has been easy work, except for the legs," Major Warrener said, as he sat with his sons and his officers on the evening of the 13th; "but it will be very different work now. These scoundrels are fighting with ropes round their necks; they know that every Cawnpore Sepoy who falls into our hands will have but a short shrift, and they can't help fighting. Altogether, they have something like five times our force; and as they have all been most carefully drilled and trained by ourselves, the scoundrels ought to make a good fight of it."

"I don't mind the fighting," Ned said, "so much as the heat; it is awful."

"It is hot, Ned," Captain Dunlop said; "but at rate it is better for us who sit on horseback than for the men who have to march, and carry a rifle and ammunition."

"Do you think we shall have fighting to-morrow, father?" Dick asked.

"We are certain to do so. The pandies have been intrenching themselves very strongly at Dong, which is five miles from here. But this is not the worst part. We know they have placed two heavy guns on the other side of the Pandoo Nuddee, which is a large stream three miles beyond Dong. These guns will sweep not only the bridge, but the straight road for a mile leading to it. The bridge, too, has, we know, been mined; and our only chance is to go on with the mutineers, so as to give them no time to blow it up."

The work of the 14th, however, was less severe than was expected. The enemy fought stoutly at the village, advancing beyond the inclosures to meet our troops. Our superior rifle and artillery fire, however, drove them back, and then they clung stubbornly to the village and inclosures, our advance being retarded by the threatening attitude of large bodies of the enemy's cavalry, who moved upon the flanks and menaced the baggage. The force under Havelock being so weak in cavalry—for the native irregulars had been disarmed and dismounted for their bad conduct—there remained only Warrener's Horse, who were known in the force as the "volunteers." These covered the baggage, and executed several brilliant charges on parties of the enemy's cavalry who came too boldly forward; but the artillery had to be brought from the front, and to open upon the heavy masses of the enemy's cavalry, before they would fall back. Then the column pressed forward again, captured Dong, with two guns placed there, and drove the enemy out in headlong flight.

Then the force moved forward to the capture of the Pandoo bridge. As the artillery, who were at the head of the column, debouched from a wood into the straight bit of road leading to the bridge two puffs of smoke burst from a low ridge ahead, followed by the boom of heavy guns, and the twenty-four pound shot, splendidly aimed, crashed in among the guns, bullocks, and men. Again and again the enemy's guns were fired with equal accuracy. Our light guns were at the distance no match for these twenty-four pounders, and Captain Maude ordered two guns to advance straight along the road until within easy practice distance, and two others to go across the country to the right and left, so as to take the bridge, which stood at the extremity of a projecting bend of the river, or, as it is called in military parlance, a salient angle, in flank.

The Madras Fusiliers, in skirmishing line, preceded the guns, and their Enfield fire, as soon as they were within range, astonished the enemy. Then the artillery opened with shrapnel, and nearly at the first round silenced the enemy's guns by killing the majority of the gunners and smashing the sponging rods. Then the infantry advanced at a charge, and the enemy, who were massed to defend the bridge, at once lost heart and fled. They tried to blow up the bridge, but in their haste they blundered over it; and while the parapets were injured, the arches remained intact.

After all this fighting, the British loss was but six killed and twenty-three wounded—among the latter being that brave officer Major Renaud, whose leg was broken by a musket shot while leading the Madras Fusiliers.

Finding that the resistance was becoming more and more obstinate, General Havelock sent off a horseman to Brigadier General Neil at Allahabad, begging him to send up three hundred more British troops with all speed. On receiving the message General Neil sent off two hundred and twenty-seven men of the Eighty-fourth Regiment in bullock vans, with orders to do twenty-five miles a day, which would take them to Cawnpore in less than five days. He himself came on with the reinforcements, Allahabad being by this time quiet and safe.

At daybreak next morning the troops marched fourteen miles, halted, and cooked their food; after which, at one o'clock, they prepared to attack the enemy, who were, our spies told us, in a position extremely strong in the front, but capable of being attacked by a flank movement. In the burning heat of the sun, with men falling out fainting at every step, the troops, under a heavy artillery fire of the enemy, turned off the road and swept round to execute the flank movement as calmly and regularly as if on parade.

When they reached the points assigned to them for the attack they advanced; and then, while the skirmishers and the artillery engaged the enemy, who were strongly posted in the inclosures of a village, the main body lay down. The enemy's guns were, however, too strongly posted to be silenced, and the Seventy-eighth were ordered to take the position by assault. The Highlanders moved forward in a steady line until within a hundred yards of the village; then at the word "Charge!" they went at it with a wild rush, delighted that at last they were to get hand to hand with their foe. Not a shot was fired or a shout uttered as they threw themselves upon the mutineers; the bayonet did its work silently and thoroughly.

A breach once made in the enemy's line, position after position was carried—Highlanders, Sixty-fourth men, and Sikhs vieing with each other in the ardor with which they charged the foe, the enemy everywhere fighting stubbornly, though vainly.

At last, at six in the evening, all opposition ceased, and the troops marched into the old parade ground of Cawnpore, having performed a twenty-two miles' march, and fought for five hours, beneath a sun of tremendous power.

CHAPTER XII.
DANGEROUS SERVICE.

On the morning of the 17th of July the troops rose with light hearts from the ground where they had thrown themselves, utterly exhausted, after the tremendous exertions of the previous day. Cawnpore was before them, and as they did not anticipate any further resistance—for the whole of the enemy's guns had fallen into their hands, and the Sepoys had fled in the wildest confusion at the end of the day, after fighting with obstinacy and determination as long as a shadow of hope of victory remained—they looked forward to the joy of releasing from captivity the hapless women and children who were known to have been confined in the house called the Subada Khotee, since the massacre of their husbands and friends on the river.

Just after daybreak there was a dull, deep report, and a cloud of gray smoke rose over the city. Nana Sahib had ordered the great magazine to be blown up, and had fled for his life to Bithoor. Well might he be hopeless. He had himself commanded at the battle of the preceding day, and had seen eleven thousand of his countrymen, strongly posted, defeated by a thousand Englishmen. What chance, then, could there be of final success? As for himself, his life was a thousandfold forfeit; and even yet his enemies did not know the measure of his atrocities. It was only when the head of the British column arrived at the Subada Khotee that the awful truth became known. The troops halted, surprised that no welcome greeted them. They entered the courtyard; all was hushed and quiet, but fragments of dresses, children's shoes, and other remembrances of British occupation, lay scattered about. Awed and silent, the leading officers entered the house, and, after a glance round, recoiled with faces white with horror. The floor was deep in blood; the walls were sprinkled thickly with it. Fragments of clothes, tresses of long hair, children's shoes with the feet still in them—a thousand terrible and touching mementos of the butchery which had taken place there met the eye. Horror-struck and sickened, the officers returned into the courtyard, to find that another discovery had been made, namely, that the great well near the house was choked to the brim with the bodies of women and children. Not one had escaped.

On the afternoon of the 15th, when the defeat at Futtehpore was known, the Nana had given orders for a general massacre of his helpless prisoners. There, in this ghastly well, were the remains, not only of those who had so far survived the siege and first massacre of Cawnpore, but of some seventy or eighty women and children, fugitives from Futteyghur. These had, with their husbands, fathers and friends, a hundred and thirty in all, reached Cawnpore in boats on the 12th of July. Here the boats had been fired upon and forced to put to shore, when the men were, by the Nairn's orders, all butchered, and the women and children sent to share the fate of the prisoners of Cawnpore.

Little wonder is it that the soldiers, who had struggled against heat and fatigue and a host of foes to reach Cawnpore, broke clown and cried like children at that terrible sight; that soldiers picked up the bloody relics—a handkerchief, a lock of hair, a child's sock sprinkled with blood—and kept them to steel their hearts to all thoughts of mercy; and that, after this, they went into battle crying to each other:

"Remember the ladies!" "Remember the babies!" "Think of Cawnpore!" Henceforth, to the end of the war, no quarter was ever shown to a Sepoy.

One of the first impulses of the Warreners, when the tents were pitched in the old cantonments, and the troops were dismissed, was to ride with their father to the house of the ranee. It was found to be abandoned-as, indeed, was the greater part of the town—and an old servant, who alone remained, said that two days previously the ranee had left for her country abode. Major Warrener at once drew out a paper, saying that the owner of this house had shown hospitality and kindness to English fugitives, and that it was therefore to be preserved from all harm or plunder; and having obtained the signature of the quartermaster-general in addition to his own, he affixed the paper to the door of the dwelling. The next day he rode out with his sons and twenty of his men to the house where the boys had first been sheltered. The gates were opened at his summons by some trembling retainers, who hastened to assure them that the ranee, their mistress, was friendly to the English.

"Will you tell her that there is no cause for alarm, but that we desire an interview with her?" the major said, dismounting.

In a minute the servant returned, and begged the major to follow him, which he did, accompanied by his sons. They were shown into a grand reception room, where the ranee, thickly veiled, was sitting on a couch, surrounded by her attendants, Ahrab standing beside her.

The ranee gave a little cry of pleasure on recognizing the boys, and Ahrab instantly signed to the other attendants to retire. Then the ranee unveiled, and the major, who had remained near the entrance until the attendants had left, came forward, the boys kissing the hands that the ranee held out to them.

"I have mourned for you as dead," she said. "When the news of that horrible treachery came, and I thought that I had let you go to death, my heart turned to water."

"This is our father, dear lady," Ned said; "he has come to thank you himself for having saved and sheltered us."

The interview lasted for half an hour; refreshment being served, Ned recounted the particulars of their escape. Major Warrener, on leaving, handed the ranee a protection order signed by the general, to show to any British troops who might be passing, and told her that her name would be sent in with the list of those who had acted kindly to British fugitives, all of whom afterward received honors and rewards in the shape of the lands of those who had joined the mutineers. Then, with many expressions of good-will on both sides, the major and his sons took their leave, and, joining the troops below, rode back to Cawnpore.

For three days after his arrival at Cawnpore General Havelock rested his troops, and occupied himself with restoring order in the town. Numbers of Sepoys were found in hiding, and these were, as soon as identified, all hung at once. On the third day Brigadier-General Neil arrived, with the two hundred and twenty men of the Eighty-fourth, who had been hurried forward-a most welcome reinforcement, for Havelock's force was sadly weakened by loss in battle, sunstroke, and disease. On the 20th the army marched against Bithoor, every heart beating at the thought of engaging Nana Sahib, who, with five thousand men and a large number of cannon, had made every preparation for the defense of his castle. At the approach of the avenging force, however, his courage, and the courage of his troops, alike gave way, and they fled without firing a shot, leaving behind them guns, elephants, baggage, men, and horses, in great numbers. The magazine was blown up, and the palace burned, and the force, with their captured booty, returned to Cawnpore.

During the advance to Cawnpore the zeal and bravery of the young Warreners had not escaped the notice of the general, who had named them in his official report as gentlemen volunteers who had greatly distinguished themselves. On the return from Bithoor, on the evening of the 20th, he turned to them as he dismounted, and said, "Will you come to my tent in two hours' time?"

"Young gentlemen," he said, when they presented themselves, and had at his request seated themselves on two boxes which served as chairs, "in what I am going to say to you, mind, I express no wish even of the slightest. I simply state that I require two officers for a service of extreme danger. I want to send a message into Lucknow. None of the officers of the English regiments can speak the language with any fluency, and those of the Madras Fusiliers speak the dialects of Southern India. Therefore it is among the volunteers, who all belong to the northwest, that I must look. I have no doubt that there are many of them who would undertake the service, and whose knowledge of the language would be nearly perfect, but there are reasons why I ask you whether you will volunteer for the work. In the first place, you have already three times passed, while in disguise, as natives; and in the second, your figures being slight, and still a good deal under the height you will attain, render your disguise far less easy to be detected than that of a full-grown man would be. If you undertake it, you will have a native guide, who last night arrived from Lucknow with a message to me, having passed through the enemy's lines. You understand, young gentlemen, the service is one of great honor and credit if accomplished, but it is also one of the greatest risk. I cannot so well intrust the mission to the native alone, because I dare not put on paper the tidings I wish conveyed, and it is possible, however faithful he may be, that he might, if taken and threatened with death, reveal the message with which he is charged. I see by your faces what your answer is about to be, but I will not hear it now. Go first to your father. Tell him exactly what I have told you, and then send me the answer if he declines to part with you—bring it me if he consents to your going. Remember that in yielding what I see is your own inclination, to his natural anxiety, you will not fall in the very least from the high position in which you stand in my regard. In an hour I shall expect to hear from you. Good-night, if I do not see you again."

"Of course father will let us go," Dick said when they got outside the tent. Ned did not reply.

"Dick, old boy," he said presently, as they walked along, "don't you think if I go alone it would be better. It would be an awful blow to father to lose both of us."

"No, Ned," Dick said warmly, "I hope he will not decide that. I know I can't talk the lingo as you can, and that so I add to your danger; still sometimes in danger two can help each other, and we have gone through so much together—oh, Ned, don't propose that you should go alone."

Major Warrener—or Colonel Warrener as he should now be called, for General Havelock had given him a step in rank, in recognition of the most valuable service of his troop during the battles on the road to Cawnpore—heard Ned in silence while he repeated, as nearly as possible word for word, the words of the general. For some time he was silent, and sat with his face in his hands.

"I don't like you both going, my boys," he said huskily.

"No, father," Dick said, "I feared that that was what you would say; but although in some respects I should be a hindrance to Ned from not speaking the language, in others I might help him. Two are always better than one in a scrape, and if he got ill or wounded or anything I could nurse him; and two people together keep up each other's spirits. You know, father, we have got through some bad scrapes together all right, and I don't see why we should not get through this. We shall be well disguised; and no end of Sepoys, and people from Cawnpore, must be making their way to Lucknow, so that very few questions are likely to be asked. It does not seem to me anything like as dangerous a business as those we have gone through, for the last thing they would look for is Englishmen making their way to Lucknow at present. The guide who is going with us got out, you know; and they must be looking out ten times as sharp to prevent people getting out, as to prevent any one getting in."

"I really do not think, father," Ned said, "that the danger of detection is great-certainly nothing like what it was before. Dick and I will of course go as Sepoys, and Dick can bind up his face and mouth as if he had been wounded, and was unable to speak. There must be thousands of them making their way to Lucknow, and we shall excite no attention whatever. The distance is not forty miles."

"Very well, boys, so be it," Colonel Warrener said. "There is much in what you say; and reluctant as I am to part with you both, yet somehow the thought that you are together, and can help each other, will be a comfort to me. God bless you, my boys! Go back to the general, and say I consent freely to your doing the duty for which he has selected you. I expect you will have to start at once, but you will come back here to change."

General Havelock expressed his warm satisfaction when the boys returned with their father's consent to their undertaking the adventure. "I understand from Colonel Warrener," he said, addressing Ned, "that you are intended for the army. I have deferred telling you that on the day of the first fight I sent your name home, begging that you might be gazetted on that date to a commission in the Sixty-fourth. Your name will by this time have appeared in order. There are only two ensigns now in the regiment, and ere I see you again there will, I fear, be more than that even of death vacancies, so that you will have got your step. I will do the same for you," he said, turning to Dick, "if you like to give up your midshipman's berth and take to the army."

"No, thank you, sir," Dick said, laughing. "By the time this is over, I shall have had enough of land service to last my life."

"I have already sent down a report to the admiral of your conduct," General Havelock said; "and as a naval brigade is coming up under Captain Peel, you will be able to sail under your true colors before long. Now for your instructions. You are to inform Colonel Inglis, who is in command since the death of Sir H. Lawrence, that, although I am on the point of endeavoring to push forward to his rescue, I have no hope whatever of success. Across the river large forces of Oude irregulars, with guns, are collected, and every step of the way will be contested. I must leave a force to hold Cawnpore, and I have only eleven hundred bayonets in all. With such a force as this it is impossible, if the enemy resists as stubbornly as may be expected, for me to fight my way to Lucknow, still more to force my way through the city, held by some ten or fifteen thousand men, to the Residency, I may say that I have no hope of doing this till I am largely reinforced. Still, my making a commencement of a march, and standing constantly on the offensive, will force the enemy to keep a large force on the road to oppose me, and will in so far relieve the Residency from some of its foes. You see the importance of your message. Did the enemy know my weakness, they would be able to turn their whole force against the Residency. Tell our countrymen there that they must hold out to the last, but that I hope and believe that in a month from the present time the reinforcements will be up, and that I shall be able to advance to their rescue. Colonel Inglis says that their stores will last to the end of August, and that he believes that he can repel all attacks. The native who goes with you bears word only that I am on the point of advancing to the relief of the garrison. So if the worst happens, and you are all taken, his message, if he betrays it, will only help to deceive the enemy. You will start tonight if possible. I leave it to you to arrange your disguises, and have ordered the guide to be at your father's tent at nine o'clock—that is, in an hour and a half's time—so that if you can be ready by that time, you will get well away before daybreak. There is a small boat four miles up the river, that the guide crossed in; he hid it in some bushes, so you will cross without difficulty; and even if you are caught crossing, your story that you are Sepoys who have been hiding for the last few days will pass muster. Now, good-by, lads, and may God watch over you and keep you!"

Upon their return to Colonel Warrener's tent they found their friends Captains Dunlop and Manners, and two or three of the officers most accustomed to native habits and ways, and all appliances for disguise. First the boys took a hearty meal; then they stripped, and were sponged with iodine from head to foot; both were then dressed in blood-stained Sepoy uniforms, of which there were thousands lying about, for the greater portion of the enemy had thrown off their uniforms before taking to flight. Ned's left arm was bandaged up with bloody rags, and put in a sling, and Dick's head and face were similarly tied up, though he could not resist a motion of repugnance as the foul rags were applied to him. Both had a quantity of native plaster and bandages placed next to the skin, in case suspicion should fall upon them and the outside bandages be removed to see if wounds really existed; and Dick was given a quantity of tow, with which to fill his mouth and swell out his cheeks and lips, to give the appearance which would naturally arise from a severe wound in the jaw. Caste marks were painted on their foreheads; and their disguise was pronounced to be absolutely perfect to the eye. Both were barefooted, as the Sepoys never travel in the regimental boots if they can avoid it.

At the appointed time the guide was summoned, an intelligent-looking Hindoo in country dress. He examined his fellow-travelers, and pronounced himself perfectly satisfied with their appearance.

Outside the tent six horses were in readiness. Colonel Warrener, and his friends Dunlop and Manners, mounted on three, the others were for the travelers; and with a hearty good-by to their other friends in the secret, the party started.

Half an hour's riding took them to the place where the boat was concealed in the bushes; and with a tender farewell from their father, and a hearty good-by from his companions, the three adventurers took their places in the boat and started.

Noiselessly they paddled across the Ganges, stepped out in the shallow water on the other side, turned the boat adrift to float down with the stream, and then struck across the country toward Lucknow.

They were now off the main road, on which the Oude mutineers collected to oppose the advance of General Havelock were for the most part stationed. Thus passed village after village, unchallenged and unquestioned, and morning, when it dawned, found them twenty miles on the road toward Lucknow. Then they went into a wood and lay down to sleep, for even if any one should enter accidentally and discover them, they had no fear of any suspicion arising. They were now near the main road, and when they started—just as it became dusk—they met various parties of horse and foot proceeding toward Cawnpore; sometimes they passed without a question, sometimes a word or two were said, the guide answering, and asking how things went at Lucknow.

The subject was evidently a sore one; for curses on the obstinate Feringhee dogs, and threats as to their ultimate fate, were their only reply.

Eighteen miles' walk, and a great black wall rose in front of them.

"That is the Alumbagh," the guide said; "the sahibs will have a big fight here. It is a summer palace and garden of the king. Once past this we will leave the road. It is but two miles to the canal and we must not enter the city—not that I fear discovery, but there would be no possibility of entering the Residency on this side. Our only chance is on the side I left it; that is by crossing the river. We must work round the town."

"How far are we from the Residency now? I can hear the cannon very clearly;" and indeed for the last two hours of their walk the booming of guns had been distinctly audible.

"It is about five miles in a straight line, but it will be double by the route we must take."

Turning to the right after passing the dark mass of the Alumbagh, the little party kept away through a wooded country until another great building appeared in sight.

"That is the Dilkouska," the guide said. "Now we will go half a mile further and then sleep; we cannot get in to-night."

In the afternoon they were awake again, and took their seats on a bank at a short distance from any road, and looked at the city.

"What an extraordinary view!" Ned said. "What fantastic buildings! What an immense variety of palaces and mosques! What is that strange building nearest to us?" he asked the guide.

"That is the Martinière. It was built many years ago by a Frenchman in the service of the king of Oude. Now it is a training college. All the pupils are in the Residency, and are fighting like men. Beyond, between us and the Residency, are several palaces and mosques. That is the Residency; do you not see an English house with a tower, and a flag flying over it, standing alone on that rising ground by the river?"

"And that is the Residency!" the boys exclaimed, looking at the building in which, and the surrounding houses, a handful of Englishmen were keeping at bay an army.

"That is the Residency," their guide said; "do you not see the circle of smoke which rises around it? Listen; I can hear the rattle of musketry quite distinctly."

"And how are we to get there?" the boys asked, impatient to be at work taking part in the defense.

"We will keep on here to the right; the river is close by. We will swim across after it gets dark, make a wide sweep round, and then come down to the river again opposite the Residency, swim across, and then we are safe."

CHAPTER XIII.
LUCKNOW.

Lucknow, although the capital of Oude, the center of a warlike people smarting under recent annexation, had for a long time remained tranquil after insurrection and massacre were raging unchecked in the northwest. Sir Henry Lawrence, a man of great decision and firmness united to pleasant and conciliating manners, had, when the Sepoys began to hold nightly meetings and to exhibit signs of recklessness, toward the end of April, telegraphed to government for full power to act; and having obtained the required authorization, he awaited with calmness the first sign of insubordination. This was exhibited by the men of the Seventh Oude Irregular Infantry, who on the 3d of May endeavored to seduce the men of the Forty-eighth Native Regiment from its allegiance, and broke out into acts of open mutiny. Sir Henry Lawrence the same evening marched the Thirty-second Foot and and a battery of European artillery, with some native regiments to their lines, three miles from the city, surrounded and disarmed them, and arrested their ringleaders. After this act of decision and energy, Lucknow had peace for some time. The native troops, awed and subdued, remained tranquil, and on the 27th of May Lucknow still remained quiet, whereas every other station in Oude, except Cawnpore, was in the hands of the rebels.

At the same time every preparation had been made for the struggle which all regarded as inevitable. The houses which formed two sides of the large irregular square in the center of which stood the Residency were connected by earthworks, and a breastwork, composed of sandbags and fascines, surrounded the other sides. Stores of provisions were collected, cattle driven in, and every preparation made for a lengthened defense. The cantonments were three miles distant from the Residency, and were occupied by the Thirteenth, Forty-eighth, and Seventy-first Native Infantry and Seventh Native Cavalry. Her majesty's Twenty-second Regiment, a battery of European artillery, and a small force of native horse.

On the evening of the 30th of May the revolt broke out. It began in the lines of the Seventy-first, and spread at once to the other native regiments, who took up arms, fired the bungalows, and killed all the officers upon whom they could lay hands. Happily all was in readiness, and a company of European troops, with two guns, took up their post on the road leading to the city, so as to bar the movement of the mutineers in that direction. Nothing could be done till morning, when Sir Henry Lawrence, with a portion of the Thirty-second, and the guns, moved to attack the mutineers. The British were joined by seven hundred men of the various regiments, who remained true to their colors, and the mutineers at once fled, with such rapidity that, although pursued for seven miles, only thirty prisoners were taken.

The troops then marched quickly back to the Residency, where their presence was much needed, as there was great excitement in the town, and a good deal of fighting between the police and the roughs of the city, who endeavored to get up a general rising and an indiscriminate plunder of the town. Sir Henry Lawrence upon his return restored order, erected a large gallows outside the fort and hung some of the rioters, executed a dozen of the mutinous Sepoys, rewarded those who had remained faithful, and for a time restored order. All the European residents in Lucknow were called into the lines of the Residency, the small European force being divided between that post and the Mutchee Bawn, a strong fort three-quarters of a mile distant, and the remnant of the native infantry regiments who had so far remained true, but who might at any moment turn traitors, were offered three months' leave to go home to their friends. Many accepted the offer and left, but a portion remained behind, and fought heroically through the siege by the side of the whites. Thus one source of anxiety for the garrison was removed; and safe now from treachery within, they had only to prepare to resist force from without.

So determined was the front shown by the little body of British that Lucknow, with its unruly population of over a quarter of a million, remained quiet all through the month of June. It was not until the last day of the month that the storm was to burst. On the 30th a body of insurgent Sepoys, some seven or eight thousand strong, having approached to Chinhut, within a few miles of the town, Sir Henry Lawrence, with two companies of the Thirty-second, eleven guns, some of them manned by natives, and eighty native cavalry, went out to give them battle.

The affair was disastrous; the native cavalry bolted, the native gunners fled, and after a loss of sixty men, three officers, and six guns, the British troops with difficulty fought their way back to the Residency. The rebels entered the town in triumph, and the city at once rose, the respectable inhabitants were killed, the bazaar looted, and then, assured of success, the enemy prepared to overwhelm the little British garrison.

Immediately upon the return of the defeated column, it became evident that the weakened force could not hold the two positions. Accordingly the Mutchee Bawn was evacuated, its great magazine, containing two hundred and forty barrels of powder and six hundred thousand rounds of ammunition, was blown up, and the British force was reunited in the Residency.

In order that the position of affairs in this, perhaps the most remarkable siege that ever took place, should be understood, it is as well to give a full description of the defenses. The Residency and its surroundings formed an irregular, lozenge-shaped inclosure, having its acute angles nearly north and south, the southern extremity being contiguous to the Cawnpore Road, and the northern point approaching near to the iron bridge over the river Goomtee. Near the south point of the inclosure was the house of Major Anderson, standing in the middle of a garden or open court, and surrounded by a wall; the house was defended by barricades, and loopholed for musketry, while the garden was strengthened by a trench and rows of palisades. Next to this house, and communicating with it by a hole in the wall, was a newly constructed defense work called the Cawnpore Battery, mounted with guns, and intended to command the houses and streets adjacent to the Cawnpore Road. The house next to this, occupied by a Mr. Deprat, had a mud wall, six feet high and two and a half thick, built along in front of its veranda, and this was continued to the next house, being raised to the height of nine feet between the houses, and loopholed for musketry. This next house was inhabited by the boys from the Martinière School. It was defended by a stockade and trench, both of which were continued across a road which divided this house from the next, which stood near the western angle, and was the brigade messhouse. This house had a lofty and well-protected terrace, commanding the houses outside the inclosure. In its rear were a number of small buildings, occupied by officers and their families.

Next to the brigade messhouse were two groups of low buildings, called the Sikh Squares, and on the flat roofs of these buildings sandbag parapets were raised. Next to this, at the extreme western point, stood the house of Mr. Gubbins, the commissioner, a strong building, defended with stockades, and having at the angle a battery, called Gubbins' Battery. Along the northwestern side were a number of yards and buildings, the racket-court, the sheep-pens, the slaughter-house, the cattle-yard, a storehouse for the food for the cattle, and a guardhouse; and behind them stood a strong building known as Ommaney's house, guarded by a deep ditch and cactus hedge, and defended with two pieces of artillery. A mortar battery was planted north of the slaughter-house. Next along the line was the church, converted now into a granary, and in the churchyard was a mortar battery. Next came the house of Lieutenant Innis, a weak and difficult post to hold, commanded as it was by several houses outside the inclosure. Commanding the extreme north point, which was in itself very weak, was the Redan Battery, a well-constructed work. From this point, facing the river, was a strong earthwork, and outside the sloping garden served as a glacis, and rendered attack on this side difficult. Near the eastern angle stood the hospital, a very large stone building, formerly the banqueting-hall of the British residents at the court of Oude. Near the hospital, but on lower ground, was the Bailey Guard. Dr. Fayrer's house, south of the hospital, was strongly built, and from its terraced roof an effective musketry fire could be kept up on an enemy approaching on this side. Next to it came the civil dispensary, and then the post office, a strong position, defended by a battery. Between this and the south corner came the financial office, Sago's house, the judicial office, and the jail. The Residency, a spacious and handsome building, stood in the center of the northern portion of the inclosure, surrounded by gardens. It was on elevated ground, and from its terraced roof a splendid view of the city and surrounding country could be obtained. The begum's khotee, or ladies' house, stood near the center of the inclosure; it was a large building, and was used as a commissariat store and for the dwellings of many officers' families. Thus it will be seen that the Residency at Lucknow, as defended against the insurgents, comprised a little town grouped round the dwelling of the Resident.

In this little circle of intrenchments were gathered, on the 1st of July, when the siege began, over a thousand women and children, defended by a few hundred British troops and civilians, and about a hundred and fifty men remaining faithful from the Sepoy regiments. Upon that day the enemy opened fire from several batteries. A shell penetrated the small room in the Residency in which Sir Henry Lawrence was sitting, and passed between him and his private secretary, Mr. Cowper. His officers begged him to change his room, but he declined to do so, saying laughingly that the room was so small that there was no chance of another shell finding its way in. He was, however, mistaken, for the very next day a shell entered, and burst in the room, the fragments inflicting a mortal wound upon Sir Henry, who died a few hours afterward. The loss was a heavy one indeed, both to the garrison, to whom his energy, calmness, and authority were invaluable, and to England, who lost in him one of her noblest and most worthy sons. On his death the command of the defense devolved upon Colonel Inglis, of the Thirty-second Regiment, a most gallant and skillful officer. After this, day after day the fighting had continued, the enemy ever gaining in numbers and in strength, erecting fresh batteries, and keeping up a ceaseless fire night and day upon the garrison.

The Warreners with their guide experienced the difficulties which this increased activity of the attack caused to emissaries trying to enter or leave the Residency. After it had become dark they swam the Goomtee, and made a wide circuit, and then tried to approach the river again opposite the Residency. Several batteries, however, had been erected on this side since the guide had left, five days before, and these were connected by a chain of sentries, so closely placed that it would have been madness to endeavor to pass them unseen. It was clear that the mutineers were determined to cut off all communication to or from the garrison. The little party skirted the line of sentries, a line indicated clearly enough by the bivouac fires on the near side of them. Round these large numbers of mutineers were moving about, cooking, smoking, and conversing.

"It is hopeless to attempt to get through here," said Ned.

"We will go on to the road leading to the iron bridge," the guide replied; "we can follow that to the river and then slip aside."

Here, however, they were foiled again, as fires were lighted and there were sentries on the road to forbid all except those on business to pass. Presently a body of men came along, bearing shell upon their heads for the service of the batteries on the other side of the river.

"Whence are they fetching these?" Ned asked the guide.

"From the king's magazine, a quarter of a mile away to the right. They are taking ammunition, now, for the bridge is within four hundred yards of the Redan battery, and they cannot cross at daylight under fire."

"Here is a party coming back," Ned said; "let us fall in behind them, go to the magazine and get shell, and then follow back again till we are close to the bridge, and trust to luck in getting clear."

The guide assented, and they followed the Sepoys down to the magazine, keeping a little behind the others, and being the last to enter the yard where the loaded shell were standing.

Each took a shell and followed closely upon the heels of the party. In the dark no one noticed the addition to their number, and they passed the sentries on the road without question. Then they fell a little behind. The natives paused just before they reached the bridge; for the British knowing that ammunition was nightly being carried over, fired an occasional shot in that direction. The party halted under shelter of a house until a shot flew past, and then hurried forward across the exposed spot. As they did so, the Warreners and their guide placed the shells they were carrying on the ground, turned off from the road, climbed a garden wall, and in a minute were close to the river.

"Go silently," the guide said; "there are some more sentries here."

Stealing quietly along, for they were all shoeless, they could see crouching figures between them and the water, every twenty yards apart.

"We shall have to run the gantlet, Ned," Dick said. "Our best chance will be to shove one of these fellows suddenly into the water, jump in and dive for it. You and I can dive across that river, and we shall come up under the shadow of the opposite bank."

Ned spoke to the guide.

"The water is shallow for the first few yards, sahib, but we shall get across that into two feet, which is deep enough for us, before the sentries have recovered from their surprise. They are sure to fire at random, and we shall be out of the water on the other side before they have loaded again."

The plan agreed to, they stripped off their uniforms, and crept quietly along until they were close to a sentry. Then with a bound they sprang upon him, rolled him over the bank into the shallow water, and dashed forward themselves at the top of their speed.

So sudden was their rush that they were knee-deep before the nearest sentry fired, his ball whizzing over their heads as they threw themselves face downward in the stream, and struck out under water.

Even when full the Goomtee is not more than ninety yards wide, and from the point where they started to equally shallow water on the other side was now not more than forty. The boys could both dive that distance; but their guide, although a good swimmer, was a less expert diver, and had to come twice to the surface for breath. He escaped, however, without a shot; for, as they had expected, the report of the musket was followed by a general volley in the direction of the splash, by all the sentries for some distance on either side. Therefore, when the party rose from the water, and dashed up the other bank, not a shot greeted them. It was clear running now, only a hundred yards up the slope of the garden, to the British earthwork.

"We are friends!" the boys shouted as they ran, and a cheer from the men on watch greeted them. A few shots flew after them from the other side of the river, but these were fired at random, and in another minute the party had scrambled over the earthwork and were among friends.

Hearty were the hand-shakes and congratulations bestowed upon them all; and as the news that messengers had arrived flew like wild-fire round the line of trenches, men came running down, regardless of the bullets which, now that the enemy were thoroughly roused up, sang overhead in all directions.

"We won't ask your message," was the cry, "till you have seen the colonel; but do tell us, is help at hand?"

"English general coming," the native guide said.

"Yes," Ned said, as delighted exclamations at the news arose; "but not yet. Do not excite false hopes among the ladies; some time must pass before help arrives. I must not say more till I have seen Colonel Inglis; but I should be sorry if false hopes were raised."

Cloaks were lent to the boys, and they were taken at once to the Residency, and along passages thronged with sleepers were conducted to Colonel Inglis' room. He had already heard that the native messenger had returned, with two Englishmen in disguise, and he was up and ready to receive them—for men slept dressed, and ready for action at a moment's call.

"Well done, subadar," he exclaimed, as the native entered; "you have nobly earned your step in rank and the five thousand rupees promised to you. Well, what is your message?"

"The General Sahib bids me say that he is coming on to Lucknow with all speed. Cawnpore was taken four days before I left. The Nana has fled from Bithoor, and all goes well. These officers have further news to give you."

"I am indeed glad to see you, gentlemen," Colonel Inglis said, warmly shaking them by the hand. "Whom have I the pleasure of seeing, for at present your appearance is admirably correct as that of two Sepoys?"

"Our name is Warrener," Ned said; "we are brothers. I have just been gazetted to the Sixty-fourth; my brother is a midshipman. We have a message for your private ear, sir; and if I might suggest, it would be better to keep our native friend close by for a few minutes, lest his news spread. You will see the reason when we have spoken to you."

Colonel Inglis gave the sign, and the other officers retired with the guide.

"Our message, sir, is, I regret to say, far less favorable than that transmitted by the subadar, and it was for that reason that General Havelock sent us with him. If taken, he would have told his message, for the general had ordered him to make no secret of his instructions if he fell into the enemy's hands, as it was desirable that they should believe that he was about to advance, and thus relieve the pressure upon you by keeping a large force on the road up from Cawnpore. But in fact, sir, General Havelock bids us tell you that he cannot advance. He has but a thousand bayonets fit for service. He must hold Cawnpore, and the force available for an advance would be hopelessly insufficient to fight his way through Oude and force a road through the city. The instant he receives reinforcements he will advance, and will in the meantime continue to make feints, so as to keep a large force of the enemy on the alert. He fears that it may be a month before he will be able to advance to your aid with a chance of success."

"A month!" Colonel Inglis said; "that is indeed a long time, and we had hoped that already help was at hand. Well, we must do our best. We are even now sorely pressed; but I doubt not we can hold out for a month. General Havelock cannot accomplish impossibilities, and it is wonderful that he should have recaptured Cawnpore with so small a force."

"We thought it better to give you this news privately, colonel, in order that you might, should you think fit, keep from the garrison the knowledge that so long a time must elapse without succor."

"You were quite right, sir," Colonel Inglis said; "but the truth had better be made public. It is far better that all should know that we are dependent upon our own exertions for another month than that they should be vainly looking for assistance to arrive. And now, gentlemen, I will call my officers in, and you shall get some clothes. Unhappily, death is so busy that there will be no difficulty in providing you in that respect. You must want food, too, and that, such as it is, is in plenty also."

The other officers were now called in, and the commandant told them the news that he had received from the Warreners. There was a look of disappointment for a moment, and then cheering answers that they were all good for another month's fighting were made.

"I know, gentlemen," Colonel Inglis said, "our thoughts are all the same. We are ready to fight another month, but we dread the delay for the sake of the women and children. However, God's will be done. All that men can do, this garrison will, I know, do; and with God's help, I believe that whether aid comes a little sooner or later, we shall hold these battered ruins till it arrives. Captain Fellows, will you get these officers something to eat, and some clothes? Then, if they are not too tired, they will perhaps not mind sitting up an hour or two and giving us the news from the outside world."

Daylight was breaking before Ned and Dick—who had, at Colonel Inglis' suggestion separated, Ned going to the colonel's room, while Dick formed the center of a great gathering in a hall below, in order that as many might hear the news as possible—brought to a conclusion the account of

Havelock's advance, of the awful massacre of Cawnpore, of the fresh risings that had taken place in various parts of India, of the progress of the siege of Delhi, and the arrival of reinforcements from China and England. With daybreak, the cannon, which had tired at intervals through the night, began to roar incessantly, and shot and shell crashed into the Residency.

"Is this sort of thing always going on?" Dick asked in astonishment.

"Always," was the answer, "by day, and four nights out of five. We have not had so quiet a time as last night for a week. Now I will go and ask the chief to which garrison you and your brother are to be assigned."

CHAPTER XIV.
THE BESIEGED RESIDENCY.

The Warrener's were taken to Gubbins' house, or garrison, as each of these fortified dwellings was now called; and the distance, short as it was, was so crowded with dangers and disagreeables that they were astonished how human beings could have supported them for a month, as the garrison of Lucknow had done. From all points of the surrounding circle shot and shell howled overhead, or crashed into walls and roofs. Many of the enemy's batteries were not above a hundred yards from the defenses, and the whistling of musket-balls was incessant.

Here and there, as they ran along, great swarms of flies, millions in number, rose from some spot where a bullock, killed by an enemy's shot, had been hastily buried, while horrible smells everywhere tainted the air.

Running across open spaces, and stooping along beneath low walls, the Warreners and their conductor, Captain Fellows, reached Gubbins' house. Mr. Gubbins himself—financial commissioner of Oude, a man of great courage and firmness—received them warmly.

"You will find we are close packed," he said, "but you will, I am sure, make the best of it. I am glad to have you, for every man is of value here; and after the bravery you have shown in coming through the enemy's lines you will be just the right sort of men for me. I think you will find most room here; I lost two of my garrison from this room on the 20th, when we had a tremendous attack all round."

The room was small and dark, as the window was closed by a bank of earth built against it on the outside. It was some fourteen feet by eight, and here, including the newcomers, eight men lived and slept. Here the Warreners, after a few words with those who were in future to be their comrades, threw themselves down on the ground, and, in spite of the din which raged around them, were soon fast asleep.

It was nearly dark when they awoke, and they at once reported themselves to Mr. Johnson—a police magistrate, who was the senior officer of the party in the room—as ready to begin duty.

"You will not be on regular duty till to-night," he replied. "Altogether, there are about forty men in the garrison. Eight are always on duty, and are relieved every four hours. So we go on every twenty hours. Only half our set go on duty together, as that gives room for those who remain. Two came off duty at eight this morning, four are just going on. You will go on with the two who came off this morning, at midnight. Besides their sentry work, of course every one is in Readiness to man the walls at any moment in case of alarm, and a good deal of your time can be spent at loopholes, picking off the enemy directly they show themselves. One of the party, in turn, cooks each day. Besides the fighting duty, there is any amount of fatigue work, the repairing and strengthening of the defenses, the fetching rations and drawing water for the house, in which there are over fifty women and children, the burying dead cattle, and covering blood and filth with earth. Besides defending our own post, we are, of course, ready to rush at any moment to assist any other garrison which may be pressed. Altogether, you will think yourself lucky when you can get four hours' sleep out of the twenty-four."

"Are our losses heavy?" Ned asked.

"Terribly heavy. The first week we lost twenty a day shot in the houses; but now that we have, as far as possible, blocked every loophole at which a bullet can enter, we are not losing so many as at first, but the daily total is still heavy, and on a day like the 20th we lost thirty. The enemy attacked us all round, and we mowed them down with grape; we believe we killed over a thousand of them. Unfortunately, every day our losses are getting heavier from disease, foul air, and overcrowding; the women and children suffer awfully. If you are disposed to make yourselves useful when not on duty, you will find abundant opportunity for kindness among them. I will take you round the house and introduce you to the ladies, then you can go among them as you like."

First the Warreners went to what, in happier times, was the main room of the house, a spacious apartment some thirty-five feet square, with windows opening to the ground at each end, to allow a free passage of air. These, on the side nearest the enemy, were completely closed by a bank of earth; while those on the other side were also built up within a few inches of the top, for shots and shell could equally enter them. The Warreners were introduced to such of the garrison as were in, the greater part being at work outside the house repairing a bank which had been injured during the day. Then Mr. Johnson went to one of the rooms leading off the main apartment. A curtain hung across it instead of a door, and this was now drawn aside to allow what air there was to circulate.

In Times Of Peril A Tale Of India | 143

"May I come in?" he asked.

"Certainly, Mr. Johnson," a lady said, coming to the entrance.

"Mrs. Hargreaves, let me introduce the Messrs. Warreners, the gentlemen who have so gallantly come through the enemy's lines with the message. They are to form part of our garrison."

The lady held out her hand, but with a slight air of surprise.

"I suppose our color strikes you as peculiar, Mrs. Hargreaves," Ned said, "but it will wear off in a few days; it is iodine, and we are already a good many shades lighter than when we started."

"How silly of me not to think of that," Mrs. Hargreaves said; "of course I heard that you were disguised. But please come in; it is not much of a room to receive in, but we are past thinking of that now. My daughter, Mrs. Righton; her husband is with mine on guard at present. These are my daughters, Edith and Nelly; these five children are my grandchildren. My dears, these are the Messrs. Warreners, who brought the news from General Havelock. Their faces are stained, but will be white again in time."

The ladies all shook hands with the Warreners, who looked with surprise on the neatness which prevailed in this crowded little room. On the ground, by the walls, were several rolls of bedding covered over with shawls, and forming seats or lounges. On the top of one of the piles two little children were fast asleep. A girl of six sat in a corner on the ground reading. There were two or three chairs, and these the ladies, seating themselves on the divan, as they called the bedding, asked their visitors to take.

Mrs. Hargreaves was perhaps forty-five years old, with a pleasant face, marked by firmness and intelligence. Mrs. Righton was twenty-five or twenty-six, and her pale face showed more than that of her mother the effects of the anxiety and confinement of the siege. Edith and Nelly were sixteen and fifteen respectively, and although pale, the siege had not sufficed to mar their bright faces or to crush their spirits.

"Dear me," Nelly said, "why, you look to me to be quite boys; why, you can't be much older than I am, are you?"

"My dear Nelly," her mother said reprovingly; but Dick laughed heartily.

"I am not much older than you are," he said; "a year, perhaps, but not more. I am a midshipman in the Agamemnon. My brother is a year older than I am, and he is gazetted to the Sixty-fourth; so you see, if the times were different, we should be just the right age to be your devoted servants."

"Oh, you can be that now," Nelly said. "I am sure we want them more than ever; don't we, mamma?"

"I think you have more than your share of servants now, Nelly," replied her mother. "We are really most fortunate, Mr. Johnson, in having our ayah still with us; so many were deserted by their servants altogether, and she is an admirable nurse. I do not know what we should do without her, for the heat and confinement make the poor children sadly fractious. We were most lucky yesterday, for we managed to secure a dobee for the day, and you see the result;" and she smilingly indicated the pretty light muslins in which her daughters were dressed. "You see us quite at our best," she said, turning to the boys. "But we have, indeed," she went on seriously, "every reason to be thankful. So far we have not lost any of our party, and there are few indeed who can say this. These are terrible times, young gentlemen, and we are all in God's hands. We are exceptionally well off, but we find our hands full. My eldest daughter has to aid the ayah with the children; then there is the cooking to be done by me, and the room to be kept tidy by Edith and Nelly, and there are so many sick and suffering to be attended to. You will never find us all here before six in the evening; we are busy all day; but we shall always be glad to see you when you can spare time for a chat in the evening. All the visitors we receive are not so welcome, I can assure you;" and she pointed to three holes in the wall where the enemy's shot had crashed through.

"That is a very noble woman," Mr. Johnson said, as they went out. "She spends many hours every day down at the military hospital where, the scenes are dreadful, and where the enemy's shot and shell frequently find entry, killing alike the wounded and their attendants. The married daughter looks after her children and the neatness of the rooms. The young girls are busy all day about the house nursing sick children, and yet, as you see, all are bright, pleasant, and the picture of neatness, marvelous contrasts indeed to the disorder and wretchedness prevailing among many, who might, by making an effort, be as bright and as comfortable as they are. There are, as you will find, many brilliant examples of female heroism and self-devotion exhibited here; but in some instances women seem to try how helpless, how foolish a silly woman can be. Ah," he broke off, as a terrific crash followed by a loud scream was heard, "I fear that shell has done mischief."

"Mrs. Shelton is killed," a woman said, running out, "and Lucy Shelton has had her arm cut off. Where is Dr. Topham?"

Mrs. Hargreaves came out of her door with a basin of water and some linen torn into strips for bandages just as the doctor ran in from the Sikh Square, where he had been attending to several casualties.

"That is right," he nodded to Mrs. Hargreaves; "this is a bad business, I fear."

"All hands to repair defenses!" was now the order, and the boys followed Mr. Johnson outside.

"The scoundrels are busy this evening," he observed.

"It sounds like a boiler-maker's shop," Dick said; "if only one in a hundred bullets were to hit, there would not be many alive by to-morrow morning."

"No, indeed," Mr. Johnson replied; "they are of course firing to some extent at random, but they aim at the points where they think it likely that we may be at work, and their fire adds greatly to our difficulty in setting right at night the damage they do in the daytime."

For the next four hours the lads were hard at work with the rest of the garrison. Earth was brought in sacks or baskets and piled up, stockades repaired, and fascines and gabions mended. The work would have been hard anywhere; on an August night in India it was exhausting. All the time that they were at work the bullets continued to fly thickly overhead, striking the wall of the house with a sharp crack, or burying themselves with a short thud in the earth. Round shot and shell at times crashed through the upper part of the house, which was uninhabited; while from the terraced roof, and from the battery in the corner of the garden, the crack of the defenders' rifles answered the enemy's fire.

By the time that the work was done it was midnight, and the Warreners' turn for guard. They had received rifles, and were posted with six others in the battery. There were three guns here, all of which were loaded to the muzzle with grape; three artillerymen, wrapped in their cloaks, lay asleep beside them, for the number of artillerymen was so small that the men were continually on duty, snatching what sleep they could by their guns during the intervals of fighting. The orders were to listen attentively for the sound of the movement of any body of men, and to fire occasionally at the flashes of the enemy's guns. The four hours passed rapidly, for the novelty of the work, the thunder of cannon and crackling of musketry, all round the Residency, were so exciting that the Warreners were surprised when the relief arrived. They retired to their room, and were soon asleep; but in an hour the alarm was sounded, and the whole force at the post rushed to repel an attack. Heralded by a storm of fire from every gun which could be brought to bear upon the battery, thousands of fanatics rushed from the shelter of the houses outside the intrenchments and swarmed down upon it. The garrison lay quiet behind the parapet until the approach of the foe caused the enemy's cannon to cease their fire. Then they leaped to their feet and poured a volley into the mass. So great were their numbers, however, that the gaps were closed in a moment, and with yells and shouts the enemy leaped into the ditch, and tried to climb the earthwork of the battery. Fortunately at this moment the reserve of fifty men of the Thirty-second, which were always kept ready to launch at any threatened point, came up at a run, and their volley over the parapet staggered the foe. Desperately their leaders called upon them to climb the earthworks, but the few who succeeded in doing so were bayoneted and thrown back into the ditch, while a continuous musketry fire was poured into the crowd. Over and over again the guns, charged with grape, swept lines through their ranks, and at last, dispirited and beaten, they fell back again to the shelter from which they had emerged. The Thirty-second men then returned to the brigade messroom, and the garrison of the fort were about to turn in when Mr. Gubbins said cheerfully:

"Now, lads, we have done with those fellows for to-day, I fancy. I want some volunteers to bury those horses which were killed yesterday; it's an unpleasant job, but it's got to be done."

The men's faces testified to the dislike they felt for the business; but they knew it was necessary, and all made their way to the yard, where, close by the cattle, the horses were confined. The boys understood at once the repugnance which was felt to approaching this part of the fort. The ground was covered deep with flies, who rose in a black cloud, with a perfect roar of buzzing.

Lucknow was always celebrated for its plague of flies, but during the siege the nuisance assumed surprising proportions. The number of cattle and animals collected, the blood spilled in the slaughter-yard, the impossibility of preserving the cleanliness so necessary in a hot climate, all combined to generate swarms of flies, which rivaled those of Egypt. The garrison waged war against them, but in vain. Powder was plentiful, and frequently many square yards of infected ground, where the flies swarmed thickest, would be lightly sprinkled with it, and countless legions blown into the air; but these wholesale executions, however often repeated, appeared to make no impression whatever on the teeming armies of persecutors.

Their task finished, the fatigue party returned to their houses, and then all who had not other duties threw themselves down to snatch a short sleep. In spite of a night passed without rest, sleep was not easily wooed. The heat in the open air was terrific, in the close little room it was stifling; while the countless flies irritated them almost to madness. There was indeed but the choice of two evils: to cover closely their faces and hands, and lie bathed in perspiration; or to breathe freely, and bear the flies as best they might. The former alternative was generally chosen, as heat, however great, may be endured in quiet, and sleep may insensibly come on; but sleep with a host of flies incessantly nestling on every exposed part of the face and body was clearly an impossibility.

That day was a bad one for the defenders of Gubbins' garrison, for no less than twelve shells penetrated the house, and five of the occupants were killed or wounded. The shells came from a newly erected battery a hundred and fifty yards to the north. Among the killed was one of Mrs. Righton's children; and the boys first learned the news when, on rising from a fruitless attempt to sleep, they went to get a little fresh air outside. Edith and Nelly Hargreaves came out from the door, with jugs, on their way to fetch water.

The Warreners at once offered to fetch it for them, and as they spoke they saw that the girls' faces were both swollen with crying.

"Is anything the matter, Miss Hargreaves?" Ned asked.

"Have you not heard," Edith said, "how poor little Rupert has been killed by a shell? The ayah was badly hurt, and we all had close escapes; the shells from that battery are terrible."

Expressing their sorrow at the news, the boys took the jugs, and crossing the yard to the well, filled and brought them back.

"I wish we could do something to silence that battery," said Dick; "it will knock the house about our ears, and we shall be having the women and children killed every day."

"Let's go and have a look at it from the roof," replied Ned.

The roof was, like those of most of the houses in the Residency, flat, and intended for the inmates to sit and enjoy the evening breeze. The parapet was very low, but this had been raised by a line of sandbags, and behind them five or six of the defenders were lying, firing through the openings between the bags, in answer to the storm of musketry which the enemy were keeping up on the post.

Stooping low to avoid the bullets which were singing overhead, the Warreners moved across the terrace, and lying down, peered out through the holes which had been left for musketry. Gubbins' house stood on one of the highest points of the ground inclosed in the defenses, and from it they could obtain a view of nearly the whole circle of the enemy's batteries. They were indeed higher than the roofs of most of the houses held by the enemy, but one of these, distant only some fifty yards from the Sikh Square, dominated the whole line of the British defenses on that side, and an occasional crack of a rifle from its roof showed that the advantage was duly appreciated.

"What do they call that house?" Ned asked one of the officers on the terrace.

"That is Johannes' house," he answered. "It was a terrible mistake that we did not destroy it before the siege began; it is an awful thorn in our side. There is a black scoundrel, a negro, in the service of the king of Oude, who has his post there; he is a magnificent shot, and he has killed a great number of ours. It is almost certain death to show a head within the line of his fire."

"I wonder we have not made a sortie, and set fire to the place," said Ned.

"The scoundrels are so numerous that we could only hope to succeed with considerable loss, and we are so weak already that we can't afford it. So the chief sets his face against sorties, but I expect that we shall be driven to it one of these days. That new battery is terribly troublesome also. There, do you see, it lies just over that brow, so that the shot from our battery cannot touch it, while it can pound away at our house, and indeed at all the houses along this line."

"I should have thought," Dick said, "that a rush at night might carry it, and spike the guns."

"No; we should be certain to make some sort of noise, however quiet we were. There are six guns, all loaded at nightfall to the muzzle with grape; we know that, for once they fancied they heard us coming, and they fired such a storm of grape that we should have been all swept away; besides which, there are a large number of the fellows sleeping round; and although sometimes the battery ceases firing for some hours, the musketry goes on more or less during the night."

The Warreners lay wistfully watching the battery, whose shots frequently struck the house, and two or three times knocked down a portion of the sandbag parapet—the damage being at once repaired with bags lying in readiness, but always under a storm of musketry, which opened in the hopes of hitting the men engaged upon the work; these were, however, accustomed to it, and built up the sandbags without showing a limb to the enemy's shot.

"There were two children killed by that last shot," an officer said, coming up from below and joining them; "it made its way through the earth and broke in through a blocked-up window."

"We must silence that battery, Ned, whatever comes of it," Dick said in his brother's ear.

"I agree with you, Dick; but how is it to be done? have you got an idea?"

"Well, my idea is this," the midshipman said. "I think you and I might choose a dark night, as it will be to-night. Take the bearings of the battery exactly; then when they stop firing, and we think the gunners are asleep, crawl out and make for the guns. When we get there we can make our way among them, keeping on the ground so that the sentry cannot see us against the sky; and then with a sponge full of water we can give a squeeze on each of the touchholes, so there would be no chance of their going off till the charges were drawn. Then we could make our way back and tell Gubbins the guns are disabled, and he can take out a party, carry them with a rush, and spike them permanently."

"Capital, Dick; I'm with you, old boy."

"Now let us take the exact bearings of the place. There was a lane, you see, before the houses were pulled down, running along from beyond that corner nearly to the guns. When we get out we must steer for that, because it is comparatively clear from rubbish, and we ain't so likely to knock a stone over and make a row. We must choose some time when they are pounding away somewhere else, and then we shan't be heard even if we do make a little noise. We will ask Mrs. Hargreaves for a couple of pieces of sponge; we need not tell her what we want them for."

"And you think to-night, Dick?"

"Well, to-night is just as likely to succeed as any other night, and the sooner the thing is done the better. Johnson commands the guard from twelve to four, and he is an easy-going fellow, and will let us slip out, while some of the others wouldn't."

CHAPTER XV.
SPIKING THE GUNS.

As soon as night fell a little procession with three little forms on trays covered with white cloths, and two of larger size, started from Gubbins' house to the churchyard. Mr. and Mrs. Hargreaves, and Mrs. Righton and her husband, with two other women, followed. That morning all the five, now to be laid in the earth, were strong and well; but death had been busy. In such a climate as that, and in so crowded a dwelling, no delay could take place between death and burial, and the victims of each day were buried at nightfall. There was no time to make coffins, no men to spare for the work; and as each fell, so were they committed to the earth.

A little distance from Gubbins' house the procession joined a larger one with the day's victims from the other parts of the garrison—a total of twenty-four, young and old. At the head of the procession walked the Rev. Mr. Polehampton, one of the chaplains, who was distinguished for the bravery and self-devotion with which he labored among the sick and wounded. The service on which they were now engaged was in itself dangerous, for the churchyard was very exposed to the enemy's fire, and— for they were throughout the siege remarkably well-informed of what was taking place within the Residency—every evening they opened a heavy fire in the direction of the spot where they knew a portion of the garrison would be engaged in this sad avocation. Quietly and steadily the little procession moved along, though bullets whistled and shells hissed around them. Each stretcher with an adult body was carried by four soldiers, while some of the little ones' bodies were carried by their mothers as if alive. Mrs. Hargreaves and her daughter carried between them the tray on which the body of little Rupert Righton lay. Arrived at the churchyard, a long shallow trench, six feet wide, had been prepared, and in this, side by side, the dead were tenderly placed. Then Mr. Polehampton spoke a few words of prayer and comfort, and the mourners turned away, happily without one of them having been struck by the bullets which sang around, while some of the soldiers speedily filled in the grave.

While the sad procession had been absent, the boys had gone to Mrs. Hargreaves' room. The curtain was drawn, and they could hear the girls sobbing inside.

"Please, Miss Hargreaves, can I speak to you for a moment?" Ned said. "I would not intrude, but it is something particular."

Edith Hargreaves came to the door.

"Please," Ned went on, "will you give us two good-sized pieces of sponge? We don't know any one else to ask, and—but you must not say a word to any one—my brother and myself mean to go out to-night to silence that battery which is doing such damage."

"Silence that battery!" Edith exclaimed in surprise. "Oh, if you could do that; but how is it possible?"

"Oh, you dear boy," Nelly, who had come to the door, exclaimed impetuously, "if you could but do that, every one would love you. We shall all be killed if that terrible battery goes on. But how are you going to do it?"

"I don't say we are going to do it," Ned said, smiling at the girl's excitement, "but we are going to try to-night. We'll tell you all about it in the morning when it is done; that is," he said seriously, "if we come back to tell it. But you must not ask any questions now, and please give us the pieces of sponge." Edith disappeared for a moment, and came back with two large pieces of sponge.

"We will not ask, as you say we must not," she said quietly, "but I know you are going to run some frightful danger. I may tell mamma and Carrie when they come back that much, may I not? and we will all keep awake and pray for you tonight—God bless you both!" And with a warm clasp of the hands the girls went back into their room again.

"I tell you what, Ned," the midshipman said emphatically, when they went out into the air, "if I live through this war I'll marry Nelly Hargreaves; that is," he added, "if she'll have me, and will wait a bit. She is a brick, and no mistake. I never felt really in love before; not regularly, you know."

At any other time Ned would have laughed; but with Edith's farewell words in his ear he was little disposed for mirth, and he merely put his hand on Dick's shoulder and said:

"There will be time to talk about that in the future, Dick. There's the battery opening in earnest. There! Mr. Gubbins is calling for all hands on the roof with their rifles to try and silence it. Come along."

For an hour the fire on both sides was incessant. The six guns of the battery concentrated their fire upon Gubbins' house, while from the walls and houses on either side of it the fire of the musketry flashed unceasingly, sending a hail of shot to keep down the reply from the roof.

On their side the garrison on the terrace disregarded the musketry fire, but, crowded behind the sandbags, kept up a steady and concentrated fire at the flashes of the cannon; while from the battery below, the gunners, unable to touch the enemy's battery, discharged grape at the houses tenanted by the enemy's infantry. The Sepoys, carefully instructed in our service, had constructed shields of rope to each gun to protect the gunners, but those at the best could cover but one or two men, and the fire from the parapet inflicted such heavy losses upon the gunners that after a time their fire dropped, and an hour from the commencement of the cannonade all was still again on both sides. The Sepoy guns were silenced.

It was now ten o'clock, and the Warreners went and lay down quietly for a couple of hours. Then they heard the guard changed, and after waiting a quarter of an hour they went out to the battery, having first filled their sponges with water. There they joined Mr. Johnson.

"Can't sleep, boys?" he asked; "those flies are enough to drive one mad. You will get accustomed to them after a bit."

"It is not exactly that, sir," Ned said, "but we wanted to speak to you. Dick and I have made up our minds to silence that battery. We have got sponges full of water, and we mean to go out and drown the priming. Then when we come back and tell Mr. Gubbins, I dare say he will take out a party, make a rush, and spike them."

"Why, you must be mad to think of such a thing!" Mr. Johnson said in astonishment.

"I think it is easy enough, sir," Ned replied; "at any rate, we mean to try."

"I can't let you go without leave," Mr. Johnson said.

"No, sir, and so we are not going to tell you we are going," Ned laughed. "What we want to ask you is to tell your men not to fire if they hear a noise close by in the next few minutes, and after that to listen for a whistle like this. If they hear that they are not to fire at any one approaching from the outside. Good-by, sir."

And without waiting for Mr. Johnson to make up his mind whether or not his duty compelled him to arrest them, to prevent them from carrying out the mad scheme of which Ned had spoken, the Warreners glided off into the darkness.

They had obtained a couple of native daggers, and took no other arms. They did not take off their boots, but wound round them numerous strips of blanket, so that they would tread noiselessly, and yet if obliged to run for it would avoid the risk of cutting their feet and disabling themselves in their flight. Then, making sure that by this time Mr. Johnson would have given orders to his men not to fire if they heard a noise close at hand, they went noiselessly to the breastwork which ran from the battery to the house, climbed over it, and dropped into the trench beyond.

Standing on the battery close beside them, they saw against the sky the figure of Mr. Johnson.

"Good-by, sir," Ned said softly; "we will be back in half an hour if we have luck."

Then they picked their way carefully over the rough ground till they reached the lane, and then walked boldly but noiselessly forward, for they knew that for a little way there was no risk of meeting an enemy, and that in the darkness they were perfectly invisible to any native posted near the guns. After fifty yards' walking, they dropped on their hands and knees. Although the guns had been absolutely silent since their fire ceased at ten o'clock, a dropping musketry fire from the houses and walls on either side had, as usual, continued. This indicated to the boys pretty accurately the position of the guns. Crawling forward foot by foot, they reached the little ridge which sheltered the guns from the battery in Gubbins' garden.

The guns themselves they could not see, for behind them was a house, and, except against the sky line, nothing was visible. They themselves were, as they knew, in a line between Gubbins' house and any one who might be standing at the guns, so that they would not show against the sky. They could hear talking among the houses on either side of the guns, and could see the light of fires, showing that while some of their enemies were keeping up a dropping fire, others were passing the night, as is often the native custom, round the fires, smoking and cooking. There was a faint talk going on ahead, too, beyond the guns; but the enemy had had too severe a lesson of the accuracy of the English rifle-fire to dare to light a fire there.

Having taken in the scene, the boys moved forward, inch by inch. Presently Ned put his hand on something which, for a moment, made him start back; an instant's thought, however, reassured him; it was a man, but the hardness of the touch told that it was not a living one. Crawling past it, the lads found other bodies lying thickly, and then they touched a wheel. They had arrived at the guns, and the bodies were those of the men shot down a few hours before in the act of loading.

Behind the guns a number of artillerymen were, as the boys could hear, sitting and talking; but the guns themselves stood alone and unguarded. A clasp of the hand, and the boys parted, one going, as previously arranged, each way. Ned rose very quietly by the side of the gun, keeping his head, however, below its level, and running his hand along it until it came to the breech. The touch-hole was covered by a wad of cloth to keep the powder dry from the heavy dew. This he removed, put up his hand again with the wet sponge, gave a squeeze, and then cautiously replaced the covering.

Dick did the same with the gun on the right, and so each crept along from gun to gun, until the six guns were disabled. Then they crawled back and joined each other.

A clasp of the hands in congratulation, and then they were starting to return, when they heard a dull tramp, and the head of a dark column came along just ahead of them. The boys shrank back under the guns, and lay flat among the bodies of the dead. The column halted at the guns, and a voice asked:

"Is the colonel here?"

"Here am I," said a voice from behind the guns, and a native officer came forward.

"We are going to make an attack from the house of Johannes. We shall be strong, and shall sweep the Kaffirs before us. It is the order of the general that you open with your guns here, to distract their attention."

"Will it please you to represent to the general that we have fought this evening, and that half my gunners are killed. The fire of the sons of Sheitan is too strong for us. Your excellency will see the ground is covered with our dead. Bring fire," he ordered, and at the word one of the soldiers lighted a torch made of straw, soaked in oil, which threw a lurid flame over the ground. "See, excellency, how we have suffered."

"Are they all dead?" asked the officer, stepping nearer.

The boys held their breath, when there was a sharp cracking of musketry, the man with the torch fell prostrate, and several cries arose from the column. The watchers on the roof of Gubbins' house had been quick to discern their enemy.

"Move on, march!" the officer exclaimed hastily, "double. Yes, I see, it is hot here; but when we have attacked, and their attention is distracted, you may do something."

So saying, he went off at a run with his regiment.

The boys lost no time in creeping out again, and making the best of their way back; once fairly over the crest, they rose to their feet and ran down toward the intrenchment. As they neared this Ned whistled twice.

The whistle was answered, and in a minute hands were stretched down to help them to scramble over the earthwork.

"All right," Ned said to Mr. Johnson; "the guns are useless, and weakly guarded. There are lots of infantry on both sides, but some of them will be drawn off, for they are going to make an attack from Johannes' house. Where is Mr. Gubbins?"

"He has just made his rounds," Mr. Johnson said; "I will take you to him."

Mr. Gubbins was astonished when he heard from the boys that they had been out, and rendered the guns temporarily useless. "You were wrong to act without orders," he said, "but I can't scold you for such a gallant action. We must act on it at once. I would send for a reinforcement, but we must not lose a moment. If the attack from Johannes' house begins before our attack, the artillerymen will prepare for action, and may discover that the breeches of their guns are wet. Call up every man at once, Mr. Johnson, and let them fall in on the battery; and do you," he turned to another, "run down to the Sikh Square and Martinière garrison, and warn them that a great attack is just going to be made. Tell them that we are making a sortie, and ask them to bring every rifle to bear on the houses to the left of the guns, so as to keep down the infantry fire there."

In two minutes every man of the garrison was assembled in the battery, even those from the roof being called down.

"Bring a dark lantern," Mr. Gubbins said; "it may be useful. Now, lads, we are going to spike the guns; they have been rendered useless, so we have only got to make a dash for them. The moment they are in our possession, you, Mr. Johnson, with ten men, will clear the house immediately behind it, and look for the magazine. Mr. Leathes, you, with fifteen men, will move to the right a little; and you, Mr. Percival, with your command, to the left. Do not go far, but each carry a house or two, set them on fire, and fall back here when you hear the bugle. I have got the hammer and spiking nails. Now, as quietly as you can till you hear that we are discovered, and then go with a rush at the guns."

In fact, they had gone very few paces before there was a shout in the enemy's line. The noise of so many men stumbling over the *débris* of leveled houses was heard in an instant in the night air.

"Forward!" Mr. Gubbins shouted; "don't fire, give them the bayonet."

At a charge the little party rushed along. They were in the lane now, and were able to run fast. The shout had been followed by a shot, then by a dozen others, and then a rapid fire broke out from the houses and walls in front.

They were still invisible, however, and the balls whistled overhead. They heard the voice of the officer at the guns shout to his men:

"Steady; don't fire till they are on the crest, then blow them into dust."

They topped the crest and rushed at the guns.

"Fire!" shouted the officer, but a cry of dismay alone answered his words, and in a moment the British rushed on to the guns, and bayoneted the astonished and dismayed enemy.

Then they separated each to the work assigned to them, while Mr. Gubbins, with a man with the lantern, went from gun to gun and drove a nail down the touchhole of each. Then he followed into the house behind. Here a short but furious fight had taken place. The Sepoys lodged there fought desperately but unavailingly. A few leaped from the windows, but the rest were bayoneted. The fight was stern and silent; no words were spoken, for the Sepoys knew that it was useless to ask for quarter; the clashing of sabers against muskets, an occasional sharp cry, and the sound of the falling of heavy bodies alone told of the desperate struggle.

It ended just as Mr. Gubbins entered.

"Look about," he said; "they must have a magazine somewhere here; perhaps a large one."

There was a rapid search.

"Here it is," Ned said, as he looked into a large outhouse behind the building. "There are some twenty barrels of powder and a large quantity of shot and shell."

"Break open a barrel, quick!" Mr. Gubbins said. "Mr. Johnson, I will do this with the Warreners. Do you line that low wall, and keep back the pandies a minute or two; they will be on us like a swarm of bees. Run into the house," he said to Dick, as Mr. Johnson led his men forward to the wall, "you will see a bucket of water in the first room. Bring it here quick. Now then," he said, "empty this barrel among the others; that's right, smash in the heads of three or four others with this hammer. That's right," as Dick returned with the water. "Now fill your cap with powder."

Dick did so, and Mr. Gubbins poured some water into it, stirred them together till the powder was damped through, and with this made a train some five feet long to the dry powder.

The party at the wall were now hotly engaged with a mass of advancing enemy.

"Fall back, Mr. Johnson, quickly. Sound the retreat, bugler. Go along, lads; I'll light the train."

He waited until the last man had passed, applied a lighted match to the train, which began to fizz and sputter, and then ran out and followed the rest, shutting the door of the magazine as he went out, in order that the burning fuse should not be seen.

By this time the houses on either side were alight, and the whole party were returning at a double toward the intrenchments.

As they neared the lines the enemy swarmed out from their cover, and the head of the reinforcements were pouring out through the house into the battery, when the earth shook, a mighty flash of fire lit the sky; there was a roar like thunder, and most of the retreating party were swept from their feet by the shock, while a shower of stones and timber fell in a wide circle. They were soon up again, and scrambled over the earthworks.

For a minute the explosion was succeeded by a deathlike stillness, broken only by the sound of the falling fragments; then from the whole circle of the British lines a great cheer of triumph rose up, while a yell of fury answered them from the enemy's intrenchments.

"Any loss?" was Mr. Gubbins' first question.

"No one killed," was the report of the officers of the three sections.

"Any wounded?"

Four of the men stepped forward; two were slightly wounded only; two were seriously hit, but a glance showed that the wounds were not of a nature likely to be fatal.

"Hurrah! my lads," Mr. Gubbins said cheerily; "six guns spiked, our garrison freed from that troublesome battery, a lesson given to the enemy, and I expect a few hundred of them blown up, and all at the cost of four wounded."

"Well done, indeed," a voice said; and General Inglis, with two or three of his officers, stepped forward. "Gallantly done; but how was it that the guns were silent? you could hardly have caught them asleep."

"No, sir," Mr. Gubbins said; "the gentlemen who brought in the message from General Havelock, two days ago, went out on their own account, and silenced the guns by wetting the priming."

A suppressed cheer broke from the whole party; for until now only Mr. Johnson and those on guard with him knew what had happened, and the silence of the guns had been a mystery to all.

"Step forward, young gentlemen, will you?" General Inglis said. "You have done a most gallant action," he went on, shaking them by the hand, "a most gallant action; and the whole garrison are greatly indebted to you. I shall have great pleasure in reporting your gallant conduct to the commander-in-chief, when the time comes for doing so. I will not mar the pleasure which all feel at your deed by blaming you for acting on your own inspiration, but I must do so to-morrow. Good fortune has attended your enterprise, but the lives of brave men are too valuable to allow them to undertake such risks as this on their own account. And now that I have said what I was obliged to say, I ask you all to give three cheers for our gallant young friends."

Three hearty cheers were given, and then the general hurried off to superintend the preparations for the defense of the quarter threatened by the attack from Johannes' house, if indeed that attack should not be postponed, owing to the discouragement which the blow just inflicted would naturally spread. Surrounded by their comrades, the Warreners re-entered the house.

"What was that terrible explosion?" "What has happened?" was asked by a score of female voices as they entered.

"Good news," Mr. Gubbins said; "you can sleep in peace. The guns of the battery which has annoyed us are all spiked, and their magazine blown up, and all this without the loss of a man, thanks to the Warreners, who went out alone and disabled all the guns, by wetting the primings. All your thanks are due to them."

There was a general cry of grateful joy; for since the battery had begun to play upon the house, no one had felt that his own life or the lives of those dearest to him were safe for a moment. All were dressed, for in these times of peril no one went regularly to bed; and they now crowded round the boys, shaking them by the hand, patting them on the shoulders, many crying for very joy and relief.

Mrs. Hargreaves was standing at the door, and the boys went up to her. She drew back the curtain for them to enter; for, sure that the boys intended to carry out some desperate enterprise, none of her family had even lain down. Mr. Hargreaves and Mr. Righton followed them in.

"We were all praying for you," she said simply, "as if you had been my own sons; for you were doing as much for me and mine as my own could have done;" and she kissed both their foreheads.

"I think, Mrs. Hargreaves," said Dick, with the demure impudence of a midshipman, "that that ought to go round."

"I think you have fairly earned it, you impudent boy," Mrs. Hargreaves said, smiling.

Mrs. Righton kissed Dick tearfully, for she was thinking that, had the battery been silenced only one day earlier, her little one would have been saved. Edith glanced at her mother, and allowed Dick to kiss her; while Nelly threw her arms round his neck and kissed him heartily, telling him he was a darling boy.

Ned, who possessed none of the impudence of his brother, and who was moreover at the age when many boys become bashful with women, contented himself with shaking hands with Mrs. Righton and Edith, and would have done the same with Nelly, but that young lady put up her cheek with a laugh.

"I choose to be kissed, sir," she said; "it is not much kissing that we get here, goodness knows."

CHAPTER XVI.
A SORTIE AND ITS CONSEQUENCES.

The night passed off without the expected attack from Johannes' house, the rebels being too much disconcerted by the destruction of the battery, and the loss of so many men, to attempt any offensive operations. The destruction of the house behind the guns, and of all those in its vicinity, deterred them from re-establishing a battery in the same place, as there would be no shelter for the infantry supporting the guns; and after the result of the sortie it was evident to them that a large force must be kept in readiness to repel the attacks of the British.

For a few days life was more tolerable in Gubbins' garrison; for although shot and shell frequently struck the house, and batteries multiplied in the circle around, none kept up so deadly and accurate a fire as that which they had destroyed.

The Warreners took their fair share in all the heavy fatigue work, and in the picket duty in the battery or on the roof; but they enjoyed their intervals of repose, which were now always spent with Mr. Hargreaves' family.

Mr. Hargreaves was collector of a district near Lucknow, and was high in the Civil Service. He was a fit husband for his kindly wife; and as Mr. Righton was of a cheerful and hopeful disposition, the boys found themselves members of a charming family circle. Often and often they wished that their father, sister, and cousin could but join them; or rather, as Ned said, they could join the party without, for no one could wish that any they loved should be at Lucknow at that time.

One evening late they were sitting together in a group outside the house, the enemy's fire being slack, when Mr. Johnson came up from the battery to Mr. Gubbins, who formed one of the party.

"I am afraid, sir, they are mining again; lying on the ground, we think we can hear the sound of blows."

"That is bad," Mr. Gubbins said; "I heard this afternoon that they believe that two mines are being driven from Johannes' house in the direction of the Martinière, and the brigade messhouse; now we are to have our turn, eh?

Well, we blew in the last they tried, and must do it again; but it is so much more hard work. Now, gentlemen, let us see who has the best ears. Excuse us, Mrs. Hargreaves, we shall not be long away."

On entering the battery they found the men on guard all lying down listening, and were soon at full length with their ears to the ground. All could hear the sound; it was very faint, as faint as the muffled tick of a watch, sometimes beating at regular intervals of a second or so, sometimes ceasing for a minute or two.

"There is no doubt they are mining," Mr. Gubbins said; "the question is, from which way are they coming."

None could give an opinion. The sound was so faint, and seemed to come so directly from below, that the ear could not discriminate in the slightest.

"At any rate," Mr. Gubbins said, "we must begin at once to sink a shaft. If, when we get down a bit, we cannot judge as to the direction, we must drive two or three listening galleries in different directions. But before we begin we must let Major Anderson, of the Royal Engineers, know, and take his advice; he is in command of all mining operations."

In ten minutes Major Anderson was on the ground.

"The fellows are taking to mining in earnest," he said; "this is the third we have discovered to-day, and how many more there may be, goodness only knows. I think you had better begin here," he said to Mr. Gubbins. "You have got tools, I think. Say about six feet square, then two men can work at once. I will be here the first thing in the morning, and then we will look round and see which is the likeliest spot for the fellows to be working from. Will you ask your sentries on the roof to listen closely to-night, in order to detect, if possible, a stir of men coming or going from any given point."

Picks and shovels were brought out, the garrison told off into working parties of four each, to relieve each other every hour, and the work began. Well-sinking is hard work in any climate, but with a thermometer marking a hundred and five at night, it is terrible; and each set of workers, as they came up bathed in perspiration, threw themselves on the ground utterly exhausted. Mr. Hargreaves and a few of the elders of the garrison were excused this work, and took extra duty on the terrace and battery.

The next day it was decided that the enemy were probably working from a ruined house near their former battery, and a gallery was begun from the bottom of the shaft. This was pushed on night and day for three days, the workers being now certain, from the rapidly increasing sound of the workers, that this was the line by which the enemy was approaching. The gallery was driven nearly twenty yards, and then three barrels of powder were stored there, and the besieged awaited the approach of the rebels' gallery.

The Sepoys had now erected batteries whose cross fire swept the ground outside the intrenchments, so that a sortie could no longer be carried out with any hope of success. Had it been possible to have attempted it, a party would have gone out, and driving off any guard that might have been placed, entered the enemy's gallery and caught them at their work. A sentry was placed continually in the gallery, and each hour the sound of the pick and crowbar became louder.

On the fifth day the engineers judged that there could not be more than a yard of earth between them. The train was laid now, and a cautious watch kept, until, just at the moment when it was thought that an opening would be made, the train was fired. The earth heaved, and a great opening was made, while a shower of stones flew high in the air. The enemy's gallery was blown in, and the men working destroyed, and a loud cheer broke from the garrison at the defeat of another attempt upon them.

The month of August began badly in Lucknow. Major Banks, the civil commissioner named by Sir Henry Lawrence to succeed him, was shot dead while reconnoitering from the top of an outhouse. The Reverend Mr. Polehampton, who had been wounded at the commencement of the siege, was killed, as were Lieutenants Lewin, Shepherd, and Archer.

On the 8th large bodies of Sepoys were observed to enter the city, and on the 10th a furious attack was made all round the British line. Every man capable of bearing arms stood at his post, and even the sick and wounded crawled out of hospital and took posts on housetops wherever they could fire on the foe. The din was prodigious—the yells of the enemy, their tremendous fire of musketry, the incessant roar of their cannon, but they lacked heart for close fighting.

Frequently large bodies of men showed from behind their shelter, and, carrying ladders, advanced as if with the determination of making an assault. Each time, however, the withering fire opened upon them from the line of earthworks, from the roof of every house, and the storm of grape from the batteries, caused them to waver and fall back. Each fresh effort was led by brave men, fanatics, who advanced alone far in front of the rest, shrieking, "Death to the infidel!"

But they died, and their spirit failed to animate their followers. Only once or twice did the assailing parties get near the line of intrenchments, and then but to fall back rapidly after heavy loss.

Day after day the position of the besieged grew more unendurable. The buildings were crumbling away under the heavy and continued fire; and as one after another became absolutely untenable, the ladies and children were more closely crowded in those which still offered some sort of shelter. Even death, fearful as were its ravages, did not suffice to counteract the closeness of the packing. Crowded in dark rooms, living on the most meager food—for all the comforts, such as tea, sugar, wine, spirits, etc., were exhausted, and even the bread was made of flour ground, each for himself, between rough stones—without proper medicines, attendance, or even bedding; tormented by a plague of flies, sickened by disgusting smells, condemned to inaction and confinement, the women and children died off rapidly, and the men, although better off with regard to light and air, sickened fast. Half the officers were laid up with disease, and all were lowered in health and strength.

On the 18th, as the Warreners had just returned from a heavy night's work, strengthening the defenses, and burying horses and cattle, a great explosion was heard, and one of those posted on the roof ran down shouting:

"To arms! they have fired a mine under the Sikh Square!"

Every man caught up his rifle and rushed to the spot. The mine had carried away a portion of the exterior defense, and the enemy, with yells of triumph, rushed forward toward the opening. Then ensued a furious *mêlée*; each man fought for himself, hand to hand, in the breach; Mussulmen and Englishmen struggled in deadly combat; the crack of the revolver, the thud of the clubbed guns, the clash of sword against steel, the British cheer and the native yell, were mingled in wild confusion. While some drove the enemy back, others brought boxes and beams, fascines and sandbags, to repair the breach. The enemy were forced back, and the British poured out with shouts of triumph.

Our men's blood was up, and they followed their advantage. Part of the engineers, ever on the alert, joined the throng with some barrels of powder, and the enemy were pushed back sufficiently far to enable some of the houses, from which we had been greatly annoyed by the enemy's sharpshooters, to be blown up.

This success cheered the besieged, and on the 20th, when it was discovered that the enemy were driving two new mines, a fresh sortie was determined upon.

The garrison of Gubbins' house had now less cover than before, for the building had been reduced almost to a shell by the enemy's fire, and all the women and children had the day before been removed to other quarters. The Residency itself was a tottering mass of ruins, and this also had been emptied of its helpless ones, who were crowded in a great underground room in the Begum Khotee. It is difficult to form an idea of the storm of shot and shell which swept the space inclosed within the lines of defense, but some notion may be obtained from the fact that an officer had the curiosity to count the number of cannon balls of various sizes that fell on the roof of the brigade messhouse in one day, and found that they amounted to the almost incredible number of two hundred and eighty. Living such a life as this, the Warreners were rejoiced when they received orders, with ten of the other defenders of the ruins of Gubbins' house, to join in the sortie on the 20th of August. About a hundred of the garrison formed up in the Sikh Square, and at the word being given dashed over the stockade and intrenchment, and made a charge for Johannes' house. This had throughout the siege been the post from which the enemy had most annoyed them, the king of Oude's negro in particular having killed a great many of our officers and men. It was from this point that the mines being driven, and it was determined at all hazards to destroy it.

The rush of the British took the enemy by surprise. Scarce a shot was fired until they had traversed half the distance, and then a heavy fire of musketry opened from all the houses held by the enemy. Still the English pushed on at full speed, without pausing to return a shot. With a cheer they burst into the inclosure in which the house stood, and while half the party entered it and engaged in a furious combat with those within, the others, in accordance with orders, pressed forward into the houses beyond, so as to keep the enemy from advancing to the assistance of their friends, thus caught in a trap. The Warreners belonged to the party who advanced, and were soon engaged in a hand-to-hand fight with the enemy. Scattering through the houses, they drove the Sepoys before them. The Warreners were fighting side by side with Mr. Johnson, and with him, after driving the enemy through the next house, they entered an outhouse beyond it.

Mr. Johnson entered first, followed by Ned, Dick being last of the party. Dick heard a sudden shout and a heavy blow, and rushed in. Mr. Johnson lay on the ground, his skull beaten in with a blow from the iron-bound staff of a dervish, a wild figure with long hair and beard reaching down to his waist. Dick was in time to see the terrible staff descend again upon Ned's head. Ned guarded it with his rifle, but the guard was beaten down and Ned stretched senseless on the ground. Before the fakir had time to raise his stuff again, Dick drove his bayonet through his chest, and the fakir fell prostrate, his body rolling down some steps into a cellar which served as a woodstore.

As he fell Dick heard a fierce growl, and a bear of a very large size, who was standing by the fakir, rose on his hind legs. Fortunately Dick's rifle was still loaded, and, pointing it into the fierce beast's mouth, he fired, and the bear rolled down the wooden steps after his master. Throwing aside his rifle, Dick turned to raise his brother. Ned lay as if dead.

Dick leaped to his feet, and ran out to call for succor. He went into the house, but it was empty. He rushed to the door, and saw the rest of the party in full retreat. He shouted, but his voice was lost in the crackle of musketry fire. He ran back to Ned and again tried to lift him, and had got him on his shoulders, when there was a tremendous explosion. Johannes' house had been blown up.

Following close upon the sound came the yells of the enemy, who were flocking up to pursue the English back to their trenches. Escape was now hopeless. Dick lowered Ned to the ground, hastily dragged the body of Mr. Johnson outside the door, and then, lifting Ned, bore him down the steps into the cellar into which the fakir and the bear had fallen. He carried him well into the cellar, took away the wooden steps, and then, with great difficulty, also dragged the bodies of the fakir and the bear further in, so that any one looking down into the hole from the outside would observe nothing unusual.

Then, as he lay down, faint from his exertions, he could hear above the tread of a great number of men, followed by a tremendous musketry fire from the house. Once or twice he thought he heard some one come to the door of the outhouse; but if so, no one entered.

Beyond rubbing Ned's hands, and putting cold stones to his forehead, Dick could do nothing; but Ned breathed, and Dick felt strong hopes that he was only stunned. In a quarter of an hour he showed signs of reviving, and in an hour was able to hear from Dick an account of what had happened, and where they were.

"We are in a horrible fix this time, Dick, and no mistake; my head aches so, I can hardly think; let us be quiet for a bit, and we will both try to think what is best to be done. There is no hurry to decide. No one is likely to come down into this place, but we may as well creep well behind this pile of wood and straw, and then we shall be safe."

Dick assented, and for an hour they lay quiet, Ned's regular breathing soon telling his brother that he had dropped off to sleep. Then Dick very quietly crept out again from their hiding-place.

"It is a grand idea," he said to himself; "magnificent. It's nasty, horribly nasty; but after three weeks of what we have gone through in the Residency one can see and do things which it would have made one almost sick to think of a month back; and as our lives depend upon it we must not stand upon niceties. I wish, though, I had been brought up a red Indian; it would have come natural then, I suppose."

So saying, he took out his pocket-knife, opened it, and went to the body of the dead fakir. He took the long, matted hair into his hand with an exclamation of disgust, but saw at once that his idea was a feasible one. The hair was matted together in an inextricable mass, and could be trusted to hang together.

He accordingly set to work to cut it off close to the head; but although his knife was a sharp one it was a long and unpleasant task, and nothing but the necessity of the case could have nerved him to get through with it.

At last it was finished, and he looked at his work with complacency.

"That's a magnificent wig," he said. "I defy the best barber in the world to make such a natural one. Now for the bear."

This was a long task; but at last the bear was skinned, and Dick set to to clean, as well as he could, the inside of the hide. Then he dragged into a corner and covered up the carcass of the bear and the body of the fakir, having first stripped the clothes off the latter, scattered a little straw over the bear's skin, and then, his task being finished, he crept behind the logs again, lay down, and went off to sleep by the side of Ned. It was getting dark when he awoke. Ned was awake, and was sitting up by his side. Outside, the din of battle, the ceaseless crack of the rifle, and the roar of cannon was going on as usual, without interruption.

"How do you feel now, Ned?" Dick asked.

"All right, Dick. I have got a biggish bump on the side of my head, and feel a little muddled still, but that is nothing. I can't think of any plan for escaping from this place, Dick, nor of getting hold of a disguise; for even if we could get out of this place and neighborhood we must be detected, and in this town it is of no use trying to beg for shelter or aid."

"It is all arranged," Dick said cheerfully. "I have got two of the best disguises in the world, and we have only to dress up in them and walk out."

Ned looked at Dick as if he thought that he had gone out of his mind.

"You don't believe me? Just you wait, then, two minutes, till I have dressed up, and then I'll call you;" and without waiting for an answer, Dick went out.

He speedily stripped to the waist, rubbed some mud from the damp floor on his arms, wound the fakir's rags round his body with a grimace of disgust, put the wig on his head—his hair, like that of all the garrison, had been cut as close to the head as scissors would take it—shook the long, knotted hair over his face and shoulders—behind it hung to the waist—took the staff in his hand, and called quietly to Ned to come out. Ned crept out, and remained petrified with astonishment.

"The fakir!" he exclaimed at last. "Good heavens, Dick! is that you?"

"It's me, sure enough," Dick said, taking off his wig. "Here is a wig in which the sharpest eyes in the world could not detect you."

"But where—" began Ned, still lost in surprise.

"My dear Ned, I have borrowed from the fakir. It was not quite a nice job," he went on, in answer to Ned's astonished look, "but it's over now, and we need not say any more about it. The hair and rags are disgustingly filthy, there is no doubt about that. Their late owner never used a comb, and was otherwise beastly in his habits; still, old man, that cannot be helped, and if you like, when we once get out of the town, we can put them in water for twenty-four hours, or make a sort of oven, and bake them to get rid of their inhabitants. Our lives are at stake, Ned, and we must not mind trifles."

"Right, old boy," Ned said, making a great effort to overcome his first sensation of disgust. "As you say, it is a trifle. You have hit upon a superb idea, Dick, superb; and I think you have saved our lives from what seemed a hopeless scrape. But what is your other disguise?"

"This," Dick said, lifting the bear's skin. "I can get into this, and if we travel at night, so that I can walk upright, for I never could travel far on all-fours, I should pass well enough, as I could lie curled up by your side in the daytime, and no one will ask a holy fakir any troublesome questions. I don't think you could get into the skin, Ned, or I would certainly take the fakir for choice; for it will be awfully hot in this skin."

"I don't mind doing the fakir a bit," Ned said. "Fortunately the sun has done his work, and the color of our skins can be hidden by a good coat of dirt, which will look as natural as possible. Now let us set about it at once."

It took an hour's preparation; for, although Ned's toilet was quickly made, needing in fact nothing but a coating of mud, it took some time to sew Dick up in the skin, the opening being sewn up by means of the small blade of the knife and some string. It was by this time quite dark, and the operation had been completed so perfectly that once Ned was dressed they had no fear whatever of interruption.

"Now, Ned, before we go I will set fire to the straw. I don't suppose any one will go down and make any discoveries, but they may be looking for wood, so it's as well to prevent accidents. We will throw that big piece of matting over the opening in the floor, so the light won't show till we get well away."

He ran down the ladder, struck a match, lit the straw, and then ran quickly up again. The mat was dragged across the opening, and then the boys went boldly out into the yard, Ned striding along, and Dick trotting on all-fours beside him. The night was dark, and although there were many men in the yard, sitting about on the ground round fires, no one noticed the boys, who, turning out through a gateway, took the road into the heart of Lucknow.

CHAPTER XVII.
OUT OF LUCKNOW.

One hundred yards or so after starting the disguised fakir and his bear entered a locality teeming with troops, quartered there in order to be close at hand to the batteries, to assist to repel sorties, or to join in attacks. Fortunately the night was very dark, and the exceedingly awkward and unnatural walk of the bear passed unseen. Over and over again they were challenged and shouted to, but the hoarse "Hoo-Hac," which is the cry of the fakirs, and the ring of the iron-bound staff with its clanking rings on the ground, were a sufficient pass.

Ned guessed, from the fact of their having been met with so close to the fort, that the fakir and his bear would be well known to the mutineers; and this proved to be the case.

Several of the men addressed him, but he waved his arm, shook his head angrily, and strode on; and as fakirs frequently pretend to be absorbed in thought, and unwilling to converse, the soldiers fell back. Beyond this, the streets were deserted. The most populous native quarter lay far away, and few of the inhabitants, save of the lowest classes, cared to be about the streets after nightfall.

The instant that they were in a quiet quarter Dick rose on to his feet.

"My goodness," he whispered to Ned, "that all-fours' work is enough to break one's back, Ned."

They now struck sharply to the left, presently crossed the wide street leading from the Cawnpore Bridge, and kept on through quiet lanes until they came to the canal. This would be the guide they wanted, and they followed it along, taking nearly the route which General Havelock afterward followed in his advance, until they came to a bridge across the canal. Once over, they were, they knew, fairly safe. They kept on at a rapid walk until well in the country, and then sat down by the roadside for a consultation as to their best course of proceeding. The lads were both of opinion that the dangers which would lie in the way of their reaching Cawnpore would be very great. This road was now occupied by great numbers of troops, determined to bar the way to Lucknow against General Havelock. They had advanced without question, because it was natural that Sepoys should be making their way from Cawnpore to Lucknow; but it would not be at all natural that a fakir should at this time be going in the opposite direction. Moreover—and this weighed very strongly with them—they knew that General Havelock would advance with a force wholly inadequate to the task before him; and they thought that even should he succeed in getting into Lucknow, he would be wholly unable to get out again, hampered, as he would be, with sick, wounded, women, and children. In that case he would have to continue to hold Lucknow until a fresh relieving force arrived, and the lads had already had more than enough of the confinement and horrors of a siege such as that of Cawnpore.

Animated by these considerations, they determined to push to Delhi, where they hoped that they might arrive in time to see the end of the siege, at whose commencement they had been present.

No suspicion would be likely to be excited by their passage through that line of country, which, indeed, would be found altogether denuded of the enemy's troops, for all the regiments that had mutinied along this line had marched off, either to Delhi or Lucknow, and the country was in the hands of the zemindars, who would neither suspect nor molest a wandering fakir. It certainly was unusual for a fakir to be accompanied by a bear, but as the fakir they had killed had a bear with him, it was clearly by no means impossible. Dick protested that it was absolutely essential that they should walk at night, for that he would be detected at once in the day.

"I vote that we walk all night, Ned, and make our thirty-five or forty miles, then turn in, hide up all day. In the evening when it gets quite dusk, we can go into the outskirts of a village. Then you will begin to shout, and I will lie down, as if tired, by you. They will bring you lots of grub, under the idea that you will give them charms, and so on, next day. When the village is asleep, we will go on. You can easily ask for cloth—I am sure your rags are wretched enough—and then I can dress at night, after setting out from each village, in native dress, for it would be awful to walk far in this skin; besides, my feet are as uncomfortable as possible."

This plan was agreed upon, and they struck across country for the main Delhi road, Dick slipping out of his bear's skin, and simply wearing it wrapped loosely round him.

The Warreners had been accustomed to such incessant labor at Lucknow that they had no difficulty in keeping going all night. As day was breaking they retired into a tope of trees and threw themselves down, Dick first taking the precaution to get into the bear's skin and lace it up, in case of surprise. It was of course hot, but at least it kept off flies and other insects;

and as it was quite loose for him, it was not so hot as it would have been had it fitted more tightly. The lads were both utterly fatigued, and in a very few minutes were fast asleep.

It was late in the afternoon before they awoke, and although extremely hungry, they were forced to wait until it became dusk before proceeding on their way.

At the first village at which they arrived they sat down near the first house, and Ned began to strike his staff to the ground and to shout "Hoo-Hac" with great vehemence. Although the population were for the most part Mussulmen, there were many Hindoos everywhere scattered about, and these at once came out and formed a ring round the holy man. Some bore torches, and Dick played his part by sitting up and rocking uneasily, in the manner of a bear, and then lying down and half-covering his face with his paw, went apparently to sleep.

"The servant of Siva is hungry," Ned said, "and would eat. He wants cloth;" and he pointed to the rags which scarce held together over his shoulder. Supplies of parched grain and of baked cakes were brought him, and a woman carried up a sick child and a length of cloth. Ned passed his hand over the child's face, and by that and the heat of her hand judged that she had fever. First, after the manner of a true fakir, he mumbled some sentence which no one could understand. Then in silence he breathed a sincere prayer that the child might be restored to health. After this he bade the mother give her cooling drinks made of rice water and acid fruit, to keep her cool, and to damp her hands and face from time to time; and then he signified by a wave of his hand that he would be alone.

The villagers all retired, and the lads made a hearty meal; then taking what remained of the food, they started on their night's journey, pausing in a short time for Dick to get out of his skin, and to wrap himself from head to foot in the dark blue cotton cloth that the woman had given.

"I felt like an impostor, getting that cloth under false pretenses, Dick."

"Oh, nonsense," Dick said. "The woman gave it for what the fakir could do, and I am sure your advice was better than the fakir would have given, so she is no loser. If ever we come on one of these sort of trips again we will bring some quinine and some strong pills, and then we really may do some good."

Dick took no pains about coloring his face or hands, for both were burned so brown with exposure to the sun that he had no fear that a casual glance at them at night, even in torchlight, would detect that he was not a native.

"Now, Ned, I promised to stop for twenty-four hours, if you liked, to soak that head of hair in a pond; what do you say?"

"No," Ned said; "it is terribly filthy, but we will waste no time. To-morrow, when we halt, we will try and make an oven and bake it. I will try to-morrow to get a fresh cloth for myself, and throw these horrible rags away. Even a fakir must have a new cloth sometimes."

They made a very long march that night; and had the next evening a success equal to that of the night before. Another long night-tramp followed, and on getting up at the end of the day's sleep Ned collected some dry sticks and lit a fire. Then he made a hole in the ground, and filled it with glowing embers. When the embers were just extinct he cleared them out, took off his wig, rolled it up, and put it into the hot oven he had thus prepared, and covered the top in with a sod. Then carefully looking to see that no natives were in sight, he threw away his old rags, and Dick and he enjoyed a dip in a small irrigation tank close to the wood. After this Ned again smeared himself over with mud, and sat down in the sun to dry. Then he dressed himself in the cloth that had been given him the night before, opened his oven, took out the wig, gave it a good shake, and put it on, saying, "Thank God, I feel clean again; I have had the horrors for the last three days, Dick."

In the three nights' journey the boys had traveled a hundred and eleven miles, and were now close to Ferruckabad, a town of considerable size. They pursued their usual tactics—entered it after dusk, and sat down near the outskirts. The signal calls were answered as before, and a number of the faithful gathered round with their simple offerings of food.

As they began stating their grievances, Ned as usual warned them off with a brief "to-morrow" when he saw outside the group of Hindoos two or three Mussulman troopers.

These moved closely up, and contemplated the wild-looking fakir, with his tangled hair and his eyes peering out through the tangle. One of them looked at the bear for some time attentively, and then said:

"That is no bear; it is a man in a bear's skin."

Ned had feared that the discovery might be made, and had from the first had his answer ready.

"Fool," he said in a loud, harsh voice, "who with his eyes in his head supposed that it was a bear? It is one who has sinned and is under a vow. Dogs like you know naught of these things, but the followers of Siva know."

"Do you call me a dog?" said the Mussulman angrily, and strode forward as if to strike; but Ned leaped to his feet, and twirling his staff round his head, brought it down with such force on the soldier's wrist that it nearly broke the arm. The Hindoos began to shout "Sacrilege!" as the Mussulman drew his pistol. Before he could fire, however, his comrades threw themselves upon him. At this time it was the policy of Hindoos and Mussulmans alike to drop all religious differences, and the troopers knew that any assault upon a holy fakir would excite to madness the Hindoo population.

The furious Mohammedan was therefore dragged away by his fellows, and Ned calmly resumed his seat. The Hindoos brought a fresh supply of food for the holy man expiating his sin in so strange a way, and then left the fakir to his meditation and his rest.

Half an hour later the Warreners were on their way, and before morning congratulated themselves upon having done more than half of the two hundred and eighty miles which separate Lucknow from Delhi. The remaining distance took them, however, much longer than the first part had done, for Dick cut his foot badly against a stone the next night, and was so lamed that the night journeys had to be greatly shortened. Instead, therefore, of arriving in eight days, as they had hoped, it was the 3d of September—that is, thirteen days from their start—before they saw in the distance the British flag flying on the watch tower on the Ridge. They had made a long detour, and came in at the rear of the British position. On this side the country was perfectly open, and the villagers brought in eggs and other produce to the camp.

Upon the 25th of August the enemy had sent a force of six thousand men to intercept the heavy siege train which was on its way to the British camp from the Punjaub. Brigadier-General Nicholson, one of the most gallant and promising officers of the British army, was sent out against them with a force of two thousand men, of which only one-fourth were British. He met them at Nujufghur and routed them, capturing all their guns, thirteen in number. A curious instance here occurred of the manner in which the least courageous men will fight when driven to bay. The army of six thousand men had made so poor a fight that the British loss in killed and wounded amounted to only thirty-three men. After it was over it was found that a party of some twenty rebels had taken shelter in a house in a village in the British rear. The Punjaub infantry was sent to drive them out, but its commanding officer and many of its men were killed by the desperate handful of mutineers. The Sixty-first Queen's was then ordered up, but the enemy was not overpowered until another officer was dangerously wounded and many had fallen. Altogether the victory over this little band of men cost us sixteen killed and forty-six wounded — that is to say, double the loss which had been incurred in defeating six thousand of them in the open. The result of this engagement was that the road in the rear of the British camp was perfectly open, and the Warreners experienced no hindrance whatever in approaching the camp.

Dick had, after crossing the Oude frontier, left his bear's skin behind him, and adopted the simple costume of a native peasant, the blue cloth and a white turban, Ned having begged a piece of white cotton for the purpose. Traveling only at night, when the natives wrap themselves up very much, there was little fear of Dick's color being detected; and as he kept himself well in the background during the short time of an evening when Ned appeared in public, he had passed without attracting any attention whatever.

The Warreners' hearts leaped within them on beholding, on the afternoon of the 3d of September, a party of British cavalry trotting along the road, two miles from camp.

"It is the Guides," Ned said. "We know the officer, Dick. Keep on your disguise a minute longer; we shall have some fun."

Ned accordingly stood in the middle of the road and shouted his "Hoo-Hac!" at the top of his voice.

"Get out of the way, you old fool," the officer riding at its head said, as he drew up his horse on seeing the wild figure, covered with shaggy hair to the waist, twirling his formidable staff.

Ned stopped a moment. "Not a bit more of an old fool than you are yourself, Tomkins," he said.

The officer reined his horse back in his astonishment. He had spoken in English unconsciously, and being answered in the same language, and from such a figure as this, naturally petrified him.

"Who on earth are you?" he asked.

"Ned Warrener; and this is my brother Dick;" and Ned pulled off his wig.

"By Jove!" the officer said, leaping from his horse; "I am glad to see you. Where on earth have you come from? Some one who came up here from Allahabad had seen some fellow there who had come down from Cawnpore, and he reported that you had gone on into Lucknow in disguise, and that news had come you had got safely in."

"So we did," Ned said; "and as you see, we have got safely out again. We left there on the night of the 20th."

"And what was the state of things then?" Lieutenant Tomkins asked. "How long could they hold out? We know that it will be another three weeks before Havelock can hope to get there."

"Another three weeks!" Ned said. "That is terrible. They were hard pushed indeed when we left; the enemy were driving mines in all directions; the garrison were getting weaker and weaker every day, and the men fit for duty were worked to death. It seems next to impossible that they could hold out for another four or five weeks from the time we left them; but if it can be done, they will do it. Do you happen to have heard of our father?"

"The man that brought the news about you said he was all right and hearty, and the troop was doing good work in scouring the country round Cawnpore. Now will you ride back and report yourself to General Wilson?" So saying, he ordered two of the troopers to dismount and walk back to camp.

Ned had thrown down the wig when he took it off; but before mounting Dick picked it up, rolled it up into a little parcel, and said:

"It is my first effort in wig-making, and as it has saved our lives I'll keep it as long as I live, as a memento; besides, who knows? it may be useful again yet."

Quite an excitement was created in the camp behind the Ridge by the arrival of the Guide cavalry with two Englishmen in native dress, and the news that they were officers from Lucknow quickly spread.

The cavalry drew up at their own lines, and then dismounting, Lieutenant Tomkins at once sent an orderly to the general with the news, while the boys were taken inside a tent, and enjoyed the luxury of a bath, and a message was sent round to the officers of the regiment, which rapidly resulted in sufficient clothes being contributed to allow the boys to make their appearance in the garb of British officers.

A curry and a cup of coffee were ready for them by the time they were dressed, and these were enjoyed indeed after a fortnight's feeding upon uncooked grain, varied only by an occasional piece of native bread or cake. The hasty meal concluded, they accompanied Lieutenant Tomkins to the general's tent.

They were most cordially received by General Wilson; and omitting all details, they gave him an account of their having been cut off during a successful sortie from Lucknow, and having made their way to Delhi in disguise. Then they proceeded to describe fully the state of affairs at Lucknow, a recital which was at once interesting and important, inasmuch as though several native messengers had got through from Lucknow to

General Havelock, as none of them carried letters—for these would have insured their death if searched—they had brought simply messages from General Inglis asking for speedy help, and their stories as to the existent state of things in the garrison were necessarily vague and untrustworthy.

The most satisfactory portion of the boys' statement was, that although the garrison were now on short rations, and that all the comforts, and many of what are regarded as almost the necessaries of life, were exhausted, yet that there was plenty of grain in the place to enable the besieged to exist for some weeks longer.

"The great fear is that some essential part of the defense may be destroyed by mines," Ned concluded. "Against open attacks I think that the garrison is safe; but the enemy are now devoting themselves so much to driving mines that however great the care and vigilance of the garrison, they may not be always able to detect them, or, even if they do so, to run counter-mines, owing to the numerical weakness of our force."

"Thanks for your description, gentlemen; it throws a great light upon the state of affairs, and is very valuable. I will at once telegraph a resumé of it to the central government and to General Havelock. The pressing need of aid will no doubt impress the Calcutta authorities with the urgent necessity to place General Havelock in a position to make an advance at the earliest possible moment. He will, of course, communicate to Colonel Warrener the news of your safe arrival here. You have gone through a great deal indeed since you left here, while we have been doing little more than hold our own. However, the tide has turned now. We have received large reinforcements and our siege train; and I hope that in the course of a fortnight the British flag will once again wave over Delhi. In the meantime you will, at any rate for a few days, need rest. I will leave you for a day with your friends of the Guides, and will then attach you to one of the divisional staffs. I hope that you will both dine with me to-day."

That evening at dinner the Warreners met at the general's table General Nicholson, whose chivalrous bravery placed him on a par with Outram, who was called the Bayard of the British army. He was short of staff officers, and did not wish to weaken the fighting powers of the regiments of his division by drawing officers from them. He therefore asked General Wilson to attach the Warreners to his personal staff. This request was at once complied with. Their new chief assured them that for the present he had no occasion for their services, and that they were at liberty to do as they pleased until the siege operations began in earnest. The next few days were accordingly spent, as Dick said, in eating and talking.

Every regiment in camp was anxious to hear the tale of the siege of Lucknow, and of the Warreners' personal experience in entering and leaving the besieged Residency; and accordingly they dined, lunched, or breakfasted by turns with every mess in camp. They were indeed the heroes of the day; and the officers were much pleased at the simplicity with which these gallant lads told their adventures, and at the entire absence of any consciousness that they had done anything out of the way. In fact, they rather regarded the whole business as two schoolboys might regard some adventure in which they had been engaged, Dick, in particular, regarding all their adventures, with the exception only of the sufferings of the garrison of Lucknow, in the light of an "immense lark."

In the meantime, the troops were working day and night in the trenches and batteries, under the directions of the engineer officers; and every heart beat high with satisfaction that, after standing for months on the defensive, repelling continual attacks of enormously superior numbers, at last their turn had arrived, and that the day was at hand when the long-deferred vengeance was to fall upon the bloodstained city.

CHAPTER XVIII.
THE STORMING OF DELHI.

On the morning of the 8th of September the battery, eight hundred yards from the Moree gate of Delhi, opened fire, and sent the first battering shot against the town which had for three months been besieged. Hitherto, indeed, light shot, shell, and shrapnel had been fired at the gunners on the walls to keep down their fire, and the city and palace had been shelled by the mortar batteries; but not a shot had been fired with the object of injuring the walls or bringing the siege to an end.

For three months the besiegers had stood on the offensive, and the enemy not only held the city, but had erected very strong works in the open ground in front of the Lahore gate, and had free ingress and egress from the town at all points save from the gates on the north side, facing the British position on the Ridge. During these three long months, however, the respective position of the parties had changed a good deal. For the first month the mutineers were elated with their success all over that part of India. They were intoxicated with treason and murder; and their enormous numbers in comparison with those of the British troops in the country made them not only confident of success, but arrogant in the belief that success was already assured. Gradually, however, the failure of all their attempts, even with enormously superior forces, to drive the little British force from the grip which it so tenaciously held of the hill in front of Delhi, damped the ardor of their enthusiasm. Doubts as to whether, after all, their mutiny and their treachery would meet with eventual success, and fear that punishment for their atrocities would finally overtake them, began for the first time to enter their minds.

Quarrels and strife broke out between the various leaders of the movement, and pitched battles were fought between the men of different corps. Then came pestilence and swept the crowded quarters. A reign of terror prevailed throughout the city; the respectable inhabitants were robbed and murdered, shops were burst open and sacked, and riot and violence reigned supreme.

The puppet monarch, terrified at the disorder that prevailed, and finding his authority was purely nominal—the real power resting in the hands of his own sons, who had taken a leading share in getting up the revolt, and in those of the Sepoy generals—began to long for rest and quiet. The heavy shell which from time to time crashed into his palace disturbed his peace, and, through his wives, he secretly endeavored to open negotiations with the British. These overtures were, however, rejected. The king had no power whatever, and he and his household were all concerned in the massacres which had taken place in the palace itself.

It was then, by an army which, however small, was confident of victory, against one which, however large, was beginning to doubt that final success would be theirs, that the siege operations began on the morning of the 8th of September. Thenceforth the besiegers worked night and day. Every night saw fresh batteries rising at a distance of only three hundred yards from the walls; fifteen hundred camels brought earth; three thousand men filled sandbags, placed fascines, and erected traverses for the guns. The batteries rose as if by magic. The besieged viewed these preparations with a strange apathy. They might at the commencement of the work have swept the ground with such a shower of grape and musketry fire that the erection of batteries so close to their walls would have been impossible; but for the first three nights of the work they seemed to pay but little heed to what we were doing, and when at last they awoke to the nature of our proceedings, and began a furious cannonade against the British, the works had reached a height that afforded shelter to those employed upon them. Each battery, as fast as the heavy siege guns were placed in position, opened upon the walls, until forty heavy guns thundered incessantly.

The enemy now fought desperately. Our fire overpowered that of the guns at the bastions opposed to them; but from guns placed out in the open, on our flank, they played upon our batteries, while from the walls a storm of musketry fire and rockets was poured upon us. But our gunners worked away unceasingly. Piece by piece the massive walls crumbled under our fire, until, on the 13th, yawning gaps were torn through the walls of the Cashmere and Water bastions. That night four engineer officers—Medley, Long, Greathead, and Home—crept forward and examined the breaches, and returned, reporting that it would be possible to climb the heaps of rubbish and enter at the gaps in the wall. Orders were at once issued for the assault to take place at daybreak next morning.

The assaulting force was divided into four columns; the first, composed of three hundred men of the Seventy-fifth Regiment, two hundred and fifty men of the First Bengal Fusiliers, and four hundred and fifty men of the Second Punjaub Infantry—in all one thousand men, under Brigadier-

General Nicholson, were to storm the breach near the Cashmere bastion. The second column, consisting of two hundred and fifty men of the Eighth Regiment, two hundred and fifty men of the Second Bengal Fusiliers, and three hundred and fifty men of the Fourth Sikh Infantry, under Colonel Jones, Q.B., were to storm the breach in the Water bastion. The third column, consisting of two hundred men of the Fifty-second Regiment, two hundred and fifty men of the Ghoorka Kumaan battalion, and five hundred men of the First Punjaub Infantry, under Colonel Campbell, were to assault by the Cashmere gate, which was to be blown open by the engineers. The fourth column, eight hundred and sixty strong, was made up of detachments of European regiments, the Sirmoor battalion of Ghoorkas, and the Guides. It was commanded by Major Reed, and was to carry the suburb outside the walls, held by the rebels, called Kissengunge, and to enter the city by the Lahore gate. In addition to the four storming columns was the reserve, fifteen hundred strong, under Brigadier Longfield. It consisted of two hundred and fifty men of the Sixty-first Regiment, three hundred of the Beloochee battalion, four hundred and fifty of the Fourth Punjab Infantry, three hundred of the Jhind Auxiliary Force, and two hundred of the Sixtieth Rifles, who were to cover with their fire the advance of the storming column, and then to take their places with the reserves. This body was to await the success of the storming column, and then follow them into the city, and assist them as required. The cavalry and the rest of the force were to cover the flank and defend the Ridge, should the enemy attempt a counter attack.

Precisely at four o'clock on the morning of the 14th, the Sixtieth Rifles dashed forward in skirmishing order toward the walls, and the heads of the assaulting columns moved out of the batteries, which had until this moment kept up their fire without intermission.

The Warreners were on duty by the side of General Nicholson; and accustomed as they were to danger, their hearts beat fast as they awaited the signal. It was to be a tremendous enterprise—an enterprise absolutely unrivaled in history—for five thousand men to assault a city garrisoned by some thirty thousand trained troops, and a fanatical and turbulent population of five hundred thousand, all, it may be said, fighting with ropes round their necks.

As the Rifles dashed forward in front, and the head of the column advanced, a terrific fire of musketry broke out from wall and bastion, which the British, all necessity for concealment being over, answered with a tremendous cheer as they swept forward. Arrived at the ditch there was a halt. It took some time to place the ladders, and officers and men fell fast under the hail of bullets. Then as they gathered in strength in the ditch there was one wild cheer, and they dashed up the slope of rubbish and stones, and passed through the breach.

The entrance to Delhi was won.

Scrambling breathlessly up, keeping just behind their gallant general, the Warreners were among the first to win their way into the city.

An equally rapid success had attended the assault upon the breach in the Water bastion by the second column. Nor were the third far behind in the assault through the Cashmere gate, But here a deed had first to be done which should live in the memories of Englishmen so long as we exist as a nation.

As the head of the assaulting column moved forward a little party started at the double toward the Cashmere gate. The party consisted of Lieutenants Home and Salkeld, of the Royal Engineers, and Sergeants Smith and Carmichael, and Corporal Burgess, of the same corps; Bugler Hawthorne of the Fifty-second regiment; and twenty-four native sappers and miners under Havildars Mahor and Tilluh Sing. Each of the sappers carried a bag of powder, and, covered by such shelter as the fire of the Sixtieth skirmishers could give them, they advanced to the gate. This gate stands close to an angle in the wall, and from the parapets a storm of musketry fire was poured upon them. When they reached the ditch they found the drawbridge destroyed, but crossed in single file upon the beams on which it rested. The gate was of course closed, but a small postern-door beside it was open, and through this the mutineers added a heavy fire to that which streamed from above. The sappers laid their bags against the gate, and slipped down into the ditch to allow the firing party to do their work. Many had already fallen. Sergeant Carmichael was shot dead as he laid down his powder bag; Havildar Mahor was wounded. As Lieutenant Salkeld tried to fire the fuse he fell, shot through the arm and leg; while Havildar Tilluh Sing, who stood by, was killed, and Ramloll Sepoy was wounded. As he fell Lieutenant Salkeld handed the slow match to Corporal Burgess, who lit the fuse, but fell mortally wounded as he did so. Then those who survived jumped, or were helped, into the ditch, and in another moment a great explosion took place, and the Cashmere gate blew into splinters, killing some forty mutineers who were behind it. Then Lieutenant Home, seeing that the way was clear, ordered Bugler Hawthorne to sound the advance, and the assaulting column came rushing forward with a cheer, and burst through the gateway into the city.

Of the six Englishmen who took part in that glorious deed only two lived to wear the Victoria cross, the reward of valor. Two had died on the spot, and upon the other four General Wilson at once bestowed the cross; but Lieutenant Salkeld died of his wounds, and Lieutenant Home was killed within a week of the capture of the city. Thus only Sergeant Smith and Bugler Hawthorne lived to wear the honor so nobly won.

General Nicholson, who was in general command of the whole force, concentrated the two columns which had entered in a wide open space inside the Cashmere gate, and then swept the enemy off the ramparts as far as the Moree bastion, the whole of the north wall being now in the possession of our troops. Then he proceeded to push on toward the Lahore gate, where he expected to meet Major Reed with, the fourth column. This column had, however, failed even to reach the Lahore gate, the enemy's position in the suburb beyond the wall proving so strong, and being held by so numerous a force, that, after suffering very heavily, the commander had to call back his men, his retreat being covered by the cavalry.

Thus, as General Nicholson advanced through the narrow lane between the wall and the houses, the column was swept by a storm of fire from window, loophole, and housetop—a fire to which no effective reply was possible. Then, just as he was in the act of cheering on his men, the gallant soldier fell back in the arms of those behind him, mortally wounded. He was carried off by his sorrowing soldiers, and lingered until the 26th of the month, when, to the deep grief of the whole army, he expired.

It being evident that any attempt to force a path further in this direction would lead to useless slaughter, and that the place must be won step by step, by the aid of artillery, the troops were called back to the bastion.

A similar experience had befallen the third column, which had, guided by Sir T. Metcalfe, who knew the city intimately, endeavored to make a circuit so as to reach and carry the Jumma Musjid, the great mosque which dominated the city. So desperate was the resistance experienced that this column had also to fall back to the ramparts. The reserve column had followed the third in at the Cashmere gate, and had, after some fighting, possessed itself of some strong buildings in that neighborhood, most important of which was a large and commanding house, the residence of Achmed Ali Khan; and when the third column fell back Skinner's house, the church, the magazine, and the main-guard were held, and guns were planted to command the streets leading thereto. One cause of the slight advance made that day was, that the enemy, knowing the weakness of the British soldier, had stored immense quantities of champagne and other wines, beer, and spirits in the streets next to the ramparts, and the troops— British, Sikhs, Beloochees, and Ghoorkas alike—parched with thirst, and excited by the sight of these long untasted luxuries, fell into the snare, and drank so deeply that the lighting power of the force was for awhile very seriously impaired.

On the 15th the stubborn fighting recommenced. From house to house our troops fought their way; frequently, when the street was so swept by fire that it was impossible to progress there, making their way by breaking down the party walls, and so working from one house into another. During this day guns and mortars were brought into the city from our batteries, and placed so as to shell the palace and the great building called the Selimgur.

The next morning the Sixty-first Regiment and the Fourth Punjaub Rifles made a rush at the great magazine, and the rebels were so stricken by their rapidity and dash that they threw down their portfires and fled, without even once discharging the cannon, which, crammed to the muzzle with grape, commanded every approach. Here one hundred and twenty-five cannon and an enormous supply of ammunition fell into our hands, and a great many of the guns were at once turned against their late owners.

So day by day the fight went on. At night the sky was red with the flames of burning houses, by day a pall of smoke hung over the city. From either side cannon and mortars played unceasingly, while the rattle of musketry, the crash of falling houses, the shrieks of women, the screams of children, and the shouting of men mingled in a chaos of sounds. To the credit of the British soldier be it said, that infuriated as they were by the thirst for vengeance, the thought of the murdered women, and the heat of battle, not a single case occurred, so far as is known, of a woman being ill-treated, insulted, or fired upon—although the women had been present in the massacres, and had constantly accompanied and cheered on the sorties of the mutineers. To the Sepoys met with in Delhi no mercy was shown; every man taken was at once bayoneted, and the same fate befell all townsmen found fighting against us. The rest of the men, as well as the women and children, were, after the fighting was over, permitted to leave the city unmolested, although large numbers of them had taken share in the sack of the white inhabitants' houses, and the murder of every Christian, British or native, in the town. It would, however, have been impossible to separate the innocent from the guilty; consequently all were allowed to go free.

From the time that the British troops burst through the breaches, an exodus had begun from the gates of the town on the other side, and across the bridge over the Jumna. Our heavy guns could have destroyed this bridge, and our cavalry might have swept round the city and cut off the retreat on the other side; but the proverb that it is good to build a bridge for a flying foe was eminently applicable here. Had the enemy felt their retreat cut off—

had they known that certain death awaited them unless they could drive us out of the city, the defense would have been so desperate that it would have been absolutely impossible for the British forces to have accomplished it. The defense of some of the Spanish towns in the Peninsular war by the inhabitants, lighting from house to house against French armies, showed what could be effected by desperate men lighting in narrow streets; and the loss inflicted on our troops at Nujufghur by twenty Sepoys was another evidence of the inexpediency of driving the enemy to despair. As it was, the rebels after the first day fought feebly, and were far from making the most of the narrow streets and strongly-built houses. No one liked to be the first to retreat, but all were resolved to make off at the earliest opportunity. Men grew distrustful of each other, and day by day the desertions increased, the resistance diminished, and the districts held by the rebels grew smaller and smaller. It is true that by thus allowing tens of thousands of rebels to escape we allowed them to continue the war in the open country, but here, as it afterward proved, they were contemptible foes, and their defeat did not cost a tithe of the loss which would have resulted in their extermination within the walls of Delhi.

Up to the 20th the palace still held out. This was a fortress in itself, mounting many cannon on its walls, and surrounded by an open park-like space. On that morning the engineers began to run a trench, to enable a battery to be erected to play upon the Lahore gate of the palace. Before, however, they had been long at work, a party of men of the Sixty-first, with some Sikhs and Ghoorkas, ran boldly forward, and taking shelter under a low wall close to the gate, opened fire at the embrasures and loopholes. The answering fire was so weak that Colonel Jones, who was in command of the troops in this quarter—convinced that the report that the king with his wives and family, and the greater part of the garrison of the palace, had already left was true—determined upon blowing in the gate at once. Lieutenant Home was appointed to lead the party told off for the duty, which was happily effected without loss. The British rushed in, and found three guns loaded to the muzzle placed in the gateway, but fortunately the Sepoys who should have fired them had fled.

The news that the palace was taken spread rapidly, and there was a rush to share in the spoil. But few of the enemy were found inside; these were at once bayoneted, and then a general scramble ensued. The order had been given that no private plundering should be allowed, but that everything taken should be collected, and sold for the general benefit of the troops. Orders like this are, however, never observed, at any rate with portable articles; and Sikhs, Ghoorkas, and British alike, loaded themselves with spoil. Cashmere shawls worth a hundred pounds were sold for five shillings, silk dresses might be had for nothing, and jewelry went for less than the value of the setting.

The same day the headquarters of the army were removed to the palace of Delhi. As the Union Jack of England ran up the flagstaff on the palace so lately occupied by the man crowned by the rebels Emperor of India, the seat and headquarters of the revolt which had deluged the land with blood, and caused the rule of England to totter, a royal salute was fired by the British guns, and tremendous cheers arose from the troops in all parts of the city.

The raising of that flag, the booming of those guns, were the signal of the deathblow of the Indian mutiny. Over one hundred thousand rebels were still in arms against the British government, but the heart of the insurrection was gone. It was no longer a war, it was a rebellion. There was no longer a head, a center, or a common aim. Each body of mutineers fought for themselves—for life rather than for victory. The final issue of the struggle was now certain; and all the native princes who had hitherto held aloof, watching the issue of the fight at Delhi, and remaining neutral until it was decided whether the Sepoys could pluck up the British flag from the Ridge, or the British tear down the emblem of rebellion from above the palace of Delhi, hesitated no longer, but hastened to give in their allegiance to the victorious power.

Nothing has been said as to the part the Warreners bore in that fierce six days' fighting. They did their duty, as did every other man in the British army, but they had no opportunity for specially distinguishing themselves. As staff officers, they had often to carry messages to troops engaged in stubborn fight, and in doing so to dash across open spaces, and run the gantlet of a score of musket balls; both, however, escaped without a scratch. They had not been present on the occasion of the taking of the palace, for they had been at early morning on the point of going in to the headquarters for orders, when Captain Hodgson came out. They had dined with him on the day previous to the assault, and he came up them now.

"Now," he said, "I am just going on an expedition after your own hearts, lads. We have news that the king and queen have stolen away, and have gone to the palace at the Kotub Minar. I am going with my troops to bring them in. Would you like to go?"

"Oh, yes, of all things," the Warreners exclaimed. "But we have no horses."

"Oh, I can mount you," he said. "Several of my fellows slipped into the town in hopes of getting some loot, and three or four were shot; so if the general will give you leave, I will take you."

The Warreners at once went in to Brigadier-General Jones, to whom they had been attached since the fall of General Nicholson. As they were supernumeraries on his staff, the general at once gave them leave, and in high delight they followed their friend—a most gallant and fearless officer, who had greatly distinguished himself by the dashing exploits which he had executed with his troop of irregular horse—to his camp outside the walls. Half an hour later they were riding at a trot toward the spot where the ex-emperor had taken refuge. Their route lay across ground hitherto in possession of the enemy, and they rode past thousands of armed budmashes, or blackguards, of Delhi, who had left the city, and were making their way to join some of the rebel leaders in the field. These scowled and muttered curses as the little troop rode by; but the blow which had just been dealt was so crushing, the dread inspired by British valor so complete, that although apparently numerous enough to have destroyed the little band without difficulty, not a man dared raise his voice or lift a weapon.

"What are all these wonderful ruins?" Dick asked Captain Hodgson, by whose side they were riding.

"This is where old Delhi stood. These great buildings are tombs of kings and other great men; the smaller houses have gone to dust centuries ago, but these massive buildings will remain for as many centuries more. Wait till you see Kotub Minar; in my opinion there is nothing in India or in the world to equal it."

Another half-hour's riding brought them into sight of a magnificent shaft of masonry, rising far above the plain.

"That is the Minar," Captain Hodgson said; "it is the same word as minaret. Is it not magnificent?"

The Kotub Minar is an immense shaft tapering gradually toward the top. It is built in stages, with a gallery round each. Each stage is different. In one it is fluted with round columns like a huge mass of basalt. In another the columns are angular; and in the next, round and angular alternately. The highest stage is plain. The height is very great, and the solidity of execution and the strength of the edifice are as striking as its height and beauty.

They were not, however, to go so far as the Kotub, for, questioning some peasants, they learned that the king had halted at a building called Durzah-Nizam-oo-deen. The gates were shut, and it was certain that the king would have a large body of retainers with him. Matchlock men showed at the windows and on the roof, and things looked awkward for the little troop of cavalry. Captain Hodgson rode forward, however, without hesitation, and struck on the great gate. A window by the side of the gate opened, and he was asked what was wanted.

"I am come to take, and to carry into Delhi, the ex-king and his family. It is better to submit quietly, for if I have to force my way in, every soul in the place will be put to the sword."

In two minutes the postern opened, and a closely veiled figure made her appearance.

"I am the Begum," she said. And Captain Hodgson bent in acknowledgment that the favorite wife of the man who was yesterday regarded as the emperor of India, stood before him.

"The king will surrender," she said, "if you will promise that his life shall be spared; if not, he will defend himself to the last, and will die by his own hand."

"Defense would be useless," Captain Hodgson said. "The force I have would suffice amply to carry the place; and if it did not, in three hours any reinforcements I could ask for would be here. I have no authority to give such a promise."

"If you give the promise it will be kept," the Begum said. "If you refuse, the king will shoot himself when the first soldier passes the gate."

Captain Hodgson hesitated. It was true that he had no authority to make such a promise; but he felt that government would far rather have the king a captive in their hands than that he should excite a feeling of regret and admiration among the people by dying by his own hand in preference to falling into those of the British.

"I agree," he said after a pause. "I promise that the king's life shall be spared."

In a minute the gate was thrown back, and an aged man came out, followed by several women. The age of the king was nearly eighty-five, and he was from first to last a mere puppet in the hands of others. In no case would he have been executed by the government, since the old man was clearly beyond any active participation in what had taken place.

The litter in which the king and his wives had been conveyed from Delhi was again brought into requisition, and the party were soon *en route* for Delhi. The royal palace had been but a few hours in our hands before the ex-king was brought in, a prisoner where he had so lately reigned. He was lodged with his women in a small building in the palace, under a strong guard, until it should be decided what to do with him.

"I shall go out to-morrow to try and catch some of the sons of the old man. They are the real culprits in the matter. If you like to go out again, and can get off duty, well and good," Captain Hodgson said.

The boys, who were very pleased at having been present at so historical an event as the capture of the king of Delhi, warmly thanked Captain Hodgson; and, having again obtained leave, started with him on the following morning at daybreak. Some of the princes a spy had reported to Captain Hodgson as being at Humayoon's tomb, a large building near the Kotub Minar. They rode in the same direction that they had gone out on the preceding day, but proceeded somewhat further.

"That is Humayoon's tomb," Captain Hodgson said, pointing to a large square building with a domed roof and four lofty minarets, standing half a mile off the road.

The troop rode up at a gallop, and, surrounding the building, dismounted. Soldiers were placed at all the various doors of the building, with orders to shoot down any one who might come out, and Captain Hodgson sent a loyal moulvie, named Rujol Ali, who had accompanied him, into the building, to order the princes there to come out. Then arose within the building a great tumult of voices, as the question whether they should or should not surrender was argued. Several times the moulvie returned, to ask if any conditions would be given; but Hodgson said sternly that no conditions whatever would be made with them.

At last, after two hours' delay, two of the sons and a grandson of the king, all of whom had been leaders in the mutiny, and authors of massacres and atrocities, came out and surrendered. They were immediately placed in a carriage which had been brought for the purpose, a guard was placed over them, and ordered to proceed slowly toward the city.

Then Hodgson, accompanied by the Warreners, entered the inclosure which surrounded the tomb. Here from five to six thousand of the refuse of the city, many of them armed, were assembled. A yell of hate arose as the little band entered; guns were shaken defiantly; sabers waved in the air. The odds were tremendous, and the Warreners felt that nothing remained but to sell their lives dearly.

"Lay down your arms!" Captain Hodgson shouted in a stentorian voice.

Eight or ten shots were fired from the crowd, and the bullets whistled over the heads of the horsemen, but fortunately none were hit.

"Lay down your arms!" he shouted again. "Men, unsling your carbines. Level."

As the carbines were leveled, the bravery of the mob evaporated at once. Those nearest threw down their arms, and as with leveled guns the horsemen rode through the crowd, arms were everywhere thrown down, and resistance was at an end. Over a thousand guns, five hundred swords, and quantities of daggers and knives were collected; and a number of elephants, camels, and horses were captured.

Ordering the native lieutenant to remain with the troop in charge of these things until some carts could be sent out for the arms, Captain Hodgson, accompanied by the boys, rode off after the carriage, which had started two hours before.

They rode rapidly until they neared Delhi, when they saw the carriage, surrounded by a great mob. Captain Hodgson set spurs to his horse and galloped forward at full speed, followed by the boys. They burst through the crowd, who were a large body of ruffians who had just left the city, where the fighting was even now not over, and who were all armed. A defiant cry broke from them as the three horsemen rode up to the carriage, from which with the greatest difficulty the guard had so far kept the crowd.

There was not a moment for hesitation. Captain Hodgson raised a hand, and a momentary silence reigned.

"These men in the carriage," said he in loud tones, "have not only rebelled against the government, but have ordered and witnessed the massacre and shameful treatment of women and children. Thus, therefore, the government punishes such traitors and murderers!"

Then drawing his revolver, before the crowd could move or lift a hand he shot the three prisoners through the head. The crowd, awed and astonished, fell back, and the carriage with the dead bodies passed into the city.

CHAPTER XIX.
A RIOT AT CAWNPORE.

While the guns of Delhi were saluting the raising of the British flag over the royal palace, General Havelock and his force were fighting their way up to Lucknow. On the 19th of September he crossed the Ganges, brushed aside the enemy's opposition, and, after three days' march in a tremendous rain, found them in force at the Alumbagh. After a short, sharp fight they were defeated, and the Alumbagh fell into our hands. All the stores and baggage were left here, with a force strong enough to hold it against all attacks; and after a day to rest his troops, General Havelock advanced on the 22d, defeated the enemy outside Lucknow, and then, as the direct route was known to be impassable, he followed the canal as far as the Kaiserbagh, and there turning off, fought his way through the streets to the Residency, where he arrived only just in time, for the enemy had driven two mines right under the defenses, and these would, had the reinforcements arrived but one day later, have been exploded, and the fate of the garrison of Cawnpore might have befallen the defenders of Lucknow.

The desperate street fighting had, however, terribly weakened the little force which had performed the feat. Out of fifteen hundred men who had entered the city, a third were killed or wounded, among the former being the gallant Brigadier-General Neil.

With so weak a force it was evident that it would be hopeless to endeavor to carry off the sick, the wounded, the women, and children through the army of rebels that surrounded them, and it was therefore determined to continue to hold the Residency until further aid arrived. The siege therefore recommenced, but under different conditions, for the increased force enabled the British to hold a larger area; and although the discomforts and privations were as great as before—for the reinforcements had brought no food in with them—the danger of the place being carried by assault was now entirely at an end.

One noble action connected with the relief of Lucknow will never be forgotten. Before General Havelock started up from Cawnpore, General Sir James Outram, his senior officer, arrived, with authority to take the command. Upon his arrival, however, he issued a general order, to say that to General Havelock, who had done such great deeds to relieve Lucknow, should be the honor of the crowning success; and that he therefore waived his seniority, and would fight under General Havelock as a volunteer until Lucknow was relieved. A more generous act of self-negation than this was never accomplished. To the man who relieved Lucknow would fall honor, fame, the gratitude of the English people, and all this General Outram of his own accord resigned. He was worthy indeed of the name men gave him— the "Bayard of India."

The news that Lucknow was relieved caused almost as much delight to the troops at Delhi as their own successes had given them, for the anxiety as to the safety of the garrison was intense. To the Warreners the news gave an intense pleasure, for the thought of the friends they had left behind in that terrible strait had been ever present to their mind. The faces of the suffering women, the tender girls, the delicate children, had haunted them night and day; and their joy at the thought that these were rescued from the awful fate impending over them knew no bounds.

It was not at Delhi, however, that the Warreners heard the news; for on the 23d, only three days after the occupation of the city, they left with the flying column of Colonel Greathead, which was ordered to march down to Agra, clearing away the bands of mutineers which infested the intervening country, and then to march to Cawnpore, to be in readiness to advance on Lucknow. The boys had no difficulty in obtaining leave to accompany this column, as Ned would naturally on the first opportunity rejoin his regiment, which was at Cawnpore, while Dick was longing to form one of the naval brigade, which, under Captain Peel, was advancing up the country.

The rebels were found in force at Allyghur, and were defeated without difficulty; and after several minor skirmishes the force marched hastily down to Agra, which was threatened by a large body of the enemy. Without a halt they marched thirty miles to Agra, and encamped in the open space outside the fort.

Just as they were cooking their meals a battery of artillery opened upon them, an infantry fire broke out from the surrounding houses, and a large body of cavalry dashed in among them.

For a moment all was confusion; but the troops were all inured to war; with wonderful rapidity they rallied and attacked the enemy, who were over five thousand strong, and finally defeated them with great slaughter, and captured fourteen guns. Agra saved, the column started two days later for Cawnpore; upon the way it defeated bodies of rebels, and punished some zemindars who had taken part against us, and arrived at Cawnpore on the 26th of October.

At Majupoorie, halfway up from Agra, the force had been joined by a brigade under Colonel Hope Grant, who, as senior officer, took the command of the column. They marched into Cawnpore three thousand five hundred strong, all troops who had gone through the siege of Delhi; and Ned at once joined his regiment, where he was warmly received.

On the following day the Ninety-third Highlanders and a part of the naval brigade, two hundred strong, arrived; and Dick's delight as the column marched in was unbounded. He reported himself for duty at once, and, as among the officers were some of his own shipmates, he was at once at home.

There was little sleep in the tents of the junior officers of the brigade that night. Dick's name had been twice mentioned in dispatches, and all sorts of rumors as to his doings had reached his comrades. The moment, therefore, that dinner was over, Dick was taken to a tent, placed on a very high box on a table, supplied with grog, and ordered to spin his yarn, which, although modestly told, elicited warm applause from his hearers.

On the 30th Colonel Grant's column moved forward, and arrived after three days' march within six miles of the Alumbagh. They had with them a great convoy of siege material and provisions, and these were next day escorted safely into the Alumbagh, where the little garrison had held their own, though frequently attacked, for six weeks. The Sixty-fourth Regiment had already done so much fighting that it was not to form part of the advance. The naval brigade was increased on the 1st of November by the arrival of Captain Peel himself, with two hundred more sailors and four hundred troops. They had had a heavy fight on the way up, and had protected the convoy and siege guns of which they were in charge, and had defeated the enemy, four thousand strong, and captured all his guns, but with a loss to themselves of nearly one hundred men. Soon after the commencement of the engagement, Colonel Powell, who was in command of the column, was killed; and Captain Peel then took command of the force, and won the victory.

The astonishment of the people of Cawnpore at the appearance of the brawny tars was unbounded. The sailors went about the streets in knots of two or three, staring at the contents of the shops, and as full of fun and good humor as so many schoolboys. Greatly delighted were they when the natives gave them the least chance of falling foul of them—for they knew that the people of the town had joined the mutineers—and were only too glad of an excuse to pitch into them. They all carried cutlasses, but these they disdained to use, trusting, and with reason, to their fists, which are to the natives of India a more terrible, because a more mysterious weapon than the sword. A sword they understand; but a quick hit, flush from the shoulder, which knocks them off their feet as if struck by lightning, is to them utterly incomprehensible, and therefore very terrible.

One day the Warreners were strolling together through the town, and turned off from the more frequented streets, with a view of seeing what the lower-class quarters were like. They had gone some distance, when Ned said:

"I think we had better turn, Dick. These scowling scoundrels would be only too glad to put a knife into us, and we might be buried away under ground in one of these dens, and no one be ever any the wiser for it. I have no doubt when we have finished with the fellows, and get a little time to look round, there will be a clear sweep made of all these slums."

The lads turned to go back, when Dick said, "Listen!"

They paused, and could hear a confused sound of shouting, and a noise as of a tumult. They listened attentively.

"Ned," Dick exclaimed, "I am sure some of those shouts are English. Some of our fellows have got into a row; come on!"

So saying, he dashed off up the narrow street, accompanied by his brother. Down two more lanes, and then, in an open space where five or six lanes met, they saw a crowd. In the midst of it they could see sabers flashing in the air, while British shouts mingled with the yells of the natives.

"This is a serious business," Ned said, as they ran; "we are in the worst part of Cawnpore."

Three or four natives, as they approached the end of the lane, stepped forward to prevent their passage; but the lads threw them aside with the impetus of their rush, and then, shoulder to shoulder, charged the crowd.

Expecting no such assault, the natives fell aside from the shock, and in a few seconds the boys stood by their countrymen. There were six in all—sailors, as the boys had expected. The fight had evidently been a sharp one. Four or five natives lay upon the ground, and two of the sailors were bleeding from sword-cuts. The tars gave a cheer at the sight of this reinforcement, especially as one of the newcomers was a naval officer—for Dick had bought the uniform of a naval officer killed in the fight of the 1st.

The infuriated crowd drew back for a moment; but seeing that the reinforcement consisted only of two lads, again attacked fiercely. The boys had drawn their swords, and for a minute the little party fought back to back. It was evident, however, that this could not last, for every moment added to the number of their foes, the budmashes flocking down from every quarter.

"Now, lads," Ned shouted, "get yourselves ready, and when I say the word make a dash all together for that house at the left corner. The door is open. Once in there, we can hold it till help comes. Press them a bit first, so as to scatter them a little, and then for a rush. Are you all ready? Now!"

With a cheer the sailors hurled themselves upon the crowd in a body. The surprise, added to the weight and force of the charge, was irresistible; the natives were sent flying like ninepins, and before the enemy quite understood what had happened, the whole party were safe in the house, and the door slammed-to and bolted.

"See if there are any windows they can get in at."

The men ran into the two rooms of which, on the ground floor, the house consisted; but the windows in these, as is often the case in Indian towns, were strongly barred. There was a furious beating at the door.

"It will give in a minute," Dick said. "Upstairs, lads; we can hold them against any number."

"It's lucky they did not use their pistols," Ned said, as they gathered in the upper room; "we should have been polished off in no time had they done so."

"I expect they made sure of doing for us with their swords and knives," Dick replied, "and did not like to risk calling attention by the sound of pistol-shots. Now, lads, how did you get into this row?"

"Well, your honor," said one of the tars, "we were just cruising about as it might be, when we got down these here lanes, and lost our bearings altogether. Well, we saw we had fallen among land pirates, for the chaps kept closing in upon us as if they wanted to board, and fingering those long knives of theirs. Then one of them he gives a push to Bill Jones, and Bill gives him a broadside between the eyes, and floors him. Then they all begins to yell, like a pack o' they jackals we heard coming up country. Then they drew their knives, and Bill got a slash on his cheek. So we, seeing as how it were a regular case of an engagement all along the line, drew our cutlasses and joins action. There were too many of them, though, and we were nigh carried by the pirates, when you bore up alongside."

At this moment a crash was heard below; the door had yielded, and the crowd rushed into the lower part of the house. When it was found to be empty there was a little delay. No one cared to be the first to mount the stairs, and encounter the determined band above. Dick stepped forward to glance at the state of things below, when half a dozen pistol-shots were fired. One inflicted a nasty cut on his cheek, and another struck him on the hand.

"Are you hurt, Dick?" Ned said, as his brother leaped back.

"No, nothing to speak of; but it was a close shave. Perkins, pick up my sword, will you? I didn't think of their firing."

"Being indoors, they are not afraid of the pistols being heard any distance," Ned said. "Keep a sharp lookout, lads, in case they make a rush upstairs, while I tie up my brother's hand and face."

"They are coming, sir," the sailors cried, as the house shook with the rush of a body of men up the stairs.

"Stand well back, lads, and cut them down as they enter the door."

Pushed from behind, five or six of the enemy burst simultaneously into the room; but ere they could fire a pistol, or even put themselves into an attitude of defense, they were cut down or run through the body. Then a tremendous crash and a wild cry was heard.

"Hurrah!" Dick shouted, "the staircase has given way."

Many groans and shrieks were heard below; then there was a sound of persons being carried out, and for awhile, quiet below, while outside the hubbub became greater.

"What is going on outside?" Ned said, and Dick and he peered through the closed jalousies into the street.

A number of budmashes were bringing bundles of bamboos from a basket-maker's shop opposite; some of the crowd were opposing them.

"They are going to fire the house," Dick exclaimed. "The people opposing are the neighbors, no doubt. They'll do it, though," he added, as the fiercer spirits drove the others back. "What's best to be done, Ned?"

Ned looked round, and then up.

"Let us cut through the bamboo ceiling, Dick; there must be a space between that and the roof. The wall won't be thick between that and the next house, and we can work our way from house to house; and if the flames gain—for they are sure to spread—we can but push off the tiles and take to the roofs, and run the gantlet of their pistols and muskets. Their blood's up now, and they will shoot, to a certainty. Do you think that the best plan?"

"That's it. Now, lads, two of you stand close together; now, Perkins, you jump on their shoulders and cut a hole through the bamboos with your cutlass. Quick, lads, there's no time to lose;" for they could hear the tramping of feet below, and the sound as the bundles of bamboo were thrown down.

"Now, lads," Dick went on—for as a naval officer he was naturally in command of the men—"take two or three of those rugs on that couch there, and knot them together. Shut the door, to keep the smoke out. There, they've lit it!"—as a shout of pleasure rose from below.

The bamboos were tough, and Perkins could not use his strength to advantage. Smoke curled up through the crevices of the floor, and all watched anxiously the progress made.

"That's big enough," Dick cried at last; "we have not a moment to lose, the flames are making through the floor. Now, Perkins, climb through the hole; now, lads, follow in turn."

Four of the sailors were rapidly through the hole.

"Now, lads, one of you two; don't waste time. Now, Ned, catch hold of this man's legs and give him a hoist; that's right. Now drop that rope, lad. Now, Ned, I'm in command; go on. Now, lads, catch this bundle of rugs; that's right. Give me one end. There we are. Now spread one of those rugs over the hole, to keep the smoke out. Now, lads, how is the wall?"

"Quite soft, your honor; we'll be through in a minute."

In accordance with orders, those first up had begun at once with their cutlasses to pick a hole through the mud wall which formed the partition between the houses. Although thicker below, the divisions between what may be called the lofts of the houses were made but of a single brick of unbaked clay or mud, and as Dick clambered up through the hole, the sailors had already made an opening quite large enough to get through. All crept through it, and again Dick hung a rug over the hole to keep out the smoke.

"Now, lads, attack the next wall again; but don't make more noise about it than you can help. The people below will be removing what things they can, and making a row; still, they might hear us; and it is as well they should think us burned in the house where we were. But you must look sharp, lads, for the fire spreads through these dried-up houses as if they were built of straw."

The sailors labored hard, and they worked their way from house to house; but the flames followed as fast; and at last, almost choked by smoke and dust, Dick said:

"Quick, my men, knock off some tiles, and get on the roof, or we shall be burned like rats in a trap. This side, the furthest from the street."

The tiles gave way readily; and each man thrust his head out through the hole he had made, for a breath of fresh air. In a minute all were on the roof.

"Crouch down, lads; keep on this side of the roof; people are not likely to be looking out for us this side, they will be too busy moving their furniture. Move on, boys; the fire is spreading now pretty nearly as fast as we can scramble along."

It was already a great fire; down both the lanes at whose junction the house first fired stood, the flames had spread rapidly, and leaping across the narrow streets had seized the opposite houses. Already fifty or sixty houses were in a blaze, although it was not five minutes from the beginning of the fire.

"There is a cross lane about ten houses ahead, Dick," Ned said.

"We will stick on the last house as long as we can, Ned, and then slide down by the rope on to that outhouse. They are too busy now with their own affairs to think about us; besides, they suppose we are dead long ago, and the fellows who are at the head of it will have made off to look after their own houses, for the wind is blowing fresh, and there is no saying how far the fire may spread. Besides, we shall have our fellows up in a few minutes. Directly the fire is seen, they are sure to be sent down to preserve order."

They were soon gathered on the roof of the last house in the lane, and three minutes later were driven from it by the flames. One by one they scrambled down by the aid of the rope on to the outhouse, and thence to the ground. Then they passed through the house into the lane beyond. Looking up the lane, it was an arch of fire; the flames were rushing from every window and towering up above every roof, almost meeting over the lane. Upon the other hand, all was wild confusion and terror; men were throwing out of upper windows bedding and articles of furniture; women laden with household goods, and with children in their arms and others hanging to their clothes, were making their way through the crowd; bedridden people were being brought out; and the screams, shrieks, and shouts mingled with the roaring of flames and the crashes of falling roofs. As in great floods in India, the tiger and the leopard, the cobra and the deer, may all be seen huddled together on patches of rising ground, their mutual enmity forgotten in the common danger, so no one paid the slightest attention to the body of Englishmen who so suddenly joined the crowd.

"Sheathe your cutlasses, my lads," Dick said. "There's no more fighting to be done. Lend a hand to help these poor wretches. There, two of you take up that poor old creature; they have carried her out, and then left her; take her on till you find some open space to set her down in. Now, Ned, you take a couple of men and work one side of the lane, I will take the opposite side with the others. Let us go into every room and see that no sick people or children are left behind. There, the flames have passed the cross lane already; the corner house is on fire."

For quarter of an hour the tars labored assiduously; and many a bedridden old woman, or a forgotten baby, did they bring out. Fortunately at the end of the lane was an open space of some extent, and here piles of household goods and helpless people were gathered.

At the end of a quarter of an hour they heard a deep tramp, and the naval brigade, led by Captain Peel, filed up through the lane. The sailors burst into a cheer as they saw their friends arrive, and these responded upon seeing some of their comrades at work carrying the sick and aged. Dick at once made his way to Captain Peel, and reported briefly that the fire was in the first place lighted with the purpose of burning him and his party; but that they had escaped, and had since been at work helping the inhabitants.

"Very well," Captain Peel said. "You can give details afterward; at present we have got to try and stop the flames. It seems a large block of fire."

"It is, sir. It extends across several lanes; there must be a couple of hundred houses in flames, and I fear, from what we have seen in the lane we have been working in, a considerable loss of life."

"Mr. Percival," Captain Peel said to one of his officers, "take your company and knock down or blow up all the houses on this side of that lane there. Mr. Wilkinson, you take number two company, and do the same with the lane to the right. The rest follow me. March!"

In five minutes all the tars and the Highlanders—who arrived on the ground immediately after the sailors—were at work pulling down houses, so as to arrest the progress of the flames by isolating the burning block. Upon three sides they succeeded, but upon the other the fire, driven by the wind, defied all their efforts, and swept forward for half a mile, until it burned itself out when it had reached the open country. In its course it had swept away a great part of the worst and most crowded quarters of Cawnpore.

All through the evening and night the troops and sailors toiled; and morning had broken before all danger of any further extension was over; the men were then ordered home, a fresh body of troops coming up to preserve order, and prevent the robbery, by the lawless part of the population, of the goods which had been rescued from the flames. Then, after a ration of grog had been first served out to each man, and breakfast hastily cooked and eaten, all sought their tents, exhausted after their labors.

It was not until evening that signs of life were visible in the camp. Then men began to move about; and an orderly presently came across to request the Warreners to go to Captain Peel's quarters to report the circumstances through which the fire arose.

The lads related the history of the affair from the time when they had come upon the scene, and Captain Peel expressed himself in terms of warm laudation of their gallantry, quickness, and presence of mind. Then the sailors were called up, and their story, although longer and more diffuse than that told by the Warreners, was yet substantially the same, and Captain Peel told the men that they ought not to have wandered in that way into the slums of Cawnpore, but that beyond that indiscretion they had acted, as reported by Mr. Warrener, with great courage, coolness, and good discipline. Then the Warreners went back to their tent, and had to go through their yarn again with great minuteness and detail.

"I do think," said Rivers, a midshipman of some two years older standing than Dick, "that you are the luckiest youngster in the service. It is not one fellow in a hundred thousand who has such chances."

"That is so, Rivers," one of the lieutenants answered; "but it is not one in a hundred thousand who, having gone through such adventures, would have been alive to tell them at the end. The getting into these scrapes may be luck, but the getting out of them demands courage, coolness, and quickness of invention, such as not one lad in a thousand possesses. Now, Rivers, tell me honestly whether you think that, had you been cut off as he was in that sortie at Lucknow, you would ever have thought of robbing that old fakir of his wig?"

"No," Rivers said; "I am quite sure it would never have occurred to me. Yes, as you say, sir, Dick Warrener has no end of luck, but he certainly deserves and makes the best of it."

CHAPTER XX.
THE RELIEF OF LUCKNOW.

On the 6th of November Captain Peel, with five hundred of his gallant bluejackets, marched from Cawnpore, taking with them the heavy siege guns. Three days later they joined General Grant's column, which was encamped at a short distance from the Alumbagh, and in communication with the force holding that position. On the 9th Sir Colin Campbell, who had come out from England with all speed to assume the chief command in India, arrived in camp, and his coming was hailed with delight by the troops, who felt that the hour was now at hand when the noble garrison of Lucknow were to be rescued.

The total force collected for the relief were: Her Majesty's Eighth, Fifty-third, Seventy-fifth, and Ninety-third regiments of infantry; two regiments of Punjaub infantry; and a small party of native sappers and miners. The cavalry consisted of the Ninth Lancers, and detachments of Sikh cavalry and Hodgson's Horse. The artillery comprised Peel's naval brigade, with eight heavy guns, ten guns of the Royal Horse Artillery, six light field guns, and a heavy battery of the Royal Artillery. A total of about twenty-seven hundred infantry and artillery, and nine hundred cavalry.

On the morning of the 10th Mr. Kavanagh, a civilian, came into camp. He had, disguised as a native, started the evening before from the Residency with a native guide, named Kunoujee Lal, had swum the Goomtee, recrossed by the bridge into the city, passed through the streets, and finally made his way in safety. He was perfectly acquainted with the city, and brought plans from Sir James Outram for the guidance of the commander-in-chief in his advance.

After an examination of the plans Sir Colin Campbell determined that, instead of forcing his way through the narrow streets as General Havelock had done, he would move partly round the town, and attack by the eastern side, where there was much open ground, sprinkled with palaces and mosques and other large buildings. These could be attacked and taken one by one, by a series of separate sieges, and thus the Residency could be approached with far less loss than must have taken place in an attempt to force a way through the crowded city.

On the 15th the troops marched to the Alumbagh, defeating a small rebel force which attempted to stop their way.

At the Alumbagh Dick Warrener—for Ned was with his regiment, which, to his great disgust, had remained at Cawnpore—had the joy of meeting his father again, as Warrener's Horse had not shared in Havelock's advance to the Residency, but had remained as part of the garrison of the Alumbagh. It is needless to tell of the delight of that meeting after all that the lads had gone through since they parted from their father, nearly four months before, at Cawnpore. Colonel Warrener had heard of the safe arrival of his sons at Delhi before he marched up from Cawnpore, but since then no word had reached him. Captains Dunlop and Manners were also delighted to meet him again; and the whole of the troop vied with each other in the heartiness of the welcome accorded to him. Disease and death had sadly lessened the ranks; and of the one hundred men who had volunteered at Meerut to form a body of horse, not more than fifty now remained in the ranks. It was very late at night—or rather, early in the morning—before the party assembled in Colonel Warrener's tent separated, to seek a few hours' sleep before the *réveillé* sounded for the troops to rise and prepare for the advance.

Soon after daybreak the column were under arms. The Seventy-fifth Regiment, to its intense disappointment, was ordered to stay and guard the Alumbagh, with its immense accumulation of stores and munitions; and the rest of the troops, turning off from the direct road and following the line the boys had traversed when they made their way into the Residency, marched for the Dil Koosha, a hunting-palace of the late king of Oude.

The enemy, who had anticipated an advance by the direct line taken by Havelock, and who had made immense preparations for defense in that quarter, were taken aback by the movement to the right, and no opposition was experienced until the column approached the beautiful park, upon an elevated spot in which the Dil Koosha stood.

Then a brisk musketry fire was opened upon them. The head of the column was extended in skirmishing order, reinforcements were sent up, and, firing heavily as they advanced, the British drove the enemy before them, and two hours after the first shot was fired were in possession of the palace. The enemy fled down the slope toward the city; but the troops pressed forward, and, with but slight loss, carried the strong position of the Martinière College, and drove the enemy across the canal. By this time the enemy's troops from the other side of the city were flocking up, and prepared to recross the canal and give battle; but some of the heavy guns were brought up to the side of the canal, and the rebels made no further attempt to take the offensive.

The result of the day's fighting more than answered the commander-in-chief's expectations, for not only had a commanding position, from which the whole eastern suburb could be cannonaded, been obtained, but a large convoy of provisions and stores had been safely brought up, and a new base of operations obtained.

The next day, the 15th of November, is celebrated in the annals of British military history as that upon which some of the fiercest and bloodiest fighting which ever took place in India occurred. At a short distance beyond the canal stood the Secunderbagh (Alexander's garden), a building of strong masonry, standing in a garden surrounded by a very high and strong wall. This wall was loopholed for musketry; the gate, which led through a fortified gateway, had been blocked with great piles of stones behind it, and a very strong garrison held it. In front, a hundred yards distant, was a fortified village, also held in great force. Separated from the garden of the Secunderbagh only by the road was the mosque of Shah Nujeeff. This building was also situated in a garden with a strong loopholed wall, and this was lined with the insurgent troops; while the terraced roof of the mosque, and the four minarets which rose at its corners, were crowded with riflemen.

The column of attack was commanded by Brigadier Hope; and as it crossed the bridge of the canal and advanced, a tremendous musketry fire was opened upon it from the village which formed the advanced post of the enemy. The column broke up into skirmishing line and advanced steadily.

"The guns to the front!" said an aide-de-camp, galloping up to the naval brigade.

With a cheer the sailors moved across the bridge, following the Horse Artillery, which dashed ahead, unlimbered, and opened fire with great rapidity. It took somewhat longer to bring the ponderous sixty-eight-pounders of the naval brigade into action; but their deep roar when once at work astonished the enemy, who had never before heard guns of such heavy metal.

The rebels fought obstinately, however; but Brigadier-General Hope led his troops gallantly forward, and after a brief, stern fight the enemy gave way and fled to the Secunderbagh.

The guns were now brought forward and their fire directed at the strong wall. The heavy cannon soon made a breach and the assault was ordered. The Fourth Sikhs had been directed to lead the attack, while the Ninety-third Highlanders and detachments from the Fifty-third and other regiments were to cover their advance, by their musketry fire at the loopholes and other points from which the enemy were firing.

The white troops were, however, too impatient to be at the enemy to perform the patient role assigned to them, and so joined the Sikhs in their charge. The rush was so fierce and rapid that a number of men pushed through the little breach before the enemy had mustered in force to repel them. The entrance was, however, too small for the impatient troops, and a number of them rushed to the grated windows which commanded the gates. Putting their caps on the ends of the muskets, they raised them to the level of the windows, and every Sepoy at the post discharged his musket at once. Before they could load again the troops leaped up, tore down the iron bars, and burst a way here also into the garden.

Then ensued a frightful struggle; two thousand Sepoys held the garden, and these, caught like rats in a trap, fought with the energy of despair. Nothing, however, could withstand the troops, mad with the long-balked thirst for vengeance, and attacked with the cry—which in very truth was the death-knell of the enemy—"Remember Cawnpore!" on their lips. No quarter was asked or given. It was a stubborn, furious, desperate strife, man to man—desperate Sepoy against furious Englishman. But in such a strife weight and power tell their tale, and not one of the two thousand men who formed the garrison escaped; two thousand dead bodies were next day counted within the four walls of the garden.

The battle had now raged for three hours, but there was more work yet to be done. From the walls and minarets of the Shah Nujeeff a terrible fire had been poured upon the troops as they fought their way into the Secunderbagh, and the word was given to take this stronghold also. The gate had been blocked up with masonry. Captain Peel was ordered to take up the sixty-eight-pounders and to breach the wall. Instead of halting at a short distance, the gallant sailor brought up his guns to within ten yards of the wall, and set to work as if he were fighting his ship broadside to broadside with an enemy. It was an action probably unexampled in war. Had such an attack been made unsupported by infantry, the naval brigade would have been annihilated by the storm of fire from the walls, and Dick Warrener's career would have come to a close. The Highlanders and their comrades, however, opened with such a tremendous fire upon the points from which the enemy commanded the battery, and at every loophole in the wall, that the mutineers could only keep up a wild and very ineffectual fire upon the gunners. The massive walls crumbled slowly but surely, and in four hours several gaps were made.

Then the guns ceased their fire, and the infantry with a wild cheer burst into the garden of the Shah Nujeeff, and filled the mosque and garden with the corpses of their defenders. The loss of the naval brigade in this gallant affair was not heavy, and Dick Warrener escaped untouched.

Evening was approaching now, and the troops bivouacked for the night. The Ninetieth and that portion of the Fifty-third not engaged in the assault of the Secunderbagh and Shah Nujeeff were now to have their turn as leaders of the attack.

The next point to be carried was the messhouse, a very strong position, situated on an eminence, with flanking towers, a loopholed mud wall, and a ditch. The naval guns began the fray, and the heavy shot soon effected a breach in the wall. The defenders of the post were annoyed, too, by a mortar battery in an advanced post of the British force in the Residency— for the space between the garrison and the relieving force was rapidly lessening. The word was given, and the Ninetieth, Fifty-third, and Sikhs dashed forward, surmounted all obstacles, and carried the position with the bayonet; and the observatory, which stood behind it, was soon afterward most gallantly carried by a Sikh regiment.

In the meantime the garrison of the Residency was not idle. On the day of the arrival of the British at Dil Koosha flag-signals from the towers of that palace had established communication with the Residency, and it was arranged that as soon as the relieving forces obtained possession of the Secunderbagh the troops of the garrison should begin to fight their way to meet them.

Delighted at taking the offensive after their long siege, Havelock's troops, on the 16th, attacked the enemy with fury, and carried two strong buildings known as Hern Khana and engine-house, and then dashed on through the Chuttur Munzil, and carried all before them at the point of the bayonet.

All the strongholds of the enemy along this line had now fallen; and on the 17th of March Sir Colin Campbell met Generals Outram and Havelock, amid the tremendous cheers of British troops, which for awhile drowned the heavy fire which the enemy was still keeping up.

The loss of the relieving column during the operations was far less than that which had befallen Havelock's force in its advance—for it amounted only to one hundred and twenty-two officers and men killed, and three hundred and forty-five wounded. The loss of the enemy considerably exceeded four thousand. The relieving force did not advance into the Residency, but were stationed along the line which they had conquered between the Dil Koosha and the Residency, for the enemy were still in enormously superior force, and threatened to cut the line by which the British had penetrated.

The first operation was to pour in a supply of luxuries from the stores at the Dil Koosha. White bread, oranges, bananas, wine, tea, sugar, and other articles were sent forward; and these, to those who had for nearly six months existed on the barest and coarsest food, were luxuries indeed. An even greater pleasure was afforded by sending in the mails which had accumulated, and thus affording the garrison the intense delight of hearing of those loved ones at home from whom they had been so long cut off.

The day that the junction was made Dick obtained leave for a few hours to visit his friends in the Residency. It was singular to the lad to walk leisurely across the open space of the Residency garden, where before it would have been death to show one's self for a minute, and to look about rather as an unconcerned spectator than as formerly, with nerves on strain night and day to repel attack, which, if successful, meant death to every soul in the place.

In the battered walls, the shattered roofs, the destruction everywhere visible, he saw how the terrors of the siege had increased after he had left; and in view of the general havoc that met his view Dick was astonished that any one should have survived the long-continued bombardment. In some respects the change had been favorable. The accession of strength after the arrival of General Havelock's force had enabled great and beneficial alteration to be made in the internal arrangements, and the extension of the lines held had also aided in improving the sanitary condition. But the change in the appearance of the place was trifling in comparison with that in the faces of the defenders. These were, it is true, still pinched and thin, for the supply of food had been reduced to a minimum, and the rations had been lowered almost to starvation point. But in place of the expression of deep anxiety or of stern determination then marked on every face, all now looked joyous and glad, for the end to the terrible trials had arrived.

As he moved along men looked at the midshipman curiously, and then, as the lad advanced with outstretched hands, greeted him with cries of astonishment and pleasure; for it was naturally supposed in the garrison that the Warreners had fallen in the sortie on Johannes' house. Very hearty were the greetings which Dick received, especially from those whom he met who had fought side by side with him at Gubbins' house. This pleasure, however, was greatly dashed by the answers to his questions respecting friends. "Dead," "dead," "killed," were the replies that came to the greater part of the inquiries after those he had known, and the family in whom he was chiefly interested had suffered heavily. Mr. Hargreaves was killed; Mr.

and Mrs. Ritchie and all their children had succumbed to the confinement and privation; but Mrs. Hargreaves and the girls were well. After briefly telling how they had escaped in disguise, after having been cut off from falling back after the successful sortie, Dick Warrener hurried off to the house where he heard that his friends were quartered.

It was outside the bounds of the old Residency, for the ground held had, since the arrival of Havelock's force, been considerably extended, and the ladies had had two rooms assigned to them in a large building. Dick knocked at the door of the room, and the ayah opened it—looked at him—gave a scream, and ran back into the room, leaving the door open. Dick, seeing that it was a sitting-room, followed her in. Mrs. Hargreaves, alarmed at the cry, had just risen from her chair, and Nelly and Edith ran in from the inner room as Dick entered. A general cry of astonishment broke from them.

"Dick Warrener!" Mrs. Hargreaves exclaimed. "Is it possible? My clear boy, thank God I see you again. And your brother?"

"He escaped too," Dick said.

Mrs. Hargreaves took him in her arms and kissed him as a dear relative would have done; for during the month they had been together the boys had become very dear to her, from their unvarying readiness to aid all who required it, from their self-devotion and their bravery. Nor were the girls less pleased, and they warmly embraced the young sailor, whom they had come to look upon as if he had been a member of the family, and whom they had wept as dead.

For a time all were too much moved to speak more than a few disjointed words, for the sad changes which had occurred since they had last met were present in all their thoughts. Nelly, the youngest, was the first to recover, and wiping away her tears, she said, half-laughing, half-crying:

"I hate you, Dick, frightening us into believing that you were killed, when you were alive and well all the time. But I never quite believed it after all. I said all along that you couldn't have been killed; didn't I, mamma? and that monkeys always got out of scrapes somehow."

Mrs. Hargreaves smiled.

"I don't think you put it in that way exactly, Nelly; but I will grant that between your fits of crying you used to assert over and over again that you did not believe that they were killed. And now, my dear boy, tell us how this seeming miracle has come about."

Then they sat down quietly, and Dick told the whole story; and Mrs. Hargreaves warmly congratulated him on the manner in which they had escaped, and upon the presence of mind they had shown. Then she in turn told him what they had gone through and suffered. Edith burst into tears, and left the room, and her mother presently went after her.

"Well, Nelly, I have seen a lot since I saw you, have I not?"

"Yes, you are a dear, brave boy, Dick," the girl said.

"Even though I am a monkey, eh?" Dick answered. "And did you really cry when you thought I was dead?"

"Yes," the girl said demurely; "I always cry when I lose my pets. There was the dearest puppy I ever had —"

Dick laughed quietly. "Who is the monkey now?" he asked.

"I am," she said frankly; "but you know I can't help teasing you, Dick."

"Don't balk yourself, Nelly, I like it. I should like to be teased by you all my life," he said in lower tones.

The girl flushed up rosy red. "If you could always remain as you are now," she said after a little pause, "just an impudent midshipman, I should not mind it. Do you know, Dick, they give terriers gin to prevent their growing; don't you think you might stop yourself? It is quite sad," she went on pathetically, "to think that you may grow up into a great lumbering man."

"I am quite in earnest, Nelly," Dick said, looking preternaturally stern.

"Yes," Nelly said, "I have always understood midshipmen were quite in earnest when they talked nonsense."

"I am quite in earnest," Dick said solemnly and fixedly again.

"No, really, Dick, we are too old for that game," Nelly said, with a great affectation of gravity. "I think we could enjoy hide-and-seek together, or even blindman's buff; but you know children never play at being little lovers after they are quite small. I remember a dear little boy, he used to wear pinafores— —"

Here Mrs. Hargreaves again entered the room, and Dick, jumping up suddenly, said that it was quite time for him to be off. "I shall only just have time to be back by the time I promised."

"Good-by, Dick. I hope to see you again tomorrow."

Edith came in, and there was a hearty shake of the hand all round, except that Dick only touched the tips of Nelly's fingers, in a manner which he imagined betokened a dignified resentment, although as he looked up and saw the girl's eyes dancing with amusement, he could scarcely flatter himself that it had produced any very serious effect. Dick returned in an indignant mood to the naval brigade, which was quartered in the Shah Nujeeff's mosque and gardens.

"You are out of sorts to-night, Dick," one of his brother midshipmen said, as they leaned together upon the parapet of the mosque, looking down on the city; "is anything the matter?"

"Were you ever in love, Harry?"

"Lots of times," Harry said confidently.

"And could you always persuade them that you were in earnest?" Dick asked.

Harry meditated. "Well, I am not quite sure about that, Dick; but then, you see, I was never quite sure myself that I was in earnest, and that's rather a drawback, you know."

"But what would you do, Harry, supposing you were really quite in earnest, and she laughed in your face and told you you were a boy?" Dick asked.

"I expect," the midshipman said, laughing, "I should kiss her straight off, and say that as I was a boy she couldn't object."

"Oh, nonsense," Dick said testily; "I want advice, and you talk bosh!"

The midshipman winked confidentially at the moon, there being no one else to wink at, and then said gravely:

"I think, Dick, the right thing to do would be to put your right hand on your heart, and hold your left hand up, with the forefinger pointing to the ceiling, and to say, 'Madam, I leave you now. When years have rolled over our heads I will return, and prove to you at once my affection and my constancy.'"

Dick's eyes opened to their widest, and it was not until his friend went off in a shout of laughter that he was certain that he was being chaffed; then, with an exclamation of "Confound you, Harry!" he made a rush at his comrade, who dodged his attack, and darted off, closely pursued by Dick. And as they dashed round the cupola and down the stairs their light-hearted laughter—for Dick soon joined in the laugh against himself—rose on the evening air; and the tars, smoking their pipes round the bivouac fires below, smiled as the sound came faintly down to them, and remarked, "Them there midshipmites are larking, just as if they were up in the maintop."

CHAPTER XXI.
A SAD PARTING.

Sir Colin Campbell had considered it possible that the enemy would, upon finding that the Residency was relieved, and the prey, of whose destruction they had felt so sure, slipped from between their fingers, leave the city and take to the open, in which case he would, after restoring order, have left a strong body of troops in the city, and have set off in pursuit of the rebels.

It soon became apparent, however, that the enemy had no intention of deserting their stronghold. Lucknow abounded with palaces and mosques, each of which had been turned into a fortress, while every street was barricaded, every wall loopholed. As from forty thousand to fifty thousand men, including many thousands of drilled soldiers, stood ready to defend the town, foot by foot, it was clear that the fighting force at Sir Colin Campbell's command was utterly inadequate to attempt so serious an operation as the reduction of the whole city. To leave a portion of the force would only have submitted them to another siege, with the necessity for another advance to their relief. The commander-in-chief therefore determined to evacuate the Residency and city altogether, to carry off the entire garrison, and to leave Lucknow to itself until the reinforcements from England should arrive, and he should be able to undertake the subjugation of the city with a force adequate for the purpose.

His intention was kept a secret until the last moment, lest the news might reach the enemy, who, from the batteries in their possession, could have kept up a terrible fire upon the road along which the women and children would have to pass, and who would have attacked with such fury along the whole line to be traversed, that it would have been next to impossible to draw off the troops.

In order to deceive the enemy, guns were placed in position to play upon the town, and a heavy fire was opened against the Kaiserbagh, or King's Palace, a fortress of great strength. In the meantime preparations for retreat were quietly carried on. Bullock hackeries were prepared for the carriage of the ladies and children; and on the morning of the 23d of

November the occupants of the Residency were informed that they must prepare to leave that afternoon, and that no luggage beyond a few personal necessaries could be carried.

The order awakened mingled emotions—there was gladness at the thought of leaving a place where all had suffered so much, and round which so many sad memories were centered; there was regret in surrendering to the foe a post which had been so nobly defended for so many months. Among many, too, there was some dismay at the thought of giving up all their movable possessions to the enemy. One small trunk was all that was allowed to each, and as each tried to put together the most valuable of his or her belongings, the whole of the buildings occupied were littered, from end to end, with handsome dresses, silver plate, mirrors, clocks, furniture, and effects of all kinds. A short time since every one would have gladly resigned all that they possessed for life and liberty; but now that both were assured, it was felt to be hard to give up everything.

Dick went in to Mrs. Hargreaves' to see if he could be of any service, but there was comparatively little to do, for that lady had lost all her portable property in the destruction of the bungalow on the estate owned by her husband, and had come into Lucknow shortly before the outbreak, when the cloud began to lower heavily, with but a small amount of baggage. Dick had not been able to see them since his first visit, being incessantly on duty.

"I was so sorry I could not come up before," he explained; "but each of the officers has been up to have a look at the Residency; and as we may be attacked at any moment, Captain Peel expects them all to be on the spot with their men."

"Shall we get away without being fired at?" Nelly asked.

"I am afraid you will have to run the gantlet in one or two places," Dick said. "The enemy keep up an almost incessant fire; and although, we must hope, they will not have an idea that any number of people are passing along the road, and their fire will therefore be only a random one, it may be a little unpleasant; but you are all accustomed to that now. I must be off again, Mrs. Hargreaves; I really only came to explain why I did not come yesterday, and only got leave for an hour, so I have come at a trot all the way."

And so Dick made off again; and as he shook hands with them, he could feel that Nelly had not yet forgiven the coldness of his last good-by.

Upon the previous day all the sick and wounded had been moved to the Dil Koosha; that done, the very large amount of money, amounting to nearly a quarter of a million, in the government treasury, was removed, together with such stores as were required. Then the guns were silently withdrawn from the batteries, and at half-past four in the afternoon the emigration of the women and children commenced. All had to walk to the Secunderbagh, along a road strewn with *débris,* and ankle deep in sand, and in some places exposed to a heavy fire. At one of these points a strong party of seamen were stationed, among whom Dick was on duty. As each party of women arrived at the spot they were advised to stoop low, and to run across at full speed, as the road being a little sunk, they thus escaped observation by the enemy, whose battery was at some little distance, but the grape whistled thickly overhead, and several were wounded as they passed.

Dick had been on the lookout for the Hargreaves party, and came forward and had a talk with them before they started across the open spot. He had quite recovered from Nelly's attack upon his dignity as a man and a naval officer, and the pair as usual had a wordy spar. Dick was, however, rather serious at the prospect of the danger they were about to run.

"Will you let me cross with you one at a time?" he asked.

"Certainly not, Dick," Mrs. Hargreaves said. "You could do us no good, and would run a silly risk yourself. Now, girls, are you ready?"

"Stoop low, for heaven's sake!" Dick urged.

Mrs. Hargreaves started at a run, accompanied by Alice. Nelly was a little behind. Dick took her hand and ran across, keeping between her and the enemy.

"Down low!" he cried, as, when they were half across, a heavy gun fired. As he spoke, he threw his arms round Nelly, and pulled her to the ground. As he did so a storm of grape swept just above them, striking the wall, and sending a shower of earth over them. Another half-minute and they were across on the other side.

"Good-by," he said to them all; "you are over the worst now."

"Good-by, my dear boy. Mind how you cross again. God bless you." And Mrs. Hargreaves and Alice shook his hand, and turned to go. Nelly held hers out to him. He took it and clasped it warmly; he was loosening his hold when the girl said: "You have saved my life, Dick."

"Oh, nonsense," he said.

"You did, sir, and—yes, I am coming, mamma"—in answer to a word from her mother. "Oh, how stupid you are, Dick!" she cried, with a little stamp of her foot; "don't you want to kiss me?"

"Of course I do," Dick said.

"Then why on earth don't you do it, sir?—There, that is enough. God bless you, dear Dick;" and Nelly darted off to join her mother.

Then he returned to his post, and the ladies went on to the Secunderbagh. Here a long halt was entailed, until all were gathered there, in order that they might be escorted by a strong guard on to the Dil Koosha. Then came an anxious journey—some in bullock-carts, some in doolies, some on foot. The Hargreaves walked, for the anxiety was less when moving on foot than if shut up in a conveyance. Several times there were long halts in expectation of attack; and a report that a great movement could be heard among the enemy at one time delayed them until reinforcements could be sent for and arrived. But about midnight all reached the Dil Koosha, where a number of tents had been erected, and refreshments prepared for the many fugitives.

Later on the troops came tramping in, having gradually, and in regular order, evacuated their posts, leaving their fires burning and moving in absolute silence, so that it was not until next morning that the enemy awoke to the knowledge that the Residency was deserted, and that their expected prey had safely escaped them.

The next day was spent quietly, all enjoying intensely the open air, the relief from the long pressure, and the good food, wine, and other comforts now at their disposal. Dick brought Colonel Warrener to make the acquaintance of his friends, and a pleasant afternoon was spent together. On the 25th a heavy gloom fell upon all, for on that day the gallant General Havelock, worn out by his labors and anxieties, was seized with dysentery, and in a few hours breathed his last. He was a good man as well as a gallant soldier, and his death just at the moment when the safety of those for whom he had done so much was assured cast a gloom not only over his comrades and those who had fought under him, but on the whole British nation. All that day the great convoy had been on the move between the Dil Koosha and the Alumbagh. Half the fighting force served as an escort, the other half stood in battle order between them and Lucknow, in case the enemy should come out to the attack. The whole road between the two stations was throughout the day covered by a continuous stream of bullock carts, palanquins, carts, camels, elephants, guns, ammunition carts, and store wagons.

Mrs. Hargreaves and her daughters were on an elephant, with their ayah; and as the Warreners had placed in the howdah a basket of refreshments, the long weary march was borne, not only without inconvenience, but with some pleasure at the novelty of the scene and the delight of air and freedom.

Sir Colin Campbell had intended to allow a halt of seven days at the Alumbagh, but on the 27th of May a continuous firing was heard in the direction of Cawnpore. Fearful for the safety of that all-important post, the commander determined to push forward his convoy at once. On the morning of the 28th they started. Dick had come soon after daybreak to the tents where the Hargreaves were, with many others, sleeping.

"There is bad news from Cawnpore," he said, "and you will have to push on. I expect that it will be a terrible two days' march with all this convoy. Pray take enough provisions with you for the two days in the howdah, and some blankets and things to make a cover at night. I am sure that the tents will not be got up, and the confusion at the halting-place will be fearful; but if you have everything with you, you will be able to manage."

It was well that they were so prepared, for the first march, owing to the immense length of the convoy, lasted until long past dark; then there was a halt for a few hours, and then a thirty miles' journey to the bridge of boats on the Ganges.

The naval brigade accompanied the convoy, but Dick had seen nothing of his friends. Colonel Warrener, however, who with his troop had moved along the line at intervals, spoke to them, and was able at the halting-place to assist them to make a temporary shelter, where they snatched a few hours' sleep.

The news that had caused this movement was bad indeed. General Wyndham, in command at Cawnpore, had been defeated by the Gwalior rebel contingent, aided by the troops of Nana Sahib and those of Koer Sing, a great Oude chief, and part of the town had been taken. Sir Colin himself pushed forward at all speed with a small body of troops and some heavy guns, so as to secure the safety of the bridge of boats; for had this fallen into the hands of the enemy the situation of the great convoy would have been bad indeed. However, the rebels had neglected to take measures until it was too late, and the approaches to the bridge on either side were guarded by our guns. The passage of the convoy then began, and for thirty-nine hours a continuous stream passed across the river.

The whole force which had accomplished the relief of Lucknow had not returned, as it was considered necessary to keep some troops to command the town, and prevent the great body of mutineers gathered there from undertaking expeditions. The Alumbagh was accordingly held by the Fifth, Seventy-eighth, Eighty-fourth, and Ninetieth Foot, the Madras Fusiliers, the Ferozepore Sikhs, and a strong artillery force, the whole under the command of Sir James Outram.

As the long day went on, and the thunder of the guns at Cawnpore grew louder and louder, Sir Colin Campbell took the naval brigade and the greater portion of the fighting troops, and pushed forward. The regiments as they arrived were hurried across the bridge, to take part in the defense of the position guarding the bridge, where General Wyndham's troops were defending themselves desperately against immense forces of the enemy.

"What has happened?" was the question the officers of the naval brigade asked those of the garrison when they first met.

"Oh, we have been fearfully licked. A series of blunders and mismanagement. We have lost all the camp equipage, all the stores—in fact, everything. It is the most disgraceful thing which has happened since the trouble began. We lost heavily yesterday, frightfully to-day. They say the Sixty-fourth is cut to pieces."

It had indeed been a wretched business, and was the only occasion when British troops were, in any force, defeated throughout the mutiny. The affair happened in this way. The British force at Cawnpore were stationed in an intrenched position, so placed as to overawe the city, and to command the river and bridge of boats, which it was all-important to keep open. The general in command received news that the mutinous Gwalior contingent, with several other rebel bodies, was on its way to Cawnpore. Unfortunately, they were approaching on the opposite side of the city to that upon which the British intrenchments were situated, and the general therefore determined to leave a portion of his force to protect the intrenchments and bridge, while with the rest he started to give battle to the enemy in the open at a distance on the other side of the city, as it was very important to prevent Cawnpore from again falling into their hands. He advanced first to Dhubarlee, a strong position on the canal, where a vigorous defense could have been made, as a cross canal covered our flank. Unfortunately, however, the next day he again marched forward eight miles, and met the advanced guard of the enemy at Bhowree. The British force consisted of twelve hundred infantry, made up of portions of the Thirty-fourth, Eighty-second, Eighty-eighth, and Rifles, with one hundred native cavalry, and eight guns. The troops advanced with a rush, carried the village, defeated the enemy, and took two guns, and then pressing forward, found themselves in face of the main body of the enemy's army. Then for the first time it appears to have occurred to the general that it was imprudent to fight so far from the city. He therefore ordered a retreat, and the British force fell back, closely followed by the enemy. Had he halted again at Dhubarlee, he might still have retrieved his error; but he continued his retreat, and halted for the night on the plain of Jewar, a short distance from the northeast angle of the city.

No preparations appear to have been made in case of an attack by the enemy, and when in the morning they came on in immense force, the British position was seriously threatened on all sides. For five hours the troops held their ground nobly, and prevented the enemy advancing by a direct attack. A large body, however, moved round to the flank and entered the city, thus getting between the British forces and their intrenchments. The order was therefore given to retire, and this was carried out in such haste that the whole of the camp equipage, consisting of five hundred tents, quantities of saddlery, uniforms for eight regiments, and a vast amount of valuable property of all kinds, fell into the hands of the mutineers. All these stores had been placed in a great camp on the plain outside the fortified intrenchments. It was a disastrous affair; and Cawnpore blazed with great fires, lighted by the triumphant mutineers.

During the retreat a gun had been capsized and left in one of the lanes of the town, and at dead of night one hundred men of the Sixty-fourth, accompanied by a detachment of sailors, went silently out, and succeeded in righting the gun, and bringing it off from the very heart of the city.

The next day the whole force moved out, and took up their position to prevent the enemy from approaching the intrenchments. The mutineers, commanded by Nana Sahib in person, advanced to the attack. One British column remained in reserve. The column under Colonel Walpole succeeded in repulsing the body opposed to it, and captured two of its eighteen-pounder guns. The column under General Carthew maintained its position throughout the day, but fell back toward the evening—a proceeding for which the officer in command was severely censured by the commander-in-chief, who, riding on ahead of his convoy, with a small body of troops, reached the scene of action just at nightfall.

But it was the division under Brigadier-General Wilson, colonel of the Sixty-fourth, that suffered most heavily. Seeing that General Carthew was hardly pressed, he led a part of his own regiment against four guns which were playing with great effect. Ned Warrener's heart beat high as the order to charge was given, for it was the first time he had been in action with his gallant regiment. With a cheer the little body, who numbered fourteen officers and one hundred and sixty men, advanced. Their way led along a ravine nearly half a mile long; and as they moved forward a storm of shot, shell, and grape from the guns was poured upon them, while a heavy musketry fire broke out from the heights on either side. Fast the men fell, but there was no wavering; on at the double they went, until within fifty yards of the guns, and then burst into a charge at full speed.

Ned, accustomed as he was to fire, had yet felt bewildered at the iron storm which had swept their ranks. All round him men were falling; a bullet knocked off his cap, and a grape-shot smashed his sword off short in his hand. The Sepoy artillerymen stood to their guns and fought fiercely as the

British rushed upon them. Ned caught up the musket of a man who fell dead by his side, and bayoneted a gunner; he saw another man at four paces off level a rifle at him, felt a stunning blow, and fell, but was up in a minute again, having been knocked down by a brick hurled by some Sepoy from a dwelling close behind the guns—a blow which probably saved his life. Two of the guns where spiked while the hand-to-hand conflict raged.

Major Stirling fell dead, Captain Murphy and Captain Macraw died fighting nobly beside him, and the gallant Colonel Wilson received three bullets through his body. From all sides masses of the enemy charged down, and a regiment of Sepoy cavalry swept upon them. Captain Sanders was now in command, and gave the word to fall back; and even faster than they had approached, the survivors of the Sixty-fourth retreated, literally cutting their way through the crowds of Sepoys which surrounded them.

Ned was scarcely conscious of what he was doing; and few could have given a detailed account of the events of that most gallant charge. The men kept well together; old veterans in fight, they knew that only in close ranks could they hope to burst through the enemy; and striking, and stabbing, and always running, they at last regained the position they had quitted. Of the fourteen officers, seven were killed and two wounded; of the one hundred and sixty men, eighteen killed and fifteen wounded; a striking testimony to the valor with which the officers had led the way. Such slaughter as this among the officers is almost without parallel in the records of the British army; and lads who went into the fray low down on the list of lieutenants came out captains. Among them was Ned Warrener, who stood fifth on the list of lieutenants, and who, by the death vacancies, now found himself a captain.

It was not until they halted, breathless and exhausted, that he discovered that he had been twice wounded; for in the wild excitement of the fight he had been unconscious of pain. A bullet had passed through the fleshy part of his left arm, while another had cut a clean gash just across his hip. Neither was in any way serious; and having had them bound up with a handkerchief, he remained with his regiment till nightfall put an end to the fighting, when he made his way to the hospital. This was crowded with badly wounded men; and Ned seeing the pressure upon the surgeons, obtained a couple of bandages, and went back to his regiment, to have them put on there. As he reached his camp, Dick sprang forward.

"My dear old boy, I was just hunting for you. We crossed to-night, and directly we were dismissed I rushed off, hearing that your regiment has suffered frightfully. I hear you are hit; but, thank God! only slightly."

"Very slightly, old boy; nothing worth talking about. It has been an awful business, though. And how are you? and how is father?"

"Quite well, Ned. Not a scratch either of us."

"And the Hargreaves?"

"Mrs. Hargreaves and the girls are all right, Ned, and will be in to-morrow; all the rest are gone."

"Gone! dear, dear! I am sorry. Now, Dick, come to the fire and bandage up my arm; and you must congratulate me, old boy, for by the slaughter to-day I have my company."

"Hurrah!" Dick exclaimed joyfully. "That is good news. What luck! not eighteen yet, and a captain."

It was only on the 1st of December that the whole of the convoy from Lucknow were gathered in tents on the parade-ground at Cawnpore, and all hoped for a short period of rest.

On the morning of the 3d, however, notice was issued that in two hours the women, children, and civilians of Lucknow would proceed to Allahabad, under escort of five hundred men of the Thirty-fourth Regiment. It would be a long march, for the convoy would be incumbered by the enormous train of stores and munitions of war, while a large number of vehicles were available for their transport.

Colonel Warrener heard the news early, and knowing how interested his sons were in the matter, he rode round to their respective camps and told them. Leaving them to follow, he then rode over to the Hargreaves' tent.

They had just heard the news, and short as the time was, had so few preparations to make that they were ready for a start. A dawk-garry, or post-carriage, was allotted to them, which, the ayah riding outside, would hold them with some comfort, these vehicles being specially constructed to allow the occupants, when two in number only, to lie down at full length. It would be a close fit for the three ladies, but they thought that they could manage; and it was a comfort to know that, even if no tents could be erected at night, they could lie down in shelter.

The young Warreners soon arrived, and while their father was discussing the arrangements with Mrs. Hargreaves, and seeing that a dozen of claret which his orderly had at his orders brought across, with a basket of fruit, was properly secured on the roof, they sauntered off with the girls, soon insensibly pairing off.

"It will be two years at least before I am home in England, Nelly," Dick said, "and I hope to be a lieutenant soon after, for I am certain of my step directly I pass, since I have been mentioned three times in dispatches. I know I am a boy, not much over sixteen, but I have gone through a lot, and am older than my age; but even if you laugh at me, Nelly, I must tell you I love you."

But Nelly was in no laughing mood.

"My dear Dick," she said, "I am not going to laugh; I am too sad at parting. But you know I am not much over fifteen yet, though I too feel older—oh, so much older than girls in England, who are at school till long past that age. You know I like you, Dick, very, very much. It would be absurd to say more than that to each other now. We part just on these terms, Dick. We know we both like each other very much. Well, yes, I will say 'love' if you like, Dick; but we cannot tell the least in the world what we shall do five years hence. So we won't make any promises, or anything else; we will be content with what we know; and if either of us change, there will be no blame and misery. Do you agree to that, Dick?"

Dick did agree very joyfully, and a few minutes later the pair, very silent now, strolled back to the tent. Ned and Edith were already there, for Ned had no idea of speaking out now, or of asking Edith to enter into an engagement which she might repent when she came to enter society in England; and yet, although he said nothing, or hardly anything, the pair understood each other's feelings as well as did Dick and Nelly.

All was now ready for the start, everything in its place, and the ayah on the seat with the driver. Then came the parting—a very sad one. Mrs. Hargreaves was much moved, and the girls wept unrestrainedly, while Colonel Warrener, who had made his adieus, and was standing a little back, lifted his eyebrows, with a comical look of astonishment, as he saw the farewell embraces of his sons with Edith and Nelly.

"Humph!" he muttered to himself. "A bad attack of calf love all round. Well," as he looked at the manly figures of his sons, and thought of the qualities they had shown, "I should not be surprised if the boys stick to it; but whether those pretty little things will give the matter a thought when they have once come out at home remains to be seen. It would not be a bad thing, for Hargreaves was, I know, a very wealthy man, and there are only these two girls."

CHAPTER XXII.
THE LAST CAPTURE OF LUCKNOW.

The women and children brought from Lucknow once sent off from the British camp, the commander-in-chief was able to direct his attention to the work before him—of clearing out of Cawnpore the rebel army, composed of the Gwalior contingent and the troops of Koer Sing and Nana Sahib, in all twenty-five thousand men. Against this large force he could only bring seventy-five hundred men; but these, well led, were ample for the purpose.

The position on the night of the 5th of December was as follows. The British camp was separated from the city by a canal running east and west. The enemy were entirely on the north of this canal, their center occupying the town. Outside the city walls lay the right of the rebel army, while his left occupied the space between the walls and the river. In the rear of the enemy's left was a position known as the Subadar's Tank. The British occupied as an advanced post a large bazaar on the city side of the river.

The operations of the 6th of December were simple. A demonstration was made against the city from the bazaar, which occupied the attention of the large force holding the town. The main body of the British were quietly massed on its left, and, crossing three bridges over the canal, attacked the enemy's right with impetuosity. These, cut off by the city wall from their comrades within, were unable to stand the British onslaught and the thunder of Peel's guns, and fled precipitately, pursued by the British for fourteen miles along the Calpee Road. Every gun and ammunition wagon of the mutineers on this side fell into the hands of the victors.

As the victorious British force swept along past the city, Sir Colin Campbell detached a force under General Mansfield to attack and occupy the position of the Subadar's Tank—which was captured after some hard fighting. Thus the British were in a position in rear of the enemy's left. The mutineers, seeing that their right was utterly defeated, and the retreat of their left threatened, lost all heart, and as soon as darkness came on, fled, a disorganized rabble, from the city they had entered as conquerors only six days before. The cavalry started next day in pursuit, cut up large numbers, and captured the greater part of their guns.

The threatening army of Gwalior thus beaten and scattered, and Cawnpore in our hands, Sir Colin Campbell was able to devote his whole attention to clearing the country in his rear, and in preparing for the great final campaign against Lucknow, which, now that Delhi had fallen, was the headquarters of the mutiny.

The next two months were passed in a series of expeditions by flying columns. In some of these the Warreners took part, and both shared in the defeats of the Sepoys and the capture of Futtyghur and Furruckabad—places at which horrible massacres of the whites had taken place in the early days of the mutiny. During these two months large reinforcements had arrived; and Jung Bahadoor, Prince of Nepaul, had come down with an army of ten thousand Ghoorkas to our aid.

On the 15th of February the tremendous train of artillery, ammunition and stores, collected for the attack upon the city, began to cross the river; and upon the 26th of the month the order was given for the army to move upon the following day.

The task before it was a difficult one. From all the various points from which the British had driven them—from Delhi, from Rohilcund, and the Doab, from Cawnpore, Furruckabad, Futtyghur, Etawah, Allyghur, Goruckpore, and other places—they retreated to Lucknow, and there were now collected sixty thousand revolted Sepoys and fifty thousand irregular troops, besides the armed rabble of the city of three hundred thousand souls. Knowing the storm that was preparing to burst upon their heads, they had neglected no means for strengthening their position. Great lines of fortifications had been thrown up; enormous quantities of guns placed in position; every house barricaded and loopholed, and the Kaiserbagh transformed into a veritable citadel. In hopes of destroying the force under General Sir James Outram, at the Alumbagh—which had been a thorn in their side for so long—a series of desperate attacks had been made upon them; but these had been uniformly defeated with heavy loss by the gallant British force. On the 3d of March the advanced division occupied the Dil Koosha, meeting with but slight resistance; and the commander-in-chief at once took up his headquarters here. The next three days were spent in making the necessary disposition for a simultaneous attack upon all sides of the town—General Outram on one side, Sir Hope Grant upon another, Jung Bahadoor, with his Nepaulese, on the third, and the main attack, under Sir Colin Campbell himself, on the fourth.

Great was the excitement in the camp on the eve of this tremendous struggle. Colonel Warrener and his sons met on the night before the fighting was to begin.

"Well, boys," he said, after a long talk upon the prospects of the fighting, "did you do as you talked about, and draw your pay and get it changed into gold?"

"Most of it," Ned said; "we could not get it all; and had to pay a tremendous rate of exchange for it."

"Here are the twenty pounds each, in gold, lads," Colonel Warrener said, "that I told you I could get for you. Now what do you want it for? You would not tell me at Cawnpore."

"Well, father, at Delhi there was lots of loot taken, quantities of valuable things, and the soldiers were selling what they had got for next to nothing. I had some lovely bracelets offered me for a few rupees, but no one had any money in their pockets. So Dick and I determined that if we came into another storming business, we would fill our pockets beforehand with money. They say that the palaces, the Kaiserbagh especially, are crowded with valuable things; and as they will be lawful loot for the troops, we shall be able to buy no end of things."

Colonel Warrener laughed.

"There is nothing like forethought, Ned, and I have no doubt that you will be able to pick up some good things. The soldiers attach no value to them, and would rather have gold, which they can change for spirits, than all the precious stones in the world. I shall be out of it, as, of course, the cavalry will not go into the city, but will wait outside to cut off the enemy's retreat."

The fighting began with General Outram's division, which worked round the city, and had on the 7th, 8th, and 9th to repulse heavy attacks of the enemy.

On the 9th Sir Colin Campbell advanced, took the Martinière with but slight opposition, crossed the canal, and occupied the Secunderbagh—the scene of the tremendous fighting on the previous advance. The Begum's palace, in front of Bank House, was then attacked, and after very heavy fighting, carried. Here Major Hodgson, the captor of the king of Delhi, was mortally wounded. General Outram's force had by this time taken up a position on the other side of the river, and this enabled him to take the enemy's defenses in flank, and so greatly to assist the advancing party.

Day by day the troops fought their way forward; and on the 14th the Imaumbarra, a splendid palace of the king of Oude, adjoining the Kaiserbagh, was breached and carried. The panic-stricken defenders fled through the court and garden into the Kaiserbagh, followed hotly by the Sikhs, Ghoorkas, and Highlanders. Such was the terror which their appearance excited that a panic seized also the defenders of the Kaiserbagh, and these too fled, deserting the fortifications raised with so much care, and the British poured into the palace. For a few minutes a sharp conflict took place in every room, and then, the Sepoys being annihilated, the victors fell upon the spoil. From top to bottom the Kaiserbagh was crowded with valuable articles, collected from all parts of the world. English furniture, French clocks and looking-glasses, Chinese porcelain, gorgeous draperies, golden thrones studded with jewels, costly weapons inlaid with gold, enormous quantities of jewelry—in fact, wealth of all kinds to an almost fabulous value. The wildest scene of confusion ensued. According to the rule in these matters, being taken by storm, the place was lawful plunder. For large things the soldiers did not care, and set to to smash and destroy all that could not be carried away. Some put on the turbans studded with jewels; others hung necklaces of enormous value round their necks, or covered their arms with bracelets. None knew the value of the costly gems they had become possessed of; and few indeed of the officers could discriminate between the jewels of immense value and those which were mere worthless imitations.

As soon as the news spread that the Kaiserbagh was taken the guns fired a royal salute in honor of the triumph; and all officers who could obtain an hour's leave from their regiments hurried away to see the royal palace of Oude.

The Warreners were both near the spot when the news came; both were able to get away, and met at the entrance to the palace. Already soldiers, British and native, were passing out laden with spoil.

"What will you give me for this necklace, sir?" a soldier asked Ned.

"I have no idea what it's worth," Ned said.

"No more have I," said the soldier; "it may be glass, it may be something else. You shall have it for a sovereign."

"Very well," Ned said; "here is one."

So onward they went, buying everything in the way of jewels offered them, utterly ignorant themselves whether the articles they purchased were real gems or imitation.

Penetrating into the palace, they found all was wild confusion. Soldiers were smashing chandeliers and looking-glasses, breaking up furniture, tumbling the contents of chests and wardrobes and caskets over the floors, eager to find, equally eager to sell what they had found.

Bitter were the exclamations of disappointment and disgust which the Warreners heard from many of the officers that they were unprovided with money—for the soldiers would not sell except for cash; but for a few rupees they were ready to part with anything. Strings of pearls, worth a thousand pounds, were bought for a couple of rupees—four shillings; diamond aigrettes, worth twice as much, went for a sovereign; and the Warreners soon laid out the seventy pounds which they had between them when they entered the palace; and their pockets and the breasts of their coats were stuffed with their purchases, and each had a bundle in his handkerchief.

"I wonder," Dick said, as they made their way back, "whether we have been fools or wise men. I have not a shadow of an idea whether these things are only the sham jewels which dancing girls wear, or whether they are real."

"It was worth running the risk, anyhow; for if only half of them are real they are a big fortune. Anyhow, Dick, let's hold our tongues about it. It's no use making fellows jealous of our good luck if they turn out to be real, or of getting chaffed out of our lives if they prove false. Let us just stow them away till it's all over, and then ask father about them."

It was calculated that twenty thousand soldiers and camp-followers obtained loot of more or less value, from the case of jewelry, valued at one hundred thousand pounds, that fell into the hands of an officer, to clocks, candelabra, and articles of furniture, carried off by the least fortunate. The value of the treasure there was estimated at ten millions of money at the lowest computation.

The fall of the Kaiserbagh utterly demoralized the enemy; and from that moment they began to leave the town by night in thousands. Numbers were cut off and slaughtered by our cavalry and artillery; but large bodies succeeded in escaping, to give us fresh trouble in the field.

Day by day the troops fought their way from palace to palace and from street to street. Day and night the cannon and mortar batteries thundered against the districts of the city still uncaptured; and great fires blazed in a dozen quarters, until gradually the resistance ceased and Lucknow was won.

It was not until a week after the storming of the Kaiserbagh—by which time everything had settled down, order was restored, and the inhabitants were, under the direction of the military authorities, engaged in clearing away rubbish, leveling barricades, and razing to the ground a considerable portion of the city—that Colonel Warrener and his sons met. The troops were now all comfortably under canvas in the cantonments, and were enjoying a well-earned rest after their labors.

"Well, boys," he said, "have you heard Warrener's Horse is to be broken up? The officers have all been appointed to regiments, the civilians are anxious to return to look after their own affairs. I am to go up to take the command of a newly-raised Punjaub regiment. Dunlop goes with me as major. Manners has been badly hit, and goes home. The greater part of the naval brigade march down to Calcutta at once. The force will be broken up into flying columns, for there is much to be done yet. The greater portion of these scoundrels have got away; and there are still considerably more than one hundred thousand of the enemy scattered in large bodies over the country. I am going to Delhi, through Agra, with Dunlop; I accompany a detachment of fifty irregular Punjaub horse, who are ordered down to Agra. Then I shall go up to Meerut, and have a week with the girls; and do you know I have seen Captain Peel and your colonel, Ned, and have got leave for you both for a month. Then you will go down to Calcutta, Dick, and join your ship; Ned will of course, rejoin his regiment."

The lads were delighted at the prospect of again seeing their sister and cousin; and Dick indulged in a wild dance, expressive of joy.

"Well, boys, and how about loot; did you lay out your money?"

"We laid it out, father; but we have not the least idea whether we have bought rubbish or not. This black bag is full of it."

So saying, Ned emptied a large handbag upon the top of a barrel which served as a table. Colonel Warrener gave a cry of astonishment, as a great stream of bracelets, necklaces, tiaras, aigrettes, and other ornaments, poured out of the bag.

"Good gracious, boys! do you mean to say all these are yours?"

"Ours and yours, father; there were forty pounds of your money, and thirty-five of ours. Do you think they are real?"

Colonel Warrener took one or two articles from the flashing heap of diamonds, emeralds, rubies, opals, and pearls.

"I should say so," he said; "some of them are certainly. But have you any idea what these are worth?"

"Not the least in the world," Ned said; "if they are real, though, I suppose they are worth some thousands of pounds."

"My boys, I should say," Colonel Warrener replied, turning over the heap, "they must be worth a hundred thousand if they are worth a penny."

The boys looked at each other in astonishment:

"Really, father?"

"Really, my boys."

"Hurrah," Dick said. "Then you can give up the service when this war is over, father, and go home and live as a rich man; that will be glorious."

"My dear boys, the prize is yours."

"Nonsense, father!" exclaimed the boys together. And then began an amicable contest, which was not finally concluded for many a long day.

"But what had we better do with all these things, father?" Dick said at last.

"We will get a small chest and put them in, boys. I will give it to the paymaster—he is sending a lot of treasure down under a strong escort—and will ask him to let it go down with the convoy. I will direct it to a firm at Calcutta, and will ask them to forward it to my agent at home, to whom I will give directions to send it to a first-class jeweler in London, to be by him opened and valued. I will tell the Calcutta firm to insure it on the voyage as treasure at twenty thousand pounds. Even if some of them turn out to be false, you may congratulate each other that you are provided for for life."

"And when do we set out, father?" Ned asked, after they had talked for some time longer about their treasure.

"In three days' time. We shall accompany a flying column for the first two days' march, and then strike across for Agra."

The next two days the Warreners spent in investigating the town, in wandering through the deserted palaces, and admiring their vast extent, and in saying good-by to their friends. A great portion of the teeming population of Lucknow had fled, and the whole city outside the original town was to be cleared away and laid out in gardens, so that henceforth Lucknow would be little more than a fifth of its former size. The ruined Residency was to be cleared of its *débris*, replanted with trees, and to be left as a memorial of British valor. The entire district through which Havelock's men had fought their way was to be cleared of its streets, and the palaces only were to be left standing, to be utilized for public purposes. The whole of the remaining male population of Lucknow was set to work to carry out these alterations. The scene was busy and amusing, and the change from the fierce fight, the din of cannon, and the perpetual rattle of musketry, to the order, regularity, and bustle of work, was very striking. Here was a party of sappers and miners demolishing a row of houses, there thousands of natives filling baskets with rubbish and carrying them on their heads to empty into bullock carts, whence it was taken to fill up holes and level irregularities. Among the crowd, soldiers of many uniforms—British infantry, Rifles, Highlanders, artillery and cavalry, sinewy Sikhs, and quiet little Nepaulese—wandered at will or worked in fatigue parties.

The three days past, Colonel Warrener, his sons, and Major Dunlop took their places on horseback with the troop of irregular cavalry commanded by Lieutenant Latham, and joined the flying column which was setting out to attack a large body of the enemy, who were reported to be gathering again near Furruckabad, while simultaneously other columns were leaving in other directions, for broken at Lucknow, the rebels were swarming throughout all Oude. The day was breaking, but the sun was not yet up, when the column started—for in India it is the universal custom to start very early, so as to get the greater part of the march over before the heat of the day fairly begins—and the young Warreners were in the highest spirits at the thought that they were on their way to see their sister and cousin, and that their nine months of marching and fighting were drawing to a close, for it is possible to have too much even of adventure. At ten o'clock a halt was called at the edge of a large wood, and after preparing breakfast there was a rest in the shade until four in the afternoon, after which a two hours' march took them to their halting-place for the night. Tents were pitched, fires lighted, and then, dinner over, they made merry groups, who sat smoking and chatting until nine o'clock, when the noise ceased, the fires burned down, and all was quiet until the *réveillé* sounded at four o'clock, after which there was an hour of busy work, getting down, rolling up, and packing the tents and baggage in the wagons.

Another day's march and halt, and then Colonel Warrener and his friends said good-by to their acquaintances in the column, and started with the troop of cavalry for Agra. Unincumbered by baggage, and no longer obliged to conform their pace to that of the infantry, they trotted gayly along, and accomplished forty miles ere they halted for the night near a village. The country through which they had passed had an almost deserted appearance. Here and there a laborer was at work in the fields, but the confusion and alarm created by the bodies of mutineers who had swept over the country, and who always helped themselves to whatever pleased them, had created such a scare that the villagers for the most part had forsaken their abodes, and driven their animals, with all their belongings, to the edge of jungles or other unfrequented places, there to await the termination of the struggle.

At the end of the day's journey they halted in front of a great mosque-like building with a dome, the tomb of some long dead prince. The doors stood open, and Colonel Warrener proposed that they should take up their quarters for the night in the lofty interior instead of sleeping in the night air, for although the temperature was still high, the night dews were the reverse of pleasant. It was evident by the appearance of the interior that it had been used as the headquarters and storehouse of some body of the enemy, for a considerable quantity of stores, military saddles, harness, coils of rope, and barrels of flour were piled against the wall. A space was soon swept, and a fire lighted on the floor. Outside the troopers dismounted, some proceeded to a wood at a short distance off to fetch fuel, others took the horses to a tank or pond to drink. It was already getting dusk, and inside the great domed chamber it was nearly dark.

"The fire looks cheerful," Colonel Warrener said, as, after seeing that the men had properly picketed their horses, and had made all their arrangements, the little group of officers returned to it. A trooper had already prepared their meal, which consisted of kabobs, or pieces of mutton—from a couple of sheep, which they had purchased at a village where they halted in the morning—a large bowl of boiled rice, and some chupatties, or griddle cakes; a pannikin of tea was placed by each; and spreading their cloaks on the ground, they set to with the appetite of travelers. Dinner over, a bottle of brandy was produced from one of Major Dunlop's holsters, the pannikin was washed out, and a supply of fresh water brought in, pipes and cheroots were lighted, and they prepared for a cheerful evening.

"I am very sorry Manners is not here," Dick said; "it would have been so jolly to be all together again. However, it is a satisfaction to know that his wound is doing well, and that he is likely to be all right in a few months."

"Yes," Colonel Warrener said, "but I believe that he will have to leave the service. His right leg will always be shorter than the left."

"I don't suppose he will mind that," Ned said. "I should think he must have had enough of India to last for his life."

"Mr. Latham," Dick said presently to the officer in command of the cavalry, "will you tell us your adventures? We know all about each other's doings."

So they sat and talked until ten o'clock, when Mr. Latham went round to see that the sentries were properly placed and alert. When he returned the door was shut, to keep out the damp air, and the whole party, rolling themselves in their cloaks, and using their saddles for pillows, laid up for the night. Dick was some time before he slept. His imagination was active; and when he at last dozed off, he was thinking what they had best do were they attacked by the enemy.

It was still dark when with a sudden start the sleeping party in the tomb awoke and leaped to their feet. For a moment they stood bewildered, for outside was heard on all sides the crack of volleys of musketry, wild yells and shouts, and the trampling of a large body of cavalry.

"Surprised!" exclaimed the colonel. "The sentries must have been asleep!"

There was a rush to the door, and the sight that met their eyes showed them the extent of the disaster. The moon was shining brightly, and by her light they could see that a large body of rebel cavalry had fallen upon the sleeping troopers, while the heavy musketry fire showed that a strong body of infantry were at work on the other side of the mosque. Lieutenant Latham rushed down the steps with his sword drawn, but fell back dead shot through the heart.

"Back, back!" shouted Colonel Warrener. "Let us sell our lives here!"

CHAPTER XXIII.
A DESPERATE DEFENSE.

In an instant the door was closed and bolted, and the four set to work to pile barrels and boxes against it. Not a word was spoken while this was going on. By the time they had finished the uproar without had changed its character; the firing had ceased, and the triumphant shouts of the mutineers showed that their victory was complete. Then came a loud thundering noise at the door.

"We have only delayed it a few minutes," Colonel Warrener said. "We have fought our fight, boys, and our time has come. Would to God that I had to die alone!"

"Look, father," Dick said, "there is a small door there. I noticed it last night. No doubt there is a staircase leading to the terrace above. At any rate, we may make a good fight there."

"Yes," Major Dunlop said, "we may fight it out to the last on the stairs. Run, Dick, and see."

Dick found, as he supposed, that from the door a narrow winding staircase led to the terrace above, from which the dome rose far into the air. The stairs were lit by an occasional narrow window. He was thinking as he ran upstairs of the ideas that had crossed his brain the night before.

"It is all right," he said, as he came down again. "Look, father, if we take up barrels and boxes, we can make barricades on the stairs, and defend them for any time almost."

"Excellent," the colonel said. "To work. They will be a quarter of an hour breaking in the door. Make the top barricade first, a few feet below the terrace."

Each seized a box or barrel, and hurried up the stairs. They had a longer time for preparation than they expected, for the mutineers, feeling sure of their prey, were in no hurry, and finding how strong was the door, decided to sit down and wait until their guns would be up to blow it in. Thus the defenders of the tomb had an hour's grace, and in that time had constructed three solid barricades. Each was placed a short distance above an opening for light, so that while they themselves were in darkness, their assailants would be in the light. They left a sufficient space at the top of each barricade for them to scramble over, leaving some spare barrels on the stairs above it to fill up the space after taking their position.

"Now for the remains of our supper, father," Dick said, "and that big water jug. I will carry them up. Ned, do you bring up that long coil of thin rope."

"What for, Dick?"

"It may be useful, Ned; ropes are always useful. Ah, their guns are up."

As he spoke a round shot crashed through the door, and sent splinters of casks and a cloud of flour flying.

"Now, Ned, come along," Dick said; and followed by Colonel Warrener and Major Dunlop, they entered the little doorway and ran up the narrow stairs.

At the first barricade, which was some thirty steps up, the officers stopped, and proceeded to fill up the passage hitherto left open, while the boys continued their way to the terrace.

"Let us have a look round, Ned; those fellows will be some minutes before they are in yet; and that barricade will puzzle them."

Day was breaking now, and the lads peered over the parapet which ran round the terrace.

"There are a tremendous lot of those fellows, Dick, four or five thousand of them at least, and they have got six guns."

"Hurrah, Ned!" Dick said, looking round at the great dome; "this is just what I hoped."

He pointed to a flight of narrow steps, only some twelve inches across, fixed to the side of the dome, which rose for some distance almost perpendicularly. By the side of the steps was a low hand-rail. They were evidently placed there permanently, to enable workmen to ascend to the top of the dome, to re-gild the long spike which, surmounted by a crescent, rose from its summit, or to do any repairs that were needful.

"There, Ned, I noticed these steps on some of the domes at Lucknow. When the worst comes to the worst, and we are beaten from the stairs, we can climb up that ladder—for it's more like a ladder than stairs—and once on the top could laugh at the whole army of them. Now, Ned, let us go down to them; by that cheering below, the artillery has broken the door open."

The mutineers burst through the broken door into the great hall with triumphant yells, heralding their entrance by a storm of musketry fire, for they knew how desperately even a few Englishmen will sell their lives. There was a shout of disappointment at finding the interior untenanted; but a moment's glance round discovered the door, and there was a rush toward it, each longing to be the first to the slaughter. The light in the interior was but faint, and the stairs were pitch dark, and were only wide enough for one man to go up with comfort, although two could just stand side by side. Without an obstacle the leaders of the party stumbled and groped their way up the stairs, until the first came into the light of a long narrow loophole in the wall. Then from the darkness above came the sharp crack of a revolver, and the man fell on his face, shot through the heart. Another crack, and the next shared his fate. Then there was a pause, for the spiral was so sharp that not more than two at a time were within sight of the defenders of the barricade.

The next man hesitated at seeing his immediate leaders fall; but pressed from behind he advanced, with his musket at his shoulder, in readiness to fire when he saw his foes; but the instant his head appeared round the corner a ball struck him, and he too fell. Still the press from behind pushed the leaders forward, and it was not until six had fallen, and the narrow stairs were impassable from the dead bodies, that an officer of rank, who came the next on the line, succeeded by shouting in checking the advance. Then orders were passed down for those crowding the doorway to fall back, and the officer, with the men on the stairs, descended, and the former reported to the leader that six men had fallen, and that the stairs were choked with their bodies. After much consultation orders were given the men to go up, and keeping below the spot at which, one after another, their comrades had fallen, to stretch out their arms and pull down the bodies. This was done, and then an angry consultation again took place. It was clear that, moving fast, only one could mount the stairs at a time, and it seemed equally certain that this one would, on reaching a certain spot, be shot by his invisible foes. Large rewards and great honor were promised by the chief to those who would undertake to lead the assault, and at last volunteers were found, and another rush attempted.

It failed, as had the first. Each man as he passed the loophole fell, and again the dead choked the stairs. One or two had not fallen at the first shot, and had got a few steps higher, but only to fall back dead upon their comrades. Again the assault ceased, and for two or three hours there was a pause. The officers of the mutineers deliberated and quarreled; the men set-to to prepare their meal. That over, one of the troopers went in to the officers and proposed a plan, which was at once approved of, and a handsome reward immediately paid him. Before enlisting he had been a carpenter, and as there were many others of the same trade, no time was lost in carrying out the suggestion. Several of the thick planks composing the door remained uninjured. These were cut and nailed together, so as to make a shield of exactly the same width as the staircase, and six feet high; on one side several straps and loops were nailed, to give a good hold to those carrying it; and then with a cheer the Sepoys again prepared for an attack. The shield was heavy, but steadily, and with much labor, it was carried up the stairs step by step, by two men, others pressing on behind.

When they reached the loophole the pistol shots from above again rang out; but the door was of heavy seasoned wood, three inches thick, and the bullets failed to penetrate. Then the shield ascended step by step, until it reached the barrier. There it stopped, for the strength that could be brought to bear upon it was altogether insufficient to move in the slightest the solid pile, and after some time spent in vain efforts, the shield was taken back again, as gradually and carefully as it had been advanced, until out of the range of the pistols of the defenders.

"What will be the next move, I wonder?" Colonel Warrener said, as the little party sat down on the stairs and waited for a renewal of the attack.

"I don't like that shield," Major Dunlop remarked; "it shows that there is some more than usually intelligent scoundrel among them, and he will be up to some new trick."

An hour passed, and then there was a noise on the stairs, and the shield was again seen approaching. As before, it advanced to the barrier and stopped. There was then a sort of grating noise against it, and the door shook as this continued.

"What on earth are they up to now?" Major Dunlop exclaimed.

"Piling fagots against it," Dick said, "or I am mistaken. I have been afraid of fire all along. If they had only lit a pile of damp wood at the bottom of the stairs, they could have smoked us out at the top; and then, as the smoke cleared below, they could have gone up and removed the barricade before the upper stairs were free enough from smoke for us to come down. There, I thought so! Make haste!" and Dick dashed up the stairs, followed by his friends, as a curl of smoke ascended, and a loud cheer burst from the Sepoys below.

Quickly as they ran upstairs, the smoke ascended still more rapidly, and they emerged upon the terrace half-suffocated and blinded.

"So ends barricade number one," Major Dunlop said, when they had recovered from their fit of coughing. "I suppose it will be pretty nearly an hour before the fire is burned out."

"The door would not burn through in that time," said Major Warrener; "but they will be able to stand pretty close, and the moment the fagots are burned out they will drag the screen out of the way, and, with long poles with hooks, or something of that sort, haul down the barricade. Directly the smoke clears off enough for us to breathe, we will go down to our middle barricade. They may take that the same way they took the first, but they cannot take the last so."

"Why not, father?" Ned asked.

"Because it's only ten steps from the top, Ned; so that, however great a smoke they make, we can be there again the instant they begin to pull it down."

It was now past midday, and the party partook sparingly of their small store of food and water. The smoke continued for some time to pour out of the door of the stairs in dense volumes, then became lighter. Several times the lads tried to descend a few steps, but found that breathing was impossible, for the smoke from the green wood was insupportable. At last it became clear enough to breathe, and then the party ran rapidly down to their second barricade. That, at least, was intact, but below they could hear the fall of heavy bodies, and knew that the lower barricade was destroyed.

"I don't suppose that screen of theirs was burned through, father, so very likely they will try the same dodge again. Of course they don't know whether we have another barricade, or where we are, so they will come on cautiously. It seems to me than if you and Dunlop were to take your place a bit lower than this, stooping down on the stairs, and then when they come were boldly to throw yourselves with all your weight suddenly against the shield, you would send it and its bearers headlong downstairs, and could then follow them and cut them up tremendously."

"Capital, Dick! that would be just the thing; don't you think so, Dunlop? If they haven't got the shield, we can shoot them down, so either way we may as well make a sortie."

"I think so," Major Dunlop said. "Here goes, then."

Halfway down they heard the trampling of steps again. The Sepoys had extinguished the fires with buckets of water, had put straps to the door again, and were pursuing their former tactics. The two officers sat down and awaited the coming of their foes. Slowly the latter ascended, until the door was within two steps of the Englishmen. Then the latter simultaneously flung all their weight against it.

Wholly unprepared for the assault, the bearers were hurled backward, with the heavy shield upon them, knocking down those behind them, who, in turn, fell on those below. Sword in hand, Colonel Warrener sprang upon the hindmost of the falling mass, while, pressing just behind him, and firing over his shoulder, Major Dunlop followed.

Shrieks of dismay rose from the Sepoys who crowded the stairs, as the bodies of those above were hurled upon them; flight or defense was equally impossible; turning to descend, they leaped upon their comrades below. A frightful scene ensued—such a scene as has sometimes been seen on the stairs of a theater on fire. What was the danger above, none thought; a wild panic seized all; over each other they rolled, choking the stairs and obstructing all movement, until the last twenty feet of the stairs were packed closely with a solid mass of human beings, lying thickly on each other, and stifling each other to death. On reaching this mass Colonel Warrener and his friend paused. There was nothing more to be done. Over fifty human beings lay crushed together; those on the top of the heap were shot, and then the officers retraced their steps. Many lay on the stairs, but Major Dunlop had passed his sword through their bodies as he passed them. Four muskets were picked up, and all the ammunition from the pouches; and then, with the boys, who had followed closely behind them, they again ascended to the terrace and sat down.

"We are safe now for some time," Colonel Warrener said. "It will take them a long time to clear away that heap of dead, and they won't try the shield dodge again."

It was indeed late in the afternoon before the Sepoys made any fresh move against the defenders of the stairs. The time, however, had not passed idly with the latter. One of them keeping watch at the barrier, the others had maintained a steady musketry fire through the open work of the parapet upon the enemy below. The Sepoys had answered with a scattering fire; but as the defenders were invisible behind the parapet, and could move from one point to another unobserved, there was but little fear of their being hit; while their steady fire did so much execution among the throng of Sepoys that these had to move their camping ground a couple of hundred yards back from the tomb.

It was nearly dark, when several men, bearing large bundles of straw and bamboos, ran across the open ground and entered the mosque, and the besieged guessed that another attempt was to be made to smoke them out. There had been much consultation on the part of the enraged mutineers, and this time two men, with their muskets leveled at their shoulders, led the advance. Very slowly they made their way up, until a pistol shot rang out, and one of the leaders, discharging his musket before him, fell. Then there was a halt. Another Sepoy, with fixed bayonet, took the place in front, and over the shoulders of him and his comrade those behind threw bundles of straw mixed with wet leaves; a light was applied to this, and with a sheet of flame between themselves and the besieged, they had no fear. Now they pressed forward, threw on fresh straw, and then, knowing that the besieged would have fled higher, reached through the flames with a pole with a hook attached to it, and hauled down the barricade. The moment the fire burned a little low, two men lighted fresh bundles, and, stamping out the fire, advanced up the stairs, carrying before them the blazing bundles like torches, the volumes of smoke from these of course preceding them.

The party on the terrace had noticed the smoke dying down, and had prepared to descend again, when a fresh addition to the smoke convinced them that the enemy were still piling on bundles, and that there was nothing to fear. So they sat, quietly chatting until Ned, who was sitting next to the door, exclaimed:

"Listen! They are pulling down our top barricade."

Sword in hand, he rushed down, the others closely following him. Just as he turned the spiral which would bring him in sight of the upper barricade a musket was fired, and Ned would have fallen forward had not Major Dunlop seized him by the collar, and pulled him backward.

"Hold the stairs, colonel!" he said; "they are at the barricade, but are not through yet; I will carry Ned up. He's hit in the shoulder."

Major Dunlop carried Ned to the platform, and, laying him down, for he had lost consciousness, rushed back to assist to hold the stairs, for the crack of Colonel Warrener's and Dick's revolvers could be heard. The advantage, however, was so great with them, standing above the others, and so placed as to be able to fire the instant that their foes came round the corner, that the Sepoys, after losing several of their number, ceased their attack.

The defenders hurried up to Ned, confident that the enemy would not renew the assault again for the moment, as they could not tell whether there was yet another barrier to be stormed. Dick stood sentry at the door, and the colonel and Major Dunlop examined Ned's wound. It was a serious one; the ball had entered the chest below the collarbone; had it been fired from a level it would have been fatal; but the Sepoy having stood so much below it had gone out near the neck, smashing the collar-bone on its way. Ned had become unconscious from the shock to the system.

"We must take to the dome at once," Colonel Warrener said. "The next assault those fellows will gain the terrace. I will carry Ned up."

"No, colonel, I will take him," Major Dunlop said. "I can carry him over my shoulders as easily as possible."

"Well, Dunlop, you are the younger man, so I will hand him over to you. I will put this coil of rope round my neck, and will take the water and food. It is so dark now that they will not see us from below. If those fellows had but waited half an hour we could have gained the top without this sad business. Will you go first, Dunlop?"

Major Dunlop, who was a very powerful and active man, lifted Ned on his shoulders, and began to ascend the narrow steps to the dome. It was hard work at first, but as he got on the ascent became less steep, and the last part was comparatively easy. Colonel Warrener mounted next, also heavily laden. Dick remained on guard at the door until he saw his father pass the shoulder of the dome, out of sight from those on the terrace; he then slung two muskets and cartridge pouches on his shoulders, briskly climbed the steps, and was soon by his father.

In three minutes the party were gathered round the central spike of the dome. Suddenly a loud cheer was heard from below.

"They are out on the terrace," Dick said. "I will go down a bit to guard the steps; you will be more use with Ned than I should."

The shouts on the terrace were answered by a great cheer of exultation from the Sepoy host around, who had been chafed almost to madness at the immense loss which was being caused by three or four men, for they knew not the exact strength of the party. The shouts of exultation, however, were silenced when, rushing round the terrace, the Sepoys found that their foes had again evaded them. There was no other door, no hiding-place, nowhere, in fact, that the besieged could have concealed themselves; but the ladder-like steps soon met the eye of the searchers. A yell of anger and disappointment arose. Not even the bravest among them thought for a moment of climbing the stairs, for it would indeed have been clearly impossible for men forced to climb in single file to win their way against well-armed defenders, who would simply shoot them down from above as fast as a head appeared over the shoulder of the dome.

The position was indeed practically impregnable against assault, although exposed to artillery fire, and to distant musketry. It was for this reason that the defenders of the stairs had not taken to it at once. They felt confident in their ability to defend the stair all day, and to inflict heavy loss upon the enemy; whereas, by climbing up the dome in daylight, they would have been a target to all those below while climbing, and would have been exposed all day to a distant fire. That they would have to support it for two or three days was nearly certain, but clearly the less time the better.

The enemy, consoling themselves with the thought that on the morrow their cannon would finish the contest which had thus far cost them so dearly, placed a guard of fifty men on the terrace at the foot of the steps, lighted a large fire there, in order that they could see any one attempting to descend long before he reached the level, and then retired below.

By this time Ned had recovered consciousness, and having taken a drink of water, was able to understand what had happened. His father had cut his uniform off his shoulder and arm, and having also cut off one of his own shirt sleeves, had soaked it in water, and applied it as a bandage on the wound.

"I am very glad we had agreed that only Dick should go," Ned said, "otherwise I should have blamed myself for keeping you here."

"No, we could not have gone in any case," Colonel Warrener said, "as there would have been no one to have lowered the rope here; besides which, it is only a sailor or a practiced gymnast who can let himself down a rope some eighty feet."

"When will Dick try?"

"As soon as the camp gets quiet. The moon will be up by twelve o'clock, and he must be off before that. Are you in much pain, old boy?"

"Not much, father; I feel numbed and stupid."

"Now, Dunlop," Colonel Warrener said, "will you relieve Dick on guard at the steps? You may as well say good-by to him. It is about eight o'clock now, and in a couple of hours he will be off. After he has gone I will relieve you. Then a four hours' watch each will take us to daylight; there won't be much sleeping after that."

By ten o'clock the noise in the rebel camp had nearly ceased. Groups still sat and talked round the campfires, but the circle was pretty large round the tomb, for the Sepoys had fallen back when the musketry fire was opened upon them from the parapet, and had not troubled to move again afterward.

"Now," Dick said, "it is time for me to be off. I have got a good seventy miles to ride to Lucknow. It is no use my thinking of going after the column, for they would be some fifty miles away from the place where we left them by to morrow night. If I can get a good horse I may be at Lucknow by midday to-morrow. The horses have all had a rest to-day. Sir Colin will, I am sure, send off at once, and the troops will march well to effect a rescue. They will make thirty-five miles before they halt for the night, and will be here by the following night."

"We must not be too sanguine, Dick. It is just possible, dear boy, that if all goes well you may be back as you say, in forty-eight hours, but we will make up our minds to twice that time. If you get here sooner, all the better; but I don't expect that they will hit us, and after tiring a bit the chances are they will not care to waste ammunition, and will try to starve us out."

CHAPTER XXIV.
BEST AFTER LABOR.

With a tender farewell of his father and brother, the midshipman prepared for his expedition. One end of the rope had been fastened round the large mast which rose from the dome. Holding the coil over his shoulder, Dick made his way down the dome, on the side opposite that at which they had ascended, until it became too steep to walk; then he lay down on his back, and paying the rope out gradually, let himself slip down. The lower part of the descent was almost perpendicular; and Dick soon stood safely on the terrace. It was, as he expected confidently that it would be, quite deserted on this side. Then he let go of the rope, and Major Warrener, who was watching it, saw that the strain was off it, pulled it up a foot to make sure, and then untied the knot. Dick pulled it gently at first, coiling it up as it came down, until at last it slid rapidly down. He caught it as well as he could, but he had little fear of so slight a noise being heard on the other side of the great dome; then he tied the rope to the parapet, lowered it carefully down, and then, when it was all out, swung himself out over the parapet, and slid down the rope. The height was over eighty feet; but the descent was a mere nothing for Dick, accustomed to lark about in the rigging of a man-o'-war.

He stood perfectly quiet for a minute or two after his feet touched the ground, but outside everything was still. Through the open-carved stonework of a window he could hear voices inside the tomb, and had no doubt that the leaders of the enemy's force were there.

From the parapet, in the afternoon, he had gained an accurate idea of the position of the cavalry, and toward this he at once made his way. He took off his boots and walked lightly until he approached the enemy's bivouac. Then he went cautiously. The ground was covered with sleeping figures, all wrapped like mummies in their clothes; and although the night was dusk, it was easy in the starlight to see the white figures. Even had one been awake, Dick had little fear, as, except near a fire, his figure would have been indistinguishable. There was no difficulty, when he neared the spot, in finding the horses, as the sound of their pawing the ground, eating, and the occasional short neigh of two quarreling, was clearly distinguishable.

Their position once clear, Dick moved round them. He had noticed that four officers' horses were picketed further away, beyond the general mass of the men's, and these could therefore be more easily removed, and would, moreover, be more likely to be fast and sound. They had, too, the advantage of being placed close to the road by which the English force had marched on the day before.

Dick was some time in finding the horses he was on the lookout for; but at last he heard a snorting at a short distance off, and on reaching the spot found the horses he was in search of. They were all saddled, but none had bridles. It would be, Dick knew, useless to look for them, and he felt sure that the halter would be sufficient for well-trained horses.

Before proceeding to work he reconnoitered the ground around. He found the way to the road, which was but twenty yards distant, and discovered also that the syces, or grooms, were asleep close by the horses; a little further off were a party of sleeping troopers. Dick now cut off the heel ropes by which two of the horses were picketed, and then, leading them by the halters, moved quietly toward the road. To get upon this, however, there was a ditch first to be passed, and in crossing it one of the horses stumbled.

"What is that?" exclaimed one of the syces, sitting up. "Halloo!" he continued, leaping up; "two of the horses have got loose."

The others leaped to their feet and ran in the direction whence came the noise which had awakened them, thinking that the horses had drawn their picket pegs.

By this time Dick was in the saddle, and giving a kick with his heels to the horse he was on, and striking the other with the halter which he held in his hand, dashed off into a gallop.

A shout burst from the syces, and several of the troopers, springing to their feet and seizing their arms, ran up to know what was the matter.

"Some thief has stolen the colonel's horse," exclaimed one of the syces.

The troopers did not like to fire, as it would have alarmed the camp; besides, which a random fire in the darkness would be of no avail; so, grumbling that the syces would have to answer for it in the morning, they went off to sleep again; while the men in charge of the two horses which had been taken after some consultation decided that it would be unsafe to remain to meet the anger of the officers in the morning, and so stole off in the darkness and made for their native villages.

Dick, hearing that he was not pursued, pulled up in a half a mile, and gave a loud, shrill "cooey," the Australian call. He knew that this would be heard by his father, sitting listening at the top of the dome, and that he would learn that so far he had succeeded. Then he set the horses off again in a hand gallop and rode steadily down the road. Every hour or so he changed from horse to horse, thus giving them a comparative rest by turns. Occasionally he allowed them to walk for a bit to get their wind, and then again rode on at a gallop. It was about eleven o'clock when he started on his ride. By four in the morning he was at the spot where the party had separated from the column, having thus made forty miles. After that he went more slowly; but it was a little past nine when, with his two exhausted horses, he rode into the camp at Lucknow, where his appearance created quite an excitement.

Dick's story was briefly told; and the two horses, which were both splendid animals, were taken off to be fed and rubbed down; while Dick, accompanied by the colonel of the cavalry regiment where he had halted, went at once to the camp of the commander-in-chief.

Sir Colin listened to Dick's story in silence.

"This will be the band," he said, "that Colonel Lawson's column went to attack; they must have altered their course. Something must be done at once. There shall be no delay, my lad; a force shall be ready to start in an hour. I suppose you will want to go with them. I advise you to go back to Colonel Harper's tent, get into a bath, and get a couple of natives to shampoo you. That will take away all your stiffness. By the time that's over, and you have had some breakfast, the troops will be in readiness."

Dick left Sir Colin, but delighted at the readiness and promptness of the fine old soldier; while Sir Colin called his military secretary, and at once arranged for the dispatch of a body of troops.

"There must be no delay," the commander-in-chief said. "If possible— and it is possible—these scoundrels must be attacked at daylight to-morrow morning. They will see the rope the lad escaped by, but they will not dream of an attack so early, and may be caught napping. Besides, it is all important to rescue those officers, whom they will have been making a target of all day, especially as one is badly wounded, and will be in the full blaze of the sun. See that a wagon and an ambulance accompany the column. Send a regiment of Punjaub horse, three field guns, and three hundred infantry in light marching order. Let gharries be got together at once to take the infantry forty miles, then they will start fresh for a thirty-mile march. The cavalry and guns can go on at once; let them march halfway, then, unsaddle and rest. If they are off by half-past ten, they can get to their halting-place by five. Then if they have five hours' rest they will catch the infantry up before daybreak, and attack just as it gets light. Those light Punjaub horse can do it. Now, which regiments shall we send?"

A quarter of an hour later bugles were blowing, and by ten o'clock three hundred British infantry were packed in light carts, and the cavalry and guns were drawn up in readiness. Dick took his place in the ambulance carriage, as, although greatly refreshed, he had had plenty of riding for a time, and in the ambulance he could lie down, and get through the journey without fatigue. Sir Colin himself rode up just as they were starting, and shook hands with Dick, and expressed his warm hope that he would find his friends safe at the end of the journey, and then the cavalry started.

Dick has always asserted that never in his life did he make such a short journey as that. Worn out by the excitement and fatigue of the preceding thirty hours, he fell fast asleep in the ambulance before he had gone a mile, and did not awake until the surgeon shook him by the shoulder.

"Halloo!" he cried, leaping up; "where are we?"

"We are, as far as we can tell, about half a mile from the tomb. I would not wake you when we halted, Warrener. I thought you wanted sleep more than food. We have been halting half an hour here, and the cavalry have just come up. It is about an hour before daybreak. The colonel wants you to act as guide."

"All right," Dick said, leaping out; "just to think that I have been asleep for eighteen hours!"

A hasty council was held, and it was determined that as the country was somewhat wooded beyond the tomb, but perfectly open on that side, the cavalry and artillery should remain where they were; that the infantry should make a *détour*, and attack at daybreak from the other side; and that as the enemy fell back, the artillery and cavalry should deal with them:

Not a moment was lost. The infantry, who were sitting down after their long tramp, got cheerily on to their feet again, for they knew that they were going to attack the enemy; and Dick led them off the road by a considerable *détour*, to come upon the enemy from the other side. By the moonlight the tomb was visible, and served as a center round which to march; but they were too far off to enable Dick to see whether any damage had been done to the dome.

Day was just breaking when the infantry gained the desired position; then throwing out two hundred men in skirmishing order, while the other one hundred were kept in hand as a reserve, the advance began. It was not until they were within three hundred yards of the enemy that they were perceived by the sentries. The challenge was answered by a musket shot, and as the rebels sprang to their feet a heavy fire was poured in upon them. In an instant all was wild confusion. Taken completely by surprise, and entirely ignorant of the strength of the enemy, the natives, after a wild fire in the direction of the advancing foe, fled precipitately. Their officers tried to rally them, and as the smallness of the force attacking them became visible, the Sepoys with their old habit of discipline began to draw together. But at this moment the guns, loaded with grape, poured into their rear, and with a cheer the Punjaub cavalry burst into their midst.

Thenceforth there was no longer any idea of fighting; it was simply a rout any a pursuit. The rebels' own guns fell at once into the hands of the infantry, and were quickly turned upon the masses of fugitives, who, mown down by the fire of the nine guns, and cut up by the cavalry who charged hither and thither among them, while volleys of musketry swept through them, threw away their arms and fled wildly. Over a thousand of them were left dead on the plain, and had not the horses of the cavalry been too exhausted to continue the pursuit, a far greater number would have fallen.

Dick took no part in their fighting; a company, fifty strong, with an officer, had been told off to attack and carry the tomb, under his guidance. Disregarding all else, this party with leveled bayonets had burst through the throng, and made straight for the door of the tomb. Many of the enemy's troops had run in there, and for a minute or two there was a fierce fight in the great hall; then, when the last foe had fallen, Dick led the men to the stairs, up which many of the enemy had fled.

"Quick," he shouted, "follow them close up!"

Some of them were but a few steps ahead, and Dick, closely followed by his men, burst on to the terrace at their very heels. It was well that he did so; for the guard upon the terrace, seeing that all was lost below, were preparing to sell their lives dearly, and to make a long resistance at the top of the stairs. Dick and his men, however, rushed so closely upon the heels of their own comrades from below that they were taken completely by surprise. Some turned at once to fly, others made an effort to oppose their enemy; but it was useless. Two or three of the Sepoy leaders, calling to their men to follow them, made a rush at the British, and Dick found himself engaged in a hand-to-hand contest with Aboo Raab, the rebel leader. He was a powerful and desperate man, and with a swinging blow he beat down Dick's guard and inflicted a severe wound on his head; but Dick leaped forward and ran him through the body, just as the bayonet of one of the British soldiers pierced him in the side.

For a minute or two the fight was fierce, but every moment added to the avenging force, and with a cheer the soldiers rushed at them with the bayonet. In five minutes all was over. Many of the Sepoys leaped over the parapet, and were dashed to pieces, preferring that death to the bayonet; while on the terrace no single Sepoy at the end of that time remained alive.

When all was over Dick gave a shout, which was answered from above.

"Are you all right, Dunlop?"

"Yes, thank God; but Ned is delirious. Send some water up at once."

Dick was too much shaken by the severe cut he had received in the head to attempt to climb the ladder, but the officer in command of the company at once offered to ascend. Several of the men had a little water left in their water-bottles, and from them one was filled, and slung over the officer's neck.

"I have some brandy in my flask," he said, and started up the steps.

In a few minutes he descended again.

"Your brother is wildly delirious," he said; "they have bound his injured arm to his side with a sash, but they cannot leave him. How is he to be got down?"

"There is plenty of rope and sacking down below," Dick said, after a moment's thought. "I think that they had better wrap him up in sacking, so that he cannot move his arms, tie a rope round him, and lower him down close by the side of the steps, my father coming down side by side with him, so as to speak to him and tranquillize him."

A soldier was sent below for the articles required, and with them the officer, accompanied by a sergeant to assist him in lowering Ned from above, again mounted. In a few minutes Dick's plan was carried out, and Ned was lowered safely to the terrace. Then four soldiers carried him below, and he was soon laid on a bed of sacks in the great hall, under the care of the surgeon, with cold-water bandages round his head.

Then Dick had time to ask his father how the preceding day had passed.

"First tell me, Dick, by what miracle you got back so soon. To-morrow morning was the very earliest time I thought that relief was possible!"

Dick told his story briefly; and then Colonel Warrener related what had happened to them on the dome during the day.

"As soon as day broke, Dick, they opened a heavy musketry fire at us, but they were obliged to go so far off to get a fair view of us that the smooth-bore would hardly carry up, and even had we been hit, I question if the balls would have penetrated, though they might have given a sharp knock. Half an hour later the artillery fire began. We agreed that Dunlop and I should by turns lie so as to command the stairs, while the other kept with Ned on the other side of the dome. The enemy divided their guns, and put them on each side also. Lying down, we presented the smallest possible mark for them; but for some hours it was very hot. Nine out of ten of their shot, just went over the dome altogether. The spike was hit twenty or thirty times, and lower down a good many holes were knocked in the dome; but the shots that struck near us all glanced and flew over. They fired a couple of hundred shot altogether, and at midday they stopped—for dinner, I suppose—and did not begin again. I suspect they were running short of ammunition. Once, when the firing was hottest, thinking, I suppose, to catch us napping, an attempt was made to climb the ladder; but Dunlop, who was on watch, put a bullet through the first fellow's head, and by the yell that followed I suspect that in his fall he swept all the others off the ladder. Anyhow, there was no repetition of the trial. The heat was fearful, and Dunlop and I suffered a good deal from thirst, for there was not much water left in the bottle, and we wanted that to pour down Ned's throat from time to time, and to sop his bandages with. Ned got delirious about eleven o'clock, and we had great trouble in holding him down. The last drop of water was finished in the night, and we should have had a terrible day of it if you had not arrived. And now let us hear what the surgeon says about poor Ned."

The doctor's report was not consoling; the wound was a very severe one, the collar-bone had been smashed in fragments; but the high state of fever was even a more serious matter than the wound.

"What will you do, father?"

"I must carry out my orders, Dick. Dunlop and I must go on to Agra, and then on to join our regiment. Ned will, of course, be taken back to Lucknow, and you must give up your trip, and stay and nurse him. Of course, if he gets over it, poor boy, he will be invalided home, and you can travel with him down to Calcutta. I shall send the girls home by the first opportunity. India will be no place for ladies for some time. We shall have months of marching and fighting before we finally stamp out the mutiny. There will be sure to be convoys of sick and wounded going down, and a number of ladies at Meerut who will be leaving at the first opportunity. It is very sad, old boy, leaving you and Ned at such a time; but I must do my duty, whatever happens." The British force encamped for that day and the next around the tomb which had been the scene of so much fierce fighting; for the animals were so much exhausted by their tremendous march that it was thought better to give them rest. Ned continued delirious; but he was more quiet now, as his strength diminished. Fortunately, the ambulance was well supplied; and cooling drinks were given to him, and all was done that care and attention could suggest. There were three other wounded in addition to Dick, all men who had taken part in the fight on the terrace; none had been killed. Elsewhere no casualty had happened in the force.

Early on the third morning the column was again in motion. The forty miles to the crossroads were done in two days, and here Colonel Warrener and Major Dunlop parted from Dick, going on with a small escort of cavalry to Agra.

It was a sad parting; and it is doing no injustice to Dick's manhood to say that he shed many tears. But his father promised that if the Lucknow jewels turned out to be real, he would leave the service, and come back to England at the end of the war.

The gharries were all in waiting at the crossroad, and another day brought them to Lucknow, where the news of the defeat and dispersion of the rebel force had already been sent on by a mounted orderly.

For a week Ned lay between life and death; then the fever left him, and the most critical point of his illness was reached. It was for days a question whether he had strength left to rally from his exhaustion. But youth and a good constitution triumphed at last, and six weeks from the day on which he was brought in, he started in a litter for Calcutta.

Dick had telegraphed to Captain Peel, and had obtained leave to remain with his brother, and he now started for the coast with Ned. He himself had had a sharp attack of fever—the result of his wound on the head and the exertion he had undergone; but he was now well and strong again, and happy in Ned's convalescence.

The journey was easy and pleasant. At Benares they went on board a steamer, and were taken down to Calcutta. By the time they reached the capital, Ned was sufficiently recovered to walk about with his arm in Dick's. The use of his left arm was gone, and it was a question whether he could ever recover it.

At Calcutta the Warreners had the delight of meeting their sister and cousin, who had arrived there the week previous. The next four days were happy ones indeed, and then there was another parting, for the girls and Ned sailed in a Peninsular and Oriental steamer for England. Dick remained a fortnight at Calcutta, until a sloop-of-war sailed to join the China fleet, to which his ship was now attached.

It was two years later when the whole party who had been together in the bungalow at Sandynuggher when the mutiny broke out met in London, on the return of Dick's ship from the East. The Lucknow jewels had turned out to be of immense value; and Messrs. Garrard, to whom they had been sent, had offered one hundred and thirty thousand pounds for them. The offer had been at once accepted; and the question of the division had, after an endless exchange of letters, been finally left by Colonel Warrener to the boys. They had insisted that Colonel Warrener should take fifty thousand pounds, and the remainder they had divided in four equal shares between themselves, their sister and cousin, whom they regarded as one of themselves. This had enabled the latter to marry, without delay, Captain Manners, whose wound had compelled him to leave the service; while Miss Warrener had a few months later married Major Dunlop.

Ned, too, was no longer a soldier. He had, when he arrived in England, found that his name had been included in the brevet rank bestowed upon all the captains of his regiment for distinguished service. He had a year's leave given him; but at the end of that time a medical board decided that, although greatly recovered, it would be years before he thoroughly regained his strength; and he therefore sold his commission and left the service.

Dick had passed as a lieutenant, and had immediately been appointed to that rank, with a fair prospect of getting his commander's step at the earliest possible date, as a reward for the distinguished services for which he had been several times mentioned in dispatches at the time of the mutiny.

General Sir Henry Warrener—for he received a step in rank, and knighthood, on retiring from the service—had renewed his acquaintance with Mrs. Hargreaves immediately on his return to England; and Dick, to his intense astonishment and delight, on arriving home—for he had received no letters for many months—found his old friend installed at the head of his father's establishment as Lady Warrener.

The daughters were of course inmates of the house; and Dick was not long in getting Nelly to acknowledge that so far she had not changed her mind as expressed at Cawnpore. More than that he could not get her to say. But when, three years later, he returned with commander's rank, Nelly, after much entreaty, and many assertions that it was perfectly ridiculous for a boy of twenty-one to think about marrying, consented; and as Ned and Edith had equally come to an understanding, a double marriage took place.

General Warrener and his wife are still alive. Major Warrener has a seat in Parliament; and Captain Warrener, who never went to sea after his marriage, lives in a pretty house down at Ryde, where his yacht is known as one of the best and fastest cruisers on the coast.

At Christmas the whole party—the Dunlops, Manners and Warreners—meet; and an almost innumerable troop of children of all ages assemble at the spacious mansion of General Warrener in Berkeley Square, and never fail to have a long talk of the adventures that they went through in the TIMES OF PERIL.